Su

CW01522617

Lily Easton is the pen na~~~~ ~~~~~~~ duo Katherine and Madeline. Katherine studied English Literature at Wesleyan University and enjoys reality TV in her free time. Madeline studied journalism at New York University and currently works in production. They met in their high school creative writing class and have been writing together ever since.

Lily Easton
Summer of Love

CANELO

First published in the United Kingdom in 2025 by

Canelo, an imprint of
Canelo Digital Publishing Limited,
20 Vauxhall Bridge Road,
London SW1V 2SA
United Kingdom

A Penguin Random House Company

The authorised representative in the EEA is Dorling Kindersley Verlag GmbH.
Arnulfstr. 124, 80636 Munich, Germany

A CIP catalogue record for this book is available from the British Library.

Print ISBN 978 1 83598 096 5
Ebook ISBN 978 1 83598 097 2

This book is a work of fiction. Names, characters, businesses, organizations, places
and events are either the product of the author's imagination or are used fictitiously.
Any resemblance to actual persons, living or dead, events or locales is entirely
coincidental.

Cover illustration and design by Rachel Lawston

Printed and bound in Great Britain by Clays Ltd, Elcograf S.p.A.

Look for more great books at
www.canelo.co
www.dk.com

For anyone who needs a queer story with a happy ending.

Pre-production

Paige

The season of *Summer of Love* hadn't started filming yet, but things were already falling apart. The murderous glare on Darcy Meadows's face could only foreshadow terrible things for Paige's budding career, since Darcy happened to be a giant in British reality TV, the show's host and her boss.

'Okay,' Paige said, biting back her apprehension and trying for an invigorating tone. 'So, Hastings is out. We'll just rearrange the starting cast and it'll be grand. We've got two months to sort out some new beats. Who knows, this could be a blessing in disguise.'

Darcy gave her a blank stare, as though she hadn't registered Paige's presence before that moment. And maybe she hadn't – it wasn't like she ever listened to any of Paige's ideas.

Brian, lead producer in name only, straightened and made his first contribution of the meeting: 'What's that you always say, Darce? A month for us is a year for everyone else? We'll scrape something together. We always do.'

Darcy's nostrils flared. 'The season was meant to be *centred* on Georgia Hastings. This isn't the minor setback you're making it out to be.'

Something, perhaps against her better judgement, compelled Paige to speak up. 'Yes, Hastings was a huge get. But it sounds like she's set on this Fashion Week invite, and we're not going to be able to convince her to miss out on that for only the *chance* to win £100,000. She'll make that much between a few brand deals, what with' – she glanced down at her notes – '1.2 million followers.'

'We've never had an influencer of that calibre before, and we've always done well enough with ratings,' Brian said, and Paige flashed him a grateful look.

'Let's be honest,' Paige ploughed on, encouraged that Darcy was actually looking at her now, even if her eyes were narrowed, 'Hastings was never fully committed. She only agreed to the show because of boy troubles and the need for a holiday. We want contestants who are more motivated than that – that's where the drama comes from.'

'And I rang Declan King,' Brian said. 'He's in, Hastings or no. Just think, that's a whole new demographic for us. We've not had a proper athlete before.'

Darcy sniffed. 'The point, as I think you'll recall, was to have both Hastings *and* King as starting contestants. With their rumoured romantic history and the mid-season introduction of Rowe, well, the season practically wrote itself. King and Hastings get their happy ending after years of will-they-won't-they, and their rabid fans dedicate themselves to our show for life.'

'But pivoting could work,' Paige said quickly. 'This gives us the chance to make something fresh and unexpected.'

Paige refused to be intimidated by Brian and Darcy's combined years of experience. *Summer of Love* was a massive undertaking compared to her previous gigs; producers spent eight weeks on location churning out daily episodes as the British public watched along and voted for their favourite couples. She hoped her outside perspective would prove to be an advantage.

'Maybe King will be a little more raw without Hastings around, less rehearsed,' Brian said thoughtfully.

Paige suppressed a sigh. Brian and Darcy seemed to think Declan King just needed a nudge to bare his soul on national television, but she wasn't convinced. 'Did you watch his press conference after the match with Petrovitch?' They both shook their heads. 'Well, I did. The man acted like he'd won a BAFTA, cracking jokes and graciously thanking his fans. You would never know he'd lost the fight of his career. It will take more than not having his girlfriend around to make him vulnerable.'

'He's staying in the starting cast,' Darcy said firmly. 'He may not give us as much drama as we'd like, but he'll bring in viewers.'

'Of course,' Paige said. 'All I'm saying is that we need to balance out the influencer-types with more relatable, more *real* contestants. Ones who will give us genuine emotion.'

Darcy cocked her head. 'Who did you have in mind?'

Paige carefully pulled a photo out of her stack of notes, sliding it across the table. 'Oliver Wright. He has basically no social media presence, but he's a dancer for the Royal London Ballet who just went through a rough break-up.'

Darcy's eyes lingered on the photo, just as Paige had expected – she was a sucker for a pretty face. 'How rough?'

Paige silently handed over the notes from her initial interview with Oliver and watched as Darcy skimmed the page, her eyes widening in delight.

Paige took a deep breath, knowing what she said next could determine the course of her career. 'I think he's got what it takes to win this thing, given the right coaching.'

Darcy pursed her lips. 'That's quite a statement, considering nobody even knows who he is.' She turned to Brian. 'Thoughts?'

Brian glanced up from his phone, having already bored of their conversation. 'People *do* love an underdog.'

Darcy studied Paige almost approvingly. 'I could see him working with the starting cast, adding something different to the mix. We'll see how he does.' She smiled slowly. 'And to make it more interesting for me, if he wins, we can talk about you taking on a more senior position.'

Paige tried to keep her expression impassive, even as her pulse raced in response to the first positive feedback she'd ever got from Darcy. She prided herself on her instincts, and she'd sensed in her first interview with Oliver that he would be the one to make her career. He just needed to win, and Paige would make sure he did.

Chapter 1

Declan

Eight Weeks Until Finale

Brian Burns: Tell me about yourself.

Declan King: Right, I'm Declan King, I'm twenty-seven years old and I'm a boxer. Born and raised in Manchester, and now I live in London.

Brian Burns: And why do you want to be on *Summer of Love*?

Declan King: I'm looking for that perfect girl, you know? I've been around the ring a few times, taken a few beatings, and definitely taken an L when it comes to love. But I'm ready to put my gloves back on and get back out there. Who knows, maybe the love of my life is waiting for me in paradise.

Declan closed his eyes against the harsh light of the main cabin, forcing a deep breath into his lungs. The beginnings of a headache formed at the base of his skull as a bead of sweat dripped down his back. Hot and faint and wanting nothing more than to get to his seat, Declan glowered at the petite woman further down the aisle struggling to load her carry-on into the overhead bin.

He let the breath out slowly, watching as the woman finally won the battle with her luggage and settled into her seat. The line moved forwards again, and Declan reached his still-empty row. He swung his suitcase into the overhead bin, wincing as a familiar, sharp pain shot up his left arm.

Declan didn't remember much of his title fight against Alexei Petrovitch, but he'd heard the story from his brother and father, had seen the replay on TV. It still felt disconnected from his body, like it had happened to someone else. The most important night of his life, and all he could remember were flashes: his wrist bent at an impossible angle, white bone poking through skin, his hand hanging limply.

It had been nearly four months and his chest still constricted uncomfortably at the memory, a dull pain throbbing behind his eyes. He had the fleeting, mad thought to grab his bag and run off the plane. Instead, he bit his lip and shoved himself into the aisle seat.

His phone rang and he struggled to pull it out of his pocket, annoyed that the simple task was still difficult for him.

'What?'

'Hello to you too,' drawled the voice on the other end.

'Sorry,' Declan said, softer. 'I didn't see it was you, George.'

'On the plane, then?' she asked, feigning nonchalance. Declan had met Georgia Hastings on a red carpet seven years earlier for an event neither of them could remember, and they had been inseparable ever since. The next eight weeks apart would be hard on both of them, and listening to her voice brought on another wave of panic.

He scanned the line of passengers, absently determining an escape route. 'I, uh—' He swallowed. 'I'm making a run for it, actually,' he tried, but the joke was feeble.

'You'd better not; I worked way too hard to make you *Summer of Love* material.'

It had been Georgia's idea to audition for the stupid show. She'd sold it as a two-month holiday, just a girl, her best mate and a bunch of fame-hungry strangers. Declan had gone along with it, like he did with all of Georgia's schemes. He'd wanted

6

to drop out when she had, but she hadn't let him, reminding him that he needed more followers and the UK's top reality show was the perfect way to get them.

'But honestly,' she continued more seriously, 'how are you feeling?'

'Incredibly hungover,' Declan said, closing his eyes and willing the throbbing behind them to dissipate. 'Thanks for that.'

'I wouldn't be your best mate if I didn't get you good and drunk before your big day,' Georgia said, and Declan could hear the smile in her voice. 'Buck up, Decs, and get excited. This will be huge for you. When you win, I bet you'll leave even more famous than me.'

'Oh boy,' Declan said, without a hint of enthusiasm. He continued quickly, 'Enough about me. How are you? Think you'll survive without me?'

'Maybe.' Georgia was silent for a long moment, then: 'James messaged me.'

Declan counted the few stragglers left in the aisle, worried. He'd spent too many late nights counselling Georgia through her break-up with James to believe he could talk her out of a bad decision quickly.

'It's funny,' she continued. 'You're not even out of the country and he's already crawling back into my DMs.'

Declan rubbed his eyes – talking about James was no cure for a headache. 'What did he say?'

'That he still loves me, and he's done with the cheating if I am.'

'You didn't cheat,' Declan said automatically, and Georgia gave a tired laugh.

'As if that matters.'

A decent boyfriend would have accepted Georgia's explan-ation that she and Declan had only ever been friends. But Georgia already knew that, and she'd heard what Declan thought of her ex's pathetic excuse for cheating on her.

'Just block him,' Declan said instead. 'Don't engage.' He couldn't help but feel responsible for Georgia's heartbreak and found himself desperate to prevent it from happening again. One of the reasons he'd decided to go through with the show was so he wouldn't ruin any of her future relationships. With Declan linked to someone else in the tabloids, Georgia would be free to find love elsewhere.

'You know I can't do that,' Georgia said. 'Even with all this shit, I can't cut him off.'

Declan couldn't understand Georgia's unshakable attachment to someone who had hurt her so badly. The kind of love Georgia had for James, the all-consuming and irrational kind, always seemed to end in devastation. Declan had no interest in ever trying it out for himself.

'I'm sorry,' he said finally.

There was another long pause, then Georgia cleared her throat. 'Just don't find anyone to replace me, yeah?' she said. Her tone was light, but Declan knew she meant it.

'Nobody could replace you, George.'

'Sir, I'm going to have to ask you to end your call. We're about to take off.' Declan looked up to find a flight attendant leaning over him with a firm smile fixed on her lips.

'Could you give me a second, please?' Declan asked, and she nodded before moving on.

'Don't worry about me,' Georgia said brightly. 'You're going to absolutely smash this! No one is better at working a crowd than you. Then you'll come back and punch people and it'll all be grand. Okay?'

Declan couldn't help but smile. 'Okay.'

Georgia hung up, as always, without saying goodbye.

Declan caught the flight attendant's eye again, waving his phone in her direction and making a show of putting it away. She smiled humourlessly back at him.

The final passengers had found their seats during the call. Declan was relieved that no one else had been assigned to

8

his row, a small mercy in his chaotic day. He watched the flight attendant go to shut the main cabin door and saw her nearly get trampled by a man in his haste to get on the plane. He apologised profusely before stumbling down the aisle and stopping in front of Declan, sheepishly nodding to the window seat.

Declan stood, glanced at the man's long legs, and begrudgingly muttered, 'You can have the aisle.'

'Cheers,' the man said, looking relieved. 'Sure you don't mind?'

'Not at all.' As he said it, he noticed a woman he recognised as a producer peering at them from a few rows down. He grabbed his backpack and slid to the window seat, slamming the armrest down between them.

'Thanks,' the man whispered, sitting and eyeing the producer too.

Studying his profile, Declan could admit he was attractive, but he didn't seem like the usual type for *Summer of Love*. There was no sign of hair gel or spray tan, no tacky sunglasses, no pungent scent of desperation. Instead, he had soft brown curls that fell into his face and sharp cheekbones hidden behind wire-rimmed glasses. If this was the competition, Declan would be fine.

'I'm Declan,' he said, smiling wide and putting out his hand.

The man's eyes flicked to Declan's face for only a moment before returning to the front of the plane. He took his hand, giving it one quick shake and muttering out, 'Oliver.'

'You a contestant?' Declan asked.

Oliver gave a minute nod, still looking intently ahead as the flight attendant explained the safety protocols. 'Last-minute addition,' he said out of the corner of his mouth.

Declan grinned, deciding the psychological warfare could begin early. 'No kidding,' he deadpanned, giving Oliver an obvious once-over.

Oliver adjusted his glasses, finally turning to look at him properly. Declan's breath caught as his lips pulled up in a brilliant smile, his eyes the most striking shade of green Declan had ever seen. Their gaze held for a second too long, and Declan, uncomfortable, was the one to glance away this time.

'You a gaffer, then?' Oliver's smile didn't drop, but the look in his eyes hardened a little.

'I'm Declan King,' Declan said, immediately annoyed by how petulantly the words came out.

'I have no clue who that is, mate,' Oliver said, turning back to the front of the plane. 'Thanks for the seat, though.'

Declan stared at him, feeling a familiar heat creep up his neck and realising he had signed himself up for far more trouble than he'd anticipated.

Chapter 2

Declan

The car ride to the villa was quiet and cold, the aircon blowing full blast against the Spanish summer. Feeling underdressed in his swim trunks, Declan did his best to ignore the goosebumps springing up on his skin as he peered out the window. It was his first view of Mallorca and his last glimpse of the outside world before entering the villa that would be his home for the next eight weeks.

Eight weeks. It was the first time he'd fully registered how long he'd be gone. Declan had always been good in press conferences, could play off reporters with an easy rapport, but those only lasted a few hours. This show would be the longest performance of his life, and he wasn't sure he could do it.

But Georgia had been convincing, reminding him that having options was only ever a good thing – and gaining a few million followers on Instagram would certainly give him options. Declan knew his competitive streak would win out; he wouldn't let himself get voted off just to be spared the constant scrutiny. Declan King didn't lose.

As soon as he'd adjusted to the cold, the SUV stopped in front of the villa. It was smaller than it looked on TV, but he supposed that was probably a trick of the camera angle. It was still a nice house, the giant two-storey glass entryway providing a dramatic focal point for the otherwise traditional Spanish architecture.

The driver nodded and Declan opened the car door, stepping out onto the hot asphalt.

There were cameramen on either side of the driveway, their lenses fixed on him as he collected himself. He kept his chin up, surveying the scene through his sunglasses. Desperately trying to look like he knew what he was doing, he started towards the house. As he got closer, he caught sight of a young producer with curly hair waving him over from beside the garden gate.

'Hey, Declan,' she said smoothly, and he recalled that her name was Paige. She pushed a mic set into his hands. 'Here, clip this to your trunks and put the necklace over your head. They're finishing up with Niall, then you'll be next. How are you feeling?'

'Yeah, good,' he replied, distracted. He struggled to get the clip secured but finally managed, fiddling with the wiring.

'Great! One more moment,' she said, bringing one side of her headset to her ear and listening intently. 'Ready on my mark.'

A rush of adrenaline hit him all at once, like he was about to enter the ring. He bounced from one leg to the other, trying to dispel the excess energy. He brought one smooth, even breath into his chest and held it there for a beat, and another, letting it out slow and easy. Selling the show was what he'd always excelled at.

'And... you're on,' Paige said. The patio gate swung open and she nudged him forwards, muttering, 'You'll see them out by the kitchen.'

He walked around a curtain of greenery and was met with the familiar view of the villa's spacious garden. A glistening pool sat in the centre of the lawn, with a firepit on one side and an open-air kitchen on the other. Daybeds were sprinkled throughout, and a large couch swing sat under a pergola on the back wall.

'Hello?' he called out, wandering down the steps.

'Another one!' came an excited voice, and a grinning black man with toned arms and a slight beer belly came bounding over. He threw an arm around Declan, pulling him into a half-hug and leading him to the others.

'I'm Jack,' the man said, his arm still around Declan's shoulders. He gestured towards a man with a sharp nose and a quizzical brow. 'That's Callum.'

'Hi,' Callum said flatly. Declan couldn't figure out if he was scowling or if his face settled into that pinched look naturally. 'Are you Declan King?'

He nodded, rubbing the back of his neck in an attempt to appear sheepish.

Callum squinted at him. 'I thought you'd be taller.'

Declan resisted the urge to roll his eyes. It was a comment he'd heard before – at five foot ten he was hardly short, but it seemed that his reputation made Declan King, the boxer, a larger-than-life figure in the public eye. Something that Declan King, the man, struggled to live up to.

'And I thought you'd have a face for radio, Callum,' Jack quipped.

Callum's scowl grew even more pronounced. 'No wonder your stand-up career hasn't taken off.'

Jack laughed good-naturedly as Declan turned to take stock of the competition. His eyes were immediately drawn to the man from the plane. Oliver's hair was a mess, as if he'd been running his hands through it. Declan wondered if it was from nerves or if he knew how attractive he looked when his curls hung slightly out of place.

'That one's Oliver,' Jack said, noticing Declan's attention had shifted.

'Hey there,' Oliver said, his eyes skimming over Declan and then across the garden distractedly.

'Nice to meet you,' Declan said, choosing to forget their previous encounter and doing his best to not stare at the toned body that had been hidden under frumpy clothes.

'And this big hunk of meat,' Jack said, nodding to the final man, 'is Niall.'

'Declan,' Niall bellowed, his Irish lilt coming out thick, 'good to meet you! I'm a big fan.'

Declan smiled genuinely at that. 'Do you box yourself?' he asked. Niall was a beast of a man, whose arms bore an impressive collection of tattoos, and nose looked like it may have been broken before, so it was a fair question.

Niall let out a booming laugh. 'Not in the slightest,' he said. 'More into healing than hurting. I'm a physical therapist.'

Declan found himself reconsidering his first impression, noticing Niall's kind eyes and easy smile. Still, there were other factors to consider when it came to sizing up the competition.

'Do I know you from somewhere?' he asked smoothly. 'TikTok?'

'Nah, can't be bothered with all that. My sister keeps me up to date with the trends, though.'

'That so?' Declan asked, amused.

Niall shrugged. 'But I caught the fight against Petrovitch, looked brutal. How's the wrist?' he asked with concern, nodding towards Declan's arm.

Declan took a deep breath. He had been out of the ring for nearly five months now, much longer than he had ever thought he'd be, and he had known there would be questions. He gave them the line he'd practised with his father.

'It was a tricky break,' he said, rotating his wrist to demonstrate his full range of motion and ignoring the accompanying pain. 'But I'm mostly healed. Figured I'd take the summer off before getting back to it, give the other lads a chance to win some matches.'

His eyes inadvertently met Oliver's, and he was surprised to find sympathy in the sharp planes of his face. Declan's stomach twisted uncomfortably, but he kept his expression impassive as the clacking of heels saved him from having to change the subject.

'Hello, boys,' came a sing-song voice. Darcy Meadows, the show's host, was perched in a pair of impossibly high stilettos, her platinum hair blinding. She gave the men a dazzling smile, waving them towards the pool and directing them to line up.

'Hello, Darcy, darling,' Declan said, letting his northern accent grow thicker as he winked. He was grateful to be getting to the part of the show he knew he'd be good at: charming the pants off the audience.

'Ooh,' Darcy said, clearly delighted, 'the girls will have to watch out for you.' She turned to the rest of the men with a suddenly grim expression. 'A quick word of advice before we get started... Your producers can only do so much to help you. You all know that the viewers rule this show. You'll never be sure when an elimination is coming, so every night's episode is a chance to create a compelling storyline for yourself. If the audience buys it, you're safe. If they think you're insincere or boring, you'll be voted off.'

Declan looked around and saw he wasn't the only one shaken by the abrupt turn to seriousness.

'This may be reality TV, but there's a fine line between what's real and what's not. Be sure you walk it carefully.'

Declan's producer, Brian, gave Darcy a cue and her smile reappeared with jarring suddenness. 'Welcome to *Summer of Love*, boys! Are you ready to meet your girls?'

After a confused pause, the men cheered affirmatively, and Darcy turned to the closest camera. 'Our expert matchmakers have paired you each with the perfect girl.' She smirked. 'We'll see how well they did in the next few weeks, once each relationship has been tested.' Declan doubted these so-called matchmakers even existed – he assumed the producers had paired them up for optimal drama. He knew from his sporadic viewing of the show that the original couples rarely lasted.

Darcy looked to the garden gate. 'Let's see the girls! Stella, dear, would you come out?'

Stella was stunning, with dark skin, shiny waves and a genuine air that immediately made Declan hope she wouldn't be paired up with him. There were always a few contestants who seemingly came on the show to find love, and Declan had vowed to himself that he wouldn't get involved with a girl like that. The only way he could go through with what would come next was to find someone as fake as him.

'I can tell you all want her,' Darcy sing-songed, 'but only one of you can have her. And that lucky boy is…' She paused to wink at the camera. 'Our resident hunky Irishman, Niall!'

Stella walked over to Niall, enveloping him in a hug before stepping back and beaming up at him.

'Niall,' Paige called over, 'could you put an arm around her?'

The pair shifted as the cameraman got a few different angles. It almost hurt to look at them, with how perfectly they were matched. Declan worried he'd discounted Niall too soon, that he and Stella had already become the ones to beat.

'Got it!' Paige finally called.

Darcy plastered on a smile. 'Let's meet our next girl, Holly!'

Holly was a tall blonde with lean muscles peeking out from her sleek black swimsuit. As she walked out, she met each of the boys' eyes indifferently. Declan supposed she was trying to be intimidating.

'Holly,' Darcy said, 'you've been paired up with Jack. Hope you don't make it into his next stand-up set!'

Holly considered Jack for a beat, her eyes narrowed. He gave her a small, awkward wave, and a hint of a smile played at her lips. She made her way over to him and was pulled into a bear hug as Paige directed the cameraman. After a moment, she gave Darcy a thumbs-up.

'Great,' Darcy said. 'Maeve, come on out!'

A short, olive-skinned girl strode down to the pool. As she drew closer, Declan was struck by her big brown eyes and full lips. She was dressed in a simple black bikini and a matching wide-brimmed hat, somehow making the ensemble look regal. If Declan wanted to win, which he desperately did, Maeve would be a good match, so long as she wasn't looking for anything real.

'Hello, Darcy,' Maeve said, giving the host a shy smile.

'Well, you've turned some heads, love,' Darcy said. Declan glanced around and saw Callum, Jack and Oliver all wearing similar lovestruck expressions. 'But only one of these boys can begin the show with you, and that lucky boy is… the voice of the UK's tenth most-listened-to podcast, Callum!'

Callum punched the air as Maeve looked him over dubiously. Darcy glanced at Paige, and Declan could see the impatience written across her face. Actress, she was not.

'Maeve, dear,' Paige said. 'Could you…'

'Let's keep going.' Darcy unsubtly pushed Maeve towards Callum before calling out, 'Come out and meet the boys, Lara!'

A striking woman with long black cornrows walked towards the pool. She scanned the line of boys, and when her eyes fell on Declan, she smiled in recognition.

'Well, Declan, it looks like you have a fangirl,' Darcy said. 'Which is perfect, because you two have been matched up!'

Declan smiled wide, knowing the cameras were capturing his every movement. He could only hope that Lara's ecstatic expression was because she wanted to be attached to his fanbase when the audience's votes came in at the end of the week and had nothing to do with him as a person.

Lara came over and he obediently put an arm around her shoulder, turning to the closest camera.

'Here we go, everyone!' Darcy said, with renewed energy. 'Let's meet our last girl, Zoë!'

A petite woman in a sporty swim set stepped out, her long, dark ponytail bouncing as she walked. Declan recognised her as an influencer, though he couldn't quite place her, and knew instantly she was exactly who he was looking for. He also knew it would make for a much better storyline to not be paired up with her from the beginning – the producers had given him the perfect opportunity to pursue her, to have to fight for her. The viewers loved that crap.

'Everyone's favourite fitness girl!' Darcy announced. 'Zoë, you'll have loads to chat about with Oliver over here, since he's a ballet dancer.'

Declan suppressed a snort. Here was the most damning piece of evidence that matchmakers had been nowhere to be found when the contestants had been coupled up. There couldn't be a worse match than an influencer and a guy like Oliver, who looked like he'd wandered off the set of *Bake Off* having just bungled the technical challenge.

As Zoë dutifully walked to Oliver's side, Darcy turned back to the camera, looking as relieved as Declan felt to be done with this part of the proceedings. 'Fantastic!' Darcy said. She reintroduced the couples to the cameras, then turned back to the contestants. 'Over the next eight weeks, we'll see hook-ups, breakdowns and heartbreaks as our Lovers try to navigate their way into the couple of their dreams… and the hearts of our viewers.' She turned to look directly at the camera. 'Tune in nightly to vote for your favourites and send others sailing home in defeat, on this season of *Summer of Love*!'

Paige immediately dissolved the scene, shuffling the girls upstairs to get ready for the first night party and instructing the boys to chat by the pool.

'So,' Jack said, once the boys had settled into a circle. 'Let's have it, what do we think of the girls?'

'I think Oliver's got the best of the lot,' Callum said, shooting Oliver a sour look.

'Zoë *is* quite talented,' Niall said, frowning at Callum. 'My sister loves her videos; she does the workouts every morning. But I think all the women seem like wonderful people.'

'Oh,' Declan said, finally placing her. 'She's Zoë Park!'

He regretted having said anything when Oliver caught his eye, his forehead wrinkling in confusion. 'Who?'

'She's got like half a million followers on YouTube,' Jack said, and Declan was relieved when Oliver's attention shifted away from him.

'Huh,' Oliver said. 'I'm not really online, but that sounds cool.'

Declan stared at him. Zoë couldn't possibly be on the show to find love, and someone like Oliver couldn't be there for any other reason. There was no way they would last, which made her perfect for his plans.

'Well, Maeve is a catch too,' Jack said to Callum. 'I recognise her… didn't she date the Prince of Jordan?'

'She can't be that well-connected,' Callum said dismissively. 'She didn't even know *The High-Value Man.*'

Declan snorted – Callum didn't seem to realise his podcast hadn't made the mainstream. He noticed Oliver's lips twitch as though he was trying to hide a grin, but his face shuttered when their eyes met.

Callum rounded on Declan. 'Why are you even here?' he asked. 'I thought you already had a girl. The hot one, Georgia something.'

'Hastings,' Declan supplied. 'And we're just mates.'

The line came out reflexively, but where he'd usually try to inject it with a note of coyness, this time it fell flat. Callum had hit on the confusing part of his friendship with Georgia: through strategic public appearances, social media posts and brand deals, they had been suggesting to the public for years that they were romantically involved. The truth was they never had been, since Georgia was the one person outside of his family who knew Declan King, the man half the English population worshipped for his skills in the ring, was gay.

'Sure,' Callum said, smirking. 'I'd love to have a mate like that.'

He elbowed Declan's side and laughed as if they were sharing an inside joke. Declan gritted his teeth, keeping his face relaxed. The last thing he wanted was to give the tabloids something to say about his temper; they would have a field day with that one.

The drawback of trying to make people believe you were dating your best friend, even if you never explicitly confirmed it, was that it was impossible to get them to stop. He and Georgia had always been careful to play it on the right side of deniability, but that hadn't been enough to stop rampant rumours. What had started as a lark to keep the press off his back had turned into something with real-world consequences.

'Don't be crass,' Jack said, side-eyeing Callum.

'And Holly?' Niall asked Jack, clearly trying to tactfully change the subject. 'What do you make of her?'

Jack clapped his hands together. 'Not sure yet, mate. She seems like a cool bird, maybe too cool for me. But I think I can crack her tough exterior with my lovable charm.' He threw his head back with forced laughter. 'I do believe she and I will just be in it for a laugh. But who knows? The night is young and the women are lush.'

'Stella may be the most beautiful woman I've ever seen,' Niall said, his eyes wistful.

'That she is, mate,' Jack agreed. 'And lucky for you, you friendly fucking giant, none of us have got the balls to go after her with you standing in our way.'

'Language!' the closest PA called out.

'Well, fuck,' Oliver quipped. 'There goes half my vocabulary.'

He said it with a self-deprecating smile that looked more like a wince. Niall and Jack laughed good-naturedly, but Declan found himself staring again. Oliver was absent-mindedly drumming his fingers along the tops of his knees, staring at the skyline. The setting sun cast a warm light on his face, catching the golden strands of his curls and giving his eyes an incandescent gleam.

'What about you, King?' Jack asked. 'You didn't say who you've got your eye on.'

Declan blinked at him, refocusing. 'You're mad if you think I'd tell you lot,' he said blandly.

He managed to not look at Oliver for the rest of the night.

Chapter 3

Oliver

Paige Nelson: Tell me about yourself.

Oliver Wright: I'm Oliver. I'm twenty-four years old and I'm a dancer for the Royal London Ballet.

Paige Nelson: And what are you looking for on *Summer of Love*?

Oliver Wright: I'm not sure what to expect, to be honest, but I hope I'll find love. I mean, that's the only reason someone would subject themselves to this specific kind of torture, right?

Oliver didn't sleep his first night in the villa. Every time he got close, he suddenly remembered the cameras trained on him and jerked awake. His body had been tense since he'd walked down the plane aisle. He'd nearly missed the flight because of traffic – maybe a sign, in retrospect, he should have listened to.

After counting sheep for several hours as a pink dawn spread over the sky, he gave up and automatically reached for where his phone would normally be sitting on the nightstand next to him. Of course, his hand closed around empty air. The producers had deprived him of even the opportunity to fixate on the lockscreen photo that had become his constant companion in depression. Before arriving in Mallorca, he didn't think there had been a day in the past seven months that hadn't begun with a text from Sophie.

He closed his eyes, pleading with his brain for a moment's escape, but quickly realised lying in bed would only make him feel worse. Instead, he made his way outside, sliding the glass door open and breathing in the cool morning air as his mind raced.

Coming on a reality TV show had been a terrible idea, that much was clear, but he couldn't see a way out of it now. Once it had started, the whole thing had spiralled out of control so quickly – responding to that producer's DM had been a tipsy mistake made under pressure from his mates, and he hadn't known that one message could lead him to a plane, a van and a hellish night of staring at the ceiling. He had never given a decision less thought, and the loss of control over his life had a dizzying effect.

As he filled the kitchen's kettle, hoping a cup of tea might clear his head, he saw Declan emerge from the villa. Oliver's mortifying first thought was to hope that Declan might acknowledge him in some way. He liked Jack and Niall fine, found Callum to be an uncomplicated annoyance, but something about Declan had set him on edge from their first meeting, when he had sized Oliver up and found him lacking.

Whatever his hopes had been, Declan headed straight for the pool, not sparing a glance in his direction. While Oliver was sure he looked a wreck, Declan was frustratingly handsome for so early in the morning, the slight shade of his stubble showing off an angular jaw, his hair effortlessly coiffed. There was a keen alertness in his bright blue eyes as he stretched his arms above his head, the hem of his shirt lifting to reveal sharp lines of muscle. Oliver averted his gaze as Declan stripped it off and dove into the pool. He was annoyed, wishing he'd got more sleep.

The sun continued to rise and the crew began setting up for the day. Oliver was watching them, sipping his tea and trying to keep his eyes open, when Zoë walked out onto the patio and gave him a peppy wave.

'Hello,' Oliver said, his voice coming out hoarse. 'Tea?'

She nodded, taking one of the stools across the counter from him. 'So,' she said, after a beat, probably realising Oliver had exhausted all capacity for speech with his opening line, 'how'd you sleep?'

He flipped the kettle on. 'Really well.'

She cocked her head at him, taking in his dishevelled appearance. His skin was pale and his eyes were bloodshot, that he knew without even looking in the mirror.

'It was a long day yesterday,' she said. 'I usually like to reserve a few hours for my night-time routine, but I guess that's the price we pay for a summer in paradise.'

Her cheer was abrasive. He had thought, despite their obvious differences, that they could at least agree the day before had been objectively terrible. He took a deep breath, reminding himself that it was pure luck that he'd got coupled up with Zoë, who had an established following and who he was certain was not on the show to find love. The last thing Oliver wanted was to meet someone with genuine interest in him – that had no place in his plan.

He tried for a smile. 'Yeah, it's incredible here. I mean, look at that view,' he said, gesturing towards the overlook, his eyes inadvertently falling on the pool where Declan was still swimming laps.

'Gorgeous,' she said, giving him a sidelong look, and he was relieved he'd managed to turn things around. With all the preparation he'd done for the show, he had neglected the most important thing for a *Summer of Love* winner to cultivate: the ability to not have a panic attack first thing in the morning.

Holly emerged from the villa next, yawning and plopping down next to Zoë without greeting, squinting in the sunlight. 'God, I'm not even hungover, I don't know why my head feels shit,' she announced, and Zoë giggled.

'Dance-related injury?' Oliver offered. The contestants had been forced to jump up and down for hours the night before, in some imitation of a club inhabited by only ten individuals. They had been assured this looked like a fun time on camera.

Holly grimaced. 'Maybe my brain didn't enjoy bouncing around my skull? Does this happen when you do ballet?'

Oliver found his smile turning more genuine. 'Only with Wagner.' He placed a cup of still-steeping tea in front of Zoë and gave Holly a questioning look.

'You should have green tea instead, Holls,' Stella said, approaching from the villa. The lights had come on in the bedroom, and the other contestants were trailing out. 'It's amazing for headaches; I recommend it to all my wellness clients.'

'You're a terrible Englishwoman,' Jack called over, heading towards the pool.

Stella shrugged. 'I consider myself a citizen of the world.'

Maeve nodded earnestly, leaning over the counter to snag the kettle from Oliver. 'When I travel for work, I'm always surprised by how everyone is fundamentally the same.'

Zoë stared between the two of them for a moment before turning to Oliver. 'Where are you from? I don't think you mentioned.'

'London,' Oliver said quickly, hoping she wouldn't pry further.

As the girls chatted about their recent holidays, Oliver stared at his tea in silence. He felt wildly out of his depth – he'd only travelled outside the UK once in his life, when he'd flown to New York to audition for Manhattan Ballet the month before. He had known when he'd agreed to come on the show that he was nothing like the ideal contestant, and he kept being reminded that he had little in common with these people. After all, they didn't need the prize money.

'Hey,' interrupted a voice from behind him. He turned to find a familiar face: Paige, the producer who had sent him that fateful DM.

'Hi,' Oliver said, not meeting her eye. The producers terrified him. They had got him to reveal things during the audition process that he refused to talk about with even his closest friends.

She gestured for him to move closer, away from the cameraman capturing footage of the contestants chatting around the kitchen counter, and he took a hesitant step towards her. 'Can I pull you for an interview? You didn't do one last night.'

'Ah,' he said evasively. 'I didn't? I must've forgotten.'

She gave him a knowing look. 'Or were you avoiding it?'

He flashed her his most charming smile, the one that had always won over his instructors. 'Oh, you're good. Have you thought about pursuing detective work?' She put her hands on her hips, and he added in a more serious tone, 'To be honest, it makes me a little nervous, talking at the camera.'

Paige's eyebrows drew together. 'It's not a performance, and you're not being graded.'

He disagreed, but nodded along anyway.

'The others just have a chat with me. Can you do that?'

'Probably,' he hedged.

She placed a reassuring hand on his arm. 'I'm on your side here. We want the same things, and we can help each other.'

'Oh? You're also looking for your soulmate?'

She dropped her hand, looking at him intently. 'I think you understand what I mean. If you're constantly on alert, performing, the audience is going to notice. There is no one the public turns on faster than someone looking for fame or fortune, and I don't want that to happen to you, since I know you're here for the right reasons.'

Was he imagining it, or had she put slight emphasis on *fortune*? He hesitated a moment more before following her towards the villa.

She led him to the small interview room deemed the Love Shack, and Oliver sank onto the stool in front of the camera. The red light was already on, signalling that he was being recorded. He tried to steady his breathing – each pre-show interview had left him exhausted.

'So,' Paige said, tying her shoulder-length curls into a bun and settling next to the camera. 'How are you and Zoë getting along?'

'Oh, fine,' Oliver said, trying to train his eyes on the camera lens, though they kept sliding back to Paige's face. 'I mean, she seems nice.'

'Wrong answer,' Paige said, and the camera light blinked off. 'You can't make everyone like you,' she continued in a kinder tone. 'You're a performer, and I understand where you're coming from. Your audience, the people watching ballet, they've come to see perfection. Right?'

He nodded. 'Right.' It was what he loved about ballet: there was a structure to it, an immediate knowledge if the movement had been done correctly or not. Perfect form was clearly defined for him.

'I trust you to know your audience, so please trust me to know mine. It's our job, isn't it? And I'm *very* good at my job.'

He believed her. She had the most commanding presence he'd ever encountered in someone her age.

'So, look at it this way. Your new audience is five million people, and they watch this show for romance and drama. You'll stick out to them if you have screen time, if you're funny and if you're sympathetic. Now, you are funny, a little *too* funny sometimes.' She gave him a look.

'Sorry,' he said, feeling chastened.

She gave a small nod of acknowledgement. 'And you're easy to root for; you have a great story. That's why you were chosen in the first place.'

That was an unnerving statement from someone he hardly knew. 'I was shocked when I got your DM,' he admitted. 'I thought it was a scam.'

'And *there's* the sympathy angle we're looking for,' she teased. 'Man is so down in the dumps that he assumes he's being scammed when a pretty girl DMs him.'

He grinned despite himself. 'Yes, well, I wasn't exactly feeling like luck was going my way.'

Her expression softened. 'I know you'd been going through a tough time.'

That was an understatement – in the months following his break-up with Sophie, Oliver had hardly left their once-shared flat except to work, shutting himself away from the world and avoiding his well-intentioned mates. It was easy to sit in the flat and pretend Sophie was on an extended holiday, especially when he spoke to her on the phone every day as though nothing had happened.

'Mhm,' he muttered in response to Paige's expectant face. Thinking of the flat brought the usual pang of unease. He pushed away the nagging thought of what his best mate, Will, would say to him about needing to move house. Instead, he focused on the present: what he needed to do to win the prize money, cover Sophie's portion of the rent, and move to New York. He straightened. 'I'm ready,' he said, trying to project confidence.

Paige seemed unconvinced. 'We can talk about it if you want. I know that the first few days can be difficult – this is my first season, and it's mad even for me.'

He cleared his throat. 'I'm fine.' It was an echo of what he'd been insisting to anyone who adopted that familiar pitying expression. He knew it was pathetic – to have been with Sophie for so long, to have thought there were no secrets between them, and to not have realised the most fundamental thing about her: she would leave. That one day, the life he'd worked so hard to build for himself would come to an abrupt end. People trying to help him through it only made him feel worse.

'Oliver,' Paige said softly, 'I chose you myself. I put my neck on the line for you, and I don't do that for just anyone. I have incredible instincts, and I know your story will resonate with our audience. Millions of viewers have been brutally dumped, and they'll be rooting for you to find love. It makes them think they can too.'

He swallowed. 'Right, so no pressure?'

'It's nothing you can't handle. Be yourself, and they'll fall in love with you. I guarantee it.' She smiled at him. 'Ready?'

He sighed. 'Ready.'

The red light blinked on.

Chapter 4

Oliver

After his interview with Paige, Oliver went to lift weights, hoping to quell his rising anxiety with exercise. No matter what she had said, he knew he could never be himself in this sort of environment. He hadn't felt like himself in months. The Manhattan Ballet audition had renewed his sense of purpose, and now he only had to wait for the letter that would determine his fate.

'All right?' He looked up mid-rep to find Niall grinning at him. 'Fancy a spot?'

Oliver glanced pointedly at Niall's chest. 'I'm not sure I can keep up with your programme.'

' 'Course you can,' Niall said, offering a hand. 'I'm not nearly as strong as I look.'

He let Niall pull him up, sure that he would persist in his friendliness until Oliver gave in.

He tried for a smile. 'What should we start with?'

As if in response to his question, a chime sounded over the loudspeakers. Niall frowned in disappointment as the contestants gathered around them.

'Lovers, the truth hurts,' Darcy's voice rang out. 'Only the most daring among you will make it to the end. Get ready to weed out the competition.'

Niall looked comically distraught by the interruption to their planned workout, and Oliver smiled, liking Niall more and more.

'Come on,' Oliver muttered. 'We'll pick it back up as soon as we have the chance, yeah?'

'Right,' Niall said, slinging an arm around Oliver's shoulders as though it were the most natural thing in the world. 'Let's see what they have in store for us.'

What the producers had in store, of course, was a game of truth or dare. Paige corralled them into a semi-circle around the firepit, a cameraman on each end, and, after a few minutes of awkward silence, Darcy's voice resumed over the loudspeakers.

'Lovers,' she said, 'it's time to get personal. To get us in the sharing mood, each contestant will reveal their body count.'

Oliver's stomach dropped. After a beat where the group glanced around nervously, Jack chuckled.

'Well, I've got nothing to hide,' he said, sitting back and throwing his arms around the contestants on either side of him, Declan and Maeve. He waited, building suspense, before saying, 'Twelve.'

He turned to Maeve, raising an eyebrow. 'Oh,' she said, glancing at the closest camera. 'Seven?'

Holly gave her an encouraging smile. 'I'll go next, but I have to admit I lost count somewhere in the low fifties. Such is the life of a bartender.' She rolled her eyes good-naturedly, nudging Stella.

Stella considered the question for a moment. 'Physically? Twenty-seven,' she said. 'But I'd like to believe I've had many spiritual partners.'

She didn't prompt anyone to follow her, and there was another tense pause. Oliver stared at his feet, wondering how production would edit the challenge to make it seem fun. When he looked up, he accidentally made eye contact with Declan.

He alone seemed unbothered by the silence, leaning back with a cocky smile. Oliver felt a pang of dislike, a familiar sensation from the other times he'd found Declan studying him as though he were some sort of fascinating zoo animal.

'I've had sex with 200 women,' Callum finally announced. Niall stifled a laugh, catching Oliver's eye, and Callum turned on him. 'And what about you?'

Niall shrugged. 'Couldn't say,' he said easily. 'I'm not very good with numbers. Oliver?'

Oliver's face reddened as the others turned to him. He didn't even contemplate lying. 'One.'

'One?' Callum echoed incredulously. 'Are you taking the piss?'

Before Oliver could respond, Declan cut in. 'Mine's twenty-five.'

Oliver blinked at him in surprise – it was hardly the same as admitting to having only slept with one woman, but it seemed low for a semi-famous athlete.

Declan turned to Lara. 'Your turn.'

As Lara gave her answer, Declan winked at Oliver. With the small interaction, he was certain that Declan had lied, presumably to avoid looking like a player. Oliver resented how naturally he had done it. Lying would have saved him a great deal of embarrassment.

Zoë was the final contestant to answer, and her number – three – assuaged some of Oliver's anxiety.

'Stella,' Darcy said next, 'tell the Lovers about the craziest date you've ever been on.'

Stella stared dreamily at no one in particular, an expression Oliver was beginning to associate with her. 'He made a compelling pitch to me about organic farming over dinner and convinced me to come and see the plot of land he had his family working on up in Dundee. I ended up staying for a year. In hindsight, I think it may have been a cult.'

Jack laughed loudly, opening his mouth like he wanted to ask more, but was cut off by Darcy. 'Time for a dare! Jack, choose a Lover for Holly to kiss,' she said.

Jack looked around deviously, not seeming to deliberate before saying, 'Callum, would you do the honours?'

Holly glared at Jack. 'But darling,' she said, faux-sweet, 'aren't you worried about me falling for another man?'

Jack grinned. 'I'm feeling quite secure about it, actually.'

'No need to sulk,' Callum said, standing. 'It'll be the best kiss of your life.'

Holly rolled her eyes, standing and chastely pecking Callum's lips, which he tried to extend unsuccessfully, snaking an arm around her.

'That's enough of that,' Holly said sternly, swatting at his hand.

They both sat, and Darcy called on Declan next. 'How long was your longest relationship?' she asked.

A small crease appeared between Declan's eyebrows as he heard the question, but he immediately smiled so brightly that Oliver forgot his frown. 'Ah, well,' he said, rubbing the back of his neck in what Oliver was sure was an imitation of self-consciousness. 'I've never been in a relationship.'

'Can't commit to one woman?' Jack asked jovially.

Declan shrugged. 'I think I'm finally ready to give it a try.'

Oliver translated this to mean that Declan was only interested in stringing girls along but wanted the audience to find him sympathetic.

'Niall,' Darcy said cloyingly, 'choose a boy to kiss Maeve.'

Maeve straightened, glancing around as Niall frowned at the loudspeaker.

When Niall said nothing, Jack spoke up. 'Come on, then. Who's the lucky lad?'

Niall raised his eyebrows. 'If you're so eager, why don't you do it?'

Maeve blushed, not looking at anyone. 'Oh, um, I don't—'

Jack cut her off, gently taking one of her hands and slowly bringing her palm to his lips.

'Should've been more specific,' he said, with a small smile. Maeve flushed a deeper red, pulling her hand away.

Darcy called on Holly next. 'Why did your last relationship end?'

Holly's face froze.

'Well,' she said finally, raising her head with a firm expression, 'he wasn't very nice. Constantly accusing me of cheating, needing to know where I was all the time, not trusting me at work... You know, the usual.'

Oliver studied his hands, troubled by the dark turn in conversation. He was certain Darcy had known about Holly's ex, and her callousness worried him. The producers knew things about him that could be used to elicit a similar emotional response, if they chose to use them.

Maeve hugged Holly from the side. 'On to better things, babe.'

'Oliver,' Darcy's voice said, and he waited with trepidation. 'Kiss the fittest boy in the villa on the lips.'

He was so relieved it wasn't a question about his break-up that he barely registered the words until he noticed the other contestants' expectant faces. 'Er – fittest... *boy*?' he echoed dumbly, hoping someone might tell him exactly what to do.

His eyes fell on Declan for a half-second too long, and he ran a hand through his hair distractedly. Declan's mouth twitched downwards, and Oliver had the fleeting thought that if he kissed him, at least he could make the other man as uncomfortable as he was.

He took a deep breath. 'Niall, how about it?' he said, trying for a nonchalant tone, as though he kissed men for a laugh all the time.

Niall stood, radiating good humour. 'I'm honoured.'

Oliver took two quick steps towards him, grabbed his face and pushed their lips together.

'Aw,' Jack said, as Oliver broke away and took a step back, 'now *that's* the couple to beat.'

Oliver sat, glancing anxiously at Niall, who grinned back at him, unfazed.

'Final dare, Callum,' Darcy cooed, 'choose a girl to kiss Declan.'

Callum scanned the group, his eyes coming to rest on Oliver as a grin spread across his face. 'Zoë.'

It took Oliver a moment to realise why Callum was looking at him, having temporarily forgotten the entire conceit of the show in his panic over what he would be forced to do or reveal next. Based on Callum's smirk, he had chosen Zoë to cause drama. Oliver wondered if he could drum up the energy to care, but as Declan stood, he found anger came naturally. The feeling was entirely misdirected, since Declan was only following the rules of the game. But he didn't have to do it so arrogantly.

Zoë faced Declan, smiling shyly. As Declan leaned down to kiss her, Oliver let himself stare at where his hand rested at the nape of Zoë's neck, tendons flexing as he pulled her closer. The tic in his jaw as they broke apart and the smirk playing on his lips made angry heat rush to Oliver's cheeks.

—

When Oliver woke at another ungodly early hour the next morning, Declan was already swimming laps. It was a semi-psychopathic hobby, getting up at dawn to exercise in a tiny, oblong pool, but Oliver supposed everyone had their vices.

In his state of total fatigue, he kept reaching for the phone he no longer had to check for texts that wouldn't be there anyway. He wondered if Sophie was as out of sorts as he was, not being able to talk. He had so much he wanted to tell her about the show – she loathed reality TV, and he could hear her colourful commentary about his castmates already. He wanted to go home, to call her, more than he wanted practically anything. But the one thing he wanted more kept him rooted to the spot.

'Everything okay?' came a voice from behind him. It was Paige, studying him curiously, some complicated-looking camera equipment in hand.

'Yes,' he said, his tone clipped. 'Just tired.'

'Right,' she said. 'You're a bit of a night owl?'

There was something in her expression, an understanding, that threw him off. He didn't think he'd mentioned anything about his sleep habits in the interview process. 'I tend to be.'

'Your ex, she's in New York, right?'

He blinked at her. 'She is,' he said stiffly, thinking of the late-night phone conversations that had kept him up for months. He had adjusted his life to accommodate for the time difference.

'One of your mates mentioned that you kept in pretty close contact after her move,' Paige explained, pushing a stray curl behind her ear.

Oliver cleared his throat awkwardly, surprised that Will knew how often he and Sophie spoke.

'We talk,' he said finally. 'The move's been hard on her. She'd lived in London her whole life, her friends are there, her family...' *Me*, he thought.

'That's big of you,' Paige said. 'I mean, most people...' She trailed off, uncomfortable. He was used to that – no one wanted to say it outright.

'Most people don't forgive their ex who announced a break-up and a cross-Atlantic move in one breath? Who secretly auditioned for and accepted a role in the ballet company that we'd planned to apply for together?' He gave her a wry smile. 'Yes, I'm unique in that sense.'

Her eyes widened. 'I suppose that's the more mature way of going about things. Me and my ex, we'd row every day if we talked at all.'

He couldn't tell her that he and Sophie never rowed. That she had been happy to see him in New York before his audition, and it had given him hope that if he moved things could go back to normal between them. It didn't seem like a wise thing to confide in a producer trying to manufacture a love story for him.

Instead, he told her a different sort of truth. 'She's my best friend.'

35

As Paige struggled to reply, Oliver noticed Declan approaching over her shoulder. Water dripped from the ends of his hair down his broad chest, disappearing into the waistband of his swim trunks.

'Hiya, Paige,' he said, smiling his brilliant smile. He didn't greet Oliver, though he was now directly in front of him. It was the closest they'd been since the plane, and Oliver glanced over the slight crook of his nose and the pout of his mouth, trying unsuccessfully to read his expression.

'Hi,' Paige said. 'Sorry about the shape of that pool – I don't think a contestant has ever tried to use it for exercise before you.'

He shrugged. 'I'm not much of a swimmer, so I've nothing to compare it to.'

'Your dad's gym probably has a more functional model, if you're taking up the sport,' Paige said. Oliver was relieved to hear her talk like that with the other contestants. It was like she was testing the waters, quizzing herself on their lives.

'I'm not quite ready to give up on boxing,' Declan said, winking. 'I've got a couple of good years in the ring left, no matter what the tabloids say.'

'Are you swimming because it's easy on your wrist?' Oliver asked, trying for some common ground. Ballet dancers often had their careers cut short by injuries, and he could sympathise with Declan not being in the best headspace after the fight.

'Nah,' Declan said, not turning towards him. 'My wrist is fine. Just felt like a change of pace.'

'Right,' Oliver said, not believing him.

'What have you got in store for us today, then?' Declan asked Paige, and Oliver got the feeling he was being dismissed from the conversation.

'It wouldn't make for good TV if I told you,' Paige teased.

Declan laughed, throwing his head back and showing off the long line of his throat. 'Fair enough,' he said. 'I'm gonna grab a shower. Gotta look my best for the cameras, right?'

Paige nodded, and Oliver's eyes followed Declan's retreating form.

'I'd watch out for that one,' Paige said.

Oliver pulled his gaze away from Declan with considerable effort, wondering what he could have possibly done to offend him.

Chapter 5

Declan

Seven Weeks Until Finale

Neil Steel: Welcome back, everyone, for another long, hot summer. And we're already off to the races with Niall and Stella leading right out of the gate.

Stella Reyes: 'I saw him and it was like I'd known him in another life.'

Neil Steel: But others might have had a false start…

Maeve Kostas: 'Callum would not have been my first choice.'

Callum Morgan: 'She's a frigid [bleep].'
    [Neil Steel: Yikes! Well, it's anyone's game, so place your bets now. Tune in nightly to see who comes in… and don't forget to vote for who goes home!

Declan pushed himself out of bed at dawn. He'd always been an early riser. When he was younger, his dad would wake him and his brother every morning to train before school, and the habit had stuck.

It was quiet when he walked outside; the lights were still out in the bedroom, which meant he had time to himself before the crew arrived. He cherished every moment off camera. Keeping up appearances was already exhausting him, and the charade wasn't made any easier by the proximity to a certain dancer.

Swimming had been his doctor's suggestion, an exercise designed to work his arm back into its full range of motion. Declan hadn't been excited at the prospect, but had come to love the silence of being underwater.

He slipped into the pool, treading water for a few minutes so his body could adjust to the near-frigid temperature before beginning his laps. Even though this had originally been pitched as a holiday by Georgia, he didn't intend to let himself slack off – he needed to be in top shape when he got back in the ring.

He swam until his wrist ached, then slowed, floating lazily and enjoying the quiet of the villa after the exhausting night before. They had danced for hours before they'd finally been allowed to go to bed. By the end, Declan had been hot, tired and a bit miffed that he hadn't been able to get drunk off their two-drink allowance take the edge off.

The creak of the gate announced the arrival of the production crew, and Declan pulled himself out of the pool, heading towards the kitchen to put the kettle on.

Oliver was the first to make it out of the bedroom when the lights flicked on, shuffling over to Declan and staring blankly at the kettle as it came to a boil. Rubbing at his eyes, he started to rummage through the cabinets, his oversized sleep shirt slipping to reveal a bare shoulder. He set four mugs on the counter by Declan.

'Thanks,' Declan said, awkwardly thrusting the box of tea at Oliver. He was standing close enough for Declan to feel the heat radiating off him, and when he made to take a step back, their elbows accidentally knocked together.

'S'all right,' Oliver said, tiredness giving his voice a soft timbre.

Declan poured the boiling water and retreated to the other corner of the kitchen with his two mugs, wanting to get out of Oliver's immediate vicinity.

He blew on his drink distractedly, watching Oliver pull a carton of milk out of the fridge and splash some into the tea. He held the carton out silently and Declan shook his head, trying to end the interaction. Oliver shrugged, humming and stirring absently, his delicate fingers dwarfing the mug.

Declan realised he was staring and glanced away, catching the glare of a camera hidden in the rafters above their heads. Jack had read somewhere that there were seventy-five cameras in the villa, and they'd made a game of trying to find them. Declan would have to let him know about this one.

He took a sip of his tea and grimaced, wishing he had added milk, as Lara walked out of the bedroom with Zoë. Declan dumbly pushed a mug of tea at her.

'Oh, thanks,' she said, sighing happily. 'You're such a gentleman.'

Declan inclined his head, watching Oliver present his own cup of tea to Zoë. Niall and Stella walked into the kitchen next, holding hands. There was a tension in the air brought on by what Declan supposed was the awkwardness of sharing a bed with a stranger, the stress of the competition, and the fact that they were under constant surveillance.

'So, let's have it,' Declan said brightly, 'how did you all get desperate enough for a date that you wound up here?'

Jack, who was making his way to the fridge, snorted. 'Why don't you start, King?' he said, pulling a jug of orange juice out. 'Wouldn't think a famous bloke like you would have any trouble finding a bird.'

Though he was closest to Jack in the villa, Declan was still wary of how much he seemed to know about the other contestants. He wouldn't let himself be fooled into opening up by easy smiles and wisecracks. Years of experience had taught Declan that the less people knew, the safer he was.

'Maybe I'm finally ready to settle down,' Declan said. He knew how he came off to the public; he and Georgia had done their best to construct a certain reputation for him. The reality wasn't far off, with all of Declan's romantic entanglements taking place in crowded clubs and only ever lasting the night. The difference was the level of care Declan took to make sure no one noticed him slipping out the back door with another man.

Not coming out hadn't been a conscious decision; he had just never thought it was the public's business who he saw behind closed doors. He hadn't wanted to sacrifice that final piece of information, the one thing in his life that still truly felt like his. That, and being known as *the* gay boxer was a responsibility he wasn't ready for.

'And what about you? Nobody hot for teacher?' Declan teased. Though he wanted to look like he was stirring the pot, really, he was assessing weaknesses – like he'd do with any opponent before a match.

Jack's expression transformed into mock annoyance. 'One viral video of my stand-up set on a failed engagement and suddenly the dating pool dries up. Figured I might as well take drastic action.'

Declan nodded while immediately discounting the story – being a teacher and an amateur comedian, Jack was certainly on the show for the prize money.

'Not a single woman in London left? Brutal,' Holly quipped as she joined them, Maeve scoffing at her side.

Jack pointedly ignored Holly, turning to Maeve instead. 'What about you, jetsetter? Run out of foreign dignitaries to get entangled with? Or are they all wanted for human rights violations?'

'Not all of them,' Maeve said casually.

Jack persisted. 'What's your reason for coming here, then?'

She took a long sip of tea. 'My mates signed me up. They think having a boyfriend in the UK will mean I'm in-country more often.'

Declan scanned the group, trying to figure out who would be the easiest to crack next. Niall and Stella were completely oblivious to the conversation, huddled in their own little world on the other side of the counter, while Zoë, Lara and Holly lamented the horrors of modern dating. Oliver was the only one who seemed uncomfortable with the line of questioning.

'What about you?' Declan asked, unable to help himself.

Oliver's eyebrows drew together. 'Dating would involve getting out of my flat every now and then, and that's a non-starter. I'm a bit of a hermit,' he said, hands tight around his mug. His tone was wry, and Declan couldn't tell if he'd imagined the strain in it.

'Just what a girl wants to hear,' Declan said, with a mean laugh.

'Call me a romantic.' Oliver pushed his glasses up from the tip of his nose. Green eyes met Declan's, and he swallowed.

'Zo?' Declan said, turning away.

Zoë shook her head noncommittally. 'I guess I've been a bit lonely. I'm so focused on my work, I haven't had time to meet a nice bloke.'

The way she delivered the line made Declan sure she'd rehearsed it. She was going for the workaholic angle, and that was something he could use.

'I know exactly what you mean,' he said. 'I feel like I spend all my time in the ring. It's been impossible to meet the right girl.' It was a line he used with the press often. He and Zoë locked eyes, and she gave him a tentative smile.

'Well, I've been on nearly a hundred dates this year with no luck,' Lara said, laughing at herself. 'I'm hoping being locked in a villa with someone will improve my chances significantly.' The look she threw Declan made him uncomfortable.

'Same here,' Holly said. 'I've got to beat them off with a stick at work, but as soon as it's time to actually make a go of it, it's crickets.'

Niall and Stella finally emerged from their bubble, seeming to notice the others for the first time.

'I thought it was a sign from the universe when they asked me to come on,' Stella said, glancing at Niall. 'I was perfectly happy with my life as it was.'

Niall, the absolute buffoon, was blushing. 'I thought I was too, but now...'

The two were staring at each other again. Jack made a retching noise and walked away, effectively ending the conversation.

Declan spent the rest of the morning and early afternoon working through what he'd learned. He was surprised by how genuine most of the contestants had seemed. Perhaps he'd been too quick to assume everyone had ulterior motives – he hoped their lack of strategising would make winning that much easier for him.

'Chime!' Jack yelled out from his perch on a nearby daybed, where he was lounging with Maeve and Holly.

'Yes, thank you. We can all hear it,' Callum drawled, leaning over the railing of the second-floor balcony.

Darcy's voice came through the loudspeaker. 'Jack and Callum: tonight, Poppy is entering the villa, and she's hungry for love. Do you have what it takes to satisfy her? Go and get ready for your dates; new meat is on the menu. Ta!'

There were some hoots and hollers as the two made their way inside. Moments later, a woman with a blonde pixie cut walked out onto the patio.

After introductions had been made, Paige ushered everyone except for Poppy and Callum upstairs. Apparently, the dates would take place on the patio, with other contestants watching from the balcony, light heckling encouraged. Jack took liberties with the definition of 'light', shouting increasingly distracting commentary at Callum.

The others gave up after a few minutes and took to murmuring amongst themselves. Declan glanced at Oliver, who was laughing at something Niall had said.

He had managed to stay away from Oliver all week, but that hadn't stopped him from looking – try as he might, his gaze always drifted back. Ignoring him almost made it worse, with Declan's body seemingly calibrated to know exactly where Oliver was at all times.

Jack slapped him on the shoulder, and he remembered to yell over the railing again, wrenching his eyes back to the patio. 'Callum, do try to smile. It's a date, not a dentist appointment.'

Callum turned his head to retort, but stopped himself. Poppy, to her credit, was ignoring them in a spectacular display of self-control.

Paige walked out onto the balcony, signalling to Jack. 'Your turn.'

'Wish me luck,' Jack said, giving the other Lovers a mock-salute before following her away.

Declan leaned on the railing, tipping himself forward to call out: 'Time to turn on that charm we've heard so much about.'

Jack flipped him off as he walked out to the table where Poppy sat, and Niall and Oliver snickered.

'Give Jack any tips?' Declan turned his head to see Zoë standing at his elbow. 'You seem to know what you're doing when it comes to women. I've seen the tabloids.' Her voice was soft, not drawing the others' attention.

Declan raised an eyebrow and chuckled. 'I can assure you I don't.'

'I find that hard to believe,' Zoë said, eyeing him slyly.

'Well, you've only seen me on my best behaviour…' Declan trailed off. She gave him a calculating look, assessing him as he had her that morning. He'd suspected Zoë had the competitive edge he was looking for in a partner, and now he was sure of it.

'Nothing wrong with behaving badly,' she said, giving his forearm a brief squeeze and letting her hand rest there. Declan spared a glance over his shoulder at Oliver, but he was shouting down at Jack as Niall egged him on.

'Oi, Jack, you want her to laugh with you, not *at* you.'

—

Declan hadn't expected a girl to make a move on him so early in the game, but he was relieved it had been Zoë. She may have found him attractive, but he was under no illusions that she would have gone for him without thinking through all of her options. This wasn't about finding love – as the contestant with the second-largest social media following after her, Declan was a safe bet. He had no doubt she would make a perfect fake girlfriend.

As he watched Oliver and Zoë chatting over the kitchen counter, thinking about his next move, Paige appeared at his side.

'Hey, Declan,' she said, in her typical no-nonsense way. 'Could we have a chat?'

' 'Course,' Declan said, following her into the villa. Brian, his usual interviewer, was always positively charmed by his soundbites, so he felt confident walking into the Love Shack.

'So,' Paige said, flicking on the camera, 'first week is almost over; what are your impressions of the girls?'

'The girls are great,' he said vaguely. 'I'm happy with Lara, but we agreed to keep our options open and get to know everyone.'

Unlike Brian, Paige didn't seem content with that response. 'I noticed that you and Zoë shared a nice moment the other night on the balcony,' she said, her expression like the reporters Declan had so often dealt with, pen poised on her clipboard.

'Oh? You caught that?' Declan asked, stalling. He considered the implications, but supposed there was nothing wrong with admitting it. He'd been waiting for his interest in Zoë to come up organically, and Paige was leading him right to it.

'Yes, I did,' Paige said, looking at him expectantly. 'Anything you want to talk about?'

Declan laughed, running his hand through his hair and doing his best to act bashful. 'Well… what can I say? She's obviously gorgeous, you'd have to be blind not to notice. And I think she and I understand each other, we have similar careers, we want the same things, you know.'

'You like her,' Paige said.

It wasn't a question, but Declan nodded anyway. 'Yes, I like her.'

'Enough to throw over Lara?' It was impossible to tell how she meant the question.

'Well, it's hardly throwing her over,' Declan said, back-tracking. 'I obviously would tell her before I tried anything with Zoë. It's only polite.'

Paige made a note on her clipboard. 'What about Oliver? Are you going to talk to him too?'

He shrugged, trying for nonchalance, conscious not to reveal too much. 'I'm not in a couple with Oliver. As far as I'm concerned, it's not my place to say anything to him.'

'So you don't think Oliver has any right to know?' Paige asked, straightening in her seat. Declan wished he could just ask her what she wanted him to say; she was clearly angling for something specific. He didn't mind playing the role that she wanted him to, if he knew what it was. He blinked at her, and she sighed, turning off the camera.

'If you want to go for Zoë, that's great, but be honest about it,' Paige said, studying Declan carefully. 'Sometimes you have to be the bad guy to get what you want.'

Declan thought he understood the situation now: Paige was trying to pit him against Oliver. He knew he would win that competition and shouldn't mind playing along, but he was reluctant. It meant he'd have to stop avoiding Oliver and drag them both into the spotlight.

Looking at Paige's eager expression, Declan realised he didn't have a choice, and at least this way he would know how to act towards Oliver. Rivalry was far less complicated than the twist in his gut whenever he looked at the other man.

She flipped the camera back on, giving him a nod. 'So, you don't think Zoë and Oliver make a good couple?'

'Well, I never thought they made sense together,' Declan found himself saying. 'I think Zoë needs a certain kind of man, and Oliver isn't it.'

Paige gave him a thumbs-up, and he relaxed slightly. 'And you are? That kind of man?'

Declan laughed. He wasn't the right man for Zoë either, but no one needed to know that. 'Yeah, I suppose I could be. I *am* pretty great.'

Paige smiled, glancing at her clipboard again. 'What kind of guy is Oliver?'

Declan considered the question for a moment, wishing he knew the answer. 'I'm not sure he really fits in. He's a bit awkward and shy, I guess.' He paused before adding without thinking: 'But he's charming when he doesn't mean to be.'

Paige gave a nod of approval and turned the camera off.

—

Declan leaned his head along the edge of the pool, listening to Lara and Holly chat about their preferred mascaras, trying to drum up the courage to ask Lara to speak privately. He was interrupted by a chime.

Declan pulled himself out of the pool and made his way over to where the contestants were huddling up.

'Lovers, how was your first week in paradise?' Darcy's voice asked over the loudspeaker. 'Hope you're not getting too comfortable. Tonight there will be a recoupling, and the last single girl standing will be sent home.'

Declan's heart sank. He had thought he'd have more time, but now it seemed like he would have to act sooner than expected. Glancing at Lara, who was already heading into the villa to change, he realised he'd missed his opportunity to talk to her about Zoë.

The boys got ready together and had been gathered by the firepit for several minutes when Darcy finally came through the gate. Paige was at her side, furiously writing notes on her clipboard as Darcy muttered out of the corner of her mouth. The girls filed out to stand before the fire, looking tense.

'All right,' Paige said, looking at the boys. 'You'll each give a quick speech about why you're picking your girl, saying her name last. On my mark.' She ducked behind the camera.

'Action!'

Darcy looked at the camera and smiled. 'We're coming to the close of our first week here on *Summer of Love*. Tonight, it's time for the boys to pick the girl they'd like to couple up with... and the last girl standing will be going home. Gentlemen, are you ready?'

The men nodded.

'Niall?'

Niall picked Stella, obviously. The crew did a few takes of his speech, directing the contestants to act shocked each time he called Stella's name, until finally Darcy decided they could move on.

'Declan, your turn.'

Declan stood, facing the girls. 'As soon as this girl walked into the villa, I knew she was someone I had to keep my eye on. She's gorgeous, and I can't wait to see what the two of us can do together. The girl I would like to couple up with is—'

'Cut!' Paige called. 'Just a sec, Declan.'

Declan waited impatiently as a cameraman moved to get shots of the girls doing their best to look nervous. It would have been funny if not for his very real anxiety.

'Okay, great!' Paige said. 'Declan, do that last line again.'

Declan nodded, turning back to the girls. 'So,' he said, 'the girl I'd like to couple up with is Zoë.'

Zoë beamed, walking over and pulling him into a hug, but Declan found himself glancing at Oliver over her shoulder. He looked stunned, his face frozen. It wasn't until he locked eyes with Declan that he frowned.

Jack and Callum's picks were less surprising: Jack chose to remain with Holly and Callum picked Poppy. Declan felt a brief pang of regret as he made eye contact with Lara for the first time that night.

'Maeve, Lara,' Darcy said, glancing between the two women. 'Whoever Oliver doesn't pick will pack her bags and leave the villa immediately.'

Oliver looked distraught, brushing the curls out of his face and inadvertently making them stick up on one side. Paige paused shooting so he could fix it, but he still seemed unsteady.

'Oliver,' Darcy said, regarding him gravely, 'which girl do you choose?'

Oliver took a deep breath. 'Well, this is difficult. The girl I'd like to couple up with is, um, a bit intimidating…' He trailed off. Declan could tell he was pulling the words out of thin air. 'I've only got to know her a little in this short week here, but I'm excited to see where things could go. The girl I choose is… Maeve.'

Chapter 6

Oliver

Six and a Half Weeks Until Finale

Neil Steel: Here's what you missed last week: Oliver and Zoë's romance was a tropical paradise, before Hurricane Declan swept in to shake things up. And he has something to say about Oliver...

Declan King: 'He's not the typical guy to come on here. A bit awkward and shy.'

Neil Steel: Can our shipwrecked lovers find their way back to each other, or will Oliver stay lost at sea?

Two days after the recoupling, Oliver lay wedged between Niall and Stella on a daybed, looking out across the garden at where Maeve sat by the pool with Holly and Jack. He had continuously entertained the idea of joining the three of them throughout the morning, but found he much preferred the position of relative safety that the fortress of Niall and Stella provided.

'Oliver,' Niall said, 'what do you think?'

'Hmm?' Oliver asked.

'I was asking,' Stella said, gazing serenely at the cloudless sky, 'if you're going to talk to Maeve.'

Oliver sighed, tipping his head back and letting the sun overwhelm his vision. 'I've talked to her,' he said softly.

Niall cleared his throat, and Oliver could feel him exchanging a look with Stella. 'You do know that you signed up for a dating show, right? Dating usually involves talking to people for more than two minutes. Getting to know them, their *soul*.'

Oliver had committed himself to doing anything he could to win the prize money. Anything, apparently, except for talking to a girl. Or knowing her soul, whatever that meant.

He had prepared for the show, to some extent. In the month between being cast and flying to Mallorca, he had watched a highlight reel of *Summer of Love* content curated by his reality TV-obsessed mate Will every moment he wasn't working. He had been so happy Oliver was finally responding to his texts that he'd even prepared presentations on the tactics of previous winners.

Unfortunately, Oliver hadn't practised basic social skills, and he definitely hadn't practised flirting. It didn't help that he couldn't turn off the part of his brain that constantly reminded him he was being watched by millions of people, including his mates, his family and Sophie. His feelings bottled up without release, making everything seem like the most important decision of his life, making him feel intense feelings about people he hardly knew.

He glanced over at Declan and Zoë. They had been in the weights area for hours now. A cameraman was trained on the two of them, and Declan had to keep pausing and resetting his reps at Brian's direction. Oliver could only imagine how annoying that would be to someone like Declan, who probably had a specific routine to keep himself looking so fit.

He wasn't sure what to make of Declan choosing Zoë at the recoupling. He hadn't seen it coming, but he didn't fool himself into thinking he could understand someone like Declan King, someone so different from anyone he had ever met. Oliver couldn't tell if choosing Zoë had been because of genuine feelings or a continuation of his one-sided feud.

He watched as Declan took a break from the workout to grab a towel and wipe off his sweat, starting with his face and trailing down the expanse of his chest and abs, putting on a good show – for Zoë or the cameras, Oliver could only guess.

'Oliver?'

Oliver started, tearing his eyes away from the squat rack and meeting Niall's intense gaze. 'Er, yeah. I'm sure Maeve's soul is lovely, and I'll speak with her... soon.'

'I know you two will hit it off,' Stella said, looking at him now. Oliver suddenly felt claustrophobic between the two of them. 'You're astrologically very compatible.'

Stella was only being nice, but Oliver had no delusions that the stars would align in his favour ever again.

'This is the perfect opportunity,' Niall said.

Oliver grimaced at him, grateful to have such well-meaning people to spend this strange period of time with. 'Yeah, all right,' he said, pushing himself up and heading towards the pool.

As he approached, Maeve looked up, smiling slightly. He took that as encouragement.

'Could we have a chat?' he asked, forcing his hands to stay at his sides rather than jump nervously to his hair.

She stood. 'Sure.'

'How are you liking the villa?' he asked stiffly as they walked towards the closest pair of lounge chairs.

She looked sideways at him, her brown eyes sincere. 'It's beautiful here.'

'Yeah?' He sat, wondering how on earth she could be enjoying this experience.

She nodded, sitting across from him and pulling her knees towards her chest. 'I know it's mad, but this is the first time I've taken off work since uni. I'm starting at a new job soon.'

They paused as the cameraman who had been getting the shot of Holly and Jack by the pool adjusted his position to focus on the two of them. 'So...' Oliver started awkwardly, 'how long ago did you graduate?'

Maeve tensed as soon as the camera was on her. 'Four years ago now,' she replied, eyes determinedly on his face.

He whistled. 'That's a long time without a holiday. What did you study?'

'Law,' she replied drily. 'This is quite the interrogation that you've prepared. I'm impressed.'

'Is it? I suppose I'm a bit nervous.' It took most of his concentration for his gaze to not constantly flick to the camera in the corner of his vision.

Maeve put a hand on his shoulder gently. 'It's cute,' she assured him. 'But I don't know anything about you yet. You give me your life story, and I'll give you mine.'

'Oh, uh, okay.' He thought for a moment and came up blank. All he could think of was a list of topics he didn't want to discuss. 'This is more difficult than it seems.'

'Where are you from?' she asked patiently.

He hesitated for a moment – her question fell into the category of topics he would rather avoid. 'Nottingham,' he said, though he wasn't sure why.

She raised her eyebrows. 'Oh?'

'I know, I don't have the accent any more. I moved to London when I was fourteen, to study ballet, and I've been there ever since.' Sophie was the only one who could still discern his childhood lilt. 'London is my home.'

He regretted it as soon as it was out, hoping it wouldn't get back to his parents and upset them. Oliver's family held a detached bemusement towards his life choices; of him and his three siblings, he was the only one who had left Nottingham. When he spoke with his parents – which wasn't often – he could tell that they still had no idea how their eldest boy had ended up as a ballet dancer instead of taking up a trade like he'd been meant to. Oliver had no words to explain his life choices to them. To him, staying in his suffocating hometown had never been an option.

Maeve looked, if he wasn't mistaken, impressed. 'Wow. That's a big decision.'

'Best decision I ever made.'

He had got one of the few coveted scholarship spots at the Covent Garden Ballet Conservatory, and arriving in London had felt like the start of his new life. He and Sophie had secured roles in the city after graduation, but the next step in his plan – their plan – had always been Manhattan Ballet.

She nodded. 'That's how I feel about studying law.'

'You're not one of those self-centred, soulless solicitors, then?' he joked. 'What, do you do child protection or something?'

'International human rights, actually.' Her tone was neutral, but her spine straightened as she said it, bracing for his reaction.

'Right, well, conversation over. It was nice chatting,' Oliver said, making to stand.

She grabbed his arm and tugged him back down.

'Shove off,' she said, rolling her eyes. 'I think ballet dancing is grand.'

'Sure you do.'

'I *do*,' she insisted. 'I couldn't get up in front of people and perform. I have terrible stage fright.'

That seemed a bit rich coming from someone currently in front of multiple cameras, even if she was tense. 'Don't you have to give speeches as a solicitor?'

She waved a hand dismissively. 'Only to octogenarians. I pretend that they're asleep, which they likely are. It's mostly writing and researching, all of the behind-the-scenes stuff. I'm confident in what I do, so long as I don't have to do it in front of a crowd of people.'

'Okay,' Oliver said. 'I'll accept your praise now that I understand your lowly career position.'

'To be honest,' she said, ignoring him, 'the men I've dated have always been intimidated by my work. But I don't want to hide how smart and passionate I am in order to settle down. I would rather be single.'

He nodded, appreciating how straightforward she was in comparison to most of the others he'd met. He didn't sense any hidden agenda behind her words. 'That makes sense.'

Maeve studied his face for a moment, perhaps trying to determine whether he was taking her seriously. 'I like you, Oliver,' she said finally, 'but I think we should keep our options open for now. It's early days still.' She added the last with a hint of irony.

He shrugged. 'It would do terrible things to my ego if a girl like you wanted to be with me right away, and we wouldn't want that, right?'

She smiled, flashing a dimple on her right cheek. 'Something like that.'

—

Paige didn't offer any greeting as Oliver entered the Love Shack the next morning, motioning for him to sit and flipping on the camera.

'How are things with Maeve?' she asked, without preamble.

'Well…' he stalled. The interviews were getting easier, but they were still nerve-wracking. 'We had a good chat yesterday, and I'm pleased with how we left things. We've decided to keep our options open, get to know the others. But right now, she's the girl I'm most interested in.'

Paige frowned. 'You're giving up on Zoë? You two had a good thing going before Declan stole her away.'

Oliver hesitated. Being coupled up with Zoë would certainly make winning easier, but he hadn't even considered trying to win her back. 'Yeah, we did. But she's coupled up with Declan now, so…' He shrugged.

'And you think Declan and Zoë make a good couple?'

'Er – well,' he said, looking helplessly at her impassive face, 'I don't know either of them, do I?'

Paige frowned again, and he knew immediately that the tepid response wouldn't play well with the audience. 'A guy you clearly dislike stole your girl, Oliver. The viewers will understand you being upset.'

Oliver *was* annoyed with Declan. It couldn't be too difficult to exaggerate his feelings for Zoë, especially if it would help his ratings. He swallowed.

'Okay. Er, I think what Declan did, picking Zoë, was under-handed. Zoë and I were great together, and now I feel like our chance at happiness was torn away from us because Declan thinks he's entitled to anything he wants.'

Paige's face lit up. 'You think Declan's entitled?'

Oliver thought Declan seemed like someone who had never been uncomfortable with himself a day in his life and resented anyone who had to work harder to keep up.

'He wanted Zoë, so he took her. I'm not convinced that Zoë wants to be with him, or that he particularly likes her. He only seemed interested once she and I got together.' Never mind that that had been as soon as she'd walked into the garden – it sounded good when he said it out loud.

Paige nodded, scribbling notes. 'Do you think Declan has it out for you in particular?'

Oliver found it hard to believe Declan thought about him at all, and yet, he couldn't shake the feeling that it had all started when they had locked eyes on the plane. 'It feels like it.'

'Repeat that, but as a full sentence.'

Oliver ran a hand through his hair. 'It feels like Declan has some sort of issue with me, but I'm not sure what I could have done wrong in his book. Maybe he just doesn't like the look of me, doesn't think I could pull a girl like Zoë.'

'And if Zoë wanted to get back together, would you be interested?' Paige said, in an odd, conspiratorial tone.

Oliver studied Paige's face. 'What do you mean?'

Her expression remained carefully blank. 'If she said she was still interested in pursuing things with you, would you want to try again?'

It was difficult to ignore the subtext: Zoë had told Paige she was still interested in him. That was more than he had from Maeve at the moment, and any drama with Declan would get him more valuable screen time, even if every part of his body warned him to stay away.

'Yes, I want to see where things go with Zoë.' He paused, trying to think of something more dramatic to say. 'We have so much potential as a couple that we haven't been able to explore yet. I hope we'll find our way back to each other.'

Paige smiled, and Oliver felt the same satisfaction as walking off stage after a perfectly executed routine. 'Great job – you're a natural, like I knew you would be. The audience is invested in this love triangle with Declan, so we'll keep things moving. Maybe you'll get a date with Zoë soon.'

Oliver was relieved that someone was telling him what to do. 'Thanks, Paige.'

When he exited the Love Shack and walked out onto the patio, two new contestants were being welcomed to the villa.

He went to stand by Maeve, who pointed at the redheaded man and muttered, 'That's Owen.' Owen was friendly in greeting everyone, but his eyes hardly left Holly the whole time.

Maeve gestured to the woman. 'And Imogen.' Imogen was tall, with brown skin, prominent cheekbones and a mass of curls. Her gaze flitted between the gathered contestants, and she quickly singled out Jack, batting her eyelashes up at him.

Oliver glanced sideways at Maeve, trying to gauge if she was interested in Owen. To his surprise, she wasn't looking at Owen at all, but studying Imogen with a frown.

'Anything I've got to worry about?' Oliver asked.

She arched an eyebrow at him. 'Not in the slightest. Early days, remember?'

Oliver grinned, deciding he liked Maeve. 'Yes, early days.'

Chapter 7

Oliver

Six Weeks until Finale

As promised, he got a date a few days after his interview with Paige. He had been trying to get to know Zoë more without attracting Declan's attention, and he thought it had been going well. Between a short conversation where he'd complimented how nicely she'd matched her make-up to her outfit – something Will swore girls put effort into – and her calling him funny after he'd made what he thought was a rather serious observation on the current state of the internet, Oliver considered his luck to be picking up.

'Oliver,' Darcy said, as those sprawled around the garden gathered around, 'looks like you'll be getting another chance at love. Take the Lover of your choosing on a date, and remember: hope floats. Ta for now!'

He looked at Zoë, standing to his left. 'What do you say, Zoë?'

Zoë hesitated for only a moment before replying, 'Love to!'

'Great,' Oliver said, trying not to look at Declan.

Zoë and Oliver walked towards the villa, the cameramen and contestants trailing behind for the pre-date ritual of pep talks and wardrobe advice. Oliver thought he could feel Declan's eyes boring into the back of his skull. When he looked over his shoulder to confirm his suspicions, Oliver's mouth went dry. Only Declan could make baby-blue eyes look so murderous. They would have been pretty in any other context.

The girls headed upstairs as the boys spread across the bedroom. Oliver had his limited wardrobe memorised and could probably get dressed in his sleep, but show mechanics dictated that the other boys have their say.

'Which shirt?' Oliver asked Niall, rifling through his suitcase. In the corner of his vision, he saw Paige talking to Declan.

'The white and green one, with the leaf print. That's your best,' Niall replied, studying the disorganised inside of Oliver's suitcase with mild horror.

'Right you are,' Oliver agreed, stripping his shirt off and buttoning the new one. As he turned to show off the end result, Declan was standing in front of him. One of his intimidation tactics must have been wearing less and less clothing as the show progressed; today he wore only an indecently short pair of swim trunks.

Oliver swallowed. 'Wishing me luck?'

Declan glared at him, his jaw becoming impossibly sharper as he clenched it. 'Look, mate, I get it, I stole your girl and now you want revenge.' He puffed his chest out a little, crossing his arms in a way Oliver thought was meant to emphasise an impressive set of muscles. 'But Zoë and I are sound; there's no splitting us up.'

Everything Declan did was more and more infuriating. He was only talking to Oliver now because he had strayed into his territory by asking Zoë out. Otherwise, he would have continued to pretend that he blended perfectly into the floor.

'Well, if you and Zoë are so *sound*,' Oliver said, 'why was she flirting with me all week?'

It was an exaggeration, but Paige was standing behind Declan, a cameraman at her side, and he was trying to remember what she had told him about drama. If he wanted to win, maybe feeling ridiculous was a part of the process.

Declan blinked. 'Oh, I see,' he said, gaze turning sharp, 'you're delusional. Well, that explains it, then.'

'Let's see who feels delusional when Zoë has her chance to pick,' Oliver said, trying his best to mirror Declan's signature cocky grin.

Declan's eyes narrowed. 'I'm looking forward to it,' he said, his expression mocking. 'And may the best man win.' He put out his hand, and Oliver, in some mild state of shock, shook it.

As he pulled his hand away, Paige gestured to the cameraman and Oliver watched them move to catch a shot of Zoë and the girls in the hall. He looked back to Declan, bracing himself for the other man's anger, but found none. Declan's face was relaxed, his expression oddly blank.

Utterly bewildered by the altercation, Oliver tried not to dwell on it when he met Zoë in front of the villa and they were escorted to a white van.

The ride was short, ending in front of a dock with a small yacht bobbing off its side. Zoë gave a whoop of excitement. Brian pointed at the unattached microphone packs in his hand and gestured them out of the car.

'First, you need these.' After their mics were on, he continued, 'Let's get that initial shot again. Zoë, you've just seen the boat. This is the most exciting moment of your life.' His tone was entirely deadpan, and Oliver had no idea if he was joking or not.

Zoë, however, nodded animatedly and waited for a cue before re-enacting her excitement. Brian gave a thumbs-up.

'I love boats,' Zoë said to Oliver. At Brian's signal, they started down the dock.

'I've never been on one,' Oliver admitted, taking a hesitant step onto the yacht.

This seemed like the most shocking piece of news that had ever been delivered to Zoë. 'Never?' she asked, eyes wide. 'How come?'

He focused on her face as the engine roared to life. 'I manage to stay busy enough – I don't have much time off work.'

'Oh,' she said, nodding. 'I totally get that. I feel like I'm constantly working, but since I'm in Brighton, the beach is close by. It's a great backdrop for my peaceful yoga meditation videos.'

'That sounds nice,' he said, managing to keep a straight face as he glanced off the port side. 'I'll have to try one out sometime.'

Brian handed them a champagne bottle and glasses, gesturing for them to lie out on the bow.

'Cheers,' Oliver said, and Zoë smiled again as the cameraman stepped even closer to them to catch their glasses clinking. The situation was getting claustrophobic, but he took a deep breath and ploughed on: 'I'm glad I got the chance to ask you on this date.'

'Oh yeah?' she asked, looking up at him through thick, dark lashes. 'I was disappointed that we didn't get to hang out more before Declan chose me.'

'Exactly! I think we have great potential,' he said. 'I fancied you like mad as soon as I saw you in the villa that first day and I admire your work ethic as a fitness coach.' He grinned at her, feeling like a complete idiot.

Zoë giggled. 'You're not so bad yourself. And I'm glad you acknowledge how difficult my career is. A lot of men undermine what I do, but managing a brand is difficult work.'

There was a beat of silence. 'So, you also run a brand?' Oliver asked finally.

She rolled her eyes. '*I* am the brand.'

'Right, so, you manage yourself?' He'd meant it as a joke, but he could tell by Zoë's flared nostrils that it hadn't landed.

She pasted on a smile. 'And I do it excellently. I just hit 250,000 followers on Instagram.'

Even Oliver knew that was a lot. 'Wow, that's impressive.'

When he didn't continue to congratulate her, Zoë glanced to the side for direction. Brian took a step forwards – now fully wedged between them – and grabbed the bottle of champagne, pouring them fresh glasses and looking like he would rather drown himself in the bottle than continue to watch their date.

'Zoë,' Brian muttered, 'you could ask Oliver about his job, his hobbies…' He trailed off and gave her a pleading look before stepping back.

'So,' Zoë said, her voice suddenly lower and more flirtatious, 'what's a guy like you do in his free time?'

Oliver paused for too long and Brian facepalmed.

'I, uh, volunteer as a dance instructor for kids who come from areas with fewer arts resources.' It was the only hobby Oliver had ever had, but he hoped Zoë wouldn't ask him anything about it. When he'd started, he and Sophie had been co-teachers.

'Oh! That's nice,' she said, leaning in. 'That's actually one of the reasons I started my channel. Wellness shouldn't be only for the rich. Having all my videos available online means anyone, anywhere can get fit if they want to.'

'Right, it's wonderful to see the kids connect with something that's such a big part of me.' She gave him such an unexpectedly earnest look that he continued, 'I was one of them, once. My first ballet instructor's encouragement is the only reason I have the career I do, and I want to be that source of support for them.'

'You must like kids,' Zoë said.

He nodded. 'Love 'em.'

'I have a younger sister,' she said, her face lighting up. 'She's four years old, and she's so much cooler than me already. Do you have siblings?'

'Two older sisters and a younger brother. We're not really close…' he said hesitantly, not wanting to explain that he and his siblings had never had a thing in common, 'but I love kids.'

She smiled. 'Well, we agree there.'

'All right,' Brian said, startling them into remembering that he was still only a foot away. 'We certainly got *something* that can air on television, anyway. Let's move on to B-roll.'

–

When Oliver and Zoë returned to the villa that evening, they found Niall and Stella cuddling on a daybed and Callum and Poppy having a splash-fight in the pool, with the rest of the contestants out of view.

Zoë turned to him. 'Great date today,' she said perkily. 'I'm going to head inside. I usually do my daily affirmations around sunset.'

He wasn't sure what a daily affirmation was, but he didn't know if he cared to find out either. 'Er... great. I'll see you later?'

She nodded and headed off towards the villa. As he watched her go, anxiety crept in – the date hadn't gone terribly, but it certainly wasn't the roaring success he and Paige had been hoping for. And then there was the problem of Declan, and how Oliver could pursue Zoë with him constantly around.

As soon as Oliver's thoughts turned to Declan, he seemed to materialise in the corner of his vision, sitting with a group of contestants under the pergola.

Oliver took a step in Niall and Stella's direction then turned, resigned, towards the pergola at Paige's warning look.

'All right?' he greeted, and Maeve made room for him next to her on the swing.

Jack grinned, eyebrows raised as he looked between Maeve and Oliver. 'So... no new missus, then?'

Oliver didn't want to talk about it in front of Declan, who was giving him another inscrutable look. 'She's in the house, doing her daily affirmations.'

'I thought we weren't allowed to masturbate,' Holly quipped, and Imogen laughed too loudly, throwing a wide smile to Jack.

Maeve snorted, but turned it into a conceivable coughing noise. 'Be more obvious, why don't you?' she muttered, too quietly for anyone but Oliver to hear.

Jack looked like he was going to ask what she had said, but Holly cut in first: 'We've been trying to have such a dull conversation that the producers will have trouble listening to it later,' she said.

'Why?' Oliver asked, puzzled.

'We're bored out of our minds,' Declan said, finally meeting his eye. As always, his gaze was unnerving. 'It's payback time.'

Oliver couldn't figure Declan out; the man sitting across from him didn't seem at all like the one that had blown up at him in the bedroom. He looked like he couldn't care less about Oliver's date with Zoë.

'I didn't realise the producers found anything you said interesting enough to record,' Oliver quipped. Declan's mouth twitched, and Oliver's stomach dropped, unsure if the joke had landed.

He was distracted from worrying about it by Paige walking over, whispering into her headset. Holly nodded towards an approaching cameraman. 'Gee, thanks, Oliver,' she said, without much bite. Oliver mouthed an apology.

'So, how did the date go?' Declan asked after a moment's pause, his voice holding none of the warmth from moments ago.

Oliver swallowed. 'I went on a boat for the first time,' he said, because he couldn't think of anything else to say.

'Right.' Something about the look in Declan's eyes reminded Oliver of how Paige had looked at him during their interview, expectant.

'I'm sure you lot go on boats all the time,' Oliver continued, feeling like he'd messed something up.

'Well, you've certainly nailed the boring thing,' Declan said drily. Jack and Owen laughed in appreciation.

'Man, you two are *too* good,' Jack said.

Oliver barely registered the dig. There was something he wasn't getting. Declan flicked a glance towards Paige; it was a split second of broken eye contact, but suddenly Oliver felt foolish. Because of his near-constant rehashing of their interaction on the plane, he hadn't considered the possibility that Declan was playing up the love triangle for the cameras.

'It was quite romantic, actually,' Oliver said, looking into Declan's eyes. 'Got to see the sunset over the waves and sip champagne together.'

Declan gave him an almost imperceptible nod of approval.

'I'm not sure a romantic setting would be enough to tempt Zoë,' he shot back, his face the picture of disdain. 'Unfortunately, I think she's also got to like the company.'

'I didn't hear any complaints,' Oliver said, trying to insert some heat into his voice. Paige was practically beaming at them now; he had never seen her so pleased.

'Well, let the best man win,' Declan said, leaning back on the swing with his arms behind his head in a pose that perfectly displayed his biceps.

'I wouldn't be so confident,' Oliver said, almost giddy now. Once he was in on it, Declan's performance was quite entertaining, and Oliver breathed a little easier knowing the drama would help him stay on the show. The only thing giving him pause was having no idea where the act ended and Declan's real feelings began.

'Oh, I am,' Declan said. 'Because at the end of the day, she's still sharing my bed, mate.'

—

Oliver stood in front of the firepit, running a hand through his hair distractedly until he noticed Paige glaring at him. *Sorry*, he mouthed, trying in vain to smooth his curls back into a presentable state. The boys were lined up in the flickering firelight for another recoupling ceremony. It was the night after Oliver's date with Zoë, and her choice would be the main focus.

Oliver glanced around at the guys, looking at Declan first. He wore a navy shirt, bringing out the blue of his eyes, the firelight catching on the crooked bridge of his nose. Noticing his gaze, Declan winked and Oliver looked away quickly.

Darcy entered through the garden gate, strutting towards the firepit in heels so high Oliver had a hard time comprehending how she could physically walk in them.

'Lovers,' Darcy said, her mouth pulling into a pout, 'I have some bad news. All week, the viewers have been voting for their favourite couples. We've tallied the results, and the couple with the fewest votes will be dropped from the villa immediately.' Oliver only had a few seconds to feel anxious, adrenaline pumping hard in his veins. Maeve grasped his hand, squeezing it tightly as Darcy continued, 'I'm sorry, Callum and Poppy, please pack your bags and leave.'

'What?' Callum's scowl was more pronounced than Oliver had ever seen it. 'That can't be right.'

A tear-stained Poppy dragged him back to the villa, as he cursed the lot of them, promising an exposé on male-discrimination on reality television in his next episode.

'Well then,' Darcy said, surveying the group hawkishly. 'Nice and easy recoupling from here on out. Make it pensive, make it dramatic, and for the love of God, *make it quick.*'

As the cameras rolled, Darcy asked Stella to choose one of the men in front of them. Stella gave a speech that ended with the predictable choice: 'Niall.' He walked over to give her a kiss before sliding his hand into hers and pulling her to the couch. Oliver gave them a thumbs-up.

Paige directed the cameraman closer. 'Oliver, do that again, on my count. Niall, give Oliver that gorgeous smile of yours. You two are mates.' They *were* mates, so it was weird she felt the need to tell them that. They repeated the moment until Oliver's cheeks were sore from smiling supportively.

'I think we have it,' Darcy said tightly. Paige signalled for the cameramen to reset. 'Zoë?' Darcy prompted, barely pausing to take a breath. 'Which Lover will you couple up with this week?'

Oliver glanced at Niall, who mimed taking a deep breath. He smiled gratefully.

'Close up on Zoë, Oliver and Declan,' Darcy ordered. 'Zoë, take it away.'

Zoë looked between him and Declan, uncertainty etched on her face. 'This week, I had a hard choice to make. I got to know two incredible guys, but I only get to choose one. This man has made me feel so comfortable here, I feel like he understands where I'm coming from and we can talk about anything. So this week, I've chosen to couple up with… Declan.'

Oliver was almost relieved when Zoë didn't call out his name. He knew it was coming – whatever potential they might have had quickly fizzled out after their date – but he did his best to look heartbroken for the cameras. He thought he caught an approving look from Declan as he strode over to Zoë.

'Perfect!' Darcy said, turning back to the remaining girls. 'Maeve?'

Maeve met Oliver's eye with an encouraging smile, and he let out a breath.

'Right, well, this boy has been rather good to me, which can't be said of all the men here, and he makes me laugh, which is hard to do with my rotten sense of humour. I'd like to see where things go. I pick Oliver.'

'Thank God,' he jokingly whispered in Maeve's ear when he reached her, under the guise of giving her a kiss on the cheek. They only had to repeat this exchange two times, since Darcy was so pleased with the result.

Holly swapped Jack for Owen, leaving him for an appreciative Imogen to scoop up. When all of the couples stood on the right side of the firepit, Oliver braced himself for what would come next. He may be safe for the night, but if Poppy and Callum's fate had proven anything it was that being in a couple wasn't enough to win – the audience had to root for your love. He glanced at Declan and Zoë, feeling like maybe he should've fought harder for her, and then back to Maeve, recommitting himself to making this work.

Chapter 8

Declan

Six Weeks Until Finale

Neil Steel: Well, well, looks like our budding love triangle might be losing a side. Which would make it a love...? I don't know, I was rubbish at geometry.

Zoë Park: 'I've been torn between them. I mean, Oliver is so sweet, but I think Declan and I have a more genuine connection.'

Neil Steel: What's the line? You miss 100 per cent of the shots you don't take? There's too much maths in this intro. Well, better luck next time, boyo!

Saturday had become Declan's favourite day of the week. It was their day off, so he let himself sleep until the designated wake-up time, and it also meant no cameras, no microphones and no drama. This week, the producers were driving them to a private beach while the villa got a much-needed deep cleaning.

Even the glaring lights of the villa flickering on mercilessly in the morning couldn't dampen Declan's good mood. He got up quickly, grabbing his swim trunks and sunglasses as Zoë yawned and stretched on the other side of the bed.

He was lucky to have found her so early in the game. Encouraging Oliver to try to win her back and fabricating a love triangle between the three of them had been a brilliant move on her part. Not only had it got them all more screen time, but it had given Declan an excuse to interact with Oliver.

'Ready?' Declan asked Zoë, and she nodded, following him out to the vans. He watched Oliver mumble something to Maeve as they climbed in, still seemingly half-asleep.

Avoidance was Declan's usual plan when it came to men he found attractive, but with Oliver it was harder than it had ever been before. He was always exactly where Declan didn't want him, slumped drowsily in the kitchen when Declan went for his morning swims, lying shirtless by the pool while Declan worked out, running his hands through his ridiculous hair whenever Declan happened to be close. Finally talking to him had been a relief, even if it was only to trade insults.

Declan hadn't thought Oliver would have had it in him to pick petty fights for the cameras, but he had been amazing, parrying Declan's barbs with his own sharp wit. Something about the look in his eyes, when he finally realised the game, had given Declan a twisted thrill.

When they arrived at the beach, Declan immediately ran down to the surf, diving head-first into the crystal-blue water. After so many mornings spent in a tiny pool, he revelled in the expanse of the ocean, swimming out as far as he could. Jack shouted behind him, and Declan turned to watch him flip himself forwards and land face-first in the wake of a wave.

'That's what I meant to do,' Jack said, struggling through the choppy water towards Declan.

Declan clapped him on the back. 'Sure, sure.'

Holly and Owen joined them, and they talked about their lives back home, enjoying the peace of not being recorded. Holly told them about her first job tending bar at a wild club, recounting a story about a man offering her a lap dance in exchange for another drink.

'Holy shit,' Owen said. 'That was my mate Cillian. Swear on my life.'

Holly laughed. 'It's so refreshing to be with someone who has banter. I just got out of a relationship with a man who never made me laugh.' She splashed Jack.

'Hey!' Jack yelled in mock outrage. 'I'm funny, take it back!' He lunged at Holly, lifting her and throwing her into an oncoming wave. Declan and Owen cheered him on as Holly screamed with laughter.

'Oi!' Brian called jovially from the beach. 'Save it for the cameras!'

Jack stuck his tongue out at Holly when she resurfaced, and the group agreed it was time for lunch. The production tent was stocked with snacks and alcohol, and for the first time since the beginning of filming, nobody was cutting the contestants off at two drinks. After they finished eating, Holly poured out tequila shots, and Declan quickly lost count of how many he'd had.

Full and more than a little tipsy, Declan glanced across the beach and noticed Oliver sleeping nearby on a towel. He was curled in on himself, his hands tucked under his chin and his hair mussed by the ocean breeze. Without thinking, Declan walked over.

'Hey,' he said, his eyes tracing over Oliver's bare chest. 'I think it may be time to reapply.'

Oliver blinked at him sluggishly for a moment before jerking up and adjusting his glasses. 'Oh shit. I can't burn. That'd be it for me, I'm sure of it.'

'Easy,' Declan said, grabbing the bottle of suncream nestled in the sand between them, his fingers hot from the alcohol pulsing through his veins. 'I can get your back.'

Oliver raised his eyebrows, then shrugged. 'All right.' He turned his back to Declan, who shuffled closer on his knees to get a better angle.

As he rubbed the cream into Oliver's back, fixating on a small constellation of moles on his left shoulder, Declan realised he was at least three drinks past tipsy and playing a very dangerous game. Remembering why he'd kept away from Oliver in the first place, he gruffly slapped the suncream on in a way that could only be seen as platonic and heterosexual.

'You should be all good,' he said stiffly, sitting back and plastering on a smile.

Oliver looked bemused. 'Cheers.'

Declan cleared his throat. 'So, uh…' Words usually came easily to him, but he couldn't think, the lines of Oliver's collarbone making him stupid. 'You a swimmer, then?'

'Pardon?' Oliver said, his eyebrows drawing together.

'I mean,' Declan backpedalled, waving a hand at Oliver's lean frame. 'You're built for it, right? And you're cut, so I figured maybe you were a swimmer.' His cheeks burned as his brain caught up with his words.

'I don't know how to swim,' Oliver said, still frowning. 'And I'm a ballet dancer.'

'Oh, right,' Declan said, nodding.

Oliver didn't look convinced. 'It's the running joke between Owen and Jack right now.'

'Is that why they were talking about tutus?'

'You're not that observant, are you?' Oliver teased, smiling slyly, and the tension eased from Declan's shoulders.

'When it's not about me?' he said, droll. 'Nah, can't be bothered.' Oliver let out a loud laugh at that, and Declan grinned. 'You're not bad to look at when you lighten up a little,' he said, without thinking. He blinked, not letting embarrassment show on his face, though he wished he could stop telling Oliver how attractive he was.

'It's getting easier,' Oliver said, seeming not to notice. 'All the cameras, constantly being recorded, it's not exactly my thing.'

'Shouldn't you be used to performing? You did a good job last week when we were fighting over Zoë.'

'Like I said, it's getting easier. Once I realised that's what it was, a performance, I could go through with it and not worry so much.' Oliver sighed, swatting some sand off his towel. 'I guess it's a little hard to explain, but when I'm dancing, I don't have to think. There's the routine, and I follow it. Nothing is up to me.'

Declan nodded along, caught in the striking contrast between Oliver's green eyes and the bright blue of the sky.

'But here,' he continued, 'I think about everything. I think about how I walk, and sit, and stand, not to mention I'm constantly thinking about the words coming out of my mouth.'

'Sounds to me like you're *over*thinking it,' Declan said.

'That's easy for you to say,' Oliver said. 'You never slip up. It's impossible to tell what you're thinking.'

Declan shrugged, relieved by that assessment. He'd certainly had enough practice. 'I've got used to it. My job is constant press conferences and talk shows and people feeling entitled to take my picture any time I leave my flat. But none of it's real. Sure, I can turn it on, but to be honest, I'd rather not be in the spotlight at all.'

'Then why come on reality TV?' Oliver asked.

The functioning portion of Declan's brain told him to exercise caution. 'Well, it's like I said, my career makes it difficult to meet someone.'

Oliver stared at him, biting his bottom lip, and said nothing. Incapable of doing anything other than stare back, Declan felt like all the air on earth had evaporated.

'Sure,' he continued after a moment, his tone sharper than he intended, 'I play things up for the drama, but I *like* Zoë. I want to find someone to spend my life with.' He could picture Georgia rolling her eyes, but it had the desired effect on Oliver.

'Huh,' he said, looking down. 'Between you, Niall and Stella, I seem to gravitate towards the saps.'

Declan cleared his throat, not wanting to think about Oliver gravitating towards him. 'Plus, my wrist is still useless, so I figured this would be a nice holiday.' He let out a humourless laugh. They both knew too well that this was no holiday.

He looked out at the ocean, realising that he'd just admitted for the first time that his break from boxing wasn't entirely voluntary, and didn't catch what Oliver said next.

'What?' Declan asked, but Oliver was looking somewhere slightly over his shoulder, his frown smoothing over.

'Hey, boys,' Paige said, laying a towel at their feet. 'How are we doing over here?'

'Oh, grand,' Oliver said.

'Yup,' Declan said, clapping Oliver on the knee. 'We've bonded over our athletic abilities and decided to be mates. I hope that doesn't ruin your plans for us.'

'Of course not,' she said. 'These storylines only have a shelf life of about three episodes anyway, and everyone loves a bromance.' She looked between them in her calculating way. 'Is there anything specific you bonded over?'

'I asked Declan about his last fight,' Oliver said.

'Oh?' Paige asked.

'I'm sure you know all about it,' Declan said quickly.

'I saw your press conference afterwards,' Paige said, eyes alight with interest. 'But I never saw what actually happened.'

She turned to him and Declan found it suddenly difficult to breathe. As much as his time on the show had been more difficult than he had expected, it had provided a decent distraction from his career. Now it was like he was back in the ring again, the bright lights beating down on him and the roar of the crowd echoing in his ear.

Declan cleared his throat. 'I, er, took a pretty bad beating on that one.' He scratched the back of his neck awkwardly, not looking at Paige or Oliver. 'Alexei has a killer right hook, which I, uh, underestimated. But I guess I had got a bit cocky. Thought I was invincible, right?' His cheeks flushed and he started talking faster, as if the quicker he relayed the story, the less it would hurt.

'He finally caught me across the cheek in the sixth round and I went down. I woke up with my wrist fucked… landed wrong, broke it clean through.' Declan shoved his wrist out stupidly as proof, the pink of his scar stark in the dying sunlight.

Oliver took it gently in his hands and brought it close to his face for inspection. His long fingers were cool against Declan's overheated skin, his calluses rough. Their hands touched and, for a crazed moment, Declan had the bizarre urge to lace their fingers together, wanting something to ground himself, to remind him that he wasn't still fighting.

Oliver caught his eye, and Declan, for the first time, had no idea what the other man would see in his expression. He hoped he looked normal and calm and not like he'd been pulled too thin across his skin. Oliver cracked a smile, that charming smile.

'I think you'll live,' he quipped, dropping his wrist, and Declan could breathe again.

Paige laughed at Oliver's joke, and Declan startled, remembering she was there, watching. 'Oh, this could be good.'

Chapter 9

Declan

Drinking himself to excess had been a mistake. When he didn't immediately pop out of bed for his usual early morning workout, Zoë took it upon herself to wiggle over to his side of the bed for a chat. Spotting a camera pointed at them, Declan understood this was an opportunity for screen time as a couple.

'Hello,' he muttered hoarsely, rearranging his body so Zoë could lay her head on his chest.

'Hello,' she echoed, with a soft smile. 'How are you this morning?'

'Absolutely knackered.'

'I think I know something that could help,' she said, her dark brown eyes wide. She leaned forward to plant a chaste kiss on his forehead. It was a compelling scene: the big, burly boxer with his tiny girlfriend fretting over him. The audience would love it.

'All better,' Declan declared. 'You should patent your healing technique; you'd make millions.'

Zoë giggled, sitting up and stretching her arms above her head.

'Well, the second step to this ancient healing ritual,' she said, playing along and looking over her shoulder at him, 'is piping hot tea.' She raised an eyebrow.

'God, yes, please,' Declan said, pulling himself out of bed and hoisting her into his arms, bridal-style. She shrieked with laughter. 'Shall we?' he asked, ignoring the pounding behind his eyes.

They walked out to the kitchen like that, greeted by hoots and hollers from the others.

'Oi,' Jack called over to them, as Declan placed Zoë gently on the counter. 'You two tying the knot, then?'

'If we do,' Declan called back, 'would you officiate?'

Zoë hopped down and pushed him towards the others. 'Go on, wifey can make the tea this morning,' she said, winking.

Declan laughed, heading to a daybed occupied by Holly, Maeve and Oliver.

'You up for being my best man?' Declan asked Oliver, sitting next to him.

Maeve glanced between them, confused. 'Am I missing something?'

'Oh, yeah,' Oliver cut in, slinging his arm over Declan's shoulder. Declan ignored a stab of discomfort, reminding himself that he was allowed to touch Oliver now that it was for the show. 'Declan and I are mates, didn't you get the memo?' Oliver gave a fake smile and made his eyes wide, like a hostage being held against his will.

'We talked it out like men,' Declan agreed.

'I conceded that the better man had won the girl,' Oliver said solemnly, but there was a glint of amusement in his eyes.

'Fancy a workout, mate?' Declan said, conscious of the cameras.

Zoë came over, handing a steaming mug to Declan. She perched herself next to him on the daybed and took a small sip, nodding expectantly towards the weights. Working out together had become part of their routine, but Declan didn't want to leave Oliver.

'Wait, Zo, why don't you put us through one of your boot-camps?' he said, knowing she wouldn't refuse – it was the perfect opportunity to promote her channel.

'What?' Zoë asked, taken aback.

'You know, like your videos,' Declan explained. 'Tell us what to do, critique our form, be our drill sergeant.' Zoë looked unsure, but Declan could tell she just wanted to be convinced. 'You'll get to boss us around; it'll be fun.'

'It could be a competition,' Holly added.

'Yes, Holly!' Declan said, pleased the idea was catching on.

'Er, do I get a say in this?' Oliver asked.

'No.'

Oliver laughed good-naturedly. 'Oh, it is so on, King.'

Declan looked to Zoë again, and she finally nodded, conceding. 'I actually have the perfect outfit for this,' she said earnestly, and the others laughed.

Fifteen minutes later, Declan and Oliver were standing side by side on the grass, yoga mats in front of them. Zoë stood on the patio stairs, with two cameramen trained on the developing entertainment and the rest of the contestants gathered to watch.

'All right, boys,' Zoë called in her trainer voice. 'We're doing a circuit of three minutes for each exercise: squat switches, step-back kick-ups, burpees and a two-minute plank.' She nimbly showed off each move as she explained it. 'On your marks, get set... go!' She blew on the whistle Paige had scrambled to find for her.

Declan fell quickly into the exercises, enjoying the familiar burn. It was simple enough, but it had been a long time since he'd competed with anyone, and Oliver was fast.

'Oh, come on, Decs,' Jack shouted. 'You can do better than that! Chin up, mate.'

Declan gave him the finger mid-squat. 'Why are you so good at these?' he shot at Oliver.

Oliver laughed. 'Sometimes at rehearsal, they'll make us carry the girls on our shoulders. This is nothing.'

'All right, stop!' Zoë called out. 'Two breaths, then start the kick-ups... Go!'

Oliver was killing him, his long legs kicking high into the air in perfectly straight lines. Declan, who struggled with tight hamstrings, was having difficulty getting his leg levelled above his hips.

'This is embarrassing, King,' Holly called. 'I thought you were a pro.'

'I'm not a *kick*boxer,' Declan said between breaths. 'I could still knock any of you clean out, so watch it.' None of them appeared to be sufficiently intimidated by his threat.

'Last ten seconds,' Zoë called out, chipper. 'Babes, keep your back straight, you don't want to hurt yourself.'

Owen and Jack cackled, and Declan squashed down murderous thoughts.

'Okay, stop.'

Declan sucked in a breath. He had thought he'd been staying in pretty good shape, but he was now mentally restructuring his workout routine to make up for the complete ass-kicking he was currently experiencing.

'Ready for burpees?' Zoë asked. 'Go!'

Finally, Declan had the upper hand against Oliver, and he felt giddy watching him struggle.

'Come on, Oliver,' Niall called. 'You've got this, boyo!'

'Thirty seconds,' Zoë said, pacing between the two men. 'Nice, Decs!'

'About time you caught up,' Oliver said, grinning. Declan grunted, deciding beating him would be the best comeback.

'Okay, finished,' Zoë said. 'Now the plank.'

Declan and Oliver fell to the ground, facing each other and pushing onto their forearms. 'Butts down, laddies,' Owen called, and Declan could've hit him. There was a dull ache in his wrist from the strain.

'Thirty seconds left,' Zoë called. 'Good form, both of you.' Declan tried to focus on his breathing and keeping his core tight.

'And... done,' Zoë said, blowing her whistle. Declan's muscles screamed at him to release the position, but Oliver was still holding himself up.

'All right, all right,' Jack shouted. 'Stop showing off, you two. Some of us are not Greek gods.'

Oliver huffed out a laugh but didn't concede, so neither could Declan. The two boys stared at each other, their bodies shaking with effort. A bead of sweat fell from Oliver's brow and Declan traced it as it slid down his cheekbone before getting caught between his lips. Declan stared at his mouth, feeling a burning in his core he desperately tried to convince himself was part of the workout.

'Jesus,' Holly said, exasperated. 'Why don't you both whip it out and spare us the dramatics?'

Declan adjusted his position to get a better grip on the mat, willing Oliver to concede, but something in his wrist gave and a searing pain shot up his arm. He fell to the ground, Oliver following him a split second later.

Niall and Owen ran over and grabbed Oliver, ceremoniously tossing him into the shallow end of the pool. He sprang up a moment later, shaking his hair out.

Declan got up to offer him a hand. 'Good one, yeah?'

Oliver grinned, the sunlight making him so brilliant it almost hurt to look at him. He reached out and took Declan's hand, a gleam in his eyes.

'Don't—' Declan started, but Oliver was already pulling him into the pool, the cool water soothing his overheated body.

'Get out!' Paige barked. 'You're still mic'd.'

They pulled themselves out, dutifully handing over their now water-logged microphones.

Paige's expression softened into a wry smile. 'But good stuff, keep it up.'

Oliver and Declan traded amused looks as Brian delivered a bored lecture about the importance of maintaining the equipment.

—

The crew arranged a neon party for the Lovers the next night. Brian had provided Declan with a neon pink tank top, yellow sweatband and miniscule bright green workout shorts.

Dressed and ready, Declan sat in the girls' dressing room as Zoë painted intricate designs on his arms and legs. The producers had given them Day-Glo paint, and the cameramen were manoeuvring to get shots of each couple painting one another. He looked over at Niall and Stella, and he could see how it could make for cute content. Niall was gazing at Stella adoringly as she carefully painted kitten whiskers on his face.

'There,' Zoë said, surveying her work with pride. Declan smiled at her and reached for the paint to return the favour, but she stopped him. 'Actually, do you mind if I do mine myself? I kinda have a vision for it.'

'Oh,' Declan said. 'Of course. Honestly, I'd prolly make a mess of it.' He stood. 'I'll get out of your way, then.' He dropped a kiss on the top of her head.

When he walked into the bedroom, he encountered a lone Day-Glo'd Oliver deciding between two equally horrific patterned shirts.

'Have you thought of burning both and going topless?' Declan asked, sitting on Oliver's bed. Oliver rolled his eyes, shrugging a black shirt with neon green parrots over his head and smudging the purple paint on one cheekbone.

'You're hopeless,' Declan said, with an exaggerated sigh. He stood and wiped at the smudge with his thumb, his other hand grasping Oliver by the back of the neck to hold him still. His grin faded slightly as he noticed how close the two of them were standing. Close enough that he could see the small flecks of gold in Oliver's eyes, could smell pine and amber on his skin.

'Er – sorry,' he said, backing off.

'Thanks,' Oliver said easily, glancing around the room for a cameraman that wasn't there. He turned back to Declan with a guarded look. 'Is it fine now?'

'Yes,' Declan said, looking Oliver over.

The producers had given him a similarly short pair of neon shorts, and his exposed legs were strong and lean, freckles sprinkled across pale skin. He was wearing a glowstick necklace around his head, casting his face in angelic light.

'Shall we?' Oliver asked, holding out his elbow. Declan smiled and looped his arm though Oliver's as they walked out onto the patio.

The others trickled out of the villa soon after, and music started booming over the loudspeakers, an indication for the festivities to begin.

Declan didn't think he'd ever get comfortable dancing in such a small crowd, but it was easier now that he knew everyone better. He was surprised by how comfortable he felt with them – he didn't take to people very quickly, and had few friends as a result. Georgia had once accused him of keeping the world at arm's length, and it wasn't untrue. But he laughed along as Jack and Owen attempted a breakdance fight for a few frantic minutes before settling into a two-man conga line.

Declan slung an arm over Niall's shoulders and grabbed Oliver's waist as they jumped around shouting out the lyrics to the Dua Lipa song playing over the loudspeaker. The girls were hand in hand, swinging each other around. It was absolute chaos, and Declan couldn't imagine it would look good televised, but he figured there must be some magic in the camera angle.

They danced for hours before Brian finally told them they had enough footage and the whole group sighed with relief.

The night wound down, the girls slipping off their heels and dipping their legs into the pool to soothe their aching feet. Declan and Oliver took it upon themselves to make tea for everyone. Oliver looked as tired as Declan felt, struggling to keep his eyes open as they waited for the water to boil.

'All right?' Declan asked, putting a steadying hand on Oliver's bicep.

He nodded. 'Exhausting, isn't it?' he said as the kettle beeped off. He poured the water, passing the steeping mugs off to Declan, who set them on a tray.

As Declan carried the tray across the patio, he noticed Jack and Imogen sitting in a secluded corner, while Holly and Owen snogged on the couch swing. He didn't interrupt either pair, pleased that his mates seemed happy.

Instead, he walked towards Zoë and Maeve, who were lounging by the pool.

Zoë gave him a grateful look. 'Thanks, babes.'

Declan kneeled to pass the last mug to Maeve. She took it from him, muttering her thanks as she gazed across the pool sombrely. Declan wondered whether she and Oliver were on the rocks somehow. He walked back, intending to ask Oliver about it, but he found him perched on the counter with his head back and eyes closed, asleep.

'Oliver,' Declan whispered as he drew closer. Oliver made a soft noise in the back of his throat. 'Hey, you've got to wake up.' He reached out and grasped Oliver's shoulder, shaking him slightly, and his eyes finally opened. 'I think we've probably only got a quarter of an hour before they let us go to bed,' he said, removing his hand. 'Come on, let's have a chat.'

Oliver blinked at him, bleary-eyed. 'Tell me more about boxing.' His voice was low as he lifted Declan's bad wrist and then let it drop. 'I know that's the only reason why I won yesterday. It's still hurting you, isn't it?'

Declan nodded, even though he didn't particularly want to talk about it on camera. But Oliver had asked, and Declan desperately wanted to give him whatever he asked for.

The gnarled skin where the sutures had been was stark against his otherwise unblemished arm. The doctors had inserted three pins to hold the remnants of his wrist together. Even now, months later, when he couldn't fall asleep, he thought he could feel where each individual piece of metal had punctured bone.

'They told me I was lucky,' he said, 'that for an older man it would've been a career-ender.' He didn't feel lucky, or young. He felt ancient, like his body was settling into the years of beatings it had taken.

He sat beside Oliver on the counter, swiping the last mug of tea. 'I've been boxing since I could stand,' Declan found himself saying. 'My dad was a boxer, pretty famous in his day. He taught me and my brother everything he knew.'

'Your brother's a boxer too?' Oliver asked.

Declan nodded. He was both surprised and pleased by how little Oliver knew about him and his family. It was the reason, he thought, that Oliver had always treated him like a normal person and not an icon.

'My brother's ranked eighth in the UK.' The ranking had been his before his loss to Alexei. It marked the first time his younger brother had ever outranked him. Declan had never been able to match Aaron's sheer power, instead winning matches with a combination of strategy and dumb luck. Together, they came close to the formidable boxer their dad had been; as individuals, they both fell just short and were desperately trying to make up the distance.

'So it's the family business. Sounds nice,' Oliver said, grabbing the mug out of Declan's hands and taking a sip. 'Do you love it?'

Declan didn't know how to answer. Fighting was all he knew; everything he'd got in life was brought forth by sheer force of will, early mornings and late nights training with his dad. Everything was to make him proud.

'It's been good for me,' Declan said finally, not sure how else to put it positively. 'I'm good at it. And I'm lucky. My dad didn't have it nearly as good.' Oliver watched him, lips slightly parted, and Declan didn't think before continuing, 'Boxing was his way out. He fought like he needed it, like it was the only thing he could do.'

'What about you?' Oliver asked. 'How do you fight?'

'Like it's all one big game.' And it was true; Declan's life had always felt unreal, like it was happening to someone else – none of it mattering much, and none of it touching him any deeper than the bruises that formed on his skin.

'What about your mum?' Oliver asked. 'What does she think about boxing?'

Declan always dreaded the inevitable question; it was the one answer he'd never mastered. 'Not sure. I haven't spoken to her since I was eight.'

'Oh,' Oliver said, his eyes suddenly more alert. 'I'm sorry.'

'It's not something I talk about much,' Declan said, trying to sound casual but not quite managing it.

He'd seen his dad take many beatings, but the day she had left was the only time Declan had seen him truly defeated. As a much weaker man, Declan suspected he'd never recover from that sort of heartbreak.

Oliver seemed at a loss for words. 'That must have been really hard on you and your family.'

'Yeah, it was. But he's fine now.' He reached over to grab the mug from Oliver, fingers accidentally grazing the back of his hand. 'What about your family, are they all dancers?'

Oliver didn't say anything for a moment, uncomfortably examining the contents of the nearly empty mug in Declan's hands as if it held the answer.

'No,' he said hesitantly, 'I only started dancing because my sisters were taking a class. Mum was pregnant with my brother at the time and there was some complication. She was in hospital a lot and I was stuck watching my sisters dance twice a week. Finally, the instructor took pity on me and asked me to join in.'

'And you loved it?'

He nodded. 'For the first time, I knew what I wanted. I went home from that class and planned my whole future out. I don't think I've felt so sure of myself since. No one else around me understood it, but I just knew.'

Noticing the wistful look on Oliver's face as he talked about dancing, Declan knew he'd never felt that sure of himself. He found himself trapped by Oliver's gaze, noticing the scatter of freckles on the bridge of his nose, then the blood pounding in his own ears. There was no looking away.

'Sounds nice,' Declan said, unable to do anything but echo Oliver's words.

'It wasn't easy,' Oliver said. 'My parents didn't understand why I wanted to stick with it after my sisters quit. They didn't have the time or money, so I did it all myself. I paid for classes, trained obsessively, got myself to London...' Oliver's eyes had gone glassy in the low light of the kitchen.

'I'm sorry,' Declan said, 'that you had to do it alone.' Oliver ducked his head and Declan's heart clenched. He wanted to say something to get Oliver to look at him again, but the moment had passed.

Brian's bored voice sounded over the loudspeaker. 'All right, Lovers, get some sleep.'

'Thank God!' Niall cried, grabbing Stella and running towards the villa. Oliver slipped off the counter, and Declan followed him silently.

As Declan lay down next to Zoë, he noticed a smudge of Day-Glo above her eyebrow. 'You missed a spot,' he said softly, rubbing his thumb over the paint.

'Thanks,' Zoë said, looking at him expectantly. There was a beat, and then her gaze dropped to his lips and she leaned in.

'Uh, good night, Zo,' he said, awkwardly kissing her cheek.

He pulled the covers over himself, knowing he'd messed up – he should have just let her kiss him; he had pulled away without thinking. He tried not to look over at the bed next to his, where Oliver slept.

Chapter 10

Declan

As Declan finished his laps the next morning, he noticed Oliver watching him from the far side of the pool.

'Morning,' Oliver said, his voice still thick with sleep. His hair hadn't been brushed yet, but Declan liked the look of him this way. He looked soft in the mornings.

'Morning,' Declan replied, leaning his arms along the side of the pool and resting his head on them, trying to catch his breath.

'You're beautiful in the water,' Oliver said.

Declan laughed, surprised. There was a beat where neither of them said anything, both still basking in the silence of the cool morning air. Oliver shifted next to him, pulling one of his legs out of the water and curling it under his other knee as he leaned back on his hands. The movement caused his shin to knock against Declan's arm. Neither moved away.

'How are you feeling?' Declan asked finally. Oliver looked more rested than he had since Declan had met him, which he took as a good sign.

'I'm good. Really good, honestly.' He looked like he wanted to say more, but stopped short. Then, 'I'm glad we're mates now.'

Declan's stomach flipped. 'Me too.'

Oliver nodded, turning as the bedroom lights switched on and the other contestants filtered through the sliding glass doors. 'I'll let you finish up.' He walked to meet Maeve in the kitchen.

Declan looked after him for a moment, enjoying the graceful way his body moved before shaking his head and sinking back into the water.

Later that morning, Brian waved Declan over and told him to have a chat with Holly about her budding romance with Owen. Declan rolled his eyes, tired already of the manufactured conversations, but conceded. He found Holly sitting on the balcony and joined her on the couch.

'Fancy meeting you here,' Holly drawled.

'Anything new with you?' Declan asked. 'Any bearded Irishmen come to sweep you off your feet?'

'He's right fit, isn't he?' Holly said, uncharacteristically excited. 'But does he *like* me?'

'Oh, Holls,' Declan said, putting an arm around her. 'Don't tell me you're up here looking all conflicted because you're worried he doesn't want to crack on with you.'

'No,' Holly said defensively.

It was almost funny to see the normally unflappable Holly so anxious over a man, but Declan tried to stay serious. 'You're a total catch. If he doesn't want you, he's mad. Just tell him how you feel.'

'You want us to communicate in a healthy manner about our relationship?' she joked. 'That's completely unrealistic.'

'You idiot,' Declan said, ruffling her hair with one hand. Holly stuck her tongue out at him.

'Oh, all right,' she said, standing. 'I suppose I'm off to be a grown-up. Need any romantic advice from me before I go?'

Declan shook his head. 'I'm the love expert here.'

She headed back inside, and Declan lay back on the couch for a few minutes.

While he enjoyed the solitude, he felt a sudden longing to talk through things honestly with Georgia.

He was certain that if he could curl up with her and tell her everything happening with Zoë and Oliver, she would be able to help him figure it all out. But the feeling in his chest when he was close to Oliver wasn't something he thought he could describe. The initial embarrassment of his drunken words on the beach had subsided, leaving uneasiness in its wake. Thinking back to their conversation the night before and the one that morning, Declan was letting Oliver get to him in a way he'd never allowed anyone to before, revealing things he hadn't meant to. It was throwing him off his game.

The chime sounded and Declan sighed, feeling the beginnings of a headache forming.

When he walked onto the patio, Owen's arm was around Holly's waist. Darcy's voice rang out: 'Owen, take the Lover of your choice on a romantic night out.'

He looked at Holly, a stupid smile on his face. 'Holly Henderson, will you do me the honour of going on this date?'

'I will,' Holly said, her cheeks reddening.

'Imogen,' Darcy continued. 'You and another Lover will join Owen and Holly on their date. Choose wisely!'

'What do you say, Jackie boy?' she asked.

Jack's smile was a bit too bright. ' 'Course, love.'

The boys headed into the bedroom. 'Nervous?' Declan teased Jack.

Jack shrugged, rifling through his duffel for a clean shirt. 'Low stakes, man. Imogen is fit, but it's too early to know how we'll get on.' Declan was again struck by how close to the chest Jack played certain parts of the show.

Niall frowned. 'Someone who likes Imogen should go on the date. She deserves a chance at love, too.'

'It's decided,' Declan joked. 'Who'll go on the date, though?'

'Not me,' Niall said. He went red. 'I mean, obviously.'

Declan turned to Oliver, who ran a frantic hand through his hair. 'I'm fully committed to Maeve. Can't stray.'

'Is that right?' Jack asked, narrowing his eyes.

Declan stifled a laugh; none of them wanted to admit they found Imogen to be a bit much.

'Don't look so smug, King.' Jack whipped his attention to Declan. 'I saw that swerve from Zoë this morning. Are you two having a lovers' quarrel?'

Declan's mood immediately darkened, remembering how coldly Zoë had acted towards him at breakfast. 'We're fine.' He pointed at the shirt in Jack's right hand. 'I think the blue one.'

He left the boys, only to find a sullen-looking Maeve standing alone in the kitchen. He wordlessly filled the kettle, catching her eye and giving her a questioning nod.

'Yeah, thanks,' she said.

'Everything all right?' he asked. 'You seemed upset after the party last night.'

'Oh,' she said, fidgeting. 'Just in my cups.' She gave him a weak smile, but he could tell something was still bothering her.

'I know that you and I aren't exactly close, but I'm here if you want to talk.'

'Well, it's just – last night—' She cut herself off, lips scrunching as she struggled to articulate her thoughts. 'What do you think of Imogen?'

'I suppose if Jack likes her, then I like her well enough too,' Declan said slowly.

'And does he?' Maeve asked, searching his face intently. 'Like her, I mean.'

'Uh, maybe?' Declan's brows drew together. 'Why?'

Maeve blushed and it finally clicked. 'No...' Declan gaped at her. 'Jack?' It came out too loudly and she shushed him.

'I just think he's funny.' She looked at the kettle, which had boiled already without them noticing, pressing the lever down to reheat it. 'And cute,' she added.

Declan bit back a laugh at her comically anguished expression before another thought struck him. 'What about Oliver?'

'Right,' Maeve said. 'I guess I wanted to know if there's a chance with Jack first, before telling Oliver.'

'I think Jack would be mad not to go for you,' he said, but it felt stiff, dread trickling up his spine.

'Oliver will be all right, though,' Maeve said, eyeing him with concern. Declan made a concentrated effort to smooth his expression. 'I'll talk to him, I promise.'

He nodded, thinking back to Oliver sitting by the pool, his knee touching Declan's arm. He thought about Oliver's eyes the night before, when they had been too close together. Declan would figure out a way to keep Oliver on the show. He'd fix this.

–

The next morning, Declan lingered over his workout, considering how to broach Maeve's confession with Oliver. Even though she'd told him not to, he didn't think he could go much longer without bringing it up.

He emerged from the water and walked to where Oliver was waiting with two mugs of tea in the kitchen, still unsure of what to do. Oliver wordlessly passed him a mic and Declan clipped it onto his shorts. When he said nothing, Oliver handed him his tea.

Declan took a sip and nodded his thanks. 'I want to talk to you about something,' he said finally.

Oliver absentmindedly fingered the buttons on his shirt. 'Yeah?'

'Do you like her?' Taking in Oliver's blank look, he clarified, 'Maeve.'

'Er...' Oliver's eyes flicked sideways, towards Brian and the cameraman, and he cleared his throat. 'I like Maeve a lot. I'm not sure I *fancy* her exactly...' He trailed off, seeming flustered, and Declan realised he'd been staring.

'What do you mean, you're not sure?' Declan asked, wishing they could have a moment alone. He wanted to make Oliver understand this wasn't part of their game, that he was trying to help him. 'I mean, you've not been looking at any of the other girls. And she's fit, isn't she? She's a bloody solicitor. What's not to like?'

Oliver just looked at him helplessly. 'Are you asking me if it's okay for you to crack on with her?' He gave Declan a weak smile. 'Thought we were past that.'

Declan shook his head. 'I'm trying to understand what you're looking for.'

Oliver seemed lost in thought. 'I guess it's not that simple for me, knowing if I fancy someone. I haven't felt that way since I was a teenager. I thought I would know it when it happened, but I'm a bit lost.'

'It's been that long?' Declan couldn't keep the surprise out of his voice.

Oliver adjusted his glasses self-consciously. 'I was sixteen when my ex and I got together, and we broke up a few months ago.' He paused. 'Almost eight months ago. She moved to America,' he said, as though that explained things.

'Oh,' Declan said. Oliver's decision to come on the show finally made sense – only someone in crisis would do something as mad as try to find love on a reality show. 'That must have been hard for you.'

Oliver's expression softened, some anxiety leaving his face. 'Makes my hermit comment a little less funny, to be sure.'

Declan didn't know how to process this new piece of information, trying to marry this revelation with what he'd thought he'd known about Oliver.

'How did you know that you fancied her?' he asked finally, and then immediately regretted the question. The last thing he wanted to hear about was Oliver's feelings for his ex-girlfriend.

Oliver blinked at him. 'Pardon?'

'We've got to start somewhere, don't we?' Declan said. 'I mean, it was a long time ago, but surely you remember.'

'Er...' Oliver said. 'It was easy, instant. We were paired up in class – I'd just moved to London and she took me under her wing, introduced me to her mates, never left me alone...' He struggled for a moment, but finally continued, his expression wistful, 'I felt like the luckiest person in the world. She was the first person in my life who didn't think that my plans were mad – they were the same as hers.'

Declan stared at him, thoughts racing. Oliver's raw tone in talking about this woman Declan had never met made him realise what a perilous position he had put himself in. Oliver was straight, and clearly in love with someone else, yet somehow had got past Declan's usual defences.

'It was easy to fall for her,' Oliver continued, oblivious to Declan's internal struggle. 'I mean, everyone loves Sophie – if you met her, you would love her too. She's just like that.'

Declan couldn't imagine a reality where that was true, but he politely refrained from saying so.

After a moment, he realised Oliver was waiting for a response. 'God, I didn't...'

He cleared his throat, his mouth suddenly dry. It was clear Oliver still cared for her, his love for her somehow unshakeable. It reminded him of Georgia and James; the kind of love that was wholly foreign to Declan. The transparent pain on Oliver's face made him inexplicably jealous of how he let himself be so vulnerable even after she'd broken his heart.

Declan had seen the aftermath of bad break-ups before, both Georgia's tears and his father's disengagement. The day after Declan's mother had walked out, his father had acted like nothing had happened, and so Declan had done the same. He'd never thought admitting that he needed her, that he missed her, was an option. His dad had needed him to be brave, unflinching, and then as the years passed, his career had demanded the same.

'I didn't realise you could even date someone for that long,' he finished lamely.

Oliver shrugged, examining Declan's hands rather than meeting his eye. 'Maybe you haven't found the girl that will change your mind,' he said in a strange voice.

Declan laughed softly, hoping it didn't sound hollow. 'That's what they tell me.'

'Maybe it's Zoë,' Oliver said, and winced.

Declan nodded, looking away, part of him wishing he'd never approached Oliver on the beach. Maybe then the careful lies upon which he'd constructed his entire life wouldn't feel so precarious. Talking to Oliver was like standing on a precipice.

His eyes refocused on the cameraman standing over Oliver's right shoulder. He swallowed, suddenly remembering the purpose of the conversation. 'It seems like when you fancy someone, you *really* fancy her,' he said, the facade sliding smoothly back into place. 'Enough to date her for, what, eight years? So I think if you did fancy Maeve, you would know for sure.'

Declan glanced at the cameraman again as he said it. Oliver's eyes followed his and understanding dawned in them – he'd forgotten about the cameras too.

'You have a point,' Oliver said stiffly.

Declan forced himself to smile. 'Which is excellent news, because Maeve fancies Jack!'

Oliver blinked. 'How do *you* know that?'

Declan shrugged. 'Women like to tell me about their feelings. I'm a trustworthy sort.'

Oliver ran a hand through his hair before pasting on a grin, deflecting with a joke. 'It wasn't learned under duress, then?'

'Freely volunteered,' Declan declared. Then, lowering his voice conspiratorially, 'But I think she wanted to be careful to not hurt your feelings, because she likes you.'

'So she sent you in, since you're so careful with my feelings?'

'I would guard your heart with my life,' Declan said dramatically, placing a hand on Oliver's breastbone.

That finally got Brian's attention, and he looked over at them from behind his phone. 'Good stuff, you two. Do it again, but this time try to ham it up a bit, yeah?'

Chapter 11

Oliver

Five Weeks Until Finale

Neil Steel: Things are heating up in the villa this week. Everyone's talking about the newest romance in the house, Declan King, champion boxer, and Oliver Wright, ballet dancer!

Oliver Wright: 'They say keep your enemies close. And if they know how to box, keep them even closer...'

Neil Steel: Apologies, must have read the cue card wrong... The newest BROmance in the house! Did I get it right that time?

When Paige asked Oliver to have a chat with her in the Love Shack, he wasn't sure if it would be his last. He'd successfully avoided Maeve in the days since his conversation with Declan, but he knew his time to form a plan was running out.

'Perk up,' Paige said cheerily, indicating for him to sit. The red light wasn't on yet. 'It's not your execution day yet.'

He tried to remove the worried expression that he was beginning to fear was permanently etched into his features. 'You sure about that?'

She gave him a look. 'Where's quippy Oliver? I don't like broody Oliver. That scowl doesn't suit you.'

'Maeve fancies Jack,' he said flatly. 'If they couple up, I don't know what I'll do.'

'Right,' Paige said. Oliver realised that she, of course, knew that already. 'Is that all? I wouldn't worry about it. You're in a good position with ratings, and the villa works in mysterious ways.'

He tried for a smile, figuring that complying with her optimism could only help him. 'You're not planning my dramatic exit as we speak?'

'Never,' she said. 'The audience likes you, which means I like you. If you hadn't spent the past day staring into the distance moodily, I would like you even more. Your bromance with Declan has been *massive* on socials. It's what I told you in the beginning: the audience wants to root for you. You're a likeable guy.'

'Oh,' Oliver said awkwardly. 'Um, thanks?'

She studied him, but looked more concerned than calculating. 'Is that all that's bothering you?'

He sighed. 'No, that's not all of it.' He cleared his throat, feeling like the walls might close in on him at any moment. 'I, er, forgot that Declan and I were being recorded when I told him about Sophie. About the break-up. I probably sounded pathetic.' He'd been doing so well keeping her out of his head to focus on winning, and now the hollow feeling that had consumed him since her departure was creeping back in.

Since his talk with Declan, it had sunk in how long eight months really was. The fact that he hadn't talked to Sophie in weeks felt more like closure than their break-up had.

Paige frowned. 'You didn't sound pathetic. Honestly, you gave Sophie a lot of grace, and I assumed it was because you were conscious of the viewers.'

He shrugged, not meeting her eye. 'It's how I feel. It wasn't an act.'

'You don't blame her for walking out on your relationship?' Paige asked, confused.

He'd never been in the situation of explaining his break-up to someone who didn't know him and Sophie already. It was like trying to summarise a novel in a few words.

He finally met Paige's eye and softened at her sympathetic expression. 'How can I blame her? I didn't realise how bad things were by the end, for her to feel like she had to do something like that. It was my fault.' He said it without thinking, the instinct to defend Sophie automatic.

Paige looked sceptical. 'She could have talked to you about it.'

'Could she have?' He fiddled with his glasses, pushing them higher on his nose. 'We never disagreed about anything, we didn't argue. I don't think she knew how to break up with me without moving across the world, without making our relationship unfixable.'

'So you think it's your fault, because you would have fought for your relationship?' Paige asked slowly.

The question frustrated him, but he didn't know if he was angry at Paige for trying to understand, or with Sophie for doing something so difficult to explain.

'No, it's my fault because I didn't see it coming.' With the distance between them now, Oliver could recognise that people in perfect relationships didn't break up suddenly and without explanation.

Paige raised her eyebrows. 'But she moved continents with no warning – that's on her. To go from an eight-year relationship to nothing, I can't even imagine.'

'Except it's not nothing. We talk every day,' Oliver said, feeling his irritation return, this time in the form of self-loathing. 'Or we did, until I came here. She broke up with me, and it's like we pretended it never happened. But it did happen, she did leave.'

It was like something had finally clicked, something that had evaded him for months. Sophie had left him. All the phone conversations in the world couldn't change the fact that she had walked out. Even if he moved to New York, even if they got back together, his life would always be altered by her decision. It wasn't something he could simply undo.

'I'm sorry,' he said after a moment. 'It's not something I've talked about. It's hard to put into words.'

'What about your mates?' Paige asked. 'Haven't you talked to them about it?'

'They were her mates first,' he explained. It had irrationally bothered him when their friends had immediately sided with him in the break-up, leaving him as the one defending Sophie. 'It feels wrong to talk about it with them. I can deal with it on my own.'

'Well, it gives you a good story,' Paige said gently. 'The scene with Declan already aired. There are thousands of people watching this show who have been dumped, and they want to see you find the love of your life.'

'Yeah,' Oliver said. He straightened, conscious of how much he had revealed to Paige, but the camera to her left stood idly. At the moment, she didn't look like his producer, she looked like a friend. He continued, jokingly: 'So, I've already done my piece, then. Why don't you pick on someone else for a change? I'm sure if you put your mind to it, you could make Declan talk about *his* shit.'

Her face shifted back, almost imperceptibly, to the more calculating one he was used to. 'You know, that's not a bad idea. When he talked about the fight on the beach, that was a good moment we didn't catch on camera.'

He was alarmed by how quickly she had turned his joke into something serious. 'That's not exactly entertaining drama,' he said carefully.

Paige was unfazed. 'It's good for him, too, to be more vulnerable. People will get tired of his tough jock persona. He needs another angle if he wants to keep his ratings up, and you could help him.'

Oliver knew Declan had shared that story off camera for a reason, but it would be impossible to avoid playing into Paige's

97

hand without giving up the game entirely. He needed the money, needed to win, more than he needed to protect Declan's feelings.

'What are you asking me to do?'

She shrugged. 'Try to find a good moment to ask him about the fight.'

'Sure, fine.'

Her face instantly looked softer. 'Thanks, Oliver, that'd be brill.'

'The fact remains that I could be leaving the villa any day now, and you'll lose your puppet,' he said lightly.

'Well, there will be another elimination tomorrow,' she said, and Oliver felt a pang of anxiety. She leaned in conspiratorially. 'But who knows, there may be someone in the villa who surprises you.'

He smiled tightly. 'Stranger things have certainly happened.'

—

Sure enough, Oliver and Declan were interrupted in the kitchen later that day by Imogen. Paige had all but told him to go for her, but his stomach dropped at the thought of having to share his afternoon with anyone other than Declan.

'Hello, you two,' she called, waving. 'And how's the villa's best-looking duo?'

'Just enjoying paradise,' Declan said drolly.

'All alone?' Imogen asked, looking around eagerly. Her expressive face had an almost cartoonish effect. 'Don't your girls know it's dangerous to leave their belongings unattended?' She didn't seem overly bothered by the prospect. Someone must have tipped her off to the Maeve–Jack development, and she clearly wasn't taking the setback lying down.

'Where's Jack?' Oliver returned smoothly.

She shrugged. 'I have all I need between the two of you, anyhow.' Not that she had spared Oliver more than the cursory glance – it was clear who she was talking about.

'Declan's spoken for, I'm afraid,' Oliver said, hoping it came out flirtatious.

'I didn't realise he was married already,' Imogen parried, shooting Declan an easy smile.

Oliver felt a stab of annoyance not altogether warranted by a joke, but Declan only laughed. 'All's fair in love and war,' he said, grinning. 'That said, I *am* spoken for.'

'Oh,' Imogen said, pouting.

Oliver mirrored her surprise – despite what he'd said, it was unusual for contestants to outright reject anyone unless their relationship was serious. It seemed that what Declan had confessed on the beach, that he liked Zoë, was true. From his interactions with Zoë, Oliver didn't think her motivations were quite as pure.

Imogen recovered quickly, turning to look at Oliver. He realised that it was exactly what he had asked for, but now that she was in front of him, the prospect of going on another date was exhausting. Still, lazing around the villa wasn't going to win him the prize money. Imogen might have been fake, but for now, she needed him to stay on the show. With Paige's voice in his head, he pressed on.

'So… what do you do for work?' he asked, trying to show interest, realising he didn't know a thing about Imogen even though she'd been there for nearly two weeks.

'I know what you're thinking – a girl this beautiful *must* be a model,' she teased. 'You'd be half right. I did a spot of modelling in my teens, and content creation is how I make most of my money now, but I'm saving up to start my own brand.'

'Oh.' He was having a horrible flashback to his date with Zoë, and from the smirk on Imogen's face, she'd guessed what he was thinking of. 'And are *you* the brand?' he asked.

She laughed, a tinkling, practised sound. 'You're cute. I'm launching a fashion brand.'

He let out a breath. 'That sounds interesting. I don't know much about fashion. Um, obviously,' he said, gesturing to his outfit.

Imogen gave him a once-over. 'Fine by me. I happen to enjoy dictating what my boyfriend wears.'

Oliver grinned, appreciating Imogen's ease in front of the cameras. 'You can choose what I wear any day.'

'Mate,' Declan cut in, 'maybe give Jack a shout before you move in on his girl?'

Oliver tried to meet his eye, to figure out what he was thinking, but he seemed suddenly focused on his tea, and Oliver was left feeling like he'd broken some unspoken rule between them.

The chime sounded and Darcy's voice rang out. 'Imogen, you talk a big game, but now it's time to play the field. Pick a boy to go on a date.'

She squeezed Oliver's bicep. 'What do you say? Feeling sporty?'

Oliver looked away from Declan. 'Sure am!'

—

'Where are the others, anyway?' Niall asked. 'Isn't wardrobe advice part of the contract, or something?'

'Dunno,' Oliver replied. He'd lost track of Declan as soon as Imogen had asked him out, and wherever he'd gone, Jack had disappeared with him. Owen, the last he'd seen, had been snoozing on a daybed with Holly. 'I think we can manage to dress me, if we put our minds to it.'

Niall nodded, studying the white shirt in his hands critically. He was meticulous about his ironing; he said Oliver's perpetually rumpled appearance gave him tension headaches. 'You seem nervous, Wright,' he said off-handedly.

'Am a bit,' Oliver confessed, fidgeting with his collar.

Niall put a steadying hand on his shoulder, giving him a soulful look that would make anyone feel like the most important person in the room. 'You've already got an incredible woman. How come you still think you're not good enough?'

Oliver grimaced. It was no secret to the audience any more, so he might as well clue Niall in as well. 'Declan told me Maeve fancies Jack.'

Niall's eyebrows knitted together. 'Maeve fancies... Jack?' He squinted, as though trying to picture the two of them together and failing. 'So that's what this date's all about? But are you sure? I wouldn't put it past Declan to mess with you. He doesn't always know when to end the joke.'

A week ago, Oliver would have agreed with him, but now Declan, if anything, felt surprisingly earnest in Oliver's company. Declan hadn't seemed like someone he could expose his vulnerabilities to until Oliver had seen the way his face had softened when he'd talked about Sophie.

But he didn't want to bring that up to Niall – more and more, his conversations with Declan were something he didn't want anyone else to have access to. It was unfortunate that they happened to be watched by an audience of millions.

'He wouldn't do that,' Oliver said firmly. 'I trust him.'

Niall shot him an incredulous look. 'What about the thing with Zoë?'

Oliver shook his head. Knowing Declan was genuinely interested in Zoë had changed Oliver's opinion of him. It made sense as to why he'd acted so coldly towards Oliver – he hadn't known how to pursue Zoë and make friends with Oliver at the same time.

'It doesn't matter either way,' he said. 'I don't fancy Maeve. I mean, she's undeniably fanciable, and I don't fancy her *at all*. Something must be wrong with me.'

He didn't know why he was so frustrated; he'd come on the show to win, not to fall in love. But now that he'd started getting to know the women, single for the first time in his adult life, he realised how much he *wanted* to fall for someone else. He wanted to feel like his whole life didn't revolve around Sophie. He wanted to know he had the option to move on, that he at least had some choice in the matter. But frustratingly, the only person Oliver felt like he was developing any sort of closeness with was Declan.

Niall's eyes flicked to the nearest camera, the contestants' universal signal for *mate, you're making yourself look a fool on television*. Oliver dipped his chin towards him in a subtle nod, and changed the subject: 'But who knows, maybe Imogen is the one?'

'Exactly,' Niall said. 'You two could be just like me and Stella. I just know we're it for each other.'

'Niall,' Paige said, stepping in front of the camera and sounding exasperated. 'What did we talk about earlier? You have to at least pretend to have reservations; it makes for good TV. Sometimes I feel like a preschool teacher with you lot.'

Niall's face betrayed a flash of annoyance at the interjection, but when he spoke, his tone was even. 'Isn't the whole point of this to find love?'

Paige exhaled slowly before responding. 'Of course the point is to find love,' she said, with a false smile pasted on. 'And you've already found your soulmate here. So if you could just keep me in a job, yeah?'

Niall snorted. 'You're lucky I'm such a pushover.' Turning back to Oliver: 'Well, I dunno, we'll have to see how it goes, won't we?'

Paige flashed a thumbs-up in the corner of Oliver's vision. When it became clear that Niall was done with his bit, Oliver jumped in. 'And how am I feeling about my date? I thought you'd never ask.' Niall chuckled. 'Imogen is exactly my type on paper. I think we have good chemistry already. And hey, third time's the charm, right?'

Paige gave Oliver a grateful smile. '*Much* better.'

Chapter 12

Oliver

Oliver and Declan were lounging by the pool the next day when Maeve finally approached him. She looked anxious, and Oliver knew what was coming. He wasn't dreading it any more – his date with Imogen had gone surprisingly well, and he thought his spot on the show was secure for now.

'Can we have a chat, Oliver?'

The two of them settled onto a daybed, the cameras on them in moments. Maeve drew her knees to her chest protectively.

He saved her the trouble of explaining. 'It's okay. I know that you want to break things off.' At her confused look, he continued, 'Declan told me.'

She frowned. 'I didn't mean for him to tell you. I'm sorry if he bungled it.'

'Shockingly, he didn't.' He paused, putting his hand over hers. 'Hey, I'm not upset. I'm happy for you and Jack, truly.'

She chewed on her lip. 'We're not... I wanted to talk to you about it first.'

'I'm flattered that you wanted to tell me first. Well, second,' he amended. 'Oh, by the way, I told Niall, so Stella likely knows too. And Imogen knows, I think. So, only half the villa.' He grinned.

Meave groaned. 'Oh God. I've been so mean to Imogen, for absolutely no reason other than I fancy Jack.'

'I'm sure she'll forgive you,' Oliver said. 'Are you going to talk to him now?'

'Yes,' she said firmly, as though trying to convince herself. 'I have to now, don't I? Made my bed, and all that.'

'Why are you so nervous?'

'Well, he could look at me like I'm mad, or say that I'm too serious for him, or...' She broke off, looking at him earnestly. 'We're an odd pair, aren't we? He's an amateur stand-up comedian and I'm the least funny person I know.'

Oliver put a bracing hand on her shoulder. 'Pretend he's an octogenarian,' he said solemnly.

She gave a bark of laughter. 'What?'

'Like when you give presentations at work, treat it like that. Talk to Jack like you would to them, and pretend he's asleep.'

Maeve looked caught between anxiety and amusement. 'Don't you think that's *more* likely to make him think I'm a nutter who has nothing in common with him?'

He considered it for a moment. 'Better an honest nutter than the alternative.'

'Thanks for the pep talk,' she said drily. 'I'm not sure it was altogether helpful, but it's certainly given me something to think about.'

'That's what I'm here for. Now, go and get him.' He made a shooing motion and she stood, walking over to Jack. Oliver watched her go for a moment, the cameraman following, before lying back.

'All right?' Declan asked, his shadow casting over Oliver.

'Yeah, fine,' Oliver replied blandly, glad for the distraction. 'Do you want to watch Maeve try to tell Jack that she fancies him? Could be entertaining.'

' 'Course,' Declan said, sitting beside him.

They watched as the cameraman trained his lens on the nook where Maeve and Jack had disappeared. Looking across the garden at the different couples, Oliver felt untethered. The show had been supposed to be a way for him to get back on track with Sophie, but instead it was confusing him, taking the things he had thought he'd wanted and muddling them.

He wanted to curl into a ball, but settled for turning to Declan. Looking into his eyes, Oliver felt more grounded.

'You'll find someone else,' Declan said lightly.

'It's not that,' he said, struggling with how to explain. 'I think I'm starting to recognise why I've been so unhappy the past few months. From here, it's easy to see that I've made a mess of things.'

Declan said nothing, but there was a slight tic in his jaw.

'Everything I built in London was for a life with someone who no longer wants to be in it, and instead of making it mine, I've been chasing down the next thing.'

Oddly, saying it didn't hurt; it felt matter-of-fact. He understood now what Sophie had said to him the night she'd left. He could conceptualise loving someone and still feeling suffocated by them. Maybe he too had felt suffocated, but more slowly, the weight in his chest not registering as anything abnormal until he felt its absence.

He continued: 'I didn't know how to handle a break-up. Pathetic, huh, to finally be figuring this angsty teenage shit out at my age?'

The back of Declan's head was framed by a halo of sunlight. 'If that's pathetic,' he said finally, his expression pensive, 'I'm pathetic too. I've never been through a break-up.' He paused. 'I've never even been in love before.'

'Can't commit to one woman?' Oliver teased.

Declan studied Oliver's hands. 'It's not as though I have tons of free time for dating, what with training and press and all.'

It was Declan's usual excuse. Oliver couldn't help but add wryly, 'And dating in the public eye certainly isn't easy.'

Declan nodded, thoughtful. 'People think they're entitled to know everything about me – that they get to judge me and tell me who I am.' He frowned. 'Though I'm grateful for all of the opportunities boxing has given me.' The line had a rehearsed quality.

Oliver wanted to ask more, but he didn't know how to get Declan to answer as himself rather than as a character constructed for the audience. Sometimes he worried he couldn't even tell the difference.

'But, you know, it's lonely,' Declan said, softer and with a look Oliver recognised intimately.

'Yeah,' Oliver said quietly. 'I get that.'

'You had someone constantly around for eight years,' Declan said, with a rueful smile. 'It's not exactly the same.'

Oliver pushed his hair back, sighing. 'When I was a kid, I was always alone. I felt like I would never escape it.'

Declan looked at him, his expression soft.

'But when I started dancing, I saw a way out. I made a plan.'

Declan seemed lost in his own world, his brow furrowed. 'Oh,' was all he said.

'It worked,' Oliver said. 'I know it's supposed to be stupid to run away from your problems, but it worked for me. I haven't been lonely since.' He remembered the weeks of confining himself to his apartment, of shutting everyone out. 'Except, I guess, recently.'

'Well, you can't run away now,' Declan said. 'You're stuck with me.'

'Only for a few more weeks,' Oliver said lightly. 'Then I'm moving to New York.' He liked the sound of it, decisive, on his tongue.

'Wow,' Declan said, and it looked for once like he was struggling to keep his expression impassive. 'New York. That's far. I mean, that's a massive decision.'

Oliver swallowed, thrown off by having to explain himself. It was hard to believe that there were still parts of him that Declan didn't know. Somehow, without him noticing, he'd come to regard Declan with the same intimacy he did his mates back home.

'It's hardly even a decision at this point – if I get the role, I'll go. You don't turn down Manhattan Ballet, and it's been a dream of mine since I was a kid. London, then New York. That's always been the plan.'

The plan had been cemented when twelve-year-old Oliver, tired of pretending to fit in with his schoolmates who bullied him mercilessly over dancing, had seen a flyer for Manhattan Ballet on the wall after a lesson.

Declan made a noise in the back of his throat. 'But plans can change.'

'My plans don't,' Oliver said automatically. With his plan, Oliver had found every good thing he'd ever had. With his plan, he didn't need to be paralysed in the face of everyday decisions.

Declan turned towards the sky. 'Uh-huh.'

Oliver felt a pang of annoyance at Declan's disinterest. 'You can't tell me you've had this much success without any strategy.'

'No strategy,' Declan said, his tone clipped. 'Just talent, hard work and all that.'

'Right.' He couldn't see Declan's expression, but he could imagine him with that closed-off look again.

'It's all down to what my dad's done for me.' Declan surprised him by turning back towards him. His face was impossible to read, but he was offering it to Oliver nonetheless. 'So, no, there's no plan – just winning matches, trying to make him proud.'

He thought he understood things better now – Declan's dedication to boxing was an extension of his intense loyalty. His whole life was a series of favours to the people he loved, and somehow he still felt like it wasn't enough.

Brian crossed in front of them and Oliver was startled by the reminder that they were being recorded. He fleetingly thought of Paige's suggestion to ask about Declan's future boxing prospects, but something made Oliver decide against it.

There was a beat of silence. 'You should think about New York,' Declan said finally.

Oliver laughed, surprised by the earnest advice. 'I can't *stop* thinking about it, so I've got that bit covered.'

'I mean,' Declan said, more impatiently, 'that you should actually *think* about it. As a possibility, not as the only one.'

'Fine, sure.' He thought it presumptuous for Declan to have any reaction other than encouragement. 'Is that why you don't have any plans? Too busy thinking everything through carefully?'

'I do have a plan. Falling in love is my plan,' Declan said gruffly.

Whatever glimpse of the real Declan he thought he'd seen was gone now, and Oliver found himself tiring of their conversation. He rolled over to search for Jack and Maeve, only to see them emerging from the nook. Jack spotted them and made for the daybed with Maeve on his arm.

'You've been holding out on me, King!' he boomed.

'Oh,' Declan said, going red. He shot an accusing look at Maeve. 'You told him I knew?'

Maeve laughed. 'I told him he was the last to know, thanks to the two of you.'

'Well done, you,' Oliver chimed in.

Jack clapped him on the back. 'Good man. Stole your girl and you're congratulating me!'

'She was freely given.'

'I'm not cattle!' Maeve said, indignant.

'What are you going to do about Imogen?' Declan asked.

As Jack seemed to remember Imogen's existence, Darcy's voice came over the loudspeaker. 'Lovers, it's time to shake things up.'

'That can't be good,' Declan muttered.

'Get ready to meet by the firepit in one hour,' Darcy continued, 'whether you like it shaken or stirred. Hopefully, you live to die another day.'

Oliver cleared his throat. 'Well, that's cheery.'

–

An hour later, everyone was gathered except for Darcy.

Paige ceased the hushed conversation she was having through her headset and stepped forwards. 'Darcy is running a bit late. Can you line up in couples?'

The contestants shuffled around the firepit, pairing off. Maeve turned to Oliver anxiously. 'Are you worried?'

His racing heart said yes, but he tried to give her a steady smile. 'It'll be fine.'

'Brian,' Paige called, 'could you get those establishing shots now? Oliver, a word?'

Paige guided him out of earshot of the other contestants and began rubbing her temples. 'What have I told you?'

'Er, I'm great and people love me?' he tried.

She gave him a beleaguered look. 'I'm on your side, and you need to be honest with me? Ring any bells?'

He rocked on his heels. 'I *have* been honest.'

'Yeah? It didn't seem pertinent to mention you're moving to New York and getting back together with Sophie?' she asked, her eyes narrowing.

'That's n—' he started.

She held up a hand, cutting him off. 'Even if I believed you, the audience isn't that stupid. It won't make it into the episode, but promise me you won't mention New York again. Someone will make the connection, and the viewers won't be pleased.'

'Would you let me explain?' Oliver asked, annoyed. 'I've wanted to dance for Manhattan Ballet since I was twelve. Just because she did it first doesn't mean I have to give it up.'

'Uh-huh,' Paige said. 'So you two *aren't* getting back together?'

He cleared his throat awkwardly. 'Well, um, nothing is decided.'

'Oliver,' she said, sighing, 'it really doesn't matter to me. I'm just asking you to not utter the words "New York" on camera again, okay?'

'Okay,' he agreed. 'Sorry.'

She gave him a tired nod as Darcy finally stormed onto the set in silver stilettos and a garish floral wrap dress.

'Let's get this party started,' she said, in the least party-starting voice possible, levelling a stare across the line of contestants.

'We're all set,' Paige said, shooing a PA over to mic her as Oliver went to stand by Maeve.

As soon as Darcy was mic'd, she turned to the contestants. 'Roll!' she barked, pausing for only a moment before continuing in her host voice: 'Our audience have been voting all week for their favourite Lovers. Tonight, the one with the fewest votes will be going home.'

She stared at them intently. 'Maeve, Declan, Imogen, Jack, Zoë and Oliver...' She drew out the pause as the cameras panned across them. 'You received the most audience votes, and are safe from elimination.'

Oliver sighed with relief, feeling Maeve do the same beside him. Instinctively he looked at Declan, but he was hugging Zoë, his back to Oliver.

'Please sit.'

As Oliver sat, he glanced nervously towards Niall and Stella. He was shocked they hadn't got more votes, as the strongest couple in the villa.

'Lovers...' Darcy said. 'The four of you in front of me this evening are in jeopardy of elimination.' Her eyes locked with each of the standing contestants as she said their names. 'Owen... Holly... Niall... Stella... You have received the fewest votes.'

Niall didn't look nearly as nervous as Oliver would have been, betrayed only by the slight tremor in his left hand. Oliver felt a pang, recognising how upset he would be if Niall left that night. They had only known each other for a month, but each week on the show felt like a year in real life.

'Holly, Niall and Stella,' Darcy said slowly, 'you have been saved from elimination by our audience.' Stella kissed a stunned Niall on the cheek before pulling him down to the couch.

'That means Owen, you've been dumped from the villa.'

—

After they had wrapped filming the elimination, Oliver found himself sitting with the others outside, waiting on the producers. As a special treat, Brian had announced that they had an outing planned that night for the Mallorcan holiday Nit de Foc.

'Do you think he'll make it out of there alive?' Stella asked, glancing towards the villa, where Jack had disappeared with Imogen and Paige. 'It would be a shame if he missed the fireworks.'

'Jack will be fine,' Oliver said with false confidence, glancing at Maeve.

'And you and Imogen can finally share your love with the world,' Declan teased.

Oliver rolled his eyes. 'Watch it, King.'

Maeve glanced over her shoulder. 'Should I be doing something to—' She was cut off by distant shouting.

'That's about the measure of it, I suppose,' Niall said.

'No wonder she got votes,' Holly said glumly. 'She's much more dramatic than Owen.'

Declan slung an arm around her shoulders, tucking her into his side. 'Come on, Holls, don't pout. You'll meet someone else, I'm sure of it.'

At that, Jack emerged from the villa, hands in his pockets and looking unusually sombre. When he reached the table, they all looked at him expectantly.

'It didn't go great,' he said.

Stella shrugged, standing and glancing at Niall. 'Are you coming with me?'

'To the ends of the earth,' Niall said, and Holly made a retching noise.

'Come on,' Maeve said to Jack. 'Can't leave these two alone, can we?'

'Coming?' Holly asked Declan.

He shook his head. 'Give us a bit.' His eyes were on the villa, and he looked pensive.

Holly frowned. 'Guess I'll fifth-wheel, then. You two have fun. Use protection!'

Declan huffed as she walked off with the others. 'She thinks she's funny.'

The two of them sat in silence for a moment. The swimming pool shimmered below them and the stars were bright in the sky above. It was muggy out, the oppressive heat only occasionally interrupted by a breeze through the grass.

'It's nice out here,' Oliver said softly.

'Mhm,' Declan muttered, distracted.

'All right?'

Declan shrugged, glancing sideways at a stray cameraman focused on the two of them. 'I'm nervous about something, but I'm a bit embarrassed to tell you.'

'Yeah?' Oliver could tell by the slight shifting of Declan's eyes that he was getting a performance. That, and he couldn't imagine Declan had ever been embarrassed in his life, or at least willingly ready to admit it. 'The great Declan King, nervous?'

Declan bit his lower lip, and Oliver's eyes moved to his mouth. 'I haven't kissed Zoë yet,' he said. 'I mean, not properly.'

'Um,' Oliver said, momentarily distracted by the way Declan's eyelashes cast shadows on his cheekbones in the dim light of the patio. 'What are you waiting for?'

Declan glanced towards the villa again, and Oliver followed his gaze. Paige had emerged, talking into her headset at a distance.

'Not sure how to go about it, you know?' Declan said, with his perfect smile.

Oliver resisted the urge to roll his eyes. 'What do you mean?'

'I mean, I want it to be romantic,' Declan said. 'She tried to kiss me, and I kinda left her hanging, so I've got to make it up to her with something special.'

'Why'd you leave her hanging?' Oliver asked, feeding Declan the line he needed.

Declan grinned sheepishly, rubbing his neck. 'I don't know, mate. I suppose I was a little drunk and…' He drew out the pause.

Oliver snorted. 'You chickened out?'

'I didn't chicken out,' Declan said through gritted teeth. 'I thought I had bad breath.'

Oliver laughed – it was a flimsy excuse and they both knew it. Declan grinned back at him, and Oliver's heart caught. It was the crooked smile he'd come to think of as reserved just for him.

'I guess I'm waiting for the right moment,' Declan said.

'It's more important that it's the right girl than the right moment,' Oliver said. 'If you feel like Zoë is the one, the moment will present itself.' The words felt oddly heavy coming out.

'Is that how you felt with your ex?' Declan asked.

'Yes.'

Declan stared at him, his gaze searching. For nearly Oliver's entire adolescent life, Sophie had been the exact person he was looking for, but he found that impossible to articulate while looking into Declan's eyes.

Declan didn't say anything for a long time, turning to look at the pool. Oliver watched him carefully, feeling strung out as he traced the broken curve of Declan's nose.

'I think I'm looking for something like that,' Declan said finally. 'Someone to understand me fully. But it doesn't come easily to me. I've always held myself back because I wasn't sure I could manage to give… everything.'

The raw quality to Declan's voice made Oliver certain he had forgotten they were being recorded. He pointedly glanced towards Paige, hovering in the periphery, but Declan didn't seem to notice.

'Well, it's only a kiss,' Oliver teased, trying to lighten things. 'Maybe you're scared of rejection.'

'I'm not scared. It's just—' Declan stared down at his fingers, flexing them. 'I've never had the option of the kind of love you're describing. And if I did, would it make a difference?' An expression like panic flashed across his face so quickly that Oliver hardly registered it. Then Declan glanced back up, his eyes reflecting the fairy lights in the bushes behind them. He looked lit from within.

'Yeah, it would,' Oliver said, not fully cognisant of what question he was answering.

An uncomfortable lump formed in his throat. He knew that Declan was more invested than Zoë in their relationship. That he was going to get his already fragile heart broken, and that Oliver was letting him walk into it blindly.

That, and Oliver was annoyed – jealous of the fact that Declan had found someone, while he felt more lost than ever.

'Hey, boys,' Paige interrupted. When Oliver looked over, he saw that she had moved closer. 'It's looking good, but we were hoping for more of a comedic angle on this one. Declan's fit and he's nervous about kissing a girl, so he comes to you, Oliver, for advice. You see?'

'Er, no,' Oliver replied. 'That doesn't sound funny to me.'

'Yeah, I think we've done enough for tonight,' Declan said, hoisting himself up.

Declan and Paige looked at each other for a moment, then she shrugged. 'Fine. Are you going to watch the fireworks?'

Declan nodded. 'Where's Zoë?'

'Here,' Zoë called, emerging from the villa. 'Did you know Brian's daughter is a fan of my channel?'

Brian trailed behind her with Imogen. 'If you lot don't get a move on, we'll miss the fireworks,' he complained.

'You okay?' Oliver asked haltingly. Imogen's calm demeanour showed none of the ire from minutes ago with Jack.

'Grand,' Imogen said with a wink.

Zoë linked arms with Declan, leading him to the gate, and he whispered something in her ear that made her beam up at him. The rest of them followed from a distance.

Brian looked at the sky. 'The fireworks are a pretty magical sight, I'll tell you. It's my favourite night of the summer.'

'Sounds romantic,' Imogen gushed, flashing Oliver a sly smile. He continued staring ahead, irritated by her continual insistence on cheeriness. He couldn't tell, looking at the backs of Declan and Zoë, whether they were speaking or not.

Paige looked relaxed for once. 'Hey, maybe Declan will get that kiss after all.' She nodded to the cameraman behind them. 'As long as we get a shot of it.'

'Ooh!' Imogen exclaimed, then visibly held herself back with a glance towards Zoë and Declan. 'They're going to kiss under the fireworks?' she asked, quieter.

Oliver wasn't enjoying this topic of conversation at all. 'Did you tell Declan to ask me for advice?' he asked Paige.

'No, he had the idea himself.' She gave him a sidelong look. 'Would it matter if I'd asked him?'

'No, it wouldn't have,' he lied. His annoyance had solidified into something more resolute. The manufactured scene, Declan blatantly using him for a plotline with Zoë, weighed on him more than it should have. 'I just like to know what's going on.'

She cocked her head. 'I'll be sure to clue you in in the future. I think it will be received well, though, so no worries.'

'Right. No worries,' he echoed.

They turned a corner and arrived in an open field. Oliver found himself impressed by the beauty of the night despite his foul mood. As they approached the contestants already in the middle of the field, the first fireworks soared into the night sky, exploding in a cascade of golden light. Oliver tipped his face up in appreciation, forgetting where he was for a moment.

'Wow,' Imogen said.

'Could you get shots of the couples?' Paige asked the cameraman.

Oliver followed her gaze and noticed Jack and Maeve and Niall and Stella slow dancing under the fireworks. He turned instinctively to look for Declan and Zoë and found them on the far side of the group. Zoë was hanging off Declan, long hair falling down her back, their faces close as they swayed in the evening light. Oliver's legs felt numb, as though the temperature in the field was much colder than a balmy twenty-six degrees. A group of bright fuchsia fireworks crackled above his head, and he breathed in.

'Quick – Declan and Zoë,' he heard Paige mutter.

Oliver tried to not look at them. He trained his eyes on the sky, on the treeline, on the fireworks, on anything else. But they kept sliding, against his will, over towards where they were dancing.

Imogen inhaled sharply. 'They're so beautiful, aren't they?'

His eyes swept down, and he saw Declan's face dip towards Zoë's. He watched as Declan pulled Zoë closer and kissed her. Oliver blinked, glancing away, and found that Imogen was looking back at him. Her expression was almost apologetic, and he wasn't sure why.

Chapter 13

Declan

Four Weeks Until Finale

Neil Steel: You know what they say: where there's smoke, there's fire. And we've seen quite a few sparks this past week!

Zoë Park: 'It was such a romantic first kiss! It's a moment I'll remember forever.'

Neil Steel: Sounds like Declan more than delivered on the fireworks. But the King wasn't the only one with a flair for the dramatics.

Imogen Vichare: 'I'm absolutely gutted that Jack has gone and two-timed me. You think it's all sorted, that a guy's solid, then he pulls a move like that.'

Neil Steel: I say this on behalf of all the men out there: thank God I'm not Jack Obiaka.

The group woke to a message from Darcy: 'Ladies, all this fun in the sun must be hard on you. That's why we're sending you to get primped and pampered.'

'Oi,' Jack grumbled at no one in particular, as he sank back into the duvet. 'What about us? Where's our spa day?'

The girls ignored him, murmuring excitedly as they went to get ready and leaving the boys to groggily fume at being passed over. Declan was the first among their ranks to pull himself out of bed, going to find Zoë for a touching on-camera goodbye.

The kiss under the fireworks the week before had fixed everything. On their day off, she'd admitted the whole spat had been a ploy to get them more screen time, and that the kiss had been the perfect conclusion.

Leaning against the doorframe of the dressing room, he watched as Zoë twisted her hair into a pair of effortless-looking braids. He'd always enjoyed watching Georgia get ready for events, and he found the same calm watching Zoë. She finally spotted him as she finished the second braid.

'Hi, you,' she said coyly.

Declan noticed that she had taken a seat in clear view of the camera in the corner – he envied her instinct to always place herself at the perfect angle. The past few days had reminded him how lucky he'd been to find someone with the same goals. With Zoë, he'd found everything he had come on the show for.

He came up behind her, keeping eye contact in the mirror. 'You look beautiful.'

'Aww,' Imogen cooed from the next vanity over. 'Couple goals.'

Declan leaned down and wrapped his arms around Zoë, smiling at their reflection. She turned and pecked him on the lips.

'We'd better go,' she said, standing.

Declan nodded. 'I'll walk you out.'

He escorted Zoë downstairs, the other girls trailing behind them.

'Wow,' Jack said from the bottom of the stairs, staring at Maeve, 'you look amazing.'

Maeve flushed, and Jack dropped a kiss to her cheek when she reached him.

'We'll be back soon,' she said, squeezing his hand.

The girls departed in a van, and the boys were left to sit around the pool and look bored for the cameras.

'I miss Maeve,' Jack said petulantly.

'I miss Stella,' Niall agreed.

'I hope the girls are having a good time,' Declan said.

Oliver snickered. 'You lot are pathetic; they'll be back soon enough.'

On cue, the loudspeaker chimed with a new message. 'Boys, we know you miss your girls, but love is a battlefield. The girls won't be coming back today, but we've found some new recruits to keep you busy.'

The boys traded bewildered glances.

'Hello!' a voice called, and Declan turned to see four girls walking out onto the patio. One for each of them, he noted.

The two groups made their introductions. Faye, a tall, dark-skinned expat from America, was the one who had greeted them, and a redhead named Eavie was by her side. The others, a set of identical twins, introduced themselves as Amelia and Annabelle.

From Declan's position on the patio, he could see through the large glass windows of the villa straight to the front door. The production staff was clearing out the other girls' suitcases, loading them into a van.

Paige sent the new girls upstairs to change into bathing suits and instructed the boys to have a chat.

'The crew is stretched thin between the two locations, so I'm expecting everyone to be on their best behaviour,' she said sternly. 'Your girls are in another villa right now meeting brand new boys, so it may be in your best interest to keep your options open.'

'Are the other guys as hot as me, though?' Jack joked.

'Hotter,' Paige deadpanned.

Jack had the good sense to look nervous. 'Fair enough. All right, boys, let's talk about our feelings, yeah?'

The boys nodded and Paige waved a cameraman over.

From Declan's casual viewing of the show, he knew the rival villa was the hardest test for the couples. The introduction of a new set of contestants sent specifically to try to steal them away from their established partners made for good drama, but it was also a trap. Straying from Zoë now would only make him a villain to the audience – all he could do was trust that she wanted to win as much as he did.

'So…' Jack said, after an awkward pause, 'what do we think of the new birds? Decs, what's your assessment?'

Declan straightened and raised his hand to his forehead in a mock salute, feeling ridiculous. 'Faye seems sound, Eavie is gorgeous, and who doesn't like twins, sir!'

'At ease, soldier,' Jack said, immediately taking to the bit. He turned a solemn face towards Niall. 'And you, Private O'Connell?'

'Yes, the girls are fit, sir!' Niall said, with equal commitment. Declan could see Paige roll her eyes in the corner of his vision.

'Permission to engage, sir,' Oliver cut in, sitting at attention.

'Hold tight, Sergeant, we still need to determine a plan of attack,' Jack said, throwing a look back at the villa.

Niall let out an offended huff. 'Why does he get to be a sergeant and I'm relegated to private?' he complained, dropping the charade.

'Can it! No backtalking to your superiors,' Jack said. 'We move out in five minutes. Ready, men?'

'Aye, aye, Captain!' the boys said sarcastically.

Paige sighed. 'Very funny. But give these girls a real chance; they may surprise you.' She gave Oliver a pointed look, and the two seemed to share a silent conversation.

The night progressed like all the others, with too-loud music and too little alcohol to cope with the awkwardness of having to dance in such a small group. Declan was tiring of the endless parties, even with new girls around to keep the conversation fresh.

Without Zoë to distract him, Declan found his gaze wandering to Oliver, and saw the same exhaustion reflected on his face. He inclined his head slightly and the two peeled off from the others, heading towards the pool.

As they sat, Declan struggled with what to say. It had been difficult to be around Oliver recently. Declan had avoided him since the night of the fireworks and found things noticeably easier when he concentrated on Zoë. He didn't have to worry about forgetting the cameras, and he could focus on what the audience wanted from him. But despite all that, he missed Oliver.

'So,' Declan said, reverting to the mechanics of the show to keep them in neutral territory, 'what do you think of the girls?'

Oliver didn't meet his eye. 'Well... Eavie is pretty.'

It wasn't much, but Declan could work with it. 'She is, mate,' he agreed. 'What's the plan?'

Oliver finally looked at him, his expression blank. 'I suppose I'll have a chat with her and see what happens?'

Declan already regretted bringing the girls up. He'd thought it would be a safe topic, but he detected a hint of irritation in Oliver's tone. 'Do you know what you're going to say?'

'Not really,' Oliver said lightly, 'but I'm sure I can manage on my own.'

Declan couldn't stand his affected cheer. 'Is everything all right?'

'Why wouldn't it be?' Oliver asked, not dropping the painfully polite tone.

'I don't know,' Declan said, wanting to goad him into a real response, 'there are four beautiful women for you to choose from and you don't seem excited at all.'

Oliver's eyes flashed to his, regarding him coolly.

'I mean, this isn't about the other night, is it?'

Oliver stiffened beside him. 'What do you mean?'

'With me kissing Zoë.'

Oliver gave him an odd look.

'I know you liked her before.'

'No,' Oliver sighed. He pinched his nose under his glasses and scrubbed at his eyes, looking like himself again. 'I don't know – I guess I'm just feeling a bit adrift. I haven't connected with any of the girls.' He looked at Declan, his green eyes glowing in the soft light. 'I'm not sure I will.'

'Of course you will!' Declan said, wanting to wipe away his lost look. 'Just get out of that head of yours and focus on how she makes you feel. It should feel good to be with her. She should make you happy.' He leaned towards Oliver without thinking and their bare shoulders grazed.

Oliver stared at him for a few more moments before nodding slowly. 'Focus on what makes me happy?' he said with a wry smile. 'Not exactly what I'm used to.' He stood, stretching his arms over his head, the muscles along his stomach fluttering at the movement. 'Wish me luck.'

Declan stared at him. 'Always,' he said, his throat dry.

—

Declan woke to Jack's soft snores in his ear. He had shifted during the night to Declan's side of the bed and was spooning him tightly.

When he opened his eyes, he found an amused Oliver watching from the next bed over, where he'd slept beside Niall. Paige had been cross when the boys refused to share with the new girls the night before, but they'd presented a united front and she'd eventually given in.

'Comfy?' Oliver whispered, a sly grin on his face.

Declan's brain was too soft from sleep for a witty reply. 'Piss off,' he muttered, shoving a grumbling Jack with his shoulder.

He headed outside, Oliver trailing behind him. It felt good to get back to their morning routine, and it reassured him that the awkwardness of the past few days had dissipated.

After his swim, they met by the weights as the crew set up around them.

'So,' Declan said, while Oliver lay back on the bench press, 'how'd it go with Eavie?'

Oliver's eyes shifted from where they'd been focused on the bar to Declan. He was beautiful with his hair splayed out around him, looking up at Declan like that.

'Um,' he huffed out. 'Good, I think?' He went for another rep. 'She thinks I'm funny.'

'And you? Do you like her?' he pressed.

Oliver finished his last rep and sat up. 'I think so?' he said, grabbing a towel. He wiped the sweat from his brow before turning back to Declan. 'Honestly, she's the first girl here that I could see myself with in the real world.'

He sounded wistful, and Declan prayed he was playing it up for the cameras.

'What do you like about her?' Declan asked, not wanting to hear the answer.

'She's a dancer, which is nice,' Oliver said, standing and letting Declan take his spot on the bench. That was much better – Declan could focus on lifting the weight from his chest rather than the pit in his stomach. 'Her parents are academics and thought the whole thing was silly. My parents thought I was mad and I'd be broke. So I guess we've got a shared experience to bond over.'

'She sounds like your type,' Declan said, masking his frustration with physical exertion.

Oliver frowned slightly. 'Well, yeah, isn't that the point?'

Declan shrugged as he pushed the bar back into the rack and stood to switch positions. 'I think you should keep your options open, get to know the other girls. I mean, you've got the pick of the lot.'

Oliver considered him carefully and – not for the first time – Declan worried he'd overplayed his hand. 'I'll think about it,' he said finally, and they continued in a not-quite-uncomfortable silence.

Starving after their workout, Oliver and Declan made their way to the kitchen, where Eavie and Faye were chatting over a cup of tea. The twins were nowhere in sight, which was a relief since Declan had already forgotten their names.

'Morning, you two. Fancy some breakfast?' Declan asked, grabbing a carton of eggs. 'How was your first night?'

Eavie cast a sidelong glance at Oliver. 'Oh, good. You boys sure know how to make us feel welcome.'

'Yup,' Faye agreed. 'It's like a full-service bed and breakfast.' She stole a banana from the fruit bowl and sat on the counter to watch the boys cook.

When they served breakfast, Oliver asked Faye for a chat and the two took their plates off to a corner of the patio, leaving Declan with Eavie.

'Don't worry,' Declan said gently, noticing her glum expression and nudging the loaded plate closer to her. 'He's just getting to know her a little better.'

'Right,' Eavie said, straightening. 'So, what can you tell me about him?'

'Trying to get some insider information?' Declan teased, but Eavie nodded earnestly.

'I like him,' she said simply. 'And I think he could be good for me.'

There was no doubt in Declan's mind that she was being genuine – she didn't speak with any of the practised coyness of someone like Zoë.

He swallowed, desperately trying to crush down his own feelings for Oliver. 'Yeah, well, he's a good guy,' he said, his tone coming out clipped.

Eavie gave him a funny look. 'So you're the protective type, then?'

'Something like that,' Declan said, regaining his composure.

'Don't worry,' she said, placing a reassuring hand on his shoulder. 'I'm not one to give up on a good thing. I'm not going to break his heart, or leave him behind like Zoë and Maeve.'

That, somehow, only made him feel worse. 'Oh,' Declan said dully. 'Well, good.'

Before she could reply, Jack and Niall interrupted them.

'Ooh,' Jack said, eyeing Declan's untouched plate. 'Are you planning on eating that?'

Declan pushed it towards him. 'Knock yourself out.'

Oliver and Faye were off by themselves for hours, though Declan couldn't fathom what they were talking about for so long. The afternoon found the contestants lounging by the pool, chatting inanely and feeling more than a little bored.

Like clockwork, the telltale chime went off and Darcy's voice echoed through the garden.

'Lovers,' she cooed, as Oliver and Faye walked back over and Declan tried not to analyse their body language too closely, 'we're kicking this game up a notch. Time for a relay race against the other villa. Complete challenges the quickest to win a night out on the town.'

There was a pause, before she continued, 'Jack, choose a girl...' The contestants glanced around at each other, unsure.

Jack shrugged. 'Amelia?'

One of the twins nodded.

'Now pour a condiment all over your chest, and have the girl lick it off.'

He and Amelia jumped into action immediately, running to the kitchen. Jack whipped open the fridge and grabbed the blue-raspberry-flavoured syrup from their neon party cocktails. Amelia grimaced at the selection, but Jack had already ripped off the cap and doused his chest in blue goo. She shrugged, pushing him against the fridge and dragging her tongue up his torso in long strokes.

'This tickles,' Jack said, squirming as the others laughed at them.

'Done!' Amelia called triumphantly, wiping some blue from the corners of her lips. Jack grabbed her by the hand and the two raced back to the group.

'One point to our boys!' Darcy called, and the group cheered. 'Everyone get into a sex position with someone of the opposite gender.'

The team didn't hesitate this time, each of them grabbing the closest contestant and tumbling into what could feasibly be a form of fornication.

'I don't think I've done that one, mate,' said Jack, studying the tangled mess that was Niall and Faye with horror.

Niall winked at him. 'Try it sometime, darling.'

'Looks like the girls are quicker to fall into bed, one point for the girls' villa!'

'Dammit!' Declan exclaimed, and the rest of the group stared at him. 'What?' He crossed his arms, pouting. 'I like to win.'

The next challenge came through the loudspeaker. 'The shortest girl must kiss the tallest boy.'

All heads turned to Eavie and Oliver as they leaned towards each other. It was a chaste peck, or at least that's what Declan tried to tell himself before seeing a flash of tongue. Irritation must have shown on his face, because Niall gave him a friendly slap on the arm.

'Buck up, I'm sure Zoë is only doing it for the game.'

Declan blinked at him, confused, before remembering that as the shortest girl in the other villa, Zoë would be kissing another man. Declan glanced back at Oliver and Eavie; they were blushing and not making eye contact. He needed to pull himself together.

'Right,' Declan said. He heard cheers around him, and must have missed that they'd won the point.

'All right, boys, time for the oldest among you to give the tallest girl a lap dance, and don't forget to make it sexy.'

Jack grinned at Faye, already making his way over. 'How about it?'

Watching Jack overdramatically grind, twerk and whip his non-existent hair on Faye cheered Declan up significantly. By the end of it, he was back in the competitive spirit.

'Sorry, boys, not sexy enough. Girls' point!' Darcy laughed delightedly.

'That's bollocks!' Jack shouted.

'We'll win the next one,' Annabelle said.

'The girl with the shortest name must plant twenty kisses on a boy of her choice.'

Faye turned to Oliver with a sly smile. 'Do you mind?'

'Not at all,' Oliver said, visibly gulping.

Faye sat in Oliver's lap, kissing his cheeks, his forehead, his lips, his throat. Declan watched them together, Faye's mouth on Oliver's neck, hating that he'd pushed Oliver to pursue her. He clenched his teeth, possessiveness tightening his chest.

'Oh, boys,' Darcy tsked, and Faye reluctantly slipped off Oliver. 'You'll need quicker lips to win next time.'

'This game is rigged,' Jack said, laughing. 'No way Zoë did that faster than Faye.'

Declan finally ripped his gaze away from Oliver when Darcy gave the next challenge. 'The boy with the first name alphabetically, snog the girl you fancy most.'

He glanced back up, eyes dragging over Oliver to Eavie beside him. Declan didn't think about it. He kissed her, harder than he meant to, the frustration of the day pouring out of him. When they broke apart, he forced himself not to look at Oliver.

'That's how you do it! Boys win that point.'

Declan hesitantly turned to Oliver. He looked stunned, blinking at Declan as though seeing him for the first time. Declan felt split open, his bitterness dissipating instantly.

There was a beat where no one said anything, and the contestants waited with bated breath.

'Was that i—' Faye started.

'Everyone jump in the pool!' Darcy cried.

The contestants scrambled out of their seats, tripping over each other as they ran to the pool's edge and jumped in, ignoring the shouts from Paige about their mics.

As they clambered back out of the pool, laughing and shoving each other playfully, Darcy's voice came over the loudspeaker: 'Tough luck! You weren't quite fast enough to catch the speedy lovebirds in the rival villa. Nice guys really do finish last!'

Declan had given up on the game as soon as the shame of the kiss had sunk in, so he wasn't put out by the loss. The others didn't seem to care either, and the boys spent the night getting to know the new girls better, any tension cut by the challenge of the afternoon. It turned out Annabelle and Amelia were actresses, doing mainly local commercials and modelling gigs, which led to Faye regaling them with the movie-star encounters she'd had living in LA.

'What made you move here?' Jack asked. 'You could've had George Clooney eating out of the palm of your hand with a smile like that.'

Faye flashed her teeth at him insincerely. 'I followed a man out here, if you can believe it. We were engaged and everything.' She looked away. 'He called it off two weeks before the wedding.'

'God,' Niall said, 'I can't imagine.'

She recovered quickly. 'Luckily, I'm hot as shit, drinking wine and surrounded by four gorgeous men now.'

The contestants laughed and Paige called for lights out in thirty minutes.

'Ready for a cuddle?' Jack asked, slapping Declan's knee.

Declan shook his head. 'Nah,' he said. 'If it's between your snores or the mosquitos, I'll take the mosquitos. I'm sleeping out here tonight.' He hoped that a night away from the other contestants, from Oliver, would help to clear his head.

Jack raised a hand to his chest in mock affront before shrugging. 'Whatever, more room for me.'

–

Declan avoided the others as he got ready for bed. He didn't want anyone to see the emotions he worried had been written across his face all night, the confusion and guilt over what had happened with Eavie.

He stripped down to his boxers before heading back outside, where he was startled to find Oliver sitting on one of the daybeds, Paige and a cameraman close by. Declan paused. Talking to Oliver would certainly make Declan lose his final measure of control, but he couldn't think of a way out of it in front of the cameras.

'Fancy a spoon?' Declan asked, donning his easy-going facade as he sat on the opposite side of the daybed, hoping in vain that Oliver couldn't see right through him.

Oliver was wearing his old grey T-shirt with the crew neck stretched to its limits from use. His hair was a complete wreck, sticking up on all sides, and his glasses hung low on his nose. He looked so perfect Declan could scream.

'I thought it'd be nice to chat. I could use some advice,' Oliver said, picking at a loose thread on the hem of his shirt.

'All right,' Declan said hesitantly. He was confused by Oliver seeking out his company after what had happened that afternoon.

'I'm conflicted,' Oliver said, turning to face him fully, 'between the girls. I had a good chat with Faye. We talked about her engagement ending, and I felt like we had a lot in common there.'

'Because of your ex?' Declan couldn't stop himself – he needed to hear more about Sophie, to understand why Oliver would move continents for someone who had broken his heart once already.

Oliver nodded with a far-away look in his eyes. 'We weren't engaged, obviously. But I was sure it would happen someday.'

'Right,' Declan said, ignoring the ache in his chest. Jealousy crept in, and he was surprised to find it wasn't directed at Sophie but at Oliver himself, for being capable of loving someone so wholly, for experiencing heartbreak and letting himself be open to it again. 'But how were you sure?'

'I don't know.' Oliver stared at him. 'The things I thought I was sure of then – I don't feel sure of them any more.'

'And you're okay with that?' Declan traced the line of Oliver's collarbone with his eyes, unable to comprehend how someone could be so willing to live in uncertainty. It took a form of bravery he didn't possess. Declan only felt comfortable in situations he could control.

'Yes.' Oliver glanced at Paige, and cleared his throat. 'And I think Faye understands that... but then there's Eavie.' Declan opened his mouth, ready to apologise for the kiss, but Oliver waved him off. 'It's fine. I mean, I don't have anything to worry about, right?'

'Not even a little,' Declan said. 'I'm too far gone on someone else.' Oliver could stay thinking he meant Zoë; he'd never have to know how hard it was to be this close to him and not reach out to touch him.

Oliver studied him carefully, the moon reflected in his eyes. 'It feels easy with Eavie,' he said. 'Like she understands me.'

'Other people understand you, Oliver.' Declan glanced at the cameraman, wanting to say more. 'But, mate,' he continued, forcing himself to sound positive, 'I don't think you can make a bad choice here.'

'Thanks,' Oliver said, resting a hand on Declan's shoulder. Declan stared back at him for a moment too long before clearing his throat.

'I'm knackered,' he said, and Oliver nodded, removing his hand.

'Do you mind if I sleep out here?' he asked. 'Niall kicks.'

Declan hid his expression by leaning down to remove his mic. 'Uh, yeah, 'course,' he said, turning to pull the duvet over himself like a shield. He knew the suggestion was innocent, that Oliver had no idea how close Declan was to unravelling and how he was driving him to it, but it was hard to think rationally. 'Not a problem.'

They listened awkwardly as Paige and the cameraman walked away.

'Good night,' Oliver said, when they were finally alone.

'Night,' Declan replied, and as a final cruel reminder that they were still being watched, the fairy lights above them flicked off, shrouding the patio in darkness.

Declan willed himself to sleep, but his body remained tense as the minutes dragged on, his thoughts always drifting back to the boy sleeping beside him.

He wondered what Oliver looked like, face slack with sleep and lips parted slightly. His hair was probably a mess, soft curls splaying out across his high cheekbones. Declan pictured Oliver's T-shirt hanging off his shoulders, showing the freckled skin beneath.

Oliver shifted next to him, turning over so they were facing the same direction, one of his legs pushing out and grazing Declan's calf. He waited, but Oliver didn't move away. His breathing was slow and even, and Declan was sure he'd fallen asleep.

He was acting mad. Oliver had just told him about two different girls he was interested in. Their friendship only worked when Declan kept himself, and his feelings, under control. He tried to make himself relax by taking in ten slow breaths, but he only got halfway through before getting paranoid that Oliver would hear him.

Finally, Declan gave up and turned over, but Oliver was much closer than he had thought, and they ended up almost nose-to-nose. Declan retreated, leaning his head on his forearm, trying not to disturb him, but Oliver's eyes were already on him, lit by the moonlight across his face.

'Hi,' he whispered to Declan, almost completely inaudible.

'Hi,' Declan whispered back. The two boys smiled at each other. Declan was struck that under the massive duvet and the moon, this was their first private moment since the beach. Oliver looked more relaxed than he'd ever seen him, his grin soft and inviting.

How are you? Declan mouthed.

Oliver wrinkled his nose and wiggled his head noncommittally. *So-so. You?* he mouthed back.

Declan grinned, Oliver's good mood infectious. *Never better.*

If Declan didn't know differently, he'd have thought Oliver blushed at that. Oliver moved his hand forward until it brushed against Declan's, his fingertips grazing Declan's palm. Declan found it difficult to breathe.

Oliver's eyes had starlight in them, and his gaze made Declan feel suddenly unmoored. He looked at their hands, wondering what it meant that Oliver had reached for him.

He glanced up, and Oliver's expression was dazed, as though realising what he'd done. Declan desperately wanted to look away, to shrug off Oliver's hand like it was nothing, but he couldn't. He glanced at Oliver's lips, at how they parted as he drew in a shaky breath. Their faces were closer together now, without Declan noticing he had moved at all. Overwhelmed, like some outside force was compelling him forwards, he leaned in.

And then panicked as their noses nearly collided. He shifted away, Oliver blinking at him. Declan cleared his throat roughly. Oliver let go of his hand.

'Well,' Declan whispered. 'Good night.' He turned over without waiting for a reply and didn't move for the rest of the night.

Chapter 14

Declan

Unsurprisingly, Declan woke up feeling like he hadn't got any sleep. He had been in agony the whole night, replaying what had happened over and over in his head. He couldn't believe he had tried to kiss Oliver. There was no way his intentions could have been misconstrued, nothing else he could have been doing leaning towards him like that. Declan was exposed, with no facade to hide behind any more. Oliver had stripped him of it.

He couldn't resist looking at the man sleeping soundly next to him. Aside from the small puddle of drool on his pillow, Oliver looked as perfect as he had the night before. Declan carefully slipped off the daybed to get ready for his swim.

He lingered over the workout, swimming more laps than he normally would. When he finished, it was Eavie, not Oliver, waiting poolside with a cup of tea for him. Oliver was in the kitchen with the rest of the contestants, and Declan tried not to read anything into that.

'Hi,' Eavie said, concern in her eyes as he shifted his gaze back to her. 'Are you okay?'

He smiled, trying to wipe away whatever honest emotion she had seen. 'Yes,' he said, pulling himself out of the pool and sitting beside her.

She handed the mug to him wordlessly, one eyebrow arched, and he sighed. 'You'll find, if you stick around, that this isn't exactly a holiday. The pressure has got to all of us one way or another. I guess it's finally getting to me.'

Eavie frowned. 'Having a change of heart for Zoë?'

'No,' he said emphatically. 'I'm fully committed to her.'

Her mouth pulled down at the corners. 'That's not exactly what I asked.'

And something in him broke. He wanted nothing more than to be off the island and away from Oliver and the rest of them. He was so tired of being Declan King for the cameras, pretending nothing could touch him. He wanted to go home, to see Georgia again, to train his ass off and win back his title so that no man in England could dare call him soft.

He knew he must look mad staring down Eavie, but he couldn't lie to her. He didn't want to lie to her. If she asked him again how he felt, he couldn't be sure he wouldn't blurt out every non-platonic thing he'd ever thought about or done with Oliver Wright.

To his relief, she backed off. 'It's fine,' she continued, waving dismissively. 'My real motivation for coming over here was to ask for your help in seducing Oliver to my side. Don't get me wrong, Faye is great, but Oliver is too amazing to pass up.'

'He is.'

She laughed like he'd made a joke.

'Oliver already likes you,' he said, looking her over. She really was beautiful – she and Oliver would look good together. 'No seduction necessary.'

'Well, put in a good word for me, if you can,' Eavie said. 'Based solely on what I've seen, he does have a tendency to be thick.'

Declan chuckled at that. 'Come on, let's join the others.'

The contestants were finishing their breakfast when the PA system chimed.

'Girls,' Darcy said, 'the sun may be setting on your time in the villa. Tonight, we'll see which couples stayed true and who will be saying adieu.'

'So that's it, then?' Jack asked. 'We pick our girls and hope they haven't cracked on with some new bloke?'

Niall nodded, his eyebrows drawn together, staring glumly at nothing in particular.

'Well, that's shit,' Jack said, crossing his arms and looking distraught for possibly the first time ever. Seeming to remember the new girls, he looked around sheepishly. 'No offence.'

Amelia put a hand on his shoulder. 'Jack, I had my tongue on your nipple. If that wasn't going to sway you, I don't have much else in my arsenal that would.'

Annabelle snickered, and Jack cracked a smile.

'Chin up, boys,' Declan said, looking around the table. 'Stella and Maeve are head over heels for you two. Me and Zoë are sound. We've got nothing to worry about.' At least only the newcomers were at risk of elimination, so that was one less anxiety for the boys.

'Except for whatever sorts they're flaunting in front of them,' Niall said darkly.

Paige called them into the Love Shack one by one to discuss who they were going to pick that night. When Declan arrived, she looked worn down, regarding him with a trepidation that immediately made his stomach twist.

'Nice to see you,' she said, with a tight smile. 'Right, well, have a seat and let's get through this.'

Declan slumped onto the stool. 'I'm excited to see the girls back here tonight,' he said, unprompted, plastering on his signature smile. 'I've missed Zoë; it's been so boring here without her.'

'Good,' Paige said. 'Say more about what you like about Zoë.'

Declan nodded. 'Zoë is one of the most wonderful girls I've ever met, and our connection was instant.'

'So you feel confident going into tonight?' Paige asked.

Declan wasn't sure what else he could give her. 'I'm feeling confident about Zoë and I going into tonight,' he parroted back. 'We were rock solid when she left. I have no doubt in my mind she'll come back to me.' He and Zoë had never explicitly talked about how they would manage this challenge, but sticking together was the best way to win, and he knew she wanted that as much as he did.

'Perfect,' Paige said. 'Thanks a mil. Could you send Oliver in next?'

Declan nodded, relieved to have been released so easily.

He walked out onto the patio, immediately spotting Oliver wedged between Faye and Eavie by the pool. Faye tousled Oliver's hair affectionately and he shot her one of his devastating smiles. Declan stalked over to them.

'Paige wants to see you,' he muttered. Oliver looked up at him, still grinning. Declan searched his face for any trace of what had happened the night before, but Oliver's expression remained infuriatingly calm.

'Cool,' he said, standing and gesturing for Declan to take his spot.

'God,' Faye said, looking after him as he walked away. 'This is weird.'

'It certainly is unorthodox,' Eavie agreed. 'I hope you didn't feel like I was intruding on your conversation.'

'Not at all. We've got, what, a few hours left before the recoupling? Best to spend as much time as possible with him.'

And Declan was in hell, watching two girls compete for the man he had nearly kissed the night before. 'I bet the producers would love it if you got catty,' he said unhelpfully.

Faye raised her fists and put on a fierce expression, taking a mock swing at Eavie, who laughed and swatted her hand away.

'They won't get us that easily,' Eavie said.

The rest of the afternoon passed tensely until finally Paige told them to get ready for the recoupling. Declan had managed to dodge Oliver since sending him to the Love Shack, while simultaneously trying to figure out if Oliver was avoiding him. It was almost a relief to be alone together as they picked out their outfits for the night.

'Green or blue?' Oliver asked, following the show's script perfectly and holding two shirts.

He seemed to have decided the best way to deal with what had happened the night before was to forget about it. Declan should have been relieved, should have been ecstatic honestly, since Oliver's choice kept his secret. Somehow his slip of self-control hadn't resulted in his sexuality being broadcast to millions of viewers, and yet the only thing he could think about was the fact that Oliver hadn't smiled at him all day.

'Green,' Declan said. 'It'll bring out your eyes.'

'Okay,' Oliver said, pulling it on.

'How are you feeling?' Declan asked, quickly adding, 'About tonight, I mean. Have you made your decision?'

Oliver stared at him, bottom lip caught between his teeth. 'I think so,' he said, nodding slowly. 'I know who makes me happy.'

'Right,' Declan said, his heart beating hard in his chest.

'You sticking with Zoë?' Oliver asked, seeming intently focused on cuffing his sleeves.

'Yes,' Declan said. 'She's all I want.'

Oliver looked up at that, opening his mouth like he might say something, and Declan panicked, turning to the mirror. He glanced at Oliver in the reflection, willing him to leave it alone.

'Five-minute warning!' Brian called over the speakers, and Declan was relieved for the out.

When the contestants had gathered, Paige went over some final details. The boys would be making their decision first, to stay coupled up or choose one of the new girls. Then they'd bring in the girls from the rival villa, who would either walk in alone, having chosen to stay with their man, or arm in arm with their new beau.

Darcy stepped out onto the patio wearing a mod vinyl white dress and silver go-go boots, her platinum hair piled into a gravity-defying beehive.

'Hello, lovelies,' she cooed, in a surprisingly good mood for what was sure to be an extra-long shoot. 'I hope you've all prepared for a night of drama.'

Declan shot an amused look at Oliver, but his eyes were on the girls lining up in front of them. Paige, whispering into her headset, gave Darcy a cue, and Darcy clapped her hands excitedly.

'Let's get started!' She turned to the boys. 'At least *try* to make it interesting, won't you?'

Niall went first. 'Well, I had a lot of fun getting to know these girls over the past few days, but my heart was won a long time ago. And it's the most real and rare thing of my life. So the girl I'd like to couple up with is… Stella.'

Darcy looked bored as the cameraman captured everyone's reactions. 'Great, moving on.'

Jack's speech had more intrigue, since he and Maeve were never officially coupled up.

'I'm choosing this girl because she's the most incredible woman I've ever met. She keeps me in my place, and God knows I need that. These few days apart have killed me, and I can only hope she still feels the same. So the girl I'd like to couple up with is… Maeve.'

Annabelle and Amelia grabbed each other's hands and gave wobbly smiles.

'You both are lovely girls though!' Jack said, apologetic.

'Oh, Jack!' they said in unison.

'God, I love twins,' Darcy said, staring at them. 'Always makes for good TV.'

Declan suppressed an eye roll.

Next was Oliver. 'Try to get a shot of him with both girls in the foreground,' Darcy directed. The two girls looked sideways at each other, and Declan saw Eavie mouth *good luck*.

Declan finally allowed himself to glance over at Oliver, only to find him staring back. He tried to smile encouragingly, but Oliver was already turning to the cameras.

'Over the past few days, I've felt a connection with two girls in particular.' At this, Oliver looked between Eavie and Faye. 'This is the hardest decision I've had to make.' He paused, and

Declan saw Darcy twirl her finger in a cue to wrap it up. 'The girl I'd like to couple up with, I felt like I knew instantly. I choose... Eavie.'

Declan realised he'd been dreading Oliver picking either girl, so he found himself oddly relieved it was done with. Eavie took Oliver's hand and he dropped a kiss to her cheek. Declan turned away to see Faye looking crestfallen. He thought he knew exactly how she felt.

'Oh, that's perfect,' Darcy said, gesturing for a cameraman to get a better angle of Faye. 'All right, Declan, your turn.'

Declan cleared his throat, 'Right, well, what can I say, I'm loyal to the bone. These girls are amazing, but there's only one woman I want to be with right now. It took her being gone for a few days for me to realise how much I care for her. I pick Zoë.'

Darcy smiled and turned to the three remaining girls. 'Ladies, you have not been chosen by any of our boys. Please pack your things and go.'

Faye, Annabelle and Amelia filed out with small waves. There were no touching goodbyes – it was time to find out who the girls had chosen.

Declan, Jack and Niall stood in front of the firepit as Darcy considered them.

'Boys,' she said solemnly, 'the three of you have chosen to stay true to your girls, and it's time to see if they feel the same... But first, let's see how the single girls picked! Holly, Imogen?' Darcy called. 'Come and take a seat.'

The two girls filed in, each with a new boy on their arm.

'Here we have Holly and the lovely Owen, who made a surprise reappearance in the other villa. And Imogen and Rhys.'

Holly grinned at the boys as she stepped up to the firepit, a familiar Irishman beside her. Imogen followed with her new man.

The new couples took their seats next to Oliver and Eavie. Darcy looked back at the three boys still standing. Jack shifted from one foot to the other, and Niall kept glancing at the gate as if he'd be able to catch a glimpse of Stella. Only Declan watched Darcy. She had a malicious glint in her eye that made his stomach drop.

'Now let's see about your girls,' she said. 'Stella, would you come in?'

The gate opened to reveal Stella, standing alone, a look of terror on her face that faded to relief as she ran into Niall's arms. He picked her up and spun her around, kissing her softly.

'I knew it,' she said over and over again as he pulled her to their seats.

'How adorable,' Darcy said, cloyingly sweet. 'Maeve, darling, do join us.'

Maeve walked out, her jaw hanging slightly open in shock when she saw Jack standing alone. She and Jack stared at each other for a moment before he enveloped her in a tight hug. 'Oh, thank God,' Maeve said. 'I thought I was about to make a fool of myself.'

'We're fools together, love,' Jack said, kissing her. They left Declan alone, the last man standing.

'Declan,' Darcy said, 'you've decided to remain faithful to Zoë after being coupled up with her for nearly four weeks. Let's see if she feels the same. Zoë, come on out.'

Zoë stepped out with a tall man on her arm, and bile rose in Declan's throat as he recognised him: James Rowe, Georgia's ex-boyfriend.

Chapter 15

Oliver

Neil Steel: Looks like everybody's favourite boy-toy boxer is getting a blast from his past... in the form of Alex Turner wannabe James Rowe!

James Rowe: 'I don't think my old pal Declan will be too pleased with me... but I couldn't pass on a girl like Zoë. She's a knockout.'

Neil Steel: Well, at least Declan found himself a new girl of his own, right?

Declan King: 'Zoë and I were rock solid when she left. She'll come back to me... She's all I want.'

Neil Steel: Uh... that was painful to watch. Looks like Declan might finally find his fighting spirit again. James, if I were you, I'd run – as for me, I'll be hiding in the corner.

Oliver watched Declan tense as a man entered the patio with Zoë's. He was taller than Oliver, with slicked-back dark hair, an earring in one ear and an expression of disdain.

'Is this the competition, babe?' he asked, shooting a bored look around the garden, eyes coming to rest on Declan. 'We've got it in the fucking bag.'

'*Fuck*,' Declan said, barely audible above the commotion surrounding them.

'What—' Oliver started.

He was drowned out by Darcy, who looked delighted. 'Language, James!'

'What the—' Declan started to say, louder, seemingly oblivious to Darcy's command.

'Sorry,' the man – James – said, without a hint of apology in his tone. 'Do we have to reshoot, Darce?'

She shook her head and signalled to keep rolling. The nearest camera panned over to Declan, whose mouth was moving without making a sound. Oliver instinctively stood, though he wasn't sure how he could possibly help things.

'Declan, mate, how's it going?' James said, with a wide smile. 'Nice to see a friendly face in these parts.'

Zoë frowned at James. 'You two know each other?'

'We have mutual friends in London,' James said smoothly. 'I was looking forward to catching up.'

Declan found his voice. 'Mutual *friend*,' he spat out, turning to Zoë. 'What's all this then, Zo?'

To her credit, Zoë looked apologetic as she opened her mouth to reply.

'Well,' James cut in, 'clearly she wasn't satisfied with you. What can I say? I please her much better than you did.' He winked.

Declan lunged at him, grabbing him and shaking him hard. It would have been comical, what with their height difference, but the unrestrained anger emanating from Declan put them on more even footing. Oliver felt sick, but he couldn't tear his eyes away. He'd never seen Declan act this way before, had never even seen an inkling of the rage that had taken hold of him.

James laughed, carefully fixing a lock of hair that had fallen out of place. 'Oh, that is *so* you, Decs, trying to fight your way out of this. But let's call it what it is: the better man finally winning the girl.'

'You have no fucking clue what you're talking about,' Declan said, shoving James. 'That was always your problem.'

'Now, boys,' Darcy said, trying to defuse the tension. It was clear she had wanted a fight when James entered the villa, but the situation had got out of hand. Oliver wanted to do something, anything, to help, but he felt rooted to the spot.

James looked down at Declan. 'What's this? Declan King can't handle the taste of his own medicine? Maybe now you'll learn not to touch other people's thi—'

Declan didn't let him finish, his fist flying out to meet the side of James's jaw. James fell to the ground, Declan advancing on him before Brian and a cameraman rushed in and grabbed him by the shoulders, holding him back.

'That's enough!' Darcy shrieked. 'Get him out of here!' The crew hauled Declan into the villa.

Oliver was left reeling. Declan had attacked James, had looked angrier than Oliver had ever seen him, all because of Zoë. It felt like a revelation, though he didn't know why. Declan had made his feelings for Zoë explicit to Oliver at every opportunity, and Oliver had chosen to block it out. Whatever might have happened, or he had thought might have happened, between the two of them the night before had clearly been a misunderstanding. He took a deep breath, feeling an over-whelming sense of embarrassment.

Paige emerged from the villa, flushed, her hair falling out of its customary bun. She hurried to Darcy's side, exchanged a few inaudible words with the host, then turned to the remaining group.

'All right, everyone?' she asked, her tense tone contrasting with her false smile. She seemed to genuinely expect an answer, eyes drifting between the contestants pleadingly. When she made eye contact with Oliver, he looked down.

'Uh, no,' Jack said. Maeve was clutching his arm so hard that her fingers made indentations in his skin, but he didn't seem to notice, pressing on: 'What's happened to Declan?'

'He's taking some time to cool off.' Paige glanced at Darcy. 'I'd also like to take this opportunity to remind everyone that physical violence is absolutely prohibited. If conflict occurs, please feel free to take a moment off camera to collect yourself.' She said the lines as though reciting out of the rule book.

'Is he going to be kicked off the show, then?' James asked gleefully.

Jack scowled at him, taking a step in his direction before heeding Paige's warning look.

'*Let's all mellow out.*' She stared pointedly at Jack. 'No, Declan's been given a warning. It won't happen again, I can assure you of that. Your safety is our priority.'

Part of Oliver wanted to ask if he could talk to Declan, but he had just been reminded it wasn't his place. He didn't recognise Declan at the moment; the man who'd thrown that punch was a complete stranger to him, nothing like the man who had shared his bed the night before.

Darcy stepped forward. 'I'm off. Let's keep things *civil*, shall we?' She gave them one final haughty look before walking out.

Paige sighed. 'Why don't you all sit back down?'

Oliver hesitated before sitting with Eavie. No one seemed to want to be the first one to break the silence. Usually Jack would be the one to make introductions, but he looked lost in his own world.

Finally, Zoë spoke, looking at Jack. 'I didn't mean for things to blow up,' she said quietly. 'I thought for sure he'd… I didn't know he cared that much.'

Jack ignored her, though Oliver couldn't tell if he'd even registered that she had been talking to him.

'Zoë, you're so lucky,' Imogen sighed. 'I would love to have two men fighting over me.'

There was a charged pause. 'This is Owen,' Holly joked, elbowing him in the side. She levelled a stern look at the men. 'He's already been dropped once, so I expect you all to treat him nicely.'

'Only the best behaviour for you, Holls,' Jack said, recovering slightly.

'I'll try not to attack him,' Oliver found himself saying. Without looking, he knew Paige was making a face at him.

'Hey, no hard feelings,' James said. 'I know you all have known Decs for longer, but I swear I'm a solid, no-drama type of guy.'

Imogen raised an eyebrow. 'How do you two know each other, anyway?'

James shrugged, giving her an easy smile. 'He tried to steal my girlfriend.' His tone was light, betraying no hint of deception. 'He played nice, acted like we were friends, but I all but caught them in the act when I came back from tour.'

'*Right*,' Jack muttered, just loud enough for Oliver to hear.

Oliver would have liked to share Jack's unflinching loyalty to Declan, but his feelings were more muddled. Hadn't Declan stolen Zoë from him in the first week of the show? Hadn't he insisted that they be friends? James's story only added to Oliver's sense that he had no idea who he was dealing with.

'Oliver,' Maeve said quickly, with a worried glance at James, 'I'm glad you've found someone. You two seem well-suited.'

'I'm lucky I got the chance to snap him up,' Eavie said. 'You lot are mad for not doing it sooner.'

Paige looked like she wanted a strong drink. 'Let's wrap,' she said curtly. 'Bedtime.'

As they walked towards the villa, Eavie slipped her hand into Oliver's. 'I hope it's not always this dramatic,' she said. 'I wanted to get some alone time with you.'

'Me too,' he lied. He had seen potential with Eavie only yesterday, but he couldn't manage to reconjure that feeling amongst everything else in his head.

As he crawled into bed with her, he couldn't stop thinking about the night before. When she mumbled 'Good night,' he thought of the quiet words he and Declan had exchanged on the daybed, and how the way Declan had looked at him had made his whole body feel electric.

Oliver had avoided even thinking the words in the daylight, but at night, he was able to finally admit it to himself: Declan had been about to kiss him. There was no other explanation for what had happened between them the night before. And the strangest part: Oliver had been about to let him.

He waited for panic to set in, but it didn't come. He'd been about to kiss a man, but it somehow didn't feel as life-altering as it should have. Instead, the scene played over and over in Oliver's head, now steeped in a profound confusion. In the moments after Declan had punched James, Oliver had rewritten the night before, assuming he had misinterpreted something.

But maybe he hadn't – hearing James's explanation of his history with Declan, he had to wonder if it was all part of some twisted game. He'd thought he had learned to distinguish the real Declan from the performance, but his anger when his fist connected with James's jaw? That hadn't been rehearsed; it was probably the first act he knew to be fully Declan's – and it terrified him, how foreign Declan seemed to him now.

–

When Oliver woke the next morning, he was sure he had overreacted. Trying to be rational, he formulated a plan: before assuming anything, he would talk to Declan.

The first problem presented itself when he walked out to the kitchen and didn't see him swimming laps. Instead, he found Paige sitting at the counter with two mugs in front of her.

'All right?' Oliver asked.

'Yeah, fine,' she said, not sounding it. She seemed to realise who she was talking to, straightening suddenly. 'You're looking for Declan?'

He tried to sound casual, though he felt like he might go mad if he didn't talk to Declan before the cameras arrived. 'Er, yeah. He always takes a swim about now, but...' He gestured towards the empty pool.

Paige took a sip of tea. 'I just talked to him. He's taking a shower – I gave him licence to use all the hot water, as an apology of sorts.'

Oliver tried to hide his disappointment. 'Gee, I'm sure everyone else will be pleased.'

'How's things with Eavie?' she asked, ignoring him.

'Good. I think there's a lot of potential there,' he said, feeling self-conscious in a way he hadn't for several weeks. He felt as though he was trying to convince Paige of something, reciting lines the way she'd once accused him of.

She looked at him sideways, and Oliver wasn't sure he'd sold it. 'Good. We brought her on for you. I know you like dancers,' she said.

Oliver blinked at her. 'It's creepy when you say stuff like that, just so you know.'

'Be nice to me,' Paige said, finishing her tea. 'I'm going to give you a date today.'

'Fine, you're not a stalker,' he said drily. 'Happy?'

Oliver kept an eye out for Declan as he started on breakfast and the other contestants slowly trickled out of the villa. When Eavie joined Oliver in the kitchen, he hardly noticed. As more and more of the crew arrived, the tension in his chest grew. He knew it would be impossible for him to say what he needed to in front of the cameras.

When Declan finally exited the villa, hair wet and skin glistening, Oliver abandoned his post at the stove, handing his spatula over to Eavie. He rounded the counter and took off after Declan, who stopped a few feet away from the pool, looking into its depths.

'All right?' Oliver asked.

Declan let out a weary sigh. 'I don't want to do this with you right now.' He didn't sound angry, but his tone wasn't reassuring either.

Oliver felt a flicker of annoyance. Things had irreversibly shifted for him in the last two days, and he no longer knew if Declan cared at all. 'Do *what* with me right now? You can't talk to me?'

Declan shook his head. It would have been difficult to sustain anger for someone who looked so miserable under different circumstances.

'Fine,' Oliver said tightly. 'Come and find me when you're ready to talk.'

Declan's eyes flashed to the nearest camera, then back to the water. Oliver backed off, though he wanted to scream with frustration. As he headed towards the kitchen, determined to finish making breakfast with Eavie, Paige intercepted him.

'Smile, Oliver,' she said brightly.

'Don't much feel like it,' he muttered.

'Look, I don't know exactly what's going on with you,' she said. 'But I *do* know that Declan's ratings are fine right now, so no need to worry about him.'

'Yeah, fine.' He hadn't even considered the ratings for the last few days, and now it was one more thing for him to worry about. The thought of going back home empty-handed, of the long hours he would have to put in to afford his move, seemed impossible.

She nudged his shoulder. 'You're about to go on your date,' she whispered. 'You might want to make it look like you're not walking to the executioner's block.'

Oliver did feel better at the prospect of leaving the villa for the afternoon – a date had never sounded more appealing.

'Go back behind the counter with Eavie and sell it,' Paige instructed. 'The cooking thing was cute.'

Eavie smiled at him, flipping a piece of bacon as he came up beside her. Maeve and Jack and Stella and Niall sat on either end of the counter, with Imogen happily wedged between them.

'Declan's not eating?' Eavie asked.

'Nah, he's not hungry,' Oliver said.

Jack gave a worried glance over his shoulder. 'It's not like him,' he said quietly.

'I'm sure he'll cheer up soon,' Imogen said, taking a large bite of bacon. 'Ooh, Eavie, this is delicious.'

'I think we should give him some space,' Oliver said to Jack just as the chime sounded.

'Oliver,' Darcy announced, 'time for you to get a little lucky. Take the Lover of your choice out on a date. Third time's the charm, right?'

Oliver looked at Eavie with what he hoped was a thoroughly adoring expression. 'Eavie, will you go on this date with me?'

She side-stepped towards him, their elbows knocking together. 'Of course.'

Oliver saw Paige watching them expectantly in his peripheral vision. She had told him to sell it, so he leaned down and kissed Eavie for good measure. Jack wolf-whistled, and when Oliver looked up, the other contestants were grinning.

The chime sounded again.

'Declan, you and a lucky Lover will join Oliver and Eavie on their date.'

Oliver noticed that Declan was standing behind the others, face carefully blank, his stare trained between Oliver and Eavie.

'Oh,' Oliver said, his stomach sinking. The fact that Paige had failed to mention this aspect of the date made it even more ominous.

'Imogen, how about it?' Declan asked, looking down the counter at her.

'I've been waiting my whole life for those words, Declan King,' she said dramatically. He rewarded her with a small smile.

'Let's crack on, then?' he asked, eyes back on Oliver.

Chapter 16

Oliver

By the time Oliver joined the others by the van for their double date, the sun was fully overhead, beating down ferociously on the asphalt driveway. A drop of sweat made its way from Oliver's nape to his lower back as they piled into the van. To his surprise and apprehension, both Paige and Brian had met the four of them out front, offering no explanation for the additional producer oversight. Oliver couldn't help but wonder if it had something to do with the fight.

The ride was awkward. He and Declan sat next to each other in total silence as the van made its way down the winding road. Declan was determinedly staring out the window, an unreadable expression on his face. Despite the shower, he looked like he'd just rolled out of bed, pale, with slight purple bruises under his eyes. He hadn't bothered to style his hair or shave.

Oliver's long legs meant he had to make an effort to keep his knee from touching Declan's. He had the feeling that any accidental contact between them would make the afternoon completely unbearable. He kept thinking of their hands touching when they had been in bed together.

'All right,' Paige said with forced cheer, as they finally pulled into a driveway. 'Let's get this show on the road.'

Eavie gave Oliver an encouraging smile as he helped her out of the van, which made him suspect he looked as upset as he felt. They had arrived at a stone manor house, and Paige gestured them through an intricately carved gate and into a pretty courtyard surrounded by flower bushes. The wooden table in the centre held two bottles of champagne in ice buckets. The air was hot and sticky, more suffocating than it had been since Oliver had arrived on the island, having seemingly grown even warmer during the ride.

'Just give us a moment to check camera angles.' Paige gestured to the two cameramen coming through the gate. 'You can sit, we'll get the establishing shots later. I think we should jump right into it.' She glanced at Oliver.

He didn't meet her eye, but he followed her directive. Eavie sat across from him and Imogen took the place next to her. Declan hesitated for a moment before pulling out the chair beside Oliver's and slouching into it. He looked like he was steeling himself for a few hours of torture.

'This is nice,' Imogen commented. 'Much prettier than the last date, don't you think, Oliver?'

'Er – yeah, very nice,' he said. The longer he sat, the more on edge he felt; the sun was like a spotlight on him, as though he was about to perform but had no idea of the routine.

'I guess they grouped the four of us together for optimal awkwardness,' Eavie said, with a small smile.

Oliver started. 'What do you mean?'

Imogen gave him a curious look. 'I think she's referring to our date.' She turned to Eavie. 'You don't have anything to worry about, babes. I don't fancy men who are clearly smitten with someone else.'

'Oh. Right.' Oliver ran a hand through his hair without looking at Declan.

Paige ended her consultation with the cameramen and walked over. 'Everyone ready?' She looked for confirmation from Declan, who had been staring at the table.

'Yeah,' he said, bringing his head up and giving her a bright smile, slipping effortlessly into his performance. 'Ready.'

'Rolling!' Paige called, stepping out of frame again.

'This is so gorgeous,' Imogen said, her dreamy gaze wandering around the courtyard.

'Very romantic,' Eavie agreed, with a look to Oliver.

He nodded enthusiastically. 'Great spot.'

Declan snorted softly by his side but said nothing.

Imogen reached forwards to open a bottle of champagne, pouring a glass for each of them. Oliver raised his in a wordless toast, taking a sip. 'So, Eavie,' he said, 'dancing for Rambert. What's it like?'

Imogen groaned. 'Please, no career talk. If I say one more word about fashion, I'll never sew again.'

Oliver blinked at her, losing his footing. 'Did you have something else in mind?'

She rested her elbows on the table and looked around pensively, giving the impression of deep thought.

'I'm scared,' Declan quipped, and Oliver bit back a smile, not wanting to give him the satisfaction of a reaction.

'How about this?' Imogen said, giving each of them a deliberate look. 'If you had to give up your current career, what would you do instead?'

'That's tricky,' Eavie said. 'I guess, practically, I would want to use my degree. But it's in art history, so I don't know if it would do me much good on the job market.'

Imogen pointed an accusatory finger at her. 'No practical thinking allowed.'

Eavie laughed. 'Okay, I suppose I'd want to be an archaeologist. It seems like a fascinating field.'

Imogen nodded, turning to Declan. 'What about you?'

'I'm Declan King,' he said, giving a short laugh. 'Can't be anyone else.'

Oliver rolled his eyes.

'I'd be a lion tamer, I think,' Imogen announced. 'I love a good top hat.'

'Ooh,' Eavie said, delighted. 'I think you'd smash that.'

Oliver turned back to Declan, unable to help himself. 'Sorry, I don't think that's the point of the question.'

Declan's expression was infuriatingly pleasant. 'I dunno, mate. What would you do?' Oliver's mind drew a blank, and he said nothing. 'Guess you never came up with a plan B, then?' Declan said, with a hint of irony.

Before Oliver could reply in kind, Imogen took control of the conversation again. 'Next question,' she said. 'What's your favourite spot in London?'

'Easy,' Oliver said, glad for the reminder to not antagonise Declan, 'the V&A.'

'Bit of a tourist trap, no?' Declan said.

'I haven't had as long in the city as you all,' Eavie cut in, her eyes flicking between Declan and Oliver. 'Seems like an unfair question.'

Oliver shot her a grateful look. 'I'll happily sign on as your tour guide,' he said.

'I would love that,' Eavie said, so sincerely that Oliver felt awful. He had meant it, he would enjoy showing Eavie around London, but he knew that implied much more than he was willing to give.

'Can I third-wheel on your date to the V&A?' Imogen asked.

'Why don't we all go?' Eavie turned to Declan.

'I can show you all the best gyms in London,' Declan said cheerfully. 'I know you dancers can bench press like madmen.' Oliver blinked at Declan, surprised, but Declan didn't meet his eye, chugging his remaining champagne instead.

'Mad*women*,' Imogen corrected.

'It's lucky I've found you three,' Eavie said, seeming gratified that Oliver and Declan had temporarily ceased bickering. 'Right now my main haunt is this terrible cafe in Islington serving rock-hard scones and glares from the hot barista.'

Imogen looked bewildered. 'Why do you keep going?'

'The coffee is the strongest I've found in the city so far. Can't turn down a deal like that – I need a lot of it to get through early morning rehearsals.'

'I'm the same,' Oliver said, before recognition clicked in his mind. 'Wait... terrible scones and good coffee in Islington? You're not talking about Lee's Coffee, are you?'

'That's the place,' Eavie confirmed. 'You've been? I thought I was their only customer.'

Oliver laughed, some of the tension in his body unwinding. 'My mate Will said the same. We went all the time, probably four or five times a week, when we were in school.' He ran a hand through his hair, the memories of hours spent in the cramped cafe listening to Will whinge about maths overwhelming him for a moment. He realised, with a start, that he was giving Eavie a genuine smile for the first time in days. 'I'd forgotten about that place. I'll have to go back for old times' sake.'

'I'm more of a tea man myself,' Declan chimed in.

Oliver ignored him. 'But wait – is it Samir glaring at you? Don't stress, that's just how he flirts.'

'Not a chance,' Eavie giggled. 'His brand of withering look is deadly.'

'Ah, you can't blame him, that's the way his face is.' Eavie made a disbelieving expression and he held up his hands. 'I swear! Give him a chance, he's a sweet bloke. He used to give me free scones all the time, said I needed to put on weight.'

'Oh, please,' Eavie said, rolling her eyes. 'That's not a kindness, that's biological warfare.' She and Oliver grinned at each other for a beat before Declan cleared his throat.

'Well, Oliver, you might not get a chance to go back to this place anyway, what with New York and all,' he said, his tone perfectly even.

'New York?' Eavie echoed, confused.

'Oliver didn't tell you? He's auditioned for Manhattan Ballet,' Declan said. Oliver had no idea where he was going with this, but it couldn't possibly end well for him. His eyes flicked towards Paige, hoping she would intervene.

'That's exciting!' Imogen said, leaning forward. 'I adore New York. It's like London, but with better weather. Do you love it there?'

Oliver fidgeted in his seat. 'Er – haven't spent much time there, actually. But, you know, everyone says it's nice.'

Declan laughed. 'He's clearly done his research.'

Oliver bit back his reply. A joking Declan, even one who was laughing at his expense, had to be a better sign than a brooding Declan. He'd grown accustomed to Declan's performance, but today he had little patience for it. He focused on Eavie, giving her a feeble smile, trying to block him out.

'You know how it goes – it's a toss-up if I get the role or not.'

'Mate,' Declan said, flashing a smile in Oliver's direction, 'I doubt Eavie here understands rejection quite as well as you do. I mean, look at her.' He gave Eavie a long look; Oliver felt a pang of unease. Declan was a bit *too* pleased with himself now.

'That's sweet,' Eavie said, her cheeks reddening, 'but of course I do. You can't be a dancer and not have lost out on a gig before.'

Declan pressed on with a wide smile, eyes still locked on Eavie. 'Bet you don't lose out on the blokes, though. Not looking like that.'

Eavie shot a confused glance between Declan and Oliver, seemingly waiting for someone to explain to her what exactly was going on. Oliver turned to Imogen, hoping for support. Her eyebrow was raised, but she said nothing.

'Could you not?' Oliver asked tightly, hoping Declan would realise he had touched on a nerve and lay off.

Declan didn't heed the warning. 'Calm down. I'm just getting to know her,' he said in that same grating tone, giving Oliver a friendly slap on the back. Oliver winced. They hadn't touched since the night they had shared a bed, and he couldn't think about that now. 'It's not called *Summer of Friends*.'

Eavie frowned at Imogen, as if unsure of how to proceed without offending anyone at the table. Oliver couldn't blame her; he was still holding out hope that Paige would interrupt at any moment. If this continued any longer, he didn't know what he'd do.

'Hear, hear!' Imogen said, breaking the silence and moving her glass to clink with Declan's abandoned one. She didn't look put out by Declan's attention shifting to Eavie, but rather wildly entertained by the unfolding events.

At the sound of the colliding champagne flutes, Declan seemed to recall that he hadn't had his second drink. He poured himself another, gulping it down as the rest of them stared at him, then leaning towards Eavie. 'You know, I've always fancied dancers. You lot have the most *incredible* bodies.'

Oliver felt a sinking loss of control, and that same sense of impending rejection that had accompanied his short-lived relationships with Maeve and Zoë. Here was Declan yet again messing with Oliver's chances. Even though he had a perfectly solid option in Imogen, even though he was supposedly heart-broken over Zoë, even though he had nearly kissed Oliver, he was *still* pursuing Eavie. Oliver made to stand, and in the process, his knee touched Declan's under the table. He nearly jumped out of his skin.

'Mate, everything okay?' Declan asked, grinning as though Oliver had told a particularly funny joke.

Oliver couldn't keep it together, between the accidental touch and the discordant smile on Declan's face. 'What the fuck is *wrong* with you?' he yelled, standing fully now.

Declan's grin, if anything, grew wider at the explosion, as though he had been hoping for it.

'Language!' Paige called, and the ringing in Oliver's ears quieted a bit. 'Let's take ten,' she said, and Oliver flinched away from a touch on his arm before realising it was Paige trying to steer him away from the table. He allowed her to pull him, not paying attention to where they were going.

He tried to take a deep breath, and found it stuck in his chest. They were inside the house now, in what looked like an abandoned dining room with a camera set-up. It was clear the producers had designated it as the interview room for the day.

Paige deposited him into a chair and kneeled in front of him. 'Oliver, what's going on?'

'Why don't you ask him?' he asked, his voice coming out hollow. 'He's the one who was being a prick back there, but I'm the one who has to be talked to, is that right?'

'Hey,' Paige said soothingly, 'I'm talking to you because you're upset and I care about you.'

'Oh, sure,' he replied, anger flaring in his chest again. 'But you're the one who had the idea to put me and Declan on a double date right now, aren't you?' He found that he was standing again, though he didn't remember making the decision to do so.

Paige looked into his eyes, but he couldn't read her expression. 'You *know* the audience responds to you and Declan together. That's all it was. And you're going to come out of this situation looking fantastic, by the way. You should be thanking me.'

'Right,' Oliver said sarcastically.

'Remember,' Paige said, laying a calming hand on his shoulder, 'you *care* about this opportunity. Remember what you care about, okay? And please,' she said, her tone sharpening, 'take into consideration that *I'm* not the one flirting with Eavie. If you're angry, be angry with Declan, not me.'

'Right,' Oliver said again, not thinking about what she said. The only part that stuck in his mind was *remember what you care about*. The rest was a bit fuzzy around the edges. 'Okay.'

Paige gave him a long, concerned look. 'Take a few minutes to collect yourself. You don't need to be back right away. Bathroom's down the hall.' With one last encouraging smile, Paige left the room.

Oliver felt unnerved in the interview room, even with the camera off. The thought of being recorded immediately set him on edge. The bathroom would be better. He could splash some

157

water on his face, put his cheek against the cold ceramic, look at himself in the mirror and *think*.

The door to the bathroom creaked as Oliver swung it open. He saw the silver feet of a clawfoot bath, the green tile backsplash and an ornate light fixture shining down over a smudged mirror. He noticed all of those details before he noticed Declan standing in front of the mirror, an inscrutable expression on his face.

Declan had been looking into the drain of the sink, but as Oliver entered, he glanced up and their eyes met in the glass. His expression softened into something pitiable, between the apology in his eyes, the stubble on his cheeks and the downwards turn of his mouth. Oliver was not in the mood to pity him.

'Come to yell at me?' Declan asked hoarsely, turning to face him.

'I haven't decided,' Oliver said, taking a step forwards and instinctively closing the door behind him. 'I mean, what were you doing out there? It seems to me as though as soon as I'm with a girl, you have to have her. Like you can't stand to let me have anything.' His voice was getting louder.

'That's not what's happ—' Declan started.

'I thought you were on my fucking side here,' Oliver said, cutting him off. 'And now I have no one, and I feel like I'm going mad. Between you and Paige, I don't know what to think any more. I don't know what's *real*.' He waited for Declan to say something, but he kept his head down, staring at the tiled floor. Oliver felt exhausted even looking at him. 'What are we doing?'

Declan's hands fisted by his sides. 'I don't know! I don't have any answers. I'm sorry, okay? I've fucked this all up and I'm sorry.'

'What are you sorry for?' Oliver demanded. 'I don't think you even know what I want you to apologise for.'

'I'm sorry that I—' When Declan met Oliver's eye, he broke off, looking down. 'It's my fault. All of it.'

Oliver took a staggering step forwards before realising what he had done. He was as close to Declan as he had been under the duvet. Declan's eyes pored over his face and Oliver had the feeling that he was thinking about the exact same moment.

The circles under his eyes gave him a wounded appearance. Oliver wanted to reach out and touch his cheek, to feel the roughness there. Something about an unkempt Declan made him want to lean closer, to run his hand through his thick hair, to feel the drum of his heart. He inhaled deeply, struck by the scent of spearmint.

'I should've...' Declan's lips twitched, and Oliver lost any of the composure he had left. He leaned down and kissed him.

Declan made a small noise of surprise and Oliver almost lost his nerve and pulled back, but then Declan's hand slotted into Oliver's hair, pulling at the roots. Declan let out a broken groan, deepening the kiss, nipping at Oliver's bottom lip, and Oliver sighed into his mouth, relieved at not having horribly misjudged the situation. He gripped Declan's shoulders tightly, worried he would fall without the support, and pulled his body harder against him.

All the anger and confusion of the last several days, of the last several weeks, drained out of Oliver at the press of their lips. Every glance, every touch, every word that they had spoken to each other finally clicked into place, and he could see it all perfectly in his head. He felt foolish, like he should've noticed sooner – their meeting on the plane was always going to lead here, to this moment.

Declan stumbled forwards, unsteady, pushing Oliver up against the bathroom door, his stubble scratching Oliver's cheeks. His body recognised the differences of kissing a man, the strength behind Declan's grip, the surprising smoothness of his lips, and yet Oliver was struck by the sameness of it all, the familiar swoop in his belly and racing of his heart, feelings he thought had left him for America.

A low moan rumbled out of Declan's chest as he pushed impossibly closer, the carefully constructed facade that was

Declan King crumbling as they pitched against each other, thigh catching hip bone, hands grasping bare skin, lips brushing jaw.

There was a desperation in the way their mouths slotted together. Oliver couldn't breathe. He shifted his hand to Declan's chest, pushing against it gently. Declan pulled away and made to take a step back, but Oliver stopped him, holding him there, their foreheads touching as he struggled to draw in air. When he finally glanced up, Declan's eyes were on him, a slight smile playing at his lips.

'Can you apologise now?' Oliver said, giddy laughter climbing its way up his throat. Something about snogging Declan, and him having that ridiculous smile on his face, made it impossible for him to collect himself.

'Yes,' Declan said, voice low. 'I'm so' – he dipped his head, kissing Oliver's jaw – 'so' – he placed a kiss on his throat where his pulse beat rapidly – 'so' – he mouthed at Oliver's collarbone – 'sorry I didn't kiss you the other night.'

'I forgive you,' Oliver said, leaning in to kiss him again. Declan wrapped his arm around him, hands sneaking into the back pockets of his shorts, and Oliver broke off with a groan. 'We can't.' It killed him to say it, but he knew someone would be looking for them before too long.

'You go first,' Declan said, disentangling himself.

'Right.' Oliver said, lightheaded, his heart hammering in his chest. He gave Declan one last, long look before exiting the bathroom and walking back towards the garden.

Oliver's legs felt like they were melting into the ground. He stumbled down the steps and saw Eavie and Imogen chatting away at the table as though nothing of consequence had occurred. Paige was having a hushed conversation with Brian, writing something hastily on her clipboard.

'Hi,' Oliver said, trying to sound like he was recovering from an angry outburst and not from snogging a man in the bathroom, 'I'm ready to continue the scene.'

'Oliver!' Paige said, with an encouraging smile. 'That was quick.'

Was it? He had no concept of how much time had passed between him entering the bathroom and now.

'Where's Declan?' he asked, congratulating himself on the neutral delivery and for remembering he wasn't supposed to know where Declan was.

'In the bathroom,' Imogen said, squinting at him.

'Oh. Well, I guess I'll sit, then,' he said, pulling out his chair and half-falling in.

Eavie studied him. 'Are you okay? That was a tough situation, with Declan—' She broke off, unsure of herself. 'I understand why you were upset.'

Oliver nodded, trying to remember how to frown. 'It was fucked up. But, you know, we're mates, and sometimes mates yell at each other, right?'

'So true,' Imogen said. 'Sometimes you just have to release that tension.'

'Hey there, Declan,' Brian said, looking towards the manor. 'All right?'

'Yeah, fine,' Declan replied from somewhere behind Oliver. 'I'm sorry for being such an ass.' He laid a hand on Oliver's shoulder unannounced, and he started. 'Please forgive me?' Oliver looked into Declan's eyes, which were filled with mirth.

'It's all right,' he said, shrugging. 'Happens.'

Chapter 17

Oliver

When he made his way out to the kitchen the next morning, Declan was already leaning against the stove, morning workout forgotten. Oliver circled the counter to stand directly in front of him. Declan didn't move. Oliver took a half-step closer and reached around him to grab the kettle. Declan leaned in.

He could feel the heat of Declan's body, and it took every ounce of his self-control not to press against him.

'Has the usual tea order not been meeting your standards? Must you supervise?' he quipped, retreating to the sink. The sound of water filling the kettle echoed the blood rushing in his ears.

Declan grabbed two mugs out of the cabinet and placed them deliberately on the counter before crossing the kitchen and gently prying the kettle out of Oliver's hands.

His heartbeat tripped over itself as he traced Declan's features, sure he'd somehow be different now. But no, the same blue eyes looked up at him from underneath bushy brows, his nose was still as crooked as ever, and he wore a hint of the lopsided smile that made the day before rush back to Oliver. He leaned forwards instinctively, only for Declan to push him gently towards the counter.

'Thought I could make you tea for a change.'

Oliver sat restlessly, his shoe tapping against the side of the cabinet as he watched Declan move around the kitchen. He revelled in the quiet confidence of Declan's mannerisms, strong and sure in a way Oliver only felt on stage, every movement mapped out and memorised. His gaze drifted along Declan's waist, up the muscles of his arms to his face, sticking on the pout of his lips. He felt a low ache in his stomach. His tapping became more rapid.

'What are you thinking about?' Declan asked, placing a mug in front of him and sitting beside him, his knee grazing Oliver's leg and stilling its movement.

Oliver stared at him, wondering how he could not know, sure that all the confusion and panic and want must be showing clearly on his face. Declan, in comparison, looked overly calm, eyeing Oliver with a wariness that made him wonder if this wasn't the first time he'd kissed a man before. He wished they could talk without the cameras around, felt foolish for walking out of that bathroom without discussing anything, but even more than that, he wanted to talk to Will.

'Just missing my friends,' Oliver said, and Declan's eyebrows drew together in confusion. Oliver tried to think of some way to explain in front of the cameras. 'My mate Will gives the best girl advice. Ironic, since he's gay.'

The final word hung between them.

Declan cleared his throat, staring at the steam rising from his mug. 'What do you think he'd say to you right now?' he asked neutrally. 'If he could?'

Oliver laced his fingers together, frowning at the counter in concentration. He closed his eyes, trying to conjure one of Will's signature pep talks, and then glanced back at Declan, wondering what his friend would think of him. 'He'd say to go with my gut. That if things feel good, they are good.'

Declan cocked his head to the side. 'So, you're good?'

Though his tone hadn't changed at all, Oliver could tell he needed to hear the answer. 'Yes.' He was surprised by how true that was. 'Better than I've been in a long time. And Will would be proud of me, making it this far.'

Declan nodded. 'He sounds like a good friend.'

Oliver leaned back, the side of his arm brushing Declan's in the process. He didn't move away. 'Yeah, my mates are pretty solid.'

'Tell me about them,' Declan said, turning to face him. He seemed genuinely interested, there was no ulterior motive or angle for the cameras.

'They're the best,' Oliver said simply. 'We've known each other since school, got our own sort of language. It makes making new friends terribly hard, since no one else knows what we're on about half the time.'

He felt an ache of longing – he had missed them, and not only in the weeks he'd been on the show. He had missed them since the break-up, when he'd been barely there for months, despite their insistence that he wasn't a burden, that he wasn't making them choose sides, that they wanted to help.

Declan pressed his knee more firmly into Oliver's thigh. 'That sounds really nice,' he said.

'And what about your mates?' Declan felt more real to him than ever, and he wanted to know about his life outside of the show. He finally felt like he could ask.

'Ah,' Declan said, his voice low, looking into his mug again. 'I have my best mate – we're practically attached at the hip. And, you know, my family.'

There was something in the hunch of Declan's shoulders, an almost imperceptible tensing. And Oliver understood, for the first time, that Declan's loneliness wasn't just for show, a ploy to ingratiate himself with the public and explain away his lack of romantic history.

Oliver grasped Declan's shoulder, rubbing a soft circle across his spine. 'And now… you have Jack,' he teased.

'Oi! Are you two gossiping about me?' Jack asked, walking into the kitchen with Maeve. Oliver dropped his hand, fiddling with the hem of his shirt. Almost on cue, the production team walked through the gate.

'Oliver was saying that he thinks you're next on the chopping block,' Declan said, so easily that Oliver felt whiplash.

Jack didn't rise to the bait. 'Everyone loves Maeve,' he said, peeling a banana. 'I think I'm safe.'

'Oh?' Maeve teased. 'Is that what you're doing with me, then? Playing it safe?'

Jack smiled at her fondly, wrapping his arms around her. 'I'm trying to woo the pants off you, is what I'm doing.'

'Are you thinking about becoming a nudist?' Stella said, as she and Niall joined them. 'I tried that for a year or two, but England really isn't the best climate for it. I was cold all the time.'

'Erm,' Maeve said awkwardly.

Oliver shot Declan a grin, only to find him already watching him. His cheeks flushed as Declan's hand came to rest by his own under the counter, his hand inching closer until their ring fingers tangled together.

'Actually, Jack was just revealing his master plan to win the show,' Declan said, raising his eyebrows.

'Surely you can handle a little competition,' Jack was saying, but Oliver barely heard him, his ears instead seemingly calibrated to the rush of Declan's breath, eyes trailing along the part of his lips.

'I'm not one for competition,' Niall said. 'But I do believe that true love will prevail.'

Declan huffed out a laugh and Jack rounded on them. Oliver tried to school his features, ducking his head and dropping Declan's hand.

'Who do you think will win? Us or them?' Jack joked.

Declan slung his arm over Oliver's shoulder, the heat of his skin radiating against Oliver's neck. 'I think it's us, actually.'

—

When Darcy's tinny voice called them to a recoupling ceremony at the end of the week, it was the first time Oliver hadn't been nervous about staying on the show; he'd been too wrapped up in stealing heated glances with Declan.

'This shirt?' Oliver asked Declan, holding up a navy shirt with vertical stripes and trying to suppress a giddy smile. Even surrounded by the other boys and the cameras, getting dressed with Declan felt like a moment just for them.

Declan gave a drawn-out look to Oliver's bare torso, giving the impression of deep thought. 'I've got one you could wear. I think it'd look good on you.'

Oliver felt his cheeks colour. 'Er – yeah, sure.'

Jack came over, slinging an arm over Declan's shoulder. 'All right, Decs? Remember what I said.' He gave Declan a stern look, and Oliver was reminded that in his real life, Jack was a secondary-school teacher.

'What's that?' Niall asked, looking up from buttoning his shirt.

'If Declan's going to punch someone, he needs to let me know first so I can join the fray. No good men left behind.'

Oliver couldn't guess the full story between Declan and James, but, like every other confusing aspect of their situation, it had faded into the background for the moment. That feeling grew when Declan handed him a heather-grey shirt. Oliver put on the shirt, inhaling the scent of Declan's cologne lingering on the collar, as Jack and Declan continued to banter.

'Glad you're back to normal, mate,' Jack said. 'I was starting to worry.'

'Things with Imogen must be going well for him to be looking that pleased with himself,' Niall observed.

Jack frowned. 'Have you two been sneaking off together? I haven't seen any canoodling.'

Declan's smile faded minutely, and a pang of anxiety hit Oliver; he'd been so caught up in his new-found sense of security he hadn't even considered the possibility of Declan going home. He had forgotten that Declan was no longer secure, that he was supposed to be finding someone to couple up with.

Declan cleared his throat, his eyes on Oliver. 'We talk. And I, uh, would say that the date went well. Imogen had a good time.'

Strangely, Oliver couldn't definitively say that it was a lie, remembering Imogen's contentment in the chaos of the afternoon.

'No wonder you're so confident,' Jack said, slapping him on the shoulder. 'Good on you, King. Recovering with ease.'

Declan shot a worried glance at Oliver. Oliver couldn't think of anything useful he could do or say, running through all the scenarios in which Declan could be saved and coming up blank.

'Okay, Wright?' Niall said, frowning at him.

'Er – fine,' he said.

'This should be the easiest one so far for you. Eavie's a sure thing.'

'Yeah. I'm grand, just typical nerves.'

Brian poked his head through the door. 'Ready, lads? The ladies have you beaten this evening.'

Darcy was already beside the firepit when they walked out, lecturing Paige. The women were lined up next to the couch, and Eavie flashed Oliver a smile as he approached.

'Sorry,' Paige said, having seemingly been dismissed as Darcy's attention moved to her phone. 'I'm ready. Brian, you've prepped the new folks?'

'Yes,' Brian said, chest puffing out slightly, as though doing his job was a great feat indeed.

'Roll,' Darcy said in a bored voice, stashing her phone.

Oliver hardly listened to the first few speeches, his eyes boring into Imogen, trying to figure out what she was thinking. She had been interested in Declan from the moment she walked into the villa, but he doubted it would be enough for her to choose him over Rhys, who probably hadn't hit on another woman in front of her. He kept trying to meet her eye, but she wouldn't look at him, staring straight ahead with an annoyingly serene air.

167

'Eavie,' Darcy said, snapping Oliver out of his reverie. Eavie was frowning at him in confusion, he supposed because he'd been staring at a different woman throughout the whole recoupling.

'The boy I'm choosing to couple with is just the sweetest. He says I remind him of his best mates, and he already feels like one of mine. I'm choosing to couple up with... Oliver.'

The ringing in his ears got louder. He tried to remind himself to smile, but it felt impossible to get his muscles to obey.

'Oliver,' Darcy said loudly, looking at him as though he was thick. 'Could you walk over to Eavie?'

'Right,' he said. He focused on Eavie's face, putting one foot in front of another, not letting himself look back at Declan.

When he reached her side, she pulled him into a hug, whispering, 'Nerves?'

He gave a slight nod before sliding onto the couch, facing the two remaining boys, Declan and Rhys. Declan was staring at Oliver in a way that made it difficult to breathe. He tried to present a calm front, but he knew his face was probably anything but helpful at the moment.

'Imogen,' Darcy was saying. 'You have the final choice of the night. Will it be Declan or Rhys?'

Imogen gave a satisfied, cat-like smile. 'Tonight, I am pleased to be choosing a boy who is clever, handsome and everything I could hope for in a boyfriend. I hope that's what he'll be one day. Tonight, I'm choosing to couple up with... Declan.'

Everything around Oliver froze for a moment, and then Declan smiled wide. He walked over to Imogen and embraced her, looking so at ease that Oliver considered that he had imagined their earlier panicked glances. He caught Imogen's eye over Declan's shoulder and she winked.

After Rhys's departure, the contestants were allowed to file back into the villa. Declan came up beside Oliver, slapping him on the shoulder. The brief touch snapped Oliver out of his reverie.

'All right?' he asked, as Declan's eyes met his.

' 'Course,' Declan said. 'Were you worried?'

Oliver heard a quiet cough and turned. Paige was standing behind him, bright eyes trained on the space between the two men. 'Oliver, could I pull you for a chat?'

Oliver groaned. 'It was too much to hope for sleep this early, I suppose.' He glanced at Declan. 'See you later, King.'

'Looking forward to it,' Declan said, nodding to Paige and continuing down the hall.

When they entered the Love Shack, the red light was already on. Oliver slid onto the stool. 'Hit me.'

Paige raised her eyebrows. 'You looked stressed during the recoupling – did you think there was a chance of you being dumped?'

'Well… there's always a chance. And you know how I get, I never feel safe.'

She nodded. 'But things are going well with Eavie?'

Oliver had prepared for this question. 'Things are great. I like Eavie a lot. I know I've had a tough go of it, but I feel like I've found my person now.'

'So, how did you feel about Declan flirting with her on your date?' Paige asked.

Oliver frowned – he and Paige had already discussed the date extensively in the days prior. 'Well, I wasn't pleased. But he was in a vulnerable position, with Zoë choosing James, and I guess he felt like he had to do anything he could. No harm done, ultimately.'

'You were pretty angry with him,' Paige said neutrally.

'That's not a question,' Oliver joked.

She rolled her eyes. 'Okay, why were you so upset? It seemed to me like it started before he was flirting with Eavie.'

Oliver shrugged. 'He was being a prick, wasn't he? Nothing more to it.'

'Specifically,' Paige pressed on, 'when Declan punched James, some contestants came to his defence. You stayed out of it. Why?'

'Er...' Oliver had no idea what she was getting at, asking the same questions he'd already answered. 'I don't like to get caught up in feuds that I don't know anything about.'

'And yet, it's quite clear whose side you're on,' she said, with a glance to his shirt that made the blood rush to his cheeks. He crossed his arms self-consciously.

'Yeah, Declan and I are mates. We had a bit of a row, and he apologised to me. It's all good. Sorry I can't give you more drama than that.'

Paige pursed her lips. 'I'm trying to get to the root of the conflict, that's all. No need to get defensive.'

Oliver hadn't felt like he'd been acting defensive, but he tried to soften his posture. 'What exactly do you want to hear, Paige? I'm shattered. I'll give you the clip if you ask nicely. Playing coy doesn't suit you.'

'Nor you.' She paused before asking, 'Why do you think Imogen chose him tonight?'

'Dunno,' Oliver said, relaxing slightly. 'She'd always thought Declan was fit; she flirted with him even when he was still with Zoë. So it's not shocking she's gone for him again.'

'All right,' Paige said. 'I think I've got enough to cobble something together. Thanks, Oliver.'

The red light flicked off, and Paige tucked a stray curl behind her ear. 'One more thing, before you go.' Something about her manner made him relax – it was clear the questioning was over.

'Yeah?' he asked, standing.

'How are you feeling about being this far along? There's only a couple weeks left. Do you think you have a shot at winning?'

'Well,' he said, 'you'd know that better than I would.'

'Do you still want it like you did at the beginning?' Her expression was unreadable.

He was surprised to catch himself genuinely considering her question. He'd been so distracted the last few days, he'd almost forgotten about the competition, about the whole reason he'd come on the show in the first place.

If he won, the prize money would upheave his whole life. He wouldn't have to worry about staying afloat in his crappy flat, wouldn't have to make difficult decisions every day. And, amazingly enough, it was within his grasp. Oliver was sure he could find a balance between stolen moments with Declan and his performance on the show. If he stuck with Eavie, committed to her on camera, they had a possibility of making it to the end.

He looked at her. 'Yes. I still want it.'

She nodded. 'Good. I'm rooting for you, Oliver.'

Chapter 18

Declan

Two and Half Weeks Until Finale

Neil Steel: And the hits keep coming for Declan King…

James Rowe: 'That is so you, Decs, trying to fight your way out of this.'

Neil Steel: It looks like Declan's not willing to go down without a fight – though some swings may be landing a bit too close to home.

Oliver Wright: 'What the [bleep] is wrong with you?'

Neil Steel: Watch out! Declan's on a warpath!

Declan walked into the Love Shack for the first time without having a good sound bite prepared. He had been sure it would be him, not Rhys, going home during the recoupling – fame and followers could only excuse so much, and he'd been slipping up for the last week. It had taken almost being eliminated for him to realise how much he wanted to stay, just to have more time with Oliver.

Paige watched him carefully. 'Big night for you,' she said, turning on the camera.

Declan shifted his eyes away from the blinking red light. 'Yes, it was.'

'Did you know Imogen would pick you?'

He tried to remember the few words he and Imogen had exchanged on the date to figure out what kind of edit the producers had given it, but it was useless. There was little chance they hadn't aired that scene as the absolute shit-show it was, and he had forgotten to give them any follow-up material. If he had been thinking, he would have spent the past two days focused on winning Imogen back in full view of the cameras.

'Honestly?' he said. 'Not in the slightest. But I'm grateful she did.' He'd spent the last hour trying to figure out Imogen's strategy. It made sense on a basic level: she was an influencer, and for anyone making money off Instagram, followers outweighed poor social conduct.

'I was surprised,' Paige said, 'given what happened on your date.' She inflected the sentence like it was a question, but Declan only shrugged.

'I guess she likes me enough to overlook that.'

'I guess she does,' Paige said, and Declan couldn't decipher her tone. He blinked at her and she turned the camera off, rubbing at her eyes. 'You must know your image hasn't been great recently. I mean, between the fight with James and that date with Oliver, you seem like an entitled prick who doesn't like people messing with his stuff.'

'Zoë mugged me off,' Declan said. 'I'm allowed to be upset.'

'Sure,' Paige said easily. 'But that doesn't give you the right to act like an ass.' She sighed. 'Look, people love to root for the slighted party. And if you hadn't flown off the handle, maybe the audience would still be on your side.'

That gave him pause. 'The audience isn't on my side any more?'

Paige pursed her lips. 'Your ratings aren't what they used to be.'

'What can I do?' Declan asked, realising how thoroughly he'd messed up. He'd let his guard down, operated solely on emotion, and now he was paying for it. It had been days since he'd even considered the audience.

Paige cocked her head. 'You lost Zoë because she didn't know you cared. Putting your heart on your sleeve and actually showing some vulnerability would give the viewers a reason to like you again.'

'Right,' Declan replied, dismissing that idea automatically. The last week had been the most real he'd been on the show. Clearly, his lowered ratings had to do with him dropping the act he'd been carefully crafting his entire career. And showing people the real him, all of him, wasn't an option.

Paige turned the camera back on. 'So, let's hear it honestly, how are you feeling?'

'Well, I've had quite the week…' Declan said, stalling as he figured out the exact wording and cadence of his next words to maximise sympathy. 'Zoë dumped me and I acted like a prat and pissed off one of my best mates. I'm deeply ashamed of what I've done, and I'm so glad to have this second chance at love. Imogen gave that to me, and I'm going to spend the rest of my time here making it up to her.'

Paige's eyes narrowed. 'Hmm… and what exactly was going on with you and Oliver on the date? I don't think we discussed that last time.'

Declan took a deep breath. This question he'd at least prepared for. 'It was… misplaced emotions. I was still angry about James and I took it out on Oliver.'

She stared at him for a moment too long, but just as Declan started to feel uncomfortable, she sighed. 'Fine, thank you. Off to bed.'

Declan walked back into the now-claustrophobic bedroom. An extra bed had been shoved in to accommodate the additional couple, leaving barely enough space to walk between them. Imogen was waiting for him, brushing her long curls over her shoulder. She wore a matching pale pink pyjama set and she smiled when Declan settled on his side of the bed.

'Just FYI, I'm a bit of a restless sleeper,' she said cheerily. 'I don't want to accidentally kick you, so it may be best that we don't cuddle.'

'Oh, er… sure,' he replied, taken aback.

'Great!' Imogen leaned over and kissed him on the cheek before diving over to her side and pulling the duvet up, effectively ending their nightly pleasantries. Declan turned away from her and saw Oliver lying on the opposite bed, close enough that Declan could've reached out and touched him. Their eyes met, twin smiles playing at their lips.

Hi, Oliver mouthed at him.

Hi, Declan mouthed back.

They were grinning like idiots, but Declan didn't care. Looking at Oliver's face, he knew he didn't need to take Paige's advice. No need to bare his heart on national television; that wasn't what people wanted to see from him anyway. He'd be the Declan King everyone loved, and he and Oliver could continue on the way they had been the past few days. It wasn't much, just a few stolen glances and secretive smiles, but it was more than Declan had ever let himself have before. He couldn't believe that what had started as a desperate attempt to fix his fake love life had resulted in something as real and extraordinary as Oliver.

–

'Everyone ready?' Paige asked, bouncing from one foot to the other.

Declan had never been more excited for a day off from filming. The producers had finally given in to Niall's pleas for a chance to explore the island and were taking the contestants on a hike.

As big as the villa looked on television, it was small and made even smaller by the new additions. Declan had done his best to avoid James and Zoë, but the sly smirks from James and the apologetic eyes from Zoë were slowly driving him mad. Watching Paige practically buzzing, Declan realised he wasn't the only one going stir-crazy.

'Yes?' she asked, when she received no response. 'Great, let's move.' She turned and climbed into a van, gesturing for the others to follow.

'Oliver and I can take the back,' Declan said to Imogen and Eavie, slapping Oliver on the shoulder.

'How chivalrous,' Eavie teased.

Imogen giggled. 'And that's only from one night with me. Give me a week, I'll get him back on the straight and narrow.'

Declan grinned sheepishly as he and Oliver piled into the back of the van, squeezing their bodies into the tight space. Oliver's knee pressed firmly into Declan's and their arms jammed together in a way that would have been uncomfortable if it had been anyone else. Instead, heat spread along every inch of his body.

'You two look cosy back there,' Imogen said, settling into her seat.

Eavie peered over her shoulder at them and laughed. 'Are you sure you're okay?'

'Your comfort is our utmost priority,' Oliver said, doing his best to look put out, but his dopey grin ruined the effect.

'Everyone strapped in?' Paige called from the front seat. They nodded. 'Great! We're off!' she said, turning the radio up.

Oliver shifted minutely against him so that their sides were pressed firmly together. Inane pop music blared in the background, but Declan was too fixated on Oliver to hear a word. Leaning sideways as much as he dared, he gently rested his cheek against the hot skin of Oliver's shoulder. Oliver turned his head, and Declan felt a slight pressure as Oliver pressed a kiss to his forehead. He didn't move, keeping his head perfectly still as his heartbeat rushed in his ears.

'Aww, don't you two look cute!' Imogen squealed. Declan jolted awake, opening his eyes and immediately regretting it as the daylight assaulted him. They had arrived.

He shot up straight, blinking slowly at the girls before tentatively glancing sideways at a sleep-riddled Oliver.

'What can I say,' Declan muttered, grasping desperately for a joke, 'he's so dreamy.'

The girls giggled as they piled out of the van, Declan following close behind and leaving Oliver to collect himself. He continued to blink as his eyes struggled to adjust to the bright morning sun, and he grabbed at his shorts for his sunglasses.

Jack walked over, grinning. 'Got a good nap in, then?' he said, taking in Declan's befuddled expression. 'Me and Niall spooned the whole way – the man is surprisingly comfortable for such a big hunk of muscle.'

'Yeah, snored the whole way too.' Owen quipped.

'Back off, Jack,' Oliver said, emerging from the van and slinging an arm around Declan's shoulders. 'We're the only bromance on this show.'

'All right!' Brian called out. He was dressed like he was going on a safari instead of a short walk to the cove, wearing khaki shorts and a wide-brimmed hat. 'It's an out and back trail, about two miles each way. We'll be stopping for lunch and a swim before we head back. Got it?'

'Sir, yes, sir!' called Jack. Brian gave him a tired look before turning on his heels and heading for the trailhead.

Declan and Oliver hung back with Niall and Jack, the four of them picking up the rear of the group.

'Now that we can speak freely,' Jack said, 'what's the first thing you're going to do when we finally finish this fucking torture chamber of a show?'

'Marry Stella,' Niall said, without hesitating. The boys laughed, but he continued, earnestly, 'Well, I suppose I'll have to ask her first.'

Oliver made a strangled noise. 'Marriage, already?'

Niall's eyebrows drew together. 'I came here to find someone to spend my life with. Marriage is only the beginning.' The rest of the group exchanged furtive glances, and Niall's look of confusion deepened. 'Why else would you come on this idiotic show, if not for love?'

'A laugh?' Jack offered.

'Followers,' Declan continued.

'A hundred thousand pounds would be nice,' Oliver said.

Niall looked scandalised.

'Don't get me wrong,' Jack said quickly, 'Maeve is a remarkable woman, but honestly, this was only meant to be a bit of fun. Maybe I'd get a good bit or two for my stand-up, but I didn't think I'd last a week.'

'But you and Maeve are so good together,' Niall said.

'I have no clue what she sees in me, but I'll be spending the rest of my life trying not to bugger it,' Jack said, slinging his arm around Oliver. 'You probably don't care about the money either, now Eavie's here.'

Oliver laughed and made a face at Declan. 'Spoken like someone who's taken up with a rich solicitor.'

'And you?' Niall said, turning accusingly to Declan. 'You're here for more followers?'

'Come on,' Jack said, saving Declan from having to explain the concept of dishonesty to Niall, 'that can't be surprising to you. The man is a walking Instagram ad.'

'Hey! I have depth!' Declan protested.

Jack rolled his eyes. 'Of course *you* do, but does Declan King?'

'He can put on quite the performance,' Oliver said, but he sounded more impressed than judgemental. 'He even had *me* convinced he was into Zoë.' He shot Declan a wry look.

Declan's attempt to respond was interrupted by Stella and Maeve calling for their men to join them ahead, leaving Oliver and Declan alone.

They walked in silence as the trail snaked inland, falling further and further behind the others.

Declan nudged Oliver the moment the rest of the group had drifted out of eyesight. 'I wonder if there's a nice view up that way,' he said, pointing towards a massive boulder to their right. It was a razor-thin excuse, but Declan was desperate to get Oliver alone. 'Wanna go check it out?'

They scrambled up the boulder, stopping at the top to look out over the expanse of ocean. It was Declan's first glimpse of the sea since the day at the beach, and the sight of the cresting waves unknotted some of the tension in his shoulders. He breathed in the salty air as Oliver absent-mindedly lifted his shirt to wipe the sweat from his brow. Declan stared at him, forgetting the view entirely.

Oliver grinned at his expression. 'Should we sit?'

Declan didn't understand how Oliver was acting so calm when he was vibrating out of his skin. 'Uh-huh,' he managed.

They sat. Oliver was unnervingly close again, his side brushing Declan's. They looked out at the glistening sea for a moment, and Declan was struck by how content he felt, maybe for the first time in his life. He sensed Oliver's eyes on him and turned towards him instinctively.

'Hey,' Oliver murmured, the midday sunlight filtering through the sparse trees casting his face in soft speckled light. After days of concealed glances in front of the cameras, seeing him like this, staring at Declan with such open affection, felt miraculous.

But Declan had looked for long enough. 'Come ·here,' he said, leaning in.

He could feel Oliver's smile against his lips as he snuck a hand into his hair, pulling him closer. It seemed impossible that he could already miss the feeling of Oliver's lips against his own, but he had. Declan gripped the nape of his neck and Oliver moaned, the soft sound in his throat vibrating against his lips. He grabbed at Declan, hands skating up his arms, long fingers digging into muscle.

The warm scent of amber invaded Declan's senses, and he was overcome, lost in the feeling of Oliver's hands on him. Six weeks, that was how long it had been since he'd first laid eyes on Oliver – six weeks of avoiding him, hating him, holding in his feelings, driving himself mad with want. Now he had him. Oliver was in his arms, hair a mess, eyes wild, lips pressing at Declan's neck, nipping at the junction where jaw met throat.

Oliver's hand drifted to his hip, pulling Declan firmly on top of him, thighs slotting on either side of his hips. Declan kissed him again, biting gently at his bottom lip, feeling a burning deep within him. Having spent his whole life either in pain or trying to dull it, the pleasure of feeling Oliver move against him was completely new to Declan. He ran reverent hands along Oliver's body. His fingers ghosted up Oliver's neck, resting on his cheek, his thumb grasping Oliver's chin to pull him even closer, pressing their lips together.

Oliver huffed out a laugh, leaning back. 'I thought I was going crazy,' he said, his fingers tightening on Declan's arms. 'That night you almost kissed me' – he pressed a lingering kiss onto Declan's lips – 'and then pretending like it didn't happen. And all that shit with James. I thought... honestly, I don't know what I thought, just that I must be mad.'

'Fuck,' Declan said, leaning his forehead against Oliver's shoulder and then sinking his teeth into the skin there. 'I'm sorry. I couldn't help it. After that day on the beach, when I acted like a drunken fool... Hell, even from the first day on the plane. You looked at me and I was gone.'

'From the first day on the plane?' Oliver murmured, his eyes wide.

'Yeah...' Declan said, sitting back to look at him properly. He took in Oliver's dishevelled appearance, insides knotting at the state of his hair and the pink of his cheeks. Oliver cocked his head to the side, waiting. 'I'm gay.'

Oliver didn't respond immediately, turning to look out over the water, and Declan moved off him, suddenly apprehensive. He watched Oliver's profile; it looked like he was considering his words carefully.

'I take it you're not,' Declan said slowly. 'Unless you were lying about your ex.'

Oliver shook his head. 'No, Sophie is real.' He paused for a moment, turning to consider Declan. 'That doesn't mean this' – Oliver gestured between them – 'isn't.' He looked back at the ocean, and Declan stared at where the tendons of his neck folded into his jaw. 'I suppose I figured if I liked men I would've noticed by now. But it was impossible to ignore how I felt about you. I mean, when I saw you kiss Eavie…'

Declan couldn't help but laugh. 'That's what did it?'

Oliver grinned. 'It was confusing at first. I kept getting mad at you and I couldn't understand why. First, because you stole Zoë from me, then I thought I was jealous of how well you were doing. But when you kissed Eavie, I realised I was just jealous. You're like no one I've ever met before. So infuriatingly hot and absolutely annoying – I didn't stand a chance.'

Declan ducked his head, pushing into Oliver's side. Oliver picked up his hand and studied it intently, lacing their fingers together. 'I suppose I'm a little more fluid than I originally thought,' he said. 'Bisexual, maybe.' He said it like he was testing the word out, squinting as he tilted his head back and forth. He waited for a beat before nodding. 'Yeah, pretty sure that's the one.'

Declan looked at their intertwined hands. Oliver made this all seem so easy, accepting his new sexuality with little more than a shrug and an air of certainty that terrified Declan. He turned away, glancing back towards the shade of the trees, unsure of what to say.

'If you knew you were gay, why come on the show?' Oliver asked after a moment. 'Why put yourself through this? Surely not just for followers?'

Declan shrugged. 'It was my best mate's idea, actually. We auditioned together, but she pulled out.'

'But you agreed to do it without her?' Oliver pressed.

'I'm doing it *for* her.' Declan sighed, dropping Oliver's hand to rub the back of his head, thinking of how to describe Georgia and everything they were to each other. 'She's the only person outside of my family that knows about me. We'd be photographed together to keep the tabloids off my back about my dating life, but it made things more complicated for hers.' Implied in Georgia's pitch for them to go on the show was something deeper – she couldn't play that role in his life any more, and he needed to find someone who could.

'She was your beard,' Oliver said simply.

Declan frowned at the term. 'We never confirmed anything, always kept things circumstantial. I didn't want to lie.'

'But you didn't want to tell the truth either.' Oliver said the words without malice, but Declan flushed with shame all the same.

'No, I didn't,' Declan admitted. 'But Georgia getting involved was a mistake.'

Oliver blinked. 'Georgia is James's ex?' Declan gave him what must have been a thoroughly confused look, and Oliver clarified, 'James told us that you stole his girlfriend.'

Declan gave a short, bitter laugh. 'Always playing the victim. He never believed that there was nothing going on between us, so he treated her like shit. And he came on the show to humiliate me, since it wasn't enough to make her miserable.'

'And then you punched him,' Oliver said flatly.

Declan squeezed his eyes shut. 'I'm not proud of that – I shouldn't have taken the bait. Now the whole country thinks I'm a possessive lunatic.'

'One punch won't change everyone's opinion of you,' Oliver said gently, laying a hand on his back, rubbing small circles into his shoulder. 'So, Georgia never told James about you?'

Declan shook his head. 'That's us, loyal to a tee,' he said, the words coming out bitter.

Oliver's eyebrows drew together. 'And why didn't *you* tell him?'

Declan frowned. 'Because he'd out me in a second.'

'Right,' Oliver said slowly, 'I guess my question was more… Why not just come out?'

Declan didn't know how to explain that his life wasn't his own, especially to Oliver, who had taken control of his life so easily. 'Haven't you wanted something that's just yours?'

'Even if it means being alone?' Oliver said. 'That is why, right? It's not because you're too busy.'

'People would want things from me that I don't think I can give,' Declan said, knowing it wasn't the whole truth. 'Being a gay boxer, being the face of it, that's not easy. And I'm not the right person for it.'

Coming out would mean giving up the public image he'd spent his career building, and he didn't know who he'd be without it. Disappointing the fans was one thing, but they weren't the only ones liable to be disappointed if Declan allowed himself to just *be*.

Oliver considered him intently. 'I'd never thought of it like that,' he said.

'No kidding,' Declan said wryly. 'I'm sure ballet is more accepting.'

'Practically all my friends from school are gay,' Oliver admitted. 'Sophie and I were the odd ones out.'

Declan asked the question he'd been holding back for weeks. Now felt like his only opportunity to learn everything he could about Oliver, away from the cameras. 'What happened between you two?'

'I dunno... eight years is such a long time. It was easy, until it wasn't.' Oliver frowned, studying a knot on the closest tree. 'Somewhere along the way, our lives got all twisted up; we had the same schedule, same mates, same everything. I think she didn't feel like she was her own person any more, and she didn't know how to tell me, or didn't think I would listen.'

'You would've listened,' Declan said confidently.

'I would like to think so,' Oliver said, meeting his gaze. 'But I never saw her as someone with problems. When I met her, I had nothing, and she had everything – money, friends, talent, support from her family. And I put her on a pedestal, and she couldn't stand it any more. I don't know, does that make any sense?'

'Yeah, it does,' Declan said. 'But it doesn't make it your fault. She *chose* not to talk to you.'

'Yes,' Oliver said. 'And I got lost in those hypotheticals for months. If she'd told me, if we could have talked about it... But it's been almost a year since she left, six weeks since I last spoke to her.' He made a soft noise in the back of his throat. 'It's been nice, in a way, to not rely on her for everything. I guess that was part of what drew me to the show. I needed to figure out who I was without her.'

'And I thought you were here to find love,' Declan dead-panned.

Oliver's eyes glinted in the sunlight. 'No, I've got ulterior motives,' he quipped. 'I'd sell you out in a second.'

Warmth spread through Declan's chest. 'And use the money for what?'

Oliver blushed, breaking eye contact. 'If I get the spot, I'll need the money to move to New York.'

Before Declan could reply, Oliver cursed, pointing down at the beach. Declan turned to see their group walking out into the cove.

'We should go,' Oliver said, and Declan nodded. They stared at each other for a long moment, neither of them wanting to end the brief freedom of being together. The shouts and splashes of the group below spurred them into motion.

They scrambled down the rocks and back onto the path. Before he lost his nerve, Declan pushed Oliver against the boulder, cupped his cheeks in both hands and kissed him deeply. As they pulled apart, Declan paused, trying to memorise the shape of Oliver's eyes when he smiled.

'God,' he groaned, burying his face into the crook of Oliver's neck and relishing the feeling of Oliver's hands creeping up his back. 'I don't know how I'll be able to stand not touching you now.'

'There's always next Saturday,' Oliver murmured into his hair.

They stood like that, intertwined, for a moment more before Declan said, 'Come on,' and pulled Oliver along. 'I'll race you.'

As he turned around, Declan thought he saw a flash of something in the trees. But then Oliver was pulling his hand, and they were off, running along the trail, yelling and goading each other the whole way to the beach. They were out of breath by the time they reached the group.

'Jesus,' Jack said. 'Where did you two make off to?'

Declan and Oliver collapsed in laughter, high off the endorphins.

'Got lost,' Oliver managed to say between deep gasps of breath, smiling at Declan. He couldn't help but grin stupidly back.

Chapter 19

Declan

Two Weeks until Finale

'It's been a bit boring lately,' Imogen announced a few days later, her heart-shaped sunglasses glinting in the afternoon light.

They were sitting on a daybed, Declan and Imogen on one side and Eavie and Oliver on the other. The picture of two straight couples, though he and Oliver had found a way to arrange their legs so Oliver's calf brushed his. Small moments of casual contact had become both the best and the most excruciating parts of Declan's days.

'Now you've gone and jinxed it,' Eavie said, resting her head contentedly on Oliver's shoulder. The boys smiled at each other, and Declan pressed more firmly against Oliver's leg.

The interlude on the hike had made pretending that they were mates in front of the cameras a special form of torture. They had spent the past few days dancing around each other, touching but only in a strictly platonic way, hanging out but not any more than before. It was maddening to stay at arm's length when Declan woke up every morning to Oliver's warm body just out of reach, especially now that he knew what it felt like against his own.

'Woah,' Imogen said, pointing towards the villa. 'Maybe I'm magic.'

Declan turned to see Paige making her way over to them. He groaned. 'Or maybe we're being surveilled at all times.'

Imogen gave a comical pout. 'Well, I'm going to continue to think I'm psychic.'

'I love that for you,' Eavie said.

'Hey,' Paige said. 'Declan, could you come with me?'

Declan was immediately suspicious. 'Why?'

'Zoë wants a word,' Paige said brightly.

'I'm all right, actually.' Declan hadn't spoken to Zoë since her return with James, but he had suspected the producers would eventually make them rehash the whole sordid affair for the cameras. He did not, however, have to make it easy for them.

Paige crossed her arms, her eyes narrowing.

'Oh, come on,' Imogen said, nudging his side. 'It won't be that bad.' Ultimately, it was Oliver's supportive look that gave Declan the fortitude to get up.

'Lead the way.'

Zoë was waiting for him on the couch swing, and the smile she gave him as he sat next to her was flat with nervousness. Neither spoke while Paige directed the cameraman into a position with a favourable angle.

'Right,' Zoë said, as soon as Paige signalled for them to begin. 'I wanted to say that I'm sorry for how things turned out between us.'

Declan couldn't tell if she was being honest, choosing to stare at the wall behind her instead of her face.

'Okay,' he said.

Paige sighed, and Zoë glanced her way before continuing. 'I wanted to explain my side of things.'

'Okay,' Declan said again, not managing to change his inflection.

'It's just,' Zoë said, wringing her hands together, 'I never believed you liked me.' Declan couldn't suppress a snort, and Zoë tensed. 'That's funny to you?' she asked coolly.

'No, it's not funny,' he managed, finally looking at her. 'How could you do that to me? And with *him*?'

'That's exactly what I mean,' Zoë said, voice rising. 'You only care about *who* I left you for, not that I left you.'

'Clearly I care that you left me,' Declan said. 'I thought—'

'Is it clear?' Zoë cut him off. Declan couldn't understand what had shifted between them; when Zoë had picked him all those weeks ago he thought it was because they had the same goal: winning.

'I thought we were in this together,' Declan said. 'So why did you do it?'

'For love,' Zoë said, as though it was obvious. 'I love him. And I know you and everyone else here hates him, but I can't help it, I can't control it. I love him.' Declan had nothing to say to that, watching as she closed her eyes and took a deep breath. 'Sure, he's not perfect.' Her voice went quiet. 'But he's surprisingly sweet, and he loves me, I think, better than anyone else I've ever met.'

Declan, who had plenty of experience bad-mouthing James to Georgia, still found himself speechless. He hadn't expected her feelings for James to be genuine, but he couldn't find any familiar signs of performance on her face.

'He's going to hurt you,' he said finally. 'And I don't want to see you get hurt.'

Zoë cocked her head at him. 'What do you mean?'

'He dated my friend, back in London. And he cheated on her, repeatedly.'

Zoë frowned. 'That's not how he tells it.'

'Yeah, well, he's a liar,' Declan said.

'That's rich coming from you, King,' James said, stalking towards them, a cameraman on his heels. With one glance at Paige's guilty face, Declan knew the scene had been orchestrated. 'A liar and a cheater? Pot, meet kettle.'

Declan was on his feet before he was even aware he'd moved. James towered over him, but Declan didn't give an inch, glaring up at him.

'C'mon,' Zoë said, tugging at James's arm. 'Drop it, James.'

'As I've said countless times before,' Declan gritted out. 'Nothing happened between me and Georgia.'

The other contestants had gathered around as their voices rose. Declan was keenly aware of Oliver's eyes on him.

'Right,' James said slowly. 'I know you think I'm thick, but I'm not that thick.'

'Yes, you are,' Declan said. 'And the worst part is that you made her feel like it was her fault you couldn't be faithful. Making her feel like a terrible girlfriend for daring to go out with her mates while you were God knows where drugged up and unresponsive partying with your band. You gaslighting piece of shit.'

There was a gasp from the crowd that had gathered around them, but Declan was too angry to look. Zoë dropped James's arm and was staring at them, a horrified expression on her face. Declan knew that he'd made his point, that he could stop now, but the words kept coming. It was everything he'd wanted to say to James over the months of his break-up with Georgia.

'You only care about yourself and your image. Did you even care about her feelings? Did you care that you left her alone half the time while you went on tour? How she'd make excuse after excuse for you because she loved you that much? She wanted it to work. She probably would've forgiven you too. If you weren't *such* a shit.'

James gaped at him, seemingly struck dumb for the first time since Declan had known him. Declan glanced around at the other contestants; everyone wore similar expressions, ranging from shock to mild horror. Zoë looked close to tears, her arms wrapped around her torso.

'Is that true?' she asked quietly. James turned to her.

'Baby—' James was cut off by a chime and Darcy's saccharine voice came over the loudspeaker.

'Oh Lovers, don't fight. It's not sexy. Let's have a challenge, shake things up a bit. Grab a swimsuit and meet by the pool.'

James stood there, blinking at him, until Zoë stalked away. Declan turned to Paige, but she didn't meet his eye.

'Sorry about that,' she muttered. She and the cameraman followed Zoë and James into the villa.

–

An hour later, after everyone had a chance to cool down and the producers had captured an apologetic James grovelling to Zoë, the contestants lined up by the pool. The production team had set up a bar with a row of colourful cocktails and a stack of whiteboards, which Declan eyed with trepidation. They stood there for a moment before the PA system chimed and Darcy's voice came through the loudspeakers.

'Lovers,' she read, tone cloying, 'you've been causing a buzz on social media. Let's see what the audience is saying about you. All good things… we hope. Each contestant will read a post with names redacted and guess who it's about. If they pick correctly, they get to throw a drink. If they guess wrong, they're the ones who get a drink to the face.'

Declan looked around and couldn't see one excited face. The audience votes were a fairly good indicator of popularity, but this was the first time they'd hear directly what the public thought of them.

Imogen was first, prancing to the bar in a bright red bikini. 'Not going to lie, [blank] dumping [blank] for [blank] was the biggest betrayal of my life and my wife cheated on me.'

The rest of the Lovers laughed, but Declan's ears pricked, knowing this one was about him. He glanced over at Zoë and James, and James scowled back.

Imogen shot Declan an apologetic expression before confidently calling out: 'Not going to lie, Zoë dumping Declan for James was the biggest betrayal of my life.' She pulled away the tape, revealing she was correct. Grabbing a red drink, she walked over to Zoë, smiling with faux-sweetness before lifting the drink high and pouring it over her.

'Hey, watch it!' James yelled, as some of the drink splashed on him.

'Oops,' Imogen said, the smile not dropping from her face as she walked back to Declan.

'Good one,' he whispered, fist-bumping her.

Niall read out the next post. '[blank] gives us regular men hope that we can bag a total babe like [blank] while still being a complete idiot.' He grinned. 'Well, that can only be one of us,' Niall said. 'Sorry, Jackie-boy, this is Jack and Maeve.' He was right.

'Go for her!' Jack cried, pushing Maeve in front of him as Niall walked over with a lime-green cocktail. Niall laughed and tried to throw the drink over Maeve's head at Jack, but ended up dousing both of them.

'Ooh, two for one!' Stella called, as Niall walked back and wrapped her in a bear hug.

Oliver read out, 'Okay, but [blank] and [blank] are in love. Cool, we all agree? Moving on.' His face froze in concentration as he considered each couple. 'Er, Niall and Stella?' He ripped off the tape. 'Okay, but Declan and Oliver are in love. Cool, we all agree? Moving on.'

Declan stiffened as Oliver shook his head dolefully, laughing along with the rest of the contestants and seeming completely unfazed. Thankfully, no one was looking at Declan; his cheeks were flushed, but he hoped his sunglasses covered most of his reaction.

Stella grabbed a drink off the bar, throwing it into Oliver's face. 'This'll be chakra-cleansing, babe,' she said. Oliver shook out his wet hair, managing to get some droplets on Stella in revenge.

Zoë walked over to the bar, grabbed a whiteboard and read out: 'Are the men on this show blind? When they've got a queen like [blank] right there? God save her.'

Declan could see the relief on her face when she realised the post had nothing to do with him or James. 'Oh, this has got to be my girl Holly!' She pulled off the tape to reveal Holly's name.

'The queen commands you to stop,' Holly joked as Zoë approached.

'So sorry, Your Majesty!' Zoë said, pouring the pink drink all over her.

Still dripping, Holly read the next post. '[Blank] is hot shit, can't believe [blank] let her go without a fight. They were so cute together.' Holly looked confused for a moment before saying slowly, 'Imogen and Oliver?'

She was only half right. 'Maeve is hot shit, can't believe Oliver let her go...' There were some wolf-whistles from the group.

'Sorry, Holls,' Oliver said, grabbing a drink from the bar and dumping it on her. 'My bad for fumbling two women, I guess.'

Declan was last, and his stomach twisted uncomfortably. The producers had probably saved the most egregious post for him, and he wasn't excited to find out what they had in store. He grabbed the board off the bar and read out: 'Girls, get you a man that looks at you the way [blank] looks at [blank].'

Relief flooded through him at the tame post. 'Jack and Maeve?' he guessed.

'No fair,' Jack said. 'That was an easy one!'

Declan pulled the tape off and revealed the correct answer: 'Get you a man that looks at you the way Declan looks at Oliver,' he read out. It took longer than it should have for the meaning to sink in. Then his face went numb.

Jack and Owen keeled over with laughter. 'The real fron-trunners,' Jack said between huffs.

It was Maeve who walked over to the bar and grabbed a drink, throwing it in his face with an almost sad look. Declan blinked rapidly, trying to get the sticky liquid out of his eyes as a ripple of discomfort crawled up his back.

The game ended and the contestants scattered while the production crew cleaned up, but Declan was barely aware of any of it. He sat in a nook at the edge of the garden and leaned his head against the wall, listening to the others chat in the kitchen.

He tried to take a deep breath, but the air left his lungs in a flitting, unsteady rhythm. They'd been careful, he had made sure of it. They hadn't been acting any differently. The posts had been jokes, and the producers were messing with them for laughs. Rationally, he knew that. But he was already plotting how he could do better, how to school his features even more when they were together. Declan knew how to look impassive; it was a face he'd learned long ago.

'There you are,' Imogen said. 'All right?' Declan looked up at her, her hair still dripping and chest stained red. She sat beside him, gently lacing their fingers together. He nodded.

'You sure?' she asked, cocking her head. 'You don't look like your usual peppy self.' He smiled tightly, wishing he could put her mind at ease, but there was a buzzing in his ears and he felt lightheaded. 'That bad, huh? You look miles away, love.'

'Just thinking about the posts,' Declan managed, trying to find a polite way to ask her to leave.

'Oh, they weren't that bad,' Imogen teased. 'You actually came out looking pretty good, I think.'

'Right,' he said, unsure how to talk about what was bothering him without mentioning Oliver. 'Just didn't realise I was so popular.'

Imogen's laugh was a bit too loud. 'Of course you are! You're every girl's dream.' She winked.

'Maybe I don't like how they're perceiving me,' Declan tried to explain. 'It's – it's not real.' Actually, he didn't like how close to the truth the audience had got.

'It's a reality TV show,' Imogen said, 'of course it's not real.' She pointed at the plants in the planter box behind their heads. 'See, fake.' She pointed at the blinking camera peeking out of a nearby sconce. 'Fake.' She pointed at her chest. 'These? Definitely fake.' That got a small laugh out of Declan, and Imogen grinned at him in a private way that reminded him of Georgia.

'Thanks,' he said.

'Of course,' Imogen said, leaning into his side. 'I'll always be here for you, no matter what. I'm the *perfect girl* for you, anything you need.' She was looking at him intently.

Something in the way she'd said it made Declan squint at her. She seemed to notice the change, nodding her head encouragingly as if to say, *come on, you've nearly got it*. She glanced pointedly at Oliver, laughing with the other contestants in the kitchen, then back at Declan.

'Oh,' he said, the dread he'd felt moments ago returning immediately. She squeezed his hand, but Declan hardly felt it. The buzzing in his ears started again, and he could feel his heart throbbing behind his eyelids. 'I'm, uh, gonna go and take a shower,' Declan said, patting her knee and standing.

'It's okay,' she said, frowning.

'I know,' Declan said, too quickly. 'I just hate being sticky.'

Imogen looked at a loss, her hands wringing uselessly in her lap. 'I'm here, whatever you need. We're in this together,' she said finally.

Declan walked away from her feeling unmoored. Imogen knew. And if she had figured it out, who else had noticed that there was something going on between him and Oliver?

His thoughts wandered aimlessly, not settling on anything in particular, leaving him feeling fuzzy and like he might be developing a headache. He breathed out slowly, hoping his mind would slow to a manageable speed where he could work out the problem at hand. Imogen knew and she wanted to stay with him anyway. She was offering him everything he had come on the show to find – only he wasn't sure he wanted it any more.

'Hey,' Oliver said, intercepting him before he reached the villa.

Declan didn't look at him directly, convinced one glance would unravel him. 'I'm going to shower.'

Oliver's eyebrows knitted together. 'Are you okay?' he asked, putting a hand on Declan's shoulder.

Declan shook it off and moved to get around him. 'I'm great.'

'No, you're not,' Oliver said, side-stepping back into his path.

'Look, I can't do this with you right now.' He was too strung out to talk to Oliver; he could feel it in the rush of blood through his veins.

Oliver ignored his pleading look. 'Do what?'

The throbbing in his head threatened to burst him open at any moment. 'Can't you just leave me alone?' he asked, pinching the bridge of his nose and digging his thumbs into the corners of his eyes.

'Can't you just talk to me?' Oliver asked, looming over him, standing too close. All Declan wanted was to lean in.

'No,' Declan said, glancing at his lips and then finally meeting his eye. *Like Declan looks at Oliver.* He blinked, saw a flash of concern in Oliver's gaze, and turned away quickly to look at the faint pink light of the setting sun.

'I don't think I can do this.' The words were out before he registered what he was saying. It was an instinct, somewhere deep down, to push Oliver away before they both got hurt.

Oliver raked a hand through his hair. 'Do what? Talk to me?'

Declan tried to imagine the two of them outside the confines of the villa, but he couldn't. Oliver wanted to go to New York and Declan had a career in London. He'd never had to fit someone into his life before, had never been willing to try. But Oliver had upended everything he had ever known; he'd do anything for him. And that terrified him.

'Any of it.'

Oliver had said being with Sophie had been easy – nothing about this was easy. Life didn't work like that; Declan didn't get to have what he wanted.

Oliver blinked at him incredulously for a moment before understanding hardened in his eyes. He opened his mouth to reply, then seemed to think better of it, brushing past Declan. Declan wanted to run after him, to take it back, but he was rooted to the spot. The throbbing in his head returned full force.

Chapter 20

Declan

Declan didn't get out of bed the next morning. When the lights flicked on, he threw the duvet cover over his head, willing himself back to sleep as the rest of the group got ready for the day around him. He didn't get much respite before Imogen walked in with a steaming cup of tea.

'Hi,' she said softly, placing the mug on the bedside table. 'How you feeling?'

He sat up slowly, rubbing his eyes. 'Just tired,' he said, grabbing the mug and taking a sip. 'I'll be out in a minute.'

Imogen didn't push him, putting a kind hand on his shoulder before heading back outside. Declan forced himself out of bed as Paige walked into the room.

'You okay?' she asked, looking about as tired as Declan felt.

'Yeah,' Declan said, pulling a pair of sweats over his boxers.

'It's a late morning for you,' Paige said, still studying him.

'I had an exhausting day yesterday,' Declan said, flashing her a sardonic smile. 'But you know that. You know everything, don't you?'

Paige made a noncommittal noise. 'Not everything,' she said. 'What happened with Oliver?'

Declan did his best to control his expression, telling himself there was no way she knew. 'Nothing,' he said carefully. 'Surely not anything to drop my ratings.'

Paige raised her eyebrows. 'You're worried about the audience?'

He had thought she would have been accustomed to his callousness at this point. Somehow, he had managed to fool even Paige into believing there was something good in him.

'Got to keep my eye on the prize,' he said.

'You still want that?' Paige asked, her gaze intent on his. 'You never struck me as someone who needed the money.'

'Oh, but I do like to win.' Declan couldn't keep the bitterness out of his voice. 'Oliver's in a good spot; he can look after himself.'

He didn't give her a chance to say anything more as he headed out onto the patio. He ignored Owen and Jack making a mess of breakfast, sitting alone on a daybed. After a few minutes of peace, Imogen joined him.

'There you are, babe,' he said, forcing some cheer into his voice. 'Fancy a cuddle?' Imogen climbed onto the bed, wrapping herself around him.

They spent most of the morning like that, with other contestants stopping by periodically to chat with Imogen. Declan couldn't have been more appreciative of her; save for a small squeeze of his leg, she hadn't acknowledged his foul mood at all. In fact, she was doing a great job of distracting anyone who tried to talk to him, regaling Jack and Holly with some of her wild club stories, listening intently to Maeve and Stella discuss politics and adding her own colourful commentary.

Imogen reminded him of Georgia in how nonchalantly she'd accepted his sexuality, but they could help each other in a way he and Georgia no longer could. Georgia had never needed Declan, for his fame or his money. With Imogen, it could be transactional – he'd show her off as his girlfriend, and she'd use him to grow her following. He'd train for his upcoming fight; she'd finish her fashion line. They both had something to gain, and Declan wouldn't have to feel guilty about any of it.

He didn't see Oliver all morning, having strategically picked the daybed with the worst view of the garden. He'd begun to think he could avoid him all day when he heard the chime from the PA system.

Imogen must have sensed Declan's nerves, because she clasped her hand in his and gave him an encouraging smile as they made their way over. Declan didn't particularly want to play any of the producers' games; he was still recovering from the previous day's.

Before he and Imogen had reached the group, Darcy's voice rang out. 'Lovers, all week long the audience has been voting for their favourite couples. Tonight, the two couples with the fewest votes will be dumped from the villa. Please get ready and gather around the firepit.'

Declan stopped dead in his tracks. Imogen tugged his hand, but when he looked at her he was struck by the unfamiliar anxiety in her eyes. Two couples. Four contestants. Declan should have seen it coming – there was no way the producers would keep them in such cramped quarters forever.

Imogen pulled him along until they finally made it to the others. All the skittish glances, clearly trying to work out who was going home, reminded Declan of the first elimination.

'Well,' Jack said, 'this sucks.'

Niall cracked a smile and the tension eased minutely. Declan was pointedly looking anywhere but Oliver, finding some solace in his confidence that Oliver and Eavie would be safe. Declan's position with Imogen, however, he wasn't so sure about.

They got ready in silence. The energy in the bedroom was tense, and even Jack's attempts at wisecracks fell flat. He must have realised that he was in a more secure position than the rest of them, because he shut up after a few minutes. Declan and Oliver danced around each other, Declan exerting a considerable amount of effort not to look at him in the tight space. In avoiding Oliver, his eyes fell on James and Paige talking in the corner. Declan didn't like that sight one bit, and he got out of the room as fast as he could, watching the crew set up from the kitchen.

The other contestants filed out to stand by the firepit, but Declan waited until Imogen came out to join them. Declan manoeuvred Imogen to a spot near Oliver and Eavie, but not directly next to them. That way he wouldn't have to look Oliver in the eye.

The contestants sat in silence, the tension palpable. Imogen laid her head on Declan's shoulder and he wrapped his arms around her.

'Don't worry,' he whispered. 'It'll be fine.' She nodded against his neck, and the two sat there like that for a few minutes before Darcy finally made her appearance.

She had styled her new fringe with a pair of severe black cat-eye glasses and a peacock-blue double-breasted suit, completing the bizarre ensemble with a pair of white patent-leather plat-form boots.

'Hello, Lovers.'

The cameras followed her as she walked towards the firepit, stopping in front of the six couples and taking a moment to consider each of them in turn. Declan tried his best to look impassive, and the squint she gave him made him think he'd succeeded in not giving her the reaction she wanted.

'Tonight,' she said, raising her voice and enunciating care-fully, 'is a sad night. Two couples will be going home. We will miss them dearly, but as we draw closer to the end of the summer, only one couple can be victorious. Are you ready to find out which couples will be staying and which will be leaving?'

Darcy paused so the cameramen could get shots of each couple to build suspense. Imogen grabbed Declan's hand, squeezing hard.

'We're good,' called Brian.

'Um, cut,' Darcy said suddenly. 'Why are you talking to me? Where the hell is Paige?'

'Here!' Paige called, emerging from the villa looking harried, pulling her curls back into her usual bun. 'Was just running through some old footage and got distracted.'

Darcy took a deep breath before turning to the camera and proceeding solemnly, 'Lovers, please stand.' They shuffled to their feet and she gave another dramatic pause.

'James and Zoë... Oliver and Eavie... Jack and Maeve...' Her eyes bored into each contestant as she called their name. Declan allowed himself to look over at Jack and Maeve. Jack's face was eerily blank, and Maeve gripped him tightly by the arm.

'You all are safe,' Darcy said finally. Declan heard Eavie's sigh of relief to his left. 'Please sit down.' She waited a moment for the couples to settle before sizing up the remaining contestants. A shiver made its way through Declan's body – the odds were no longer in his favour. He looked around at the others standing and his heart sank. No matter who went home tonight, it was going to hurt. Imogen squeezed his hand again, but this time he couldn't manage to offer her a comforting smile.

'Only one couple standing before me,' Darcy said, 'will be staying. The rest will pack their bags and leave immediately.'

Declan took a deep breath. Despite what he'd told Paige, winning didn't matter to him any more. If he got sent home tonight, he'd leave with only one regret.

'Declan and Imogen,' Darcy said, holding eye contact with Declan, her face completely unreadable. Imogen's grip on his hand turned painful and Declan glanced at her, but she wasn't looking at him. He followed her gaze and saw Darcy's lips twitch. 'You are safe. Please sit.' Suddenly, Imogen was in his arms and they were falling onto the couch.

'Thank God,' she whispered before pulling away.

'Niall and Stella,' Darcy said, 'and Owen and Holly. You've received the fewest votes and will be leaving the villa tonight.' The cameramen pushed in to capture the eliminated couples' reactions, but Declan couldn't bear to watch.

'But there's one twist,' Darcy said, and Declan's head shot up. 'Your fellow Lovers have the opportunity to save just one of you. Let's see who they choose, shall we?'

'All right,' Brian called out, 'those still standing, please go into the villa while the rest deliberate.'

'Oh yeah, it shouldn't be a hard decision at all.' Oliver's tone was surprisingly spiteful.

'It's okay, boyo,' Niall said.

Darcy sat next to Zoë and James at the edge of the couch, folding her legs and smiling brightly.

Declan let the others talk through all the options before adding his two cents: 'Neither Niall nor Stella would want to stay without the other.'

'All right,' Maeve said, looking around. 'So, we've decided?' They all nodded.

'Send them back in,' Darcy called, standing.

The couples returned to stand in front of the firepit.

'One of you has been saved tonight by your fellow Lovers,' Darcy said. 'The rest of you will be going home.' She gave her longest pause yet. 'Your fellow Lovers have chosen to save... Holly!'

Chapter 21

Oliver

Neil Steel: Hold on to your helmets, laddies, the villa's in for another bombshell.

Darcy Meadows: 'Two couples will be leaving tonight.'

Jack Obiaka: 'Well, this sucks.'

Neil Steel: You've got that right!

The contestants filed into the villa, Niall and Stella holding hands as though they might be forcibly separated at any moment. Oliver enveloped them in a hug as soon as they were inside, unable to say anything with the weight of emotion pressing against his chest. Losing Niall right after losing Declan felt like the end of something.

Holly ripped herself away from Owen to join their embrace, her normally tough exterior cracked by the tears falling down her face. 'It shouldn't be me staying, it should be you.'

Stella shook her head vigorously, and Oliver noticed that she was also crying. 'You need to stay, it's not your time yet.'

Niall tucked Holly under his arm. It would have been comical, with Niall being about twice her size, if both of them weren't choked up. 'We've had a good run; we're ready to take on the real world.'

Holly glanced back at Owen. 'Maybe it's my time, too.'

'Absolutely not,' Oliver said, surprising himself. 'No one else is leaving, all right? No more talk of giving up.' Stella gave Oliver a watery smile. 'I'm going to miss you both so much,' Oliver continued, since he couldn't bear silence.

'We'll see you on the other side,' Jack said, saluting Niall before wrapping his arms around him.

As they said their goodbyes, Oliver's eyes drifted to Declan. He remained at the edge of the group, studying the floor with an expression Oliver recognised as carefully smoothed-over. He was seized with the desire to reach out, to comfort him, before remembering they weren't speaking.

Niall must have noticed his panicked expression, gently prying him away. 'Everything okay?' he asked in a low voice.

'It's going to be weird without you here,' Oliver said, pushing Declan to the back of his mind.

Niall sighed. 'I hate to say it, but I'm relieved. I was tired of being told that a healthy relationship with Stella wasn't enough drama. But I'm obviously sad to leave you all.'

The lump in Oliver's throat grew. 'I'm gonna miss you.'

'I'll miss you too,' Niall said, pulling Oliver into his famous bear hug. 'And Oliver,' he said, a serious look on his face, 'if you have real feelings for someone, don't let them go, no matter what the producers throw at you. They couldn't shake me and Stella because we refused to play their game.'

'Right,' Oliver said, his eyes involuntarily flitting back to Declan. He was watching Stella and Maeve's tearful embrace expressionlessly, and Oliver's chest tightened. He looked back at Niall. 'Don't worry about me, Eavie and I are solid.'

Niall's eyebrows drew together. 'Think about it, okay?'

Oliver nodded. 'Okay.'

The two of them rejoined the group, where Zoë was now hugging Stella and whispering something in her ear.

Paige finally stepped into the scene. 'All right, lovebirds, we have to get going.'

Oliver gave Niall, Stella and Owen each a final hug as they departed the villa. Watching them go, he found Maeve at his side.

'Mad, isn't it?' she said softly. 'Guess true love doesn't make for good TV.'

'Watch out,' Oliver deadpanned. 'If you're right, you and Jack are next.'

She gave him a small smile. 'Viewers seem to like you and Eavie together, though. I've heard it's playing well with the audience.' She gave a pointed glance towards Brian. 'Little birdies.'

'Oh,' Oliver said, startled but gratified. 'But who knows, maybe me and Eavie will be just as boringly happy as Niall and Stella in a week.'

'Hmm,' Maeve said, the corners of her lips pulling down. She gave him a final pat on the arm as Brian called that it was time for lights out. Eavie glanced at Oliver and Maeve, a question in her eyes, before turning to prepare for bed.

Oliver sat in bed, anxiously waiting for Eavie to come back from the bathroom. He'd always felt at ease with her before, but he'd been too caught up with Declan to overthink anything. Now, Declan was sitting on the next bed over, staring at the ceiling, but he felt further away from Oliver than ever.

Imogen returned from the bathroom with her hair pulled back in a plait and her face shiny with product. She exchanged soft words with Declan, and Oliver couldn't stop himself from glancing sideways at them. They looked perfect together – Declan had stopped brooding to pull at one of her braids playfully. That was the difference between him and Declan: through either years of practice or natural instinct, Declan always seemed unaffected.

As Eavie joined him in bed and the lights flicked off, Oliver's mind wouldn't settle. The sick feeling in his stomach that he had carried for the past day had solidified into something resembling resentment. Declan had been spooked so easily into ending things that Oliver had to believe that his feelings were less intense, or easier to ignore. The worst part was that he'd never know the full story. He doubted that Declan would ever let him close enough to talk about it.

At the same time, Maeve and Niall were right. Oliver was doing well, by all appearances, with Eavie. He hadn't been in danger of elimination that night, which was still shocking to him. He'd never thought he could get this far on the show. He'd also never thought he would genuinely be interested in someone, or that it would end like this.

He swallowed and rolled over, wrapping his arms around Eavie. He couldn't face Declan, even in the dark. If he committed himself to Eavie, to winning the show, he could convince himself it had all been worth it. He *had* to convince himself it had all been worth it. The money to move to New York would be consolation enough for his broken heart.

—

Any semblance of Oliver's old morning routine was gone now. He lay in bed with Eavie as late as he possibly could, until the rest of the contestants had already gone out to the kitchen. Eavie seemed to take this as encouragement, snuggling closer to him.

'Sleepy?' she murmured, propping herself up on an elbow and looking down at him. She looked strikingly beautiful in the morning light, and Oliver hated himself for feeling nothing towards her. It would've been too simple, he supposed, to fall for someone he could be with publicly. 'You're usually an early riser.'

He suddenly wanted to be anywhere else. 'Everything's great,' he lied. 'Shall I make you breakfast?'

'You're the best,' she said, her hand on his cheek and her face drawing slowly closer to his. He swung himself hurriedly off the bed.

'I can hear your stomach rumbling,' he said, in response to her put-out expression. 'You need food in you.'

He gave her a parting smile, steeling himself for whatever awaited him outside. Declan was sure to be somewhere in the vicinity, and though Oliver knew he should be prepared for that eventuality, he'd been too distracted to consider what their new relationship would look like or how they would play it for the cameras. It was even stranger to think that thousands of people would be watching him, heartbroken, and not understand what had happened.

Thankfully, as he exited the villa, he was met with only Jack and Maeve in the kitchen. Jack waved him over to where he sat overlooking Maeve's attempt at cooking bacon.

'All right?' Oliver asked, as Maeve flinched away from spitting oil. 'Care for some assistance?'

'*Please* help,' Jack said. 'She's the least domestic bird I've ever met.'

'I'm the breadwinner, Jack, you can't have it all,' Maeve said, removing the burned bacon from the pan.

Oliver came to her aid. 'Shall I do a demo?' he joked, moving around the counter to put his hands on her shoulders.

Eavie exited the villa just then, heading for the counter. 'I see you haven't started,' she said, looking at where his hands rested on Maeve's shoulders.

Oliver dropped them. 'Maeve was giving it a go, but intervention was necessary,' he explained.

He started on breakfast, flipping bacon and scrambling eggs as he became increasingly frustrated that no one had mentioned where Declan was.

'Imogen,' he said, when she finally joined them, 'where's your man? Thought you would be keeping him on a tight leash.' He plated Eavie's breakfast and passed it to her across the counter.

'The producers have other ideas. They've taken him to the Love Shack,' Imogen said. 'Why? Are you looking for him?'

'No,' Oliver said quickly, in what he desperately hoped was a casual tone, 'just wondering where he is.'

'Mhm,' Imogen said, narrowing her eyes at him. Thankfully, at that moment, Maeve interrupted.

'Oliver,' she said, 'let's have a chat, okay?'

'Uh—' he started, his eyes darting to Eavie.

'Come on,' Maeve said impatiently, grabbing his hand and practically dragging him away from the kitchen. When he glanced back, Eavie was frowning at them.

Sorry, he mouthed in her direction.

Maeve settled onto a nearby couch, patting the spot beside her. She had a strange energy about her – it was clear she wanted something from him and wasn't going to leave without it.

'All right?' he asked, not sitting.

'I couldn't spend another second without you telling me what's going on. You look awful,' she said. 'Now sit, please.'

'Gee, thanks,' he said, sitting nonetheless.

She gave him a look. 'I've never seen you stab toast quite that dramatically before. Something's going on, and I'm the only person who's willing to ask.' She placed a hand on his shoulder, her eyes softening. 'Talk to me.'

'It's—' he started.

She cut him off. 'It's *not* about Niall and Stella. Don't start bullshitting with me.'

'You know Niall was one of my mates,' he said weakly. 'This place is mad, and if you don't have anyone to confide in, it's impossible.'

'So, confide away,' Maeve said dismissively. 'You have me, Jack, Eavie... you have Declan.' She gave him a pointed look, as though waiting for him to contradict her on the last.

He looked down at his hands, folding them in his lap. 'I don't know what to say – maybe the pressure's catching up to me.'

'So what did you two row about, then?' she asked matter-of-factly.

Oliver frowned at her. 'Nothing... I guess we don't get on as well as I thought.'

She raised her eyebrows. 'Why would you say that?'

'Because,' Oliver said, barely able to get the words out, 'none of this is real.'

Maeve shook her head. 'You don't believe that, I know you don't. You know how I feel about you is real. How's it any different?'

'Of course it's real with us,' Oliver said, trying to find the words to make her understand. He felt a desperate urge to tell her everything, only tempered by the knowledge of the cameras lurking in the corner of his vision. 'It's different with Declan.'

'Okay...' Maeve said. 'You know you can tell me anything, right?'

He glanced at the nearest camera and she inclined her head slightly. 'Thanks, Maeve,' he said with forced cheer, wrapping his arms around her.

'If you ever *can* talk about it, I'm here,' she murmured, just as Oliver saw Declan approaching in the corner of his vision.

He expected Declan to continue ignoring him, to have something to say to Maeve instead, but he didn't. Declan looked directly at him, and Oliver's throat went dry as he stared into bottomless blue eyes.

'Hey,' Declan said, voice low. 'Paige wants to see you in the Love Shack.' His tone was warning, and Oliver understood that nothing good was coming. Still, he felt almost relieved having Declan beside him again.

'Uh-huh,' he managed. 'Thanks for letting me know.'

'Sure,' Declan said gruffly, looking away.

When Oliver entered the Love Shack, Paige was reading notes off her clipboard. 'Hey there.' She smiled at him in a way that put him on edge. It was the sort of smile designed to make him comfortable, but he didn't know how comfortable he should be with her at the moment.

'Hi,' he said, sitting. 'How's it going?'

'Good, good,' she said absently, before fixing her intense gaze on him. The red light blinked on. 'So, how are things with Eavie?'

'Things are great,' he started cautiously. 'I think she's the girl for me.' He could hear the boredom in his own voice, the repetition of words he'd been regurgitating for two weeks. He thought of his conversation with Maeve the night before, of the fact that the audience turned on couples who weren't involved in enough drama. 'Could you...?' he asked, gesturing to the camera.

She flicked it off. 'What is it?'

'Could you tell me what you think is a good strategy?' It felt weird to ask for her advice outright.

Paige frowned. 'To be frank, your ratings aren't great at the moment. People like you, but you need to be packaged correctly, and it's not working as well as it used to with Eavie.' She paused before adding, 'I still think you have potential to win this, if you trust me.'

He was surprised by her harsh presentation of his chances. 'So... what? It doesn't matter what I say about Eavie?'

'Exactly.'

He scratched his head. 'So why ask, then?'

'Because I want to know how it's going before we jump in. Just give me your honest answer.'

Oliver wasn't convinced that honesty would work in his favour, but he nodded anyway. The red light blinked on again. 'It's been a tough week for me, and Eavie has been incredibly helpful.'

'What's been going on?'

Oliver should have anticipated that follow-up. He decided to be as vague as possible, hoping she would move on quickly. 'I guess I didn't expect to make it this far, and I didn't realise how hard it would be to be away from my mates.'

'And you've now lost Niall, and you and Declan are on the outs as well?'

Oliver stiffened. 'Yeah...' he said. 'It's been tough, since those were my two strongest friendships in the villa.'

'So... what is your relationship with Declan now?' Paige asked neutrally.

209

Oliver's heart raced – her expression was unreadable as ever, but he knew how easily she sensed weakness. 'We *were* mates,' he said, hoping in vain that she would leave it at that.

'It's clear that the two of you didn't have just any friendship.'

'Things get intense in here,' Oliver said, his face growing hot. 'I got a lot closer to people than I expected, including him.'

'How close?'

'What kind of question is that?' Oliver said, tone clipped. 'You want me to quantify how close our friendship was?'

Paige stared back at him with that same blank look. 'No, actually, I'd like it if you were honest with me.'

'What—' he started, scrambling. He took a steadying breath. 'What exactly are you asking me?'

'I'm asking you if your relationship with Declan is entirely platonic.'

Oliver lost any feeling in his face. 'Of course it is. That's ridiculous. Men can be friends and touch each other and talk about their feelings.'

'Yeah?' Paige asked, her voice growing tight, a hint of emotion finally coming out. 'How many of your mates have you been snogging?'

'Turn the camera off.' Oliver didn't realise he'd said the words, but when he heard them, he knew they were his own. He couldn't feel any part of his body other than the pounding of his heartbeat in his ears.

Paige's poker face broke, and she looked concerned. It reminded him of how she'd acted in the living room at the manor house, cajoling. 'Oliver, you're not in trouble here, okay? But I need to know what happened. That's my job.'

'Turn the camera off,' he said again, his voice firmer.

She hesitated before flicking the switch on the camera. 'I'm listening.'

'What did you see on the hike?'

She frowned. 'The hike?'

'This is bad,' he said, not thinking about who he was talking to. He knew, without any consideration, that this conversation would ruin everything.

'Oliver...' Paige said slowly, as though he might run out of the room at any provocation. 'You're not thinking this through. This doesn't have to be a bad thing. It could be a very, very good thing for you.'

'Yeah, well, it's not, okay?' he snapped, fear finally catalysing into anger. 'You knowing about... whatever it is you think you know about... is exactly what I *didn't* want to happen.'

'Why?' she asked, surprised. 'We both want the same thing, don't we?'

He sighed, running a hand through his hair. 'I doubt that.' At the moment, the only thing Oliver wanted was to be able to look at Declan without feeling a corresponding ache in his chest at the thought that he couldn't touch him.

'I have the audio feed,' she said cautiously, 'of you and Declan in the bathroom at the manor.'

'*What?*' That was worse than he'd feared. He hadn't imagined that she had proof. Evidence of his relationship with Declan could cause irreparable damage. Oliver knew well the lengths that Declan had gone to ensure his sexuality stayed a secret.

He'd turned his mic off, hadn't he? He tried to think back through all that had happened on the double date, and couldn't think of a single moment where he would have checked if they were being recorded. They were off set, and Paige and Brian weren't around. They were in the *bathroom*. Weren't there laws about that kind of thing?

'I was tipped off, and I went looking to see if it was true, or if he was making it up.'

'James,' Oliver breathed out in recognition. No one else would have gone to the producers with something like that.

Paige ignored him. 'I've been trying to get one of you to admit there was something going on, but you've given me nothing, and Declan's even worse. I mean, I never expected him to react like that to the posts,' she said, frowning. Oliver felt a jolt of understanding, of pure anger. It hadn't been bad luck, bad timing. The fight hadn't been his fault or Declan's, it had been Paige's. 'So it seems the only way is to be upfront: what are your feelings for Declan King?'

He wanted to laugh at the absurdity of her question. How she assumed he could express something that he didn't even fully understand.

'What? You thought I would sit here and admit to you that I love him if you asked nicely?'

'Are you saying you love him?'

He had never imagined he could get this angry over something that wasn't even real, over a television show, but he felt like he was about to burst out of his skin. A strangled sound came out of his mouth. 'Why didn't you *tell* me about the audio?'

He was shocked by the betrayal he felt over that small detail, but it seemed vital for him to understand. He was sure that if he'd known, he could have done things differently, could have fixed things before it was too late.

Paige pursed her lips. 'I was trying to make it easier for you, so you didn't feel threatened by me. I wanted you to feel like you could confide in me.' She paused, studying his stony expression. 'Oliver, I'm on your side here.'

'Good job,' he bit out. 'That's worked out *fantastically*, hasn't it? I don't feel threatened at all right now.'

She folded her arms. 'Can you hear me out before yelling at me?'

'Go ahead,' Oliver said woodenly, knowing he had no say in the matter.

'I have an idea,' Paige said, looking as though she'd been sitting on this speech for a long time, 'and if you agree to work with me, you're guaranteed to win this thing.'

'Does this idea involve me coming out on national television?' Oliver asked sarcastically.

'Well, yes,' Paige replied, biting her lip. 'Here's the bottom line: I can't sit on this audio. If Darcy finds out I knew about this and did nothing, it would destroy my career. I've already left it for longer than I should have.'

'You're going to air it?' he asked, his tone flat. He didn't allow himself to think too deeply about what that would mean for him or Declan.

'Yes.' She leaned in. 'But we can take control of this narrative. If you tell the world that you love Declan, that's not just good television, that's *groundbreaking*. The two of you would have this thing in the bag.'

'That's if you assume Declan reciprocates my feelings,' Oliver said, still without any emotion. 'You may have noticed we aren't speaking at the moment, which would suggest he doesn't.'

Paige sat back. 'Of course he does. Being on a straight dating show isn't the easiest way to start a gay relationship, and I'm sure that's caused problems.' She looked to Oliver, seemingly for confirmation, and he gave her a blank stare. He was beginning to suspect all of his and Declan's problems were sitting right in front of him. 'But with my support – and Darcy's blessing – the two of you could just... be together.'

'Yeah, that's grand,' he said, 'except we're not together.'

Paige waved that away as though she knew better, infuriating him further. 'If you confess your love to him, do you think he'd be able to hide his feelings for you? His choices would be to lie, badly, and make himself look like an ass, or to acknowledge what the two of you have. And when we air the audio, it will be clear that those feelings are reciprocated, so there's no chance of you looking the fool.'

Oliver thought back to the weeks in which he and Declan had been friends, before he had suspected there was anything else between them. Declan had years of practice at pretending to be straight, but Oliver had no idea how he would react to the scenario that Paige proposed. Maybe he would cave under the pressure and acknowledge that there was something between them. A part of him – a part he was immediately ashamed of – wanted confirmation from Declan that the whole thing hadn't been in his head.

'People would root for you,' Paige continued imploringly. 'The first openly gay couple on *Summer of Love*. That's *major*, Oliver. The audience is already obsessed with the two of you together. And think about after, all the sponsorship opportunities – you're looking at hundreds of thousands of pounds here.'

'And if I don't want to do it, if I'm not interested in the money?' He was surprised to find it was the truth, that there was no amount of money that would make her offer appealing.

Paige frowned. 'Like I said, I want you to be able to control this narrative, and to get everything you were hoping for. But I still have to give the audio to Darcy. It's my job on the line.'

Oliver tried to conjure the tiniest amount of sympathy for Paige's situation, but found he couldn't. She had put him in an impossible situation – he was going to be outed on television, alongside Declan. He could try to mitigate the damage, denying that anything else had happened between them. Or he could profess his love to someone who wanted nothing to do with him.

'Did you talk to Declan about this?' he asked finally, his voice coming out hoarse.

Paige looked slightly encouraged. 'No, he doesn't know anything about it. I had the feeling if one of you would act, it would be you.'

His laugh was short and sardonic. 'Right.'

She leaned forwards again, sympathetic. 'I understand this feels like a difficult decision for you right now, since it's so sudden. You have time to think about how you want to go about this. The audio clip airs on Sunday, either way. So you have some time to get ahead of it, to show your side of the story.'

He found himself nodding. Paige was still looking at him in that concerned way that made him want to scream, so he stood and let himself out of the room without another word.

He had three days to make a decision, but, if he was honest with himself, he already knew he would do nothing. If Oliver could be relied upon for anything, it was letting things happen to him.

Chapter 22

Oliver

One and Half Weeks until Finale

Over the next two days, he continued to avoid Declan, though he had the feeling his constant staring at the other man hadn't gone unnoticed. Sometimes, when he looked away, he thought he could feel Declan's eyes on him too. There was no other explanation: the show was driving him mad.

Two new contestants entered the villa, neither of them making any impression on Oliver. Shortly after their arrival, Eavie interrupted him as he lay flat on the pool deck, contemplating his life choices.

'Hey,' she said, as he reluctantly sat up. 'You seem... distracted.'

'Do I?' he asked, watching Paige approach from across the patio.

Eavie pointedly followed his stare. 'Yes,' she said bluntly.

He shrugged. 'Sure, okay.' A cameraman was trained on them now, and he could hear the buzz of Paige muttering into her headset. He was sure that she was planning on using this footage as some sort of leverage in the final reveal.

A moment of painful silence passed before Eavie spoke again. 'Elliot asked me on a date.'

'Who?'

Eavie looked as close to rolling her eyes as Oliver had ever seen her. 'Elliot? He came in earlier today? You two had a whole conversation about whether you can find decent fish and chips in London?'

'Oh,' Oliver said vacantly. From his fuzzy memory of the afternoon, Elliot had seemed nice enough. 'Great.'

'Great?' she repeated, frowning. 'That's all you have to say?'

Oliver blinked at her and she came slightly more into focus. 'Er... what?'

'You've been ignoring me for *days*, Oliver. I liked you, I thought we had genuine potential, and you've disappeared on me. Do you understand how frustrating that is?' Her cheeks were red, but Oliver couldn't tell if it was from anger or the heat.

'No...?' he tried.

'I know you haven't been toying with me for fun. I mean, you seem miserable and I think I understand why. But it *hurts* that you've been stringing me along with no intention to ever commit.'

Oliver's thoughts drifted to Declan, to the fact that he couldn't commit, to the possibility that he would have to. He felt sick and didn't even attempt to respond.

She continued, more sharply, 'Fine, don't say anything. If we're laying it all out, it's pretty obvious what's going on.'

'Uh – is it?' he asked.

'You're in love with someone else,' she said, without any accusation in her tone.

'I'm not,' he said feebly.

Eavie stared at him. 'Don't lie to me,' she snapped. 'I deserve the truth from you, don't you think?'

'Okay, sure,' he said, deciding it hardly mattered what she thought at this point. 'I'm in love with someone else. It's awful, not being able to act on your feelings. And I'm completely falling apart, so that's great.'

She shook her head. 'If I wasn't so angry with you, I would feel sorry for you. I know Jack is one of your mates.'

Oliver blinked. 'What?'

'It must be difficult, knowing if you told Maeve how you felt, you would lose Jack in the process.'

'Right...' He didn't fully register what she had said, distracted by Brian gesturing wildly in the kitchen and trying to not search in the corner of his vision for the person he always found himself searching for. 'I suppose.'

'Well, no use dwelling on it,' she said abruptly, and he looked at her again, feeling desperately sad about the situation that they both were in. It occurred to Oliver vaguely that he might have been on the verge of a panic attack for two days now.

'Eavie,' he said, emotion strangling his voice, 'I *am* sorry.'

She gave him a small nod. 'Me too.'

He stood and walked towards the villa just to get away from her, his movements mechanical and out of his control. He had gone for the bedroom, assuming it would be empty, but one couple lingered.

When he saw Declan and Imogen, Oliver nearly turned on his heel to face whatever awaited him on the patio, but his knees buckled beneath him. He flung himself onto the nearest bed so he wouldn't collapse in the middle of the room, on camera, and make himself look pathetic.

'All right there?' Imogen asked, turning. Her dark curls were haloed by the ceiling lights in his peripheral vision. He couldn't bring himself to look beside her.

'Oh, I'm grand,' Oliver said, incredibly tired of everyone asking him the same question. 'Don't I look fantastic?'

'Sorry you're feeling shit.' They were the first words Declan had spoken to him in days.

'Not your fault,' Oliver said, meeting his eye and feeling the customary pang in his chest. His anger at Declan had entirely dissipated; he could see now how they'd been doomed from the start. He could only hope that Declan would believe him, would somehow understand that Oliver's current spiral wasn't the result of their fight.

'Try to think about how it will feel when this is all over,' Imogen said, and Oliver was jarred by her voice, which had dropped low. 'God knows I am.' She turned to Declan. 'Shall I give you a moment?'

'Yeah,' Declan said, kneeling beside Oliver as Imogen left the room. They just looked at each other for a moment.

'Not thinking of running away, are you?' Declan said with a small smile, his lips lifting crookedly in a way Oliver had committed to memory. It made him feel better, if only just a bit.

'No,' Oliver said, with a wan smile, 'you're stuck with me.'

It looked like Declan wanted to say more, his lips parting slightly before he pressed them together in a thin line. He stood abruptly, his arm brushing Oliver's side, and Oliver could feel him stiffen at the unintentional contact.

As he walked away, Oliver felt certain that if he could have one conversation with Declan, off camera, he would know what to do. Part of him thought Paige was right: if he gave Declan the opportunity to offer his own response to Oliver's feelings, that might be less awful than him being blindsided by them airing the kiss without context. If Declan had to come out, at least it would be in his own words, if not on his own terms.

–

Oliver tried not to notice Declan watching him as the lights came on the next morning, or as he made his way out to the kitchen, or as he drank his tea silently at the counter. It wouldn't do him any good at this point. It was his final day to act, and he'd never felt more unsure of the right thing to do.

For better or worse, Paige seemed to have given up on him, and called the remaining five men together shortly after breakfast. 'How's everyone holding up?' she asked, her eyes sweeping across their faces and resting on Oliver.

'Why?' Jack asked, suspicious.

'Just checking in!' she said. 'Since we're only a week out from the finale, I had an idea.' Oliver snorted, and her eyes cut towards him. 'Something wrong?'

'No,' Oliver said, not bothering to hide his contempt, 'you know how much I love your ideas, Paige. Let's hear it.'

Both Declan and Jack looked taken aback by the exchange, but Paige just ignored him. 'On the last day, you're expected to exchange vows of commitment, and I thought it might be nice to have the five of you work on them together. Like, you're all bad at expressing your feelings, so you're helping each other out... you get it?'

If Oliver hadn't been sure that she was fucking with him from the start, he was now. 'Oh, *I* get it,' he said, 'but I'm not sure the rest of them have caught on.'

'I get it,' James replied, indignant. 'I'm good with words, though. I mean, my songs are a form of poetry.'

It was Declan's turn to snort. 'Yes, modern Lennon over here.'

Elliot looked overwhelmed. 'I'm, um, happy to try my best,' he said, 'but I've only been here two days? I mean' – he looked at Oliver – 'Eavie and I aren't even a couple?'

Oliver shrugged. 'No need to tiptoe around it on my account – I'm happy for you two.'

'Wait, what?' Jack asked, frowning at him. 'Since when are you and Eavie broken up?'

'Since yesterday.' Oliver turned to Paige. 'So, who am I meant to write my speech to?'

'I'm sure you'll think of someone,' Paige said drily.

She directed them over to the swing, where she had set out notepads and pens. Two cameras were already trained on the area.

The rest of the men got to work, scribbling away, while Oliver stared despondently at the blank sheet of paper. He couldn't figure out the least disastrous way to handle things, the decision that would make him feel least like he was orchestrating his own demise for public spectacle.

'Okay,' Paige said, walking back over. She glanced at Oliver's blank notepad and frowned. 'Let's hear it – James, you go.'

Though James stood and started reading, Oliver couldn't focus on the words. When he thought of coming out, he thought of telling his friends and family, and the idea of that didn't bother him. But coming out on national television would put him under a scrutiny he wasn't prepared for, his sexuality too new for even him to feel expert in.

He couldn't stop himself from looking at Declan. When the kiss aired on Sunday, Declan's whole life, the one he had worked so hard for, would fall apart. And it would be Oliver's fault – he kept thinking that if he'd acted sooner, if he'd played the game better, he would have been able to find a way out of this mess for the both of them. Instead, he was frozen, powerless, watching Paige's plan unfurl before him, and the most he'd been able to do was to sling a few barbs her way. It wasn't nearly enough.

'Declan, your turn,' Paige said.

Declan nodded, standing, and Oliver wished he could be anywhere else. Despite the torture Paige had put him through this week, he knew listening to Declan pretend to be in love with Imogen would be the thing to finally break him.

'I can admit this now, since we've come to the end,' Declan read, the words coming out stilted and awkward. 'I didn't come here to find someone. I didn't think I could. I thought I'd have a holiday, I'd get my face on TV, and then I'd go back home and that'd be it.'

He swallowed. 'Now, I'm not sure I *can* go back… Knowing you has changed me, and I don't think I'd fit there like I used to. You've shown me how to be myself, and I didn't realise how exhausted I was with pretending to be someone else,' he said, his voice growing rougher. 'I met you and it was like I could breathe.' He paused, the piece of paper fluttering in his shaking hand.

'Sorry, I'm not sure how to end this. I'm not good at saying things I actually mean. I guess I'm just glad I met you.' Declan glanced up, catching Oliver's eye, and, for a brief moment, it felt like they were alone. For once, Declan's face was open, and he was showing Oliver everything.

'Um, wow,' Jack said, breaking the silence. 'That was... deep?'

Declan held Oliver's gaze for a moment longer before sitting down.

'Oliver?' Paige said, looking at him intently.

Oliver stood and turned to face everyone, blank paper in hand. He glanced at Declan, clearing his throat, with no idea what came next. He had spent his life in a constant series of next steps, but now he wished he could stop everything from moving forwards.

He had only ever really made one decision: pursuing ballet. His family had thought he was a ridiculous dreamer, the boys at school had thought he was strange, and still Oliver had found a way to make it happen. He hadn't wanted anything like he'd wanted that in a long time. He hadn't allowed himself to. He'd made a plan and never strayed from it, paralysed by the fear of losing everything.

He'd come on the show because his friends had responded to Paige's DM and he'd gone along with it. He'd been pliant to all of Paige's manipulations, not making a single decision for himself.

But as Declan looked at him, he knew he had to fix this. He at least had to try. If not for himself, he could do it for Declan.

'Actually, I won't do this.' He turned, walking towards the villa.

Paige was immediately on his heels. 'What's going on? That was the perfect set-up.'

He turned to look at her, feeling oddly elated, despite the fact that he had no idea what he was going to do. 'I've got a plan.'

Paige studied him, eyes bright. 'Well, let's hear it, then.'

'I want to talk in the Love Shack,' he suggested.

She nodded. 'Fine by me.'

They walked through the hall and to the interview room, and Oliver sat on the stool that he'd spent so much time on over the last eight weeks.

'Camera on or off?' Paige asked, still staring at him. He knew that he looked peculiar, grinning like an idiot after days of abject misery.

'On's fine.'

'Right.' The red light blinked on. 'I assume you know where you're going with this?'

'Yes,' he said. Now, unfortunately, the hard part came. Paige would certainly not make this easy. 'I'm done playing your game. I'm not taking any more orders from you.'

Her face fell immediately, the effect almost comical. 'Be serious, Oliver.'

He continued with a straight face: 'I am serious. I'm not going to let you blackmail me, and I'm not going to waste any more of my time trying for the approval of people who don't give a shit about me. And you've got that on tape, if you'd ever like a reminder of how low you've gone in life. Watch at your leisure.'

To his surprise, shame flitted across Paige's features. 'This is my job. I know it's not pretty, and believe me, it's not easy for me to see you like this. But I want you and Declan to be together properly. It's not as though I've got an evil agenda here. *We want the same thing.*' She looked at him, pleading.

He shook his head. That refrain had never been less true than it was now. 'I want to protect Declan. You just want to use him. How is it you don't see the difference?'

'You don't know how I feel about you, about all of this,' she argued.

'I know it's your career on the line. I understand giving everything else up to go after something – that's what I've done for ballet. But there are more important things. It's Declan's entire life that you're threatening. It's my life, my livelihood, my sanity. You're manipulating me, all in the name of... what?'

'Making a point,' she snapped. 'A very important point. *That,* I thought you would understand.'

'You're not making a point,' Oliver countered. 'You're profiting off people's emotions, their vulnerabilities. If the audience knew what went on behind the scenes of the show, they would go ballistic. How do you think they would respond if they knew you offered me a good edit, fame and money to out another contestant on national television? That's not as progressive as you're telling yourself it is.'

As soon as Oliver said it, everything fell into place. He knew exactly how to get out of this, how to get almost everything he wanted. He'd lost Declan, but he had figured out how to win.

Paige's face had turned a blotchy red, and she stared at him defiantly. 'You don't know what you're talking about. Darcy's heard the audio. I can't stop it from airing, even if I wanted to.'

Oliver bit back a laugh. 'You haven't shown it to Darcy. There's no story here unless I go along with it. If you air the audio and I leave, you expose yourself for exactly what you are: an industry capitalising on traumatising people for entertainment. Outing contestants for shock value and jeopardising their wellbeing in the process. I think you're smart enough to know that's not a good look, and that's why you've kept this plan between the two of us. Isn't that right?'

Her face was all the confirmation he needed. 'Oliver – come on, we can still figure this out so we both win.'

'You never fucking *listen* to me. I'm leaving. I quit. You can't make me stay.' The words bubbled out of him. 'You can't make me do anything any more.'

Her face was stony. 'Is that all?'

'That's all. Good interview, Paige.'

The red light blinked off. He stood and walked out the door.

Chapter 23

Declan

One Week Until Finale

Neil Steel: Awkward conversations abounded in the villa last week. Let's take a look…

Eavie Laurent: 'You're in love with Maeve.'

Oliver Wright: 'I'm completely falling apart.'

Neil Steel: Uh-oh! We know Oliver doesn't handle rejection well.

Oliver Wright: 'I won't do this. I'm leaving the villa tonight.'

'So, should we keep going, or…' Elliot asked, as they watched Oliver storm off.

'No,' Declan said, heading to the kitchen.

Jack followed him. 'What the hell was that?'

Declan shrugged, opening the fridge and letting the cool air wash over him.

He leaned his head against the metal and squeezed his eyes shut. All week, he'd been rehashing the fight, watching Oliver look miserable and knowing it was his fault. He'd thought putting all his feelings out there could fix it.

'You okay?' Maeve asked. Declan wasn't sure how long she'd been standing there.

He didn't have the energy to plaster on a smile. 'I—'

'What's happening?' Imogen cut in. Her tone made Declan turn to see a cameraman jogging into the villa, a haggard-looking Brian trailing behind. Without a word, the four of them followed.

It was Oliver, racing around the bedroom, throwing his things into a suitcase.

As bad as Declan had felt before, it was nothing compared to now. 'What's going on?' he asked, not keeping the panic out of his voice.

'I'm leaving,' Oliver said.

Declan's stomach dropped. 'No, you can't.' The words were out before he could stop them.

Maeve took a step forwards, shaking her head. 'Come on, I'm sure we can talk it out,' she said calmly.

'I can't take it any more,' Oliver said, pacing around the room and running a hand through his already messy hair. 'Where's my other shoe?' He rummaged through his suitcase.

'Oliver,' Declan tried, but he got no response. He hated the way his voice sounded, hoarse and weak. This couldn't be happening. Oliver couldn't leave.

'What's going on?' Holly and Eavie came in.

'Oliver's leaving,' Imogen said, folding her arms tightly and blinking rapidly as though to hold back tears.

'Come on, mate,' Jack said, walking over to clap Oliver on the back. 'Don't be silly. We're nearly there, just a week more.'

Oliver shrugged his hand off. 'I can't stay,' he said, without any discernible emotion.

Jack didn't seem to know how to respond to that. None of them did. Oliver wasn't giving them any hope to cling to. He wasn't angry, he wasn't throwing a fit, this wasn't for the cameras. It was just over. He was finished, and that was it. They stood there for a moment, not knowing what to say, before Maeve threw her arms around Oliver.

'I'm going to miss you so much,' she said.

'Me too,' Oliver said, holding her as she cried into his shoulder.

'Great, now I'm crying,' Jack said, throwing his arms around them. 'Ollie boy, you were the best of us.'

Declan frantically searched for words that could make Oliver see reason, could make him stay. His speech had only made things worse. Oliver deserved more than disguised apologies; he deserved the truth.

'Oliver,' he said again, voice low. No one around him seemed to hear, but Oliver raised his head and their eyes finally met.

The air rushed out of his lungs, words dying on his tongue. He wanted to reach out, to touch Oliver one last time. But the glare of the camera lens kept him fixed to the spot.

–

Declan slipped out of bed the next morning as the sun peeked out over the horizon. He dove into the pool, driving his body forwards, feeling his muscles strain to their limit and pushing past even that. He swam until he couldn't any more, his wrist throbbing as he grabbed the side of the pool and gulped air into his shaking body. He wanted to punch something, to tear his hair out, to make this hurt something he could isolate.

He let himself sink to the bottom of the pool, feeling the bubbles float up around him. Lying flat along the cool tile, he stared at the water above him, the chlorine pricking his eyes. All he could see was blue, endless blue. Declan felt crushed by it. He closed his eyes, but the pressure stayed. It pressed on his lungs that were beginning to burn for want of air, but he couldn't move. His heartbeat rushed in his ears and his thoughts went fuzzy around the edges. Oliver was gone and it was his own fault.

He opened his eyes again and noticed a shadow peeking out from the side of the pool. For a moment, his oxygen-starved brain thought it was Oliver, bringing him his morning cup of tea like he'd done so many times before.

It wasn't Oliver, of course, but Imogen. He surfaced, gasping for breath and taking in her sympathetic expression.

'We're heading out in a few minutes.'

He was grateful that she didn't ask him if he was okay. But, he supposed, if you found your fake boyfriend sitting at the bottom of a pool, moping over another man, it would be correct to assume that no, he wasn't okay. He nodded and pulled himself onto the deck, taking the towel Imogen offered him.

It was the last Saturday before the finale, the final day off to relax before the hardest week of all. They were going back to the beach, and Declan was pointedly ignoring the irony. He threw on a shirt before heading out.

When they got there, the brisk ocean breeze swept over his face, catching his hair. The others raced to the water, jumping in with shouts of laughter, but he walked down the beach, ditching his shoes, his feet sinking into the sand. He sat, watching the waves crash. He couldn't be sure how long he stayed there, his thoughts circling nebulously.

Someone sat next to him. He figured it was Imogen, coming to tell him he should go for a swim. But it was Maeve.

'Hi,' she said, when he glanced over at her.

'Hi,' he replied, his voice rough with disuse. It was the first thing he'd said all morning.

'It's weird without him here, huh?'

Declan sighed. He didn't want to talk about it, didn't know what he could even say.

'I was going to talk about you with Oliver today,' she said, looking at the ocean.

Declan turned to her, but she stared steadfastly at the waves. 'What?' he asked finally.

'I could tell he was upset about something – about you – but he wouldn't say anything in front of the cameras. I was hoping to catch him alone.' Maeve squinted at him. There was something cold in her tone, and it registered that she wasn't trying to comfort him, she was upset with him.

'Oh,' Declan said, feigning ignorance.

Maeve shook her head emphatically. 'Don't do that!' she said, her nostrils flaring. 'Tell me the truth. For once in your life, stop acting the fool.'

And Declan felt so tired. He was tired of keeping secrets, tired of pretending. He was tired of holding all of himself in and keeping everything he wanted wrapped up so tightly that he might burst.

'He and I, we weren't—' Declan didn't know how to start. 'I kissed him.' He was overcome by a sense of weightlessness, the burden finally lifting.

He watched as Maeve's anger froze on her face. 'What?'

'I kissed him,' he said again, more firmly. 'And I fucked it up.'

Maeve's eyebrows shot up, the line of her mouth softening, and then, surprisingly, she laughed. 'Shit,' she said, shaking her head. 'I thought that might be it.'

It was Declan's turn to look surprised. 'You knew?'

'I suspected,' Maeve admitted. 'Male rituals are so weird, I couldn't be sure.'

Declan let out a long breath.

'You weren't obvious,' she reassured him. 'I was only trying to look out for Oliver. Jack definitely doesn't know, the dolt.' She said it with such affection that Declan's chest ached. 'So, let's have it, what happened?'

'I don't know,' Declan said.

Maeve gave him a stern look. 'Yes, you do.'

'I fucked it up,' Declan said again.

'How?'

Declan squeezed his eyes shut. His head throbbed, the ache in his chest becoming almost unbearable. He couldn't breathe. 'I backed out as soon as it got real.'

Her eyebrows drew together. 'Why would you do that?'

'Because it would never have worked. I'm Declan King. I don't get to just do whatever I want. I train, I fight, I win.'

The words tasted bitter in his mouth. 'There's no room left for anything else.'

'Sure there is,' Maeve said.

Declan looked down. 'There's a reason I was never out before this,' he said. 'They can have every other part of me if they want, but not this.'

A small frown played at Maeve's lips. 'So you gave up Oliver because you didn't want people to find out you're gay?' she asked. 'Are you just never going to date *anyone*?'

'I wasn't planning on it.' Her frown deepened, and he continued, 'It's – everyone loves me for what I *do*. My entire life, it's been about being the best, winning.' His life had stopped feeling like his own a long time ago, when his father and brother had become the priority. 'I don't think I can be vulnerable with someone in that way. Sometimes I think if I let myself be, they would see there's nothing there.'

Maeve looked at him, her mouth slightly agape. 'Are you serious? Declan, why would you ever think that?'

Declan stared out into the blue of the ocean, feeling his cheeks flush. Maeve had steered their conversation to a place Declan never ventured. His eyes pricked and he swallowed hard.

'I, um—' He let out a shaky breath. 'I'm not built for it. Other people, they've got this love built in that they're waiting to give to someone and I – I don't.'

Maeve looked livid. 'I've seen you with Oliver and trust me, you're fucking built for it. You're the one who looks after all of us – the first person to make a cup of tea, to offer advice and keep us going. We'd all have gone mad in here without you. I mean, hell, Jack and I probably wouldn't even be together if not for your meddling.'

Declan didn't know what to do with Maeve's words. Was that honestly how she saw him? Didn't she know all he was good for was a fight?

'There are too many things that could go wrong,' he said finally. 'It would've been too hard.'

Maeve scoffed. 'Relationships *are* hard.' She pointed to Jack, who was running into an oncoming wave. 'He's a teacher and I travel the world for half of the year, but we're both willing to make it work. We've got to try.'

Declan followed her gaze over to Jack. He was grinning at Holly, the sun glinting off his shoulders as he swam. He said something that made Holly throw her head back in laughter. Declan thought back to when they'd all swum together in that exact spot. He remembered it like it had happened to someone else; he had walked out of the surf and sat next to Oliver and he had changed completely.

He'd let Oliver go because he was too scared to keep him. Now he was terrified that he was going to feel like this forever, the tightness in his chest turning chronic, walking around with a crucial piece of himself missing. He thought about going home after this was all over; he thought about stepping back into his dad's gym. He thought about training; he thought about hitting the bag, over and over and over again. His body going through the motions, his eyes blank. He thought about getting hit; he thought about eating mat; he thought about tasting blood.

He did taste blood, the soft skin inside his cheek splitting under clenched teeth. He couldn't say the words; if he did he'd be done for.

'I love him,' Declan said, barely above a whisper. He wasn't sure if Maeve even heard him over the sound of the waves crashing around them. Instead, louder, he said, 'It's too late. He's already gone.'

–

For the next week, Declan woke up early. He swam laps. He lifted weights. He laughed with the other contestants. He flirted with Imogen. He answered all of Paige's interview questions. He played the game. He was charming and he was funny. He was everything that Declan King was known to be. He no longer felt like Declan King.

He sat on the couch swing with Jack and Holly, listening to them talk and idly watching a small blue bird hopping across the deck, inching its way closer to the kitchen.

'I'm just not sure,' Holly was saying. The bird made it to the side of the counter, where Maeve and Imogen were sharing a bag of crisps.

'He seems like a nice enough bloke,' Jack said. Imogen dropped a crisp and the bird descended on it, pecking at it before grabbing a piece and flying to a safe spot a few feet away to consume the stolen meal.

'Decs, what do you think?' Holly asked.

Declan startled at the sound of his name. 'Er, what?'

Jack frowned. 'Holly is trying to decide if she fancies Liam,' he explained, in a tone that made Declan feel like one of his secondary students.

'Oh, right,' Declan said, looking over at the two contestants who had arrived that morning. It was a pointless conversation – there was no way for Holly to win, with Liam coming in too late to make any impact on the audience. And if it was love she was looking for, Declan certainly couldn't help her. 'Well, how does he make you feel about yourself?' he asked. 'Does he make you laugh?'

Holly blinked at him, then threw her head in her hands. 'I don't know,' she wailed. 'I didn't expect it to be this hard!'

'Come on, Holls,' Jack said, putting an arm around her and shooting Declan an annoyed look. 'It's gonna be okay.'

'I don't know what I'm even doing here; I sure as shit haven't found love,' Holly said despondently. 'Owen was the closest I came, and he's gone!'

'Hey,' Declan said, scooting towards her and grabbing her hand. 'You've been braver than the lot of us, putting yourself out there again and again. And don't say you didn't find love here, because you have. I love you.'

'Me too,' Jack agreed.

Holly shot them both a watery smile, straightening. 'You're right. I suppose it doesn't matter who I pick. I've got you lot, and that's all the winnings I need.'

'Great stuff, you three,' Brian said. Jack hid his laugh with a coughing fit as Holly slapped their knees and got up to find Liam.

They sat in comfortable silence for a few minutes, and Declan resumed watching his new bird friend feast on a fallen grape.

Jack sighed happily next to him. 'It's pretty incredible, huh?' Declan glanced sideways and noticed he was looking at Maeve and Imogen.

'Oh,' Declan said, watching the two girls laugh. 'Yeah.'

'I never thought I'd meet someone like her,' Jack said, and he looked almost sombre. He glanced back at Declan, his eyes wistful. 'I mean, all of you. I feel so lucky to have met you, Declan.'

He didn't know what to say to that.

'Declan!' Paige called from the corner of the patio, and Declan shrugged apologetically at Jack before heading over.

'Yeah?' he asked, casting a glance at the monitor where she'd been watching them. A miniature Jack waved at him.

'We were hoping you could have a chat with James,' she said, her eyes not meeting his.

'Why?' Declan asked, more confused than angry.

'We thought it would be nice to have some closure between you two.' She still wasn't looking at Declan, turning her attention back to the monitor. It made Declan want to scream, but instead he nodded.

'Where is he?'

'In the bedroom.'

'Great,' Declan said tersely.

'Thank you.'

He walked into the villa with no clue of what to say to James.

He found him and Zoë lounging on their bed, neither looking up as he walked in. James pushed a strand of Zoë's hair behind her ear as she giggled at something he'd said. He leaned in and kissed her softly. It was surprising to see them like this – almost sweet.

Declan cleared his throat awkwardly, and Zoë sprang away as James turned to glare at Declan.

'Hi,' Zoë said. She glanced between them, her cheeks flushing. Declan supposed she was expecting another fight, but he didn't have it in him any more.

'What do you want?' James asked snidely. Zoë shot him a warning look, which he ignored.

Declan would have rather been anywhere else. 'Could we chat?'

'Are you sure that's a good idea?' Zoë asked, confused.

'I promise not to punch him,' Declan deadpanned. Zoë cracked a small smile, but James crossed his arms.

'I'd like to see you try.'

'Are you coming or not?' He headed upstairs, not waiting to see if James was following.

'What did you want?' James asked, as they stepped out onto the balcony.

'I wanted to apologise,' Declan said, and was surprised by the honesty in that statement. Looking at James now, he only felt sorry for him.

'For what?' James asked suspiciously.

'For all of it,' Declan said. 'I'm sorry for punching you, I'm sorry for making your time here harder, and I'm sorry for what happened with Georgia.'

James looked like he wanted to hit him. 'And what exactly happened with Georgia?'

Declan snorted. 'You're an idiot.' James took a step towards him, but Declan held up a hand. 'Nothing happened.'

James scoffed. 'Why should I believe you? I saw you two together; I know how close you were. You tried to make a fool out of me.'

Declan shook his head. 'You did that yourself. Why would I lie to you now?'

'To mess with my head before the finale,' James said testily. 'I know how much you like to win, King.'

Declan tried to figure out how to convince him, and settled for the truth, or at least part of it. 'It was for publicity,' he said simply. 'I had lost my last three fights and people were saying I'd lost my touch, that my career was stalling. Georgia thought we could distract everyone by giving them something more interesting to talk about. It was all a big joke, but she never meant for it to be on you.'

He said it knowing the conversation would be aired to millions of viewers. He couldn't find it within himself to care. It was one less lie he'd have to live with.

James was incredulous. 'So, what, it was just a stunt?'

Declan nodded.

'But she never said—'

'Because I asked her not to,' Declan said. 'I mean, come on, a fake relationship? It was embarrassing.'

James's lips parted slightly as he blew out a breath. It was a small movement, but it was enough to know he had got through.

'She should – she should've told me,' James stammered.

'You should've trusted her,' Declan said. 'But you couldn't let yourself be hurt, so you pushed her away.'

He tried to focus on Georgia, but instead he thought of Oliver's smile that first day on the plane; he thought of the dazed look on his face when they were in bed together. He thought of his eyes flashing after their first kiss. Declan squeezed his eyes shut, trying to block out the memories.

'That's on you.' He blinked back tears. 'And if you're miserable now without her, that's on you too.'

For the first time since Declan had met him, James looked ashamed. 'I'm sorry.' It looked like he wanted to say more, but Declan didn't wait, turning on his heel and nearly running into Paige in the doorway.

'Was that enough for you?' Declan asked, wiping at his face. 'Good shit, right? Hope that plays well with the audience.'

'I—' Paige started, but Declan didn't let her finish, walking away.

Chapter 24

Paige

Fifteen Hours Until Finale

Neil Steel: Well, folks, the summer is coming to an end… and for those of you living under a rock, here's whatcha missed!

Declan fancied Zoë but Zoë dumped him for James, now Declan's with Imogen, who used to date Oliver, who was dating Eavie, who's now dating Elliot, because Oliver was still hung up on Maeve, who's with Jack, who used to date Holly, who's now dating some fellow named Liam, I guess.

I've got a rhyme to keep them all straight:

James and Zoë are the couple to beat, Jack and Maeve come off so sweet, Declan and Imogen have been through the ringer, Elliot and Eavie have no chance, and in case you forgot, James is a singer!

Paige jolted awake, scrambling to turn her alarm off as she squinted at the bright light of her phone's lock screen. She rolled over and stared at the ceiling for a few minutes, her eyes feeling heavier with each blink. Just as her breathing slowed, the sharp horn blasted again, this time louder. She groaned. Groggily, she sat up and flicked on her bedside lamp, casting her room in a soft glow.

The place was a mess. Clothes exploded from a suitcase still sitting exactly where she'd first put it down eight weeks before. Old dishes caked with food were piled precariously next to her laptop, symmetrical to the stack of notepads on the other side of her desk.

She rummaged for clothes, grabbing a pair of black jeans and a black blouse and pulling them on.

She stumbled into the bathroom to brush her teeth and tease her hair into a presentable bun, using concealer on the dark circles that had begun to form when she'd come across that audio from the bathroom after James had tipped her off about what he'd seen on the hike.

She raced down the stairs to where Brian and the rest of the crew were waiting by idling white vans. It was 5:33 a.m.

'You're late,' Brian said, bored.

'Yes, thanks,' Paige said, waving the team into vans before climbing into the front seat of one.

She looked over her clipboard on the short drive to the villa. She'd be doing interviews that morning with the remaining couples to get final reflections on the summer. They'd do a short break for lunch and then the couples would share a romantic last dance before the crew set up for the live finale. Once she had the details for the day in hand, Paige turned to the crew and rattled off assignments.

'Be sure you have all footage submitted before twelve. We've got a quick turnaround on this one and we'll need final approvals before we go live at eight thirty. Understood?'

She received a few sleepy nods.

'It's the last day, people. Let's make it count,' were Paige's parting words of inspiration before she headed into the Love Shack.

Her first interview of the day was with the person she least wanted to see. Declan showed up to his and Imogen's interview looking more hesitant than she'd seen him all season. Her one consolation in the past week had been that though she had undeniably hurt Oliver, at least Declan had been unflappable. But when she'd asked him to talk to James – Darcy's idea – and he'd broken down, she had started to doubt even that.

'Hi there, Declan, Imogen,' she said, trying to stay upbeat. Contestants fed off the energy she gave them, which was the most exhausting part of her job. In the past week of masking her feelings, she'd become so worn down that she could only feel relief at reaching the finale.

'Morning, Paige,' Imogen said sweetly.

'Hey,' Declan said, sitting. His hesitancy vanished as he smiled at Paige, his usual charming grin. This was a man who knew exactly what it meant to mask his feelings. 'How's it going?'

'Good, good. This shouldn't take too long – we've got tons to cover today.'

Declan nodded, the smile not dropping from his face.

'So… how are you two feeling about your chances?'

Declan looked sideways at Imogen, raising his eyebrows cockily. 'Well, Imogen and I are practically shoo-ins at this point, aren't we?'

His confidence would play well with the audience; this was Declan at his best. She shouldn't have worried about him.

Imogen beamed at Declan. 'I'm so excited for what the future holds for us. It's going to be one long adventure.'

'You don't think there's a chance for any of the others? What about James and Zoë?'

Declan scowled. 'I should hope the British public hasn't stooped *that* low.'

He'd led her into it perfectly. 'Do you feel like you've not made amends with James? Thought you two understood each other better after your chat.'

'Nah,' Declan said, tone flat. 'We've got it straightened out, but we'll never be mates.'

'Nothing like a little rivalry to keep things fresh,' Imogen said.

'And when you look back on your time here,' Paige said, 'you feel it's been a good experience?' It wasn't a question she had written down, but she was curious what Declan's answer would be.

'It's been amazing,' Imogen gushed. 'I've made so many lifelong friends, plus I snagged this dreamboat.'

Paige smiled, placating, then turned to Declan.

'Uh—' Declan frowned, seeming to choose his next words carefully. 'There have been highs and lows, but it was all for a summer in paradise, all in the name of true love. Right?'

When he looked at her, she felt a pang of unease at his raw expression. The line he'd given her had been suitably cheesy, but it seemed like he wanted some sort of confirmation from her.

'Right,' she said, after a pause. 'I mean, you've found Imogen. Where do you see the two of you, after the show?'

Declan's expression eased. 'Ah, well, I've got boxing to return to. Imogen is so supportive of my career, and I hope I can do the same for her. She wants to open a clothing store, and I think she'll be brilliant at it. She says I can be one of her models, if I've got any spare time.' Declan elbowed Imogen in the side and gave a short laugh. 'I think it will be easy, with the two of us.'

Paige nodded. Giving a perfect sound bite had always been Declan's strong suit, but there was something about his smile that made her want to cry.

'All right, that's it,' she said, suddenly wanting to be anywhere else.

Oliver had accused her of trying to ruin Declan's life, something she hadn't forgotten. When she was lying in bed, trying to get the few hours of sleep she could, his voice played over and over in her head. He was self-righteous, when it came down to it.

Did it count as being self-righteous if you were in the right?

She shook her head, clearing it, and noticed Declan giving her a funny look. 'Good luck,' she said, her voice coming out slightly uneven.

'Er – thanks.' He and Imogen stood, and Paige automatically flicked the camera off. His face cleared. 'Are you rooting for us?' he asked, his cocky demeanour back.

'Of course,' Paige said. It was a lie. At this point, she didn't care who won the show. She hardly cared that it was a good show. All she wanted was one night of uninterrupted sleep.

–

Darcy arrived at 7:50 p.m., a full twenty minutes late. Paige nearly had an aneurysm, but Brian swooped in before she could get too involved, ushering Darcy to her dressing room. Paige followed after taking some calming breaths, walking through the private part of the villa that the contestants didn't have access to. It wasn't nearly as glamorous on the production side of the house, mainly another bedroom the team had been using as a supply closet, Darcy's dressing room – sometimes doubling as a much-needed nap room – and the house's indoor kitchen.

'Ready?' Paige asked as she entered the dressing room, listening to her intercom. They'd already let the live audience into the garden to find their seats.

Tonight, Darcy was in an 80s-inspired suit dress, with a vaguely floral pattern of reds, greens, purples and blues. She wore dark smoky eyeshadow and a dramatic red lip.

'Nearly,' Darcy said, adding more powder to her already-perfect make-up. 'How are our Lovers?'

'Good,' Paige said, glancing at her clipboard. 'The sound-bites from this morning have been added to the montages. Here are your questions for the live interviews.' She placed a stack of notecards on the table near Darcy's elbow. She still wasn't looking at Paige, instead tousling her hair until it reached her preferred level of dishevelledness.

'Great,' Darcy said. 'How are our numbers?'

Paige consulted her clipboard again. 'As of an hour ago, we're up 5 per cent in voting over the same time last year.'

Darcy nodded absentmindedly, bending to fiddle with her blue suede boots. 'We'd hope to be at 10 per cent over last year.'

Paige's cheeks burned. They had talked about it, and only a week ago they had been on track to meet that goal. Unfortunately, due to the untimely departure of one fan favourite and the complete disinterest of another, viewership had stalled.

'There's still time,' she replied.

'I'm sure,' Darcy said, finally straightening. She grabbed the notecards from the table and walked out of the room. 'I'll just work my arse off to get us there, hmm?'

They made their way to the girls' dressing room and Brian's voice came through Paige's headset: 'Audience has been seated.'

'Brill,' Paige said, watching as Darcy chatted with the girls still applying make-up. 'And the sizzle reel?'

'Already rolling.'

'Cheers, Bri,' she said, turning to head to the bedroom to collect any stragglers. 'I'll be out in a moment.' She caught Darcy's eye and held up a hand to signal her five-minute warning.

As Paige crossed the hall, she noticed the door to the bathroom slightly ajar. Declan was there, staring at himself in the mirror.

It was only a split-second, Paige didn't pause on her way to the bedroom, but she was struck by the expression on his face. It wasn't the Declan she'd seen through the weeks, the boisterous, cocky man who had given her so many perfect moments to air to millions, the one she'd spoken to that morning. At first glance, she assumed he'd thrown water on his face to calm his nerves before the live show, but maybe he'd been crying. His face had been twisted in pain, but it was hard to know for sure, with her guilt over Oliver warping her perception.

She reached Brian in the outdoor kitchen, the crew's makeshift backstage for the finale. He smiled faintly at her, sweat collecting on his forehead.

'Last few hours now,' he said, putting out his hand. Paige took it. 'It's been a pleasure working with you.'

Paige was touched; she'd never pegged Brian for the sentimental type, but she'd take the small kindness he offered in the sea of chaos.

Darcy came out behind her, applause from the crowd rising at her appearance.

'All set?' she asked, looking between Brian and Paige expectantly. Brian nodded. 'Great!' She threw on her most dazzling smile and strolled out onto the grandstand stage the crew had constructed for the occasion. 'Hello, everybody! Are you ready to crown our winning couple for this year's *Summer of Love*?'

The crowd shouted enthusiastically, and Paige settled into her role of producing the live show. This was always the part she'd been good at, setting cues and calling shots.

'Thirty seconds out,' she called to the controllers, 'ready pre-taped interview highlights.' She paused, counting the seconds as she scanned Darcy's script, a speech she'd already memorised. 'Okay, take highlights.'

That pre-recorded segment bought them about five minutes to get the couples ready to walk out for their introductions. Paige turned to ask Brian to round them up, but found him already ushering them into a line.

'All right,' Paige said, forcing some pep into her voice. 'This is it! Congratulations on making it this far, and no matter what happens tonight, you all have been spectacular to work with.'

Zoë and Imogen smiled politely back at her from their spots in line, but the rest of the contestants had their eyes trained on the sliver of audience visible from behind the grandstand. Paige didn't take it to heart. Living in front of cameras – the viewers becoming more and more abstract as the weeks progressed – couldn't compare to screaming fans.

Paige studied Declan. He looked nothing like what she had thought she'd seen in the bathroom. His suit jacket was perfectly pressed, his head up and eyes clear. He even smiled at Imogen and leaned down to whisper something that made her laugh. It was a shame they wouldn't win.

'Thirty seconds,' Paige called. 'Count to three before following the previous couple, like we practised. Got it?'

She saw some nods and decided that was sufficient.

'All right, ready...'

Darcy's voice rang out as she began her introductions.

'And walk.'

—

Paige had reached the final hour of the show. If she survived this last exit interview with Declan, she would have made it through the worst. She would have proven she could do this absolutely mad, exhausting job that she'd worked towards for years.

Declan walked into the Love Shack looking almost relieved. It wasn't the reaction she had expected from the man who had confidently told her he would win hours earlier. His demeanour threw her off, and her pen nearly slipped out of her fingers as she twirled it distractedly.

'Hi,' she said, tucking a loose strand of hair behind her ear. This moment was the culmination of months of work that she'd put into the show. That was why her heart was beating so loudly in her ears. 'How are we doing tonight?'

Declan pursed his lips, his eyes sliding to the flashing red light of the camera. 'Well,' he began, 'obviously, it was disappointing that Imogen and I didn't win. But our relationship is as strong as ever, and I'm excited to see what the outside world has in store for us.'

Paige wondered if Declan had a PR team at all, or if he spent all of his free time spinning this crap on his own. That propensity should have been *good* for her, for the show. There was no reason that it should make her tense with sudden frustration, especially after months of the same from him.

The words came out of her mouth unbidden: 'You're planning on continuing your relationship with Imogen?'

It was a test, and, from his expression, it looked like he knew it. He took on a soothing tone, as though he could tell how wired she was. 'Of course I am. Finding Imogen was the best thing that's ever happened to me. Plus, it's good for you – another success story in the books, right?' He had the audacity to wink at her.

She inhaled sharply. 'Could you please stop thinking about what *I* want? What do *you* want, Declan?' His gaze moved, almost imperceptibly, to the camera standing next to her. She sighed, flicking it off. 'Better? Can we be properly introduced now?'

Declan chuckled, not losing any of his amiability. 'I don't know what's got you so shaken up. Sure, I put on a show for the cameras, but it's not like I've got any dark secrets. I'm not holding back.'

She pressed him further, desperately, stupidly wanting something real from him. 'How do you feel about the end of the show, cameras off?'

He gave the question a moment of thought, looking at her more earnestly. 'I got exactly what I came here for, didn't I?'

Paige assumed Declan had come on the show as a ploy to distract the public from his downward-trending boxing career. He could live a cushy life on sponsorships alone, especially after this exposure. She had known from the beginning that he wasn't there for love – but then again, few of them were.

She had taken the job cynical about the possibility of real love forming on a TV show. And yet there were examples of those who had proved her wrong over the weeks. Niall and Stella. Jack and Maeve.

And, of course, Oliver's face came unbidden to her mind. Her head felt too heavy on her shoulders, the guilt suddenly overwhelming.

'What about Oliver?' she blurted out. She had expected to feel even worse as her veneer cracked in front of a contestant.

Instead, she felt a slight measure of relief, an uncoiling in her neck.

The corner of Declan's mouth twitched. 'What about him?'

'Do you have any regrets?'

He slowly leaned back, and Paige could almost see the memories flickering across his face.

'I suppose so,' he said softly, as though he wasn't sure he wanted her to hear. 'I feel like maybe I could have stopped him from leaving, if I'd done things differently. I mean, we had a bit of a – a row. And that's why he left.'

Paige bit the inside of her mouth, hard. 'You think he left because of something you did?'

'Um—' He glanced at the camera again, as though checking she hadn't turned it back on, then shrugged. He looked as though they were talking about nothing significant, maybe the weather or their upcoming flight numbers. His voice, when he spoke, bore the brunt of his emotion. It came out gravelly and uneven: 'Yeah. I think so.'

The admission of the pain Paige had inflicted made everything easier. There was only one way to make this feeling stop. 'Oliver didn't leave because of you. He left because of me.'

Declan gave a humourless laugh. 'No offence, Paige, but you don't know what you're on about.'

She shook her head forcefully. 'I put Oliver in an impossible position, and he had to leave; he couldn't do it any more. Because of me.'

Declan's eyes flashed with emotion for a second, and she thought she could see some understanding, or anger, there. 'What did you do?' he demanded.

'I—' She cleared her throat. 'I knew about you two.'

Realisation dawned on Declan's face, and then unmistakable anger. 'What did you *do*?' His voice was tight and low.

She swallowed. 'I wanted him to go public with your relationship, to be honest about his feelings for you. But he wouldn't do it.'

'It wasn't a relationship,' Declan bit out. 'There was nothing to tell. Isn't that what he said?'

She closed her eyes, unable to look at him. 'No. That's not what he said.' She didn't know how to make him understand what had happened when she hardly understood it herself. It had all got out of control so quickly. 'He called my bluff – he knew I couldn't do anything without his participation. Without the two of you being together, the happy ending that would justify everything else. Otherwise it would look like the show had outed you both for publicity.'

She opened her eyes and immediately regretted it. Declan wore a blank expression, but his posture was tense and his eyes held a cold fury.

'It would *look* like that?' he spat out. 'You still can't own up to it? It didn't *look* like that, it *was* like that.'

'I shouldn't have done it.' Her voice came out small. 'I shouldn't have tried to force his hand. But I didn't mean for it to all go so wrong, please believe me. I wanted the two of you to be able to be together, and I thought you both wanted that too.'

'Don't pretend to care about what *we* wanted.'

He stood, not looking at her, and offered no other parting words as he slammed the door behind him. The adrenaline that had been keeping Paige upright dissipated, and she lowered herself into the closest chair.

Darcy found her there hours later.

'Paige,' she barked. 'Where have you *been*? I've been looking everywhere.'

'Here,' Paige said, not moving.

Darcy crossed her arms, surveying the room. 'Doing what exactly?'

'Nothing.'

'Come on,' Darcy said, laying a manicured hand on her shoulder. 'We've wrapped; let's go out and celebrate!'

'I'm all right,' Paige said, barely feeling the words come out.

'Come on,' Darcy said again. 'There are some people who I want to introduce you to.'

'No,' Paige said, more forcefully. 'I'm not going.' She shrugged Darcy's hand off and stood, heading for the door.

'You *have* to go,' Darcy said, her voice taking on a hard edge. Paige turned to see her standing in the middle of the room – the one Paige had spent nearly all summer trapped in – with barely concealed outrage on her face.

'No, I don't,' she said, 'because I quit.' And she walked out the door.

Chapter 25

Oliver

One Week Until Finale

Oliver had expected relief to wash over him as soon as he got to Heathrow, but instead he just felt lost. He had spent nearly two months following strict rules, unable to make decisions for himself, and now he was returning to the mess of his real life. He did the only thing he could think of, and rang his best mate.

Will met him in the same spot of the car park as he had four months ago, when Oliver had returned from New York. When he spotted Oliver, he ran over to wrap him in a hug, clutching him tightly.

'Are those tears in your eyes?' Oliver quipped, pulling back to look at his friend's flushed face.

Will wiped a cheek with the back of his hand. 'This is the longest we've been apart in ten years. I can have a cry about it – I'm secure enough in my masculinity.' He lifted Oliver's suitcase into the boot as Oliver slid into the familiar front seat.

Will spent several minutes jiggling the boot's latch before it finally held, arriving to the driver's seat with a triumphant smile. 'Your place or mine, then?'

Oliver didn't want to face his flat, but he knew the discomfort wouldn't go away unless he acted on it. A plan was starting to form in his mind. 'Mine. I have a few things I need to sort there.'

249

'So… I know the full interrogation has to wait until the gang's assembled,' Will said, pulling out of the car park, 'but I have a few urgent matters to clear up.'

'What's that?'

'What happened at the end?' Will asked intently. 'You were doing great. Not just great, you were bloody *fantastic*.' He glanced at Oliver. 'And then, what? You had a breakdown and quit the show. So, are you in love with Maeve?'

Oliver snorted. 'Is that what's going around?'

Will shrugged. 'You were clearly losing the plot, telling Eavie you loved Maeve and then upping and leaving. What am I missing?'

'Er—' Oliver rubbed the back of his neck, apprehensive to jump right in. 'All right. Please don't freak out. I wanted to wait until you had a few pints in you.'

Will abandoned any pretence of watching the road, turning to look sharply at Oliver. 'What is it?'

He could feel his face reddening. He didn't know how to put it eloquently, so he went for direct. 'I, er, kind of fell for a man.'

'*Declan King?!*' Will bellowed, and Oliver jumped as the car swerved into the next lane over.

'Shall I take over the driving?' Oliver asked, putting a hand on the wheel.

'You can't drop *that* on me in the middle of the road. That's your foul, not mine.' Will was clearly trying hard to not turn fully towards Oliver. '*Declan King?* Who would have thought you'd go for the meatheads? Tell me everything, now.'

Oliver almost protested the meathead comment, but he didn't want to act overly defensive. He was in the middle of a balancing act. 'There's not much to tell,' he said slowly. 'I mean, you've seen everything already, haven't you?'

'Bullshit,' Will barked. 'There's a story here. How did I not see it? But… how could I have known? How did *you* know?'

'Well, it definitely wasn't an immediate realisation.' He sighed, thinking of how to explain it properly without outing

Declan. He could at least do that much for him. 'Declan had this idea that playing up a bromance would win us more screen time. And Paige – one of the producers – was on board with it.'

Will nodded. 'Yeah, people thought you two were funny together. So, was that the first time you'd ever suspected…?'

'I'm as confused as you are,' Oliver said, frowning. 'Practically all of my mates are gay. How did I never even consider the possibility?'

'Because,' Will said slowly, 'let's face it, you've only ever been attracted to one person in your life, and she happened to be a woman.' The corner of his mouth twitched. 'Speaking of Sophie, what does she have to say about all this?'

'Er—' Oliver glanced at his phone, which was sitting in his lap. Sophie: three missed calls, eight text messages, all unopened. 'I haven't spoken to her yet.'

Will gave him a long, sideways look. 'Oh, you *really* like this guy, huh?'

'What do you mean?' Oliver asked, feeling his face redden.

'You've talked to Sophie every day since the break-up.' Oliver made to protest, and Will swatted his shoulder. 'You may have lied to me about it, because you didn't want to look pathetic, but I knew.'

'Well, I've spent seven weeks *not* talking to her,' Oliver said defensively.

'Exactly,' Will said, tapping his nose. 'And you didn't call her as soon as you had your phone back.'

'Um,' Oliver muttered, unsure of how to respond. 'I had other things on my mind.'

'Will you listen to yourself? You had other things on your mind, besides your ex-girlfriend? That is *not* the bloke I said goodbye to two months ago.'

'Oh,' Oliver said. 'You're… right.'

'I mean,' Will said, becoming uncharacteristically serious, 'I'm not going to lie, we were all worried about you, much more so than we let on.'

Oliver looked out the window, pondering this, and realised they were only a minute away from his flat. 'Something else I've been thinking about…' he said. 'Could you help me move?'

Will glanced over at him, startled. 'Move? *You?*'

Oliver cracked a smile. 'Moving's a bridge too far?'

Will shook his head, looking a bit dizzy. 'You get off the plane, you fancy a man, you're not talking to Sophie, and you're moving? Did they put some sort of chip in your brain? Are you a robot now?' He waved his hand in front of Oliver's face. 'Oliver, if you're in there, blink twice.'

Oliver swatted his hand away. 'It's time, that's all.'

–

Oliver and Will stared at the mess of the flat in horror.

'Well, no wonder you would never ask me over,' Will said, clapping him on the back.

Oliver examined the dirty floors, the piles of health forms required for his dance company, haphazard stacks of Sophie's books, and one extremely dead cactus. The flat that had once been meticulously kept by him and Sophie had fallen into disarray as Oliver had stuffed his already busy schedule with odd jobs to cover her portion of the rent. Arriving there with fresh eyes made it apparent: he'd become one of the people highlighted on hoarder TV shows. There, another reality show to add to his repertoire.

'Jesus,' he said, after a long silence. 'We need industrial bin bags.'

It took the two of them a few hours to make the place more presentable, but Oliver continued on past that, packing away anything he didn't need immediately. It wasn't the most organised move in history, but at least he was trying.

Somewhere around the three-hour mark, Will let out a noise that could only be described as a mix between a squeak and a gasp.

'All right there?' Oliver called from his position half-under the sofa, reaching for his favourite jumper that had somehow got wedged between the back leg and the wall.

'You should probably come and see this.' Will's voice was strained. Oliver hoped he hadn't found any dead pests.

'I swear, if you make me touch a spider—' Oliver froze, still only half upright. Will was holding a sizable envelope.

'Is that—?' Oliver started, grabbing it from him.

The red letters on the front spelled out *Manhattan Ballet*. Oliver swallowed, hard.

'Are you breathing?' Will asked.

'Think so,' he managed.

'Can you open it?'

'Think so,' he repeated, frowning at the envelope as though it had presented him with a difficult riddle.

'Just tear it,' Will said, impatient.

Oliver did, pulling out a thick sheet of paper. 'All right... I...' He read the important bit a few times, to be sure. 'I got in. I got into Manhattan Ballet.'

'Well done,' Will said, hugging a motionless Oliver from the side.

'Hmm,' he said, squinting to read the sentence again. Yes, that was certainly what it said. How odd, that he didn't feel pure joy. 'It is good. You're right.'

'Are you... in shock?' Will asked carefully.

'Probably,' he agreed. That was the explanation. 'Wow,' he said, looking at his friend's smile and replicating it, 'this is incredible.'

'You don't know if you'll take it, do you?' Will asked, peering at him. He didn't sound altogether surprised by what should have been a ridiculous statement. Will, of all people, should be certain Oliver would take the job. He'd heard enough about it over the years.

'Of course I'm going to take it,' Oliver snapped without thinking. 'It's bloody Manhattan Ballet. People don't say no to them.'

253

'Well…' Will said, 'are you going to tell Sophie?'

Oliver nodded. 'Definitely.'

He blinked, his hands moving numbly, muscle memory taking over to dial Sophie's number. Before he had the chance to regret it, she picked up.

'Hey, you're back!' There was noise in the background, but her voice was clear.

He hadn't heard it in so long, and he was shocked he felt no pull, no tightening in his chest, nothing except for a vague and comfortable fondness. 'Hi. Shall I ring you later, when you're home?'

'It's okay, I'm on break right now. I've only got… fifteen minutes. How are you?' The voices in the background quieted, and Oliver assumed she'd found a more private spot in the studio.

He took a deep breath. 'I got in.'

There was a sharp intake of breath on the other end. 'Oh, wow. That's brilliant, Oliver!'

'Thanks.' He paused, unsure of how to continue.

Sophie seemed to sense his hesitation. 'How are you feeling?'

'I feel… good,' he said. 'I feel the way you're supposed to feel when you accomplish your biggest life goal, I think.'

'Mhmm,' Sophie said. 'And you're taking the spot?'

'Of course I am,' he said quickly. 'But, Soph – I want to be clear, I'm not moving to New York to try to win you back. When I auditioned, I thought that maybe…' He cleared his throat, pointedly not looking at Will. 'But I don't think we make sense any more.'

There was no simple way to articulate everything he felt, everything he'd learned about himself and them in the past two months.

'I never moved out of our flat,' he said finally, though he wasn't sure why that was what he'd settled on. 'I sat here every day for months, paying your part of the rent and mine, waiting for you to come back.'

'Oh God,' Sophie said. 'I made a mess of things, didn't I? I'll pay you back. You should've said, I didn't mean to—' She sighed. 'Well, anyway. I'm sorry.'

'Me too.'

They let silence creep onto the line, and Oliver thought about all the things that would remain unsaid between them. For months, he'd driven himself mad talking to her every night, unwilling to ask the question he had so desperately wanted answered. In the quiet, he realised no answer from her would ever satisfy him.

Oliver heard a loudspeaker in the background. 'They're calling us back now... But I guess I'll see you soon?'

'Yes, see you soon.'

As Oliver hung up, he made himself turn to Will, expecting either judgement or overbearing worry. Instead, he found his friend scrupulously dusting the dead cactus on his kitchen counter, clearly pretending not to be eavesdropping.

'Well?' Oliver asked.

Will looked at him with only mild concern. Oliver found that it bothered him less now, and that it looked more like compassion than pity.

Oliver smiled slowly. 'You know, I think I'll keep you around, even after the move.'

Will put a hand over his heart, feigning shock. 'And here I was, worried I would lose you to the influencer crowd.'

—

That Friday, Will insisted their friends gather to watch the finale together. They met in Oliver's nearly empty flat. He had packed almost everything already, though he was still looking for a place in New York. After things were settled, his plan in place once again, he finally felt like he could face Declan, even if it was just on screen.

'This place is a ghost town,' Divya said, dry as ever, shucking off her jacket in the doorway.

A windswept Hanna followed behind her, carrying a bottle of wine. 'Weather's mad for August, isn't it? I think a storm is brewing.'

He gave them both hugs. 'Glad you could make it. It's been too long.'

Hanna wriggled out of his grasp. 'Well, we wanted to come over sooner, but were told there might be toxic waste disposal in progress.'

They were second to arrive, after Will, who had taken to crashing most nights on Oliver's uncomfortable couch. He assured Oliver it was not an inconvenience, and Oliver, despite his months of insistence that no one help him, let Will do what he wanted. It was nice to have someone around all the time, so the flat didn't feel so empty.

'Looks *loads* better than it did before I went at it with a mop,' Will said, patting the spot next him on the couch.

'So,' Divya said, sitting beside Will and shooting Oliver a sly look, 'excited to see the man of your dreams tonight?'

Oliver blushed. His friends had been suitably shocked when he'd told them about Declan, and Will had found their reactions endlessly entertaining, insisting he hadn't been surprised, not in the slightest, when Oliver had told him he was bisexual.

'Please don't call him that.'

'Why? He's the fittest on the show, not a bad choice at all.' Her gaze was more approving than he'd expected.

Someone knocking saved Oliver from responding.

'How are we the last ones here?' Max asked, when Hanna opened the door on her way to the kitchen for a corkscrew. 'We live ten metres down the hall.'

'Why isn't it on?!' Chloe demanded from Max's side, ushering him in and closing the door behind them. 'We're going to miss the recap!'

Oliver held up a pacifying hand, turning the TV on. His friends gathered around, Hanna leaning on him from the left and Chloe rubbing the top of his head affectionately. He felt an overwhelming sense of warmth just sitting with them.

'And that's what you missed on *Summer of Love!*' Neil Steel declared over panning shots of the villa's exterior.

Oliver was startled by the longing he felt looking at the patio area where he'd spent so many afternoons lounging, the kitchen where he'd made breakfast in the mornings, the deep turquoise of the pool. Even in the comfort of his friends' company, it still felt like something was missing.

The footage seamlessly transitioned into a montage of Jack and Maeve's relationship, from Jack kissing her hand during truth or dare the first week to their final slow dance.

'He's certainly not what I expected to find when I agreed to come on this show,' Maeve was saying, gazing adoringly at Jack, who wore a ridiculously big grin.

'I think I wore her down with my boyish charm!'

'Boyish?' Maeve teased. 'You're practically an old man.'

'Take that back,' Jack said, going in as if to tickle her but instead dropping a quick kiss to her forehead.

'They're *so* cute,' Chloe gushed. 'Can't believe she started with that prick Callum and ended up with the sweetest bloke of all.'

It shouldn't have been surprising that Chloe had a perspective on his friends' public relationship, but Oliver realised he hadn't considered how weird this situation would be for him.

'Ooh,' Divya said, smirking at Oliver as Declan and Imogen appeared on screen. 'Declan's up. This should be good.'

Declan wore an expression he'd never directed at Oliver, rendering him almost unrecognisable. 'Imogen and I are practically shoo-ins at this point,' he said, with a smile that wasn't even close to the real thing.

Oliver somehow hadn't considered that the Declan on TV would be the version of him that everyone saw, not the one he knew. A lump formed in the back of his throat at the thought that he would never see that version of Declan again. He had been trying to be optimistic about the future – he had so many options ahead of him, so many directions to take his life in. And yet none of them involved the one thing he was certain he wanted.

On screen, Imogen smiled at Declan. 'I'm so excited for what the future holds. It's going to be one long adventure.'

Watching them together, with his friends representing only a sliver of the audience who had no idea what had happened, made Oliver suddenly nauseous.

'Ugh,' Chloe said, as another montage began, this time of James and Zoë. 'I wish they would stop replaying clips I've already seen. I want to know who wins.'

'Anyone want more wine?' Oliver asked feebly, heading for the kitchen without waiting for a response. He stuck his head in the fridge, keeping it in the cool air for a long moment. By the time he returned with a glass of wine, Darcy was getting ready to announce third place.

She made unnerving eye contact with the camera, and Oliver gulped involuntarily as the live crowd cheered. 'In third place...' Darcy said dramatically, 'we have... Declan and Imogen!'

Declan and Imogen smiled graciously from the side of the stage. The camera didn't have a good angle on Declan's face, but Oliver thought he looked almost relieved.

'Declan,' Darcy said cloyingly, 'how does it feel to get so close, and lose it all?'

'Well, Darcy,' Declan started, his voice oozing with charm, 'you know how much I hate to lose out on anything.' He paused to look fondly at Imogen. 'But somehow I still feel like a winner right now.'

Darcy frowned, turning to Imogen. 'Imogen, you fell for Declan the moment you entered the villa. How does it feel knowing it simply wasn't enough?'

Divya snorted. 'No holds barred, huh?'

Imogen made a face like she was stifling a laugh. 'It was enough. I have the best boyfriend in the world.' Declan draped an arm around her shoulders and she beamed.

'And now,' Darcy said abruptly, looking back at the two remaining couples, 'for your *Summer of Love* winners! Which couple has the British public voted their favourite?'

The camera cut between the final two couples: Jack and Meave and James and Zoë.

'Jack looks like he's going to piss himself,' Max said.

'The winners of *Summer of Love* Season 10 are... Jack and Maeve!'

A burst of confetti engulfed the contestants, torrents of gold paper blocking the camera's view. When it cleared, Jack and Maeve were embracing, with James scowling in the background.

'Good on them,' Oliver managed to get out. He was aware that the others were waiting for a reaction, but his eyes were trained on the sliver of Declan's face visible in the commotion.

'You okay?' Hanna asked. She turned towards Oliver, not looking at the TV.

'Great,' he muttered, knowing not a single person in the room would believe him.

Chapter 26

Oliver

Two Weeks Post-Finale

Oliver was walking back to Will's flat when Maeve called him.

'Glad to know you made it out alive,' he said wryly.

'Ha,' she said. 'Sorry I didn't call right away – it's been mad. How are you?'

'Yeah, fine,' he said, waiting for the light to change at the crossing. 'Strangers keep sending me DMs saying they want to have my babies, you know, the usual.'

'Good,' she said briskly. 'So, when are you free?'

'Oh, er, I've quit my job, so no rehearsals or anything to schedule around. But, well...' He didn't want to say it, but he knew she would find out soon enough. 'Thing is, I'm leaving for New York at the end of the month. So, if you can fit something in before then...'

There was a moment of silence on the other end. 'You're moving?' she asked finally.

'I got into Manhattan Ballet,' Oliver said in a rush. 'How's this weekend?'

'You... leaving London?'

'Yes,' he said. This was going about as poorly as possible. 'I mean, I'm sure I'll come back home to visit.' He had no idea how he would do it on his salary, but the idea of leaving London forever was too painful to contemplate. 'Trying not to think about it. Anyway, let's meet up soon.'

'Um, okay,' Maeve said, uncertain. 'What about Saturday?'

Oliver ran through his list of commitments and came up blank. 'Yeah, that's brilliant. Drinks?'

'Actually, Jack's moved to London, so I'm hosting a small welcome party for him. Are you in?'

Oliver rubbed his forehead. He didn't like where this was going. A party for Jack would certainly involve Declan. 'Er – I'm a bit under the weather, now that you mention it.'

'Oh, piss off,' Maeve replied, without any venom. 'You'd agreed to come when it was only me.'

'Yes, which was sneaky of you. I'm not sure I like cut-throat Maeve.'

'You consider me trying to get you to see your friends cut-throat? Darling, you wouldn't want to see me at work.'

He grasped for any excuse. 'I hardly think Jack wants to see me. Apparently people are saying that I'm in love with you?'

Maeve sighed. 'Don't be thick, Oliver. Jack knows you're not in love with me. *Honestly.*' She paused for a moment. 'Though I'm sure he'd love to hear why you let Eavie run with that story. As would I, if you're handing out explanations.'

Oliver arrived at Will's building and fumbled for his keys. 'I wanted her off my back,' he said feebly.

'Well, why don't you come to the party and tell Jack that?' Maeve said.

Oliver frowned, suspicious, and inserted the key into the door. 'Who else will be there?'

'Oh,' Maeve said nonchalantly, 'Holly is in town, and the London crowd will be there, of course.'

Oliver climbed the stairs, thinking quickly. 'Well, like I said, I'm coming down with something,' he tried, opening the door to the flat and giving an unconvincing cough. He had no idea what would happen to him if he was in a room with Declan without the cameras watching. He was terrified to find out.

'What's up?' Will called from the couch. Oliver waved him off, pointing at his phone and sitting at the kitchen table.

'*Oliver.*' Maeve had clearly reached the end of her rope. 'You can be honest now; no one's recording. Why are you avoiding Declan?'

'He asked me to give him space to be with Imogen,' Oliver said, in some version of the truth. 'And they're still together, aren't they?' He paused, wondering if that made him sound like a pathetic stalker. Declan and Imogen had been spotted together a few times since the show had wrapped. She was, in all ways, the new Georgia. 'Or I haven't heard that they've broken up?' he tried.

'Declan King is trending,' Will said.

Oliver waved a hand to quiet him. Declan had always had the most impeccable timing.

He could practically hear Maeve's eyes roll through the phone. 'That would be something you could ask him at the party, wouldn't it? That's the great thing about friends – you don't have to google them to find out who they're dating.'

Oliver flushed, embarrassed by the accuracy of the accusation.

'Oh shit! Declan King is retiring from boxing,' Will called over.

'Will, I'm kind of in the middle of something here,' Oliver grumbled. He couldn't focus on the conversation with Maeve if he thought about Declan retiring from boxing. Boxing was Declan's whole life. Oliver wondered how he'd decided it was time to retire, and how he'd told his dad about it.

'Sorry about that…' he continued, 'But, anyway, I don't think we're friends.'

'*Holy shit,*' Will exclaimed. 'Oliver—'

'Just a moment,' Oliver said impatiently. 'I'm on the phone.'

'Your circumstances have changed,' Maeve said. 'Even if he's been hanging out with Imogen, you don't know that he doesn't want to see you. I suspect it's quite the opposite.'

'Why?' he asked quickly. 'Has he said something?'

'*Boys,*' was all Maeve had to say to that.

'*Oliver*,' Will said, now looming over him. He placed his phone deliberately on the table, facing Oliver. The screen displayed a series of posts from the past few minutes, and Oliver scanned them, his heart racing.

'I have to go now,' he managed, dropping his phone onto the table.

He stared up at Will, dazed. 'Is this…?' He couldn't even finish the thought.

'Declan King just came out.' Will folded his arms dramatically. 'Now… is there something you want to tell me, *mate*?'

Chapter 27

Declan

Two Weeks Post-Finale

Declan breathed out slowly, trying to keep calm as he watched Imogen pace in front of him. The door behind her led to a room filled with dozens of reporters – all of them waiting for him.

'Can you not?' Georgia said, not unkindly, to Imogen. Imogen whirled around, eyes wide.

'Sorry,' she said, quickly sitting on Declan's other side. 'Didn't even realise I was doing it.'

Declan grimaced. 'It's okay,' he said. 'To be honest, I didn't notice.'

'It's going to be all right, Decs,' Georgia said.

'Yeah!' Imogen agreed.

Declan looked between them. 'You guys don't need to be so nice to me,' he said finally.

'Nonsense,' Imogen responded, as Georgia said, 'Oh, piss off.'

Declan huffed out a laugh and the girls grinned at each other. He'd been nervous to introduce Imogen to Georgia when they'd first got back to London, but he needn't have worried. They were thick as thieves now.

It had been an interesting couple of weeks. He and Imogen had exited the plane with the rest of the couples to find Georgia waiting for them. Declan hadn't even attempted to play coy, spilling his guts about everything on the drive back to his flat. Georgia hadn't looked surprised by any of it; she'd simply turned to him and asked, 'What now?'

Which was how Declan found himself wanting to completely upend his life. He stood and pressed his suit jacket down, easing imaginary wrinkles. This was what he wanted. He hadn't spent the past two weeks in prep meetings with his manager, agent and father on a passing whim. He wanted this, even though it was the most terrifying thing he'd ever done.

His dad opened the press room door, slipping into the hallway with Declan's brother at his side. His eyes were kind when they met Declan's. Jim had been understanding when Declan had told him his plan to retire and come out in one fell swoop. He hadn't been disappointed, like Declan had expected. He had simply asked if he was sure, and had hugged him after hearing that he was.

'All right,' his dad said, laying a hand on his shoulder. 'They're ready for you.'

A near-blinding cascade of camera flashes went off as Declan entered the room.

'Hello, everybody,' he said, leaning in to speak clearly into the microphone. 'Thank you for coming.'

He was met with silence as the reporters poised their pens. He saw a few lean forwards, their phones held out to record.

'Right, well,' Declan said, glancing at his hands. Imogen had suggested he bring notecards and now he wished he had listened to her, if only to keep them from shaking. 'I'll be retiring from boxing effective immediately.'

A massive roar of questions followed. He held up a hand for quiet, pointing at a slim woman in the front row.

'Declan,' she began, 'you're still a relatively young athlete – why retire at this age? Is it because of the injury you sustained earlier this year?'

'This has nothing to do with that.' Declan rolled his left wrist to display a full range of motion. 'Boxing is just no longer my main interest. I've got other priorities. Plus,' – he caught his brother's eye at the back of the room – 'I want to give Aaron a fighting chance in the ring.' Aaron grinned.

The joke got him a few laughs before more hands shot into the air. Declan pointed to a stout man towards the back.

'What are your plans for retirement? You mentioned other priorities; will you be pursuing another career?'

Declan thought for a moment. 'I have no set plans at the moment, and I reckon I've earned a bit of a break. My priorities are personal.' That caused a murmur among the crowd.

Another woman raised her hand, and Declan nodded at her.

'You were on the latest season of *Summer of Love*, where you met and were romantically connected with' – she consulted her notes – 'Imogen Vichare. Does she have anything to do with your shifting priorities?'

Declan chuckled. 'No, I'm sorry to say she does not. Imogen and I are not dating,' Declan said, for the first time looking directly at the cameras lining the back wall of the room. 'We were never dating. It was all for the show.' Another flurry of hands shot up, but Declan ignored them, clearing his throat.

'Which brings me to my next announcement,' he said. 'And I want to be clear: I'm choosing to tell you this not because I think you're entitled to know, but because I'm tired of keeping it a secret.'

Declan glanced over at Georgia, standing with his dad, his brother and Imogen. He couldn't read her expression with the lights glaring on him, but if he had to guess, he'd say she looked proud.

He took one final deep breath in and said, 'I'm gay. I never found that relevant to my career, so I didn't share it publicly. For any of my fans who are disappointed, I can honestly say I don't care.'

There was a brief moment where no one said anything. Declan could see the red blinking lights of the cameras at the back of the room. He cleared his throat again.

'And I won't be taking any questions about this, because, frankly, it's no one's business. So, um, thank you.'

—

Declan pushed the button for the fifth floor, staring at his blurry reflection in the lift's doors and trying unsuccessfully to convince himself he wasn't nervous.

Besides a string of exclamation points from Holly, a mind-blown emoji from Jack and a long text from Niall about his commitment to allyship, none of the other contestants had reached out to Declan after his press conference. It didn't do much to calm his nerves now that he was seeing them all again, and that wasn't even the night's main source of anxiety.

The lift dinged, and Declan could hear the low murmur of the party from the hallway. He knocked, steeling himself.

The door swung open to reveal a beaming Maeve. She had curled her hair and wore a champagne slip dress, and looked much livelier than she had on the show. Declan supposed they'd all got worn down by the end.

'Hi,' she said, hugging him tightly. 'I'm so glad you could make it.'

'Are you kidding?' Declan responded, handing over the bottle of wine he'd brought for the occasion. 'I wouldn't miss this.'

He meant it. When Declan had got the text from Maeve suggesting a reunion, he had hoped it would give him the opportunity to make things right with Oliver.

Maeve looked as though she knew exactly what he was thinking. 'They're straight back,' she said, stepping aside.

The flat was nice: modern features with clean lines, but filled with colourful knick-knacks and art pieces Maeve must have collected on her travels.

'There he is!' Jack yelled when Declan stepped into the living room. 'Man of the fucking hour.'

Declan was immediately engulfed in a hug.

'Welcome to London!' Declan said, scanning the rest of the room over Jack's shoulder.

Holly was there, sitting close to Owen on Maeve's sectional. Imogen, Zoë, Faye and Eavie were gathered by the kitchen island across the way. No Oliver yet. He reminded himself that it was still early.

Jack pouted comically. 'I can't believe you tried to steal my thunder,' he said. 'Coming out two days before my party. Very rude. You could've at least given me a heads up.' It was said in jest, but Declan could tell Jack was a bit hurt.

'What can I say? I live for the drama.' Declan knocked Jack's shoulder and hoped the apology was clear on his face.

'Jack, you're a terrible host. Get the man a beer!' Holly called over.

'Why don't you make him a drink?' Jack shot back. Holly stood and Declan slung an arm around her.

'Hi, you,' he whispered into her ear. 'Fancy that Owen bloke managing an invite.' She squeezed his ribs threateningly, cheeks flushed.

'Right, one old fashioned coming up,' she said, heading to the kitchen.

He followed her. 'I should come up to Manchester and get the real Holly, hot bartender experience.'

She scoffed. 'If you could make it in. Ever since I got back, it's been bedlam.' She dropped a sugar cube and a dash of bitters into the bottom of the shaker, muddling them before adding in the bourbon.

'Beating blokes off with a stick now?' he asked. She pinned him with a hard glare as she shook the cocktail, and Declan's grin widened. 'Well, I'm newly unemployed. Can I put in an application for bodyguard of one Holly Henderson?'

'Application denied,' she said, pouring his drink and sliding it across the counter. 'Besides, the pay would be shit.' With that, she turned and flounced back to Owen. Declan took a sip of his drink and immediately understood why Holly's bar was so crowded.

'Hello, stranger,' Imogen called from the other end of the counter, giving him a once-over. 'Nice outfit.'

Declan nodded to the other girls. 'Thanks, my ex picked it out.'

'Well, she has impeccable taste,' Imogen said, sipping her wine.

'In everything but men,' Declan agreed, dropping a kiss to her cheek. He glanced at Zoë, who was watching the exchange curiously.

'Hiya, Zo,' he said. 'I didn't know you'd be here. Good to see you.'

'You, too.'

'Where's James?' he asked, and caught a warning look from Faye.

'We broke up,' Zoë said flatly, taking a long pull of her drink and crossing her arms. Imogen put a hand on her shoulder.

'Oh. I'm sorry.'

Zoë shot him an incredulous look.

'No, honest. I'm not his biggest fan, but I know how you felt about him.'

Zoë swirled her drink. 'Yeah, well, I thought I did too.' She sighed. 'Turns out a three-week fling on a TV show doesn't necessarily equate to true love. I should've stuck with you and gone for the win like I'd planned.'

He grabbed her hand, squeezing it gently, and she gave him a small smile.

'We would've had it in the bag,' he said, and saw a hint of amusement creep into her eyes. He groped for something better to say. 'You're way too good for him anyway.'

'God,' Zoë said with a laugh, 'this is painful. I don't know what's worse, getting dumped by a half-rate musician or getting comforted by my gay kind-of-ex-boyfriend. I suppose I should just be happy this isn't being televised.'

Declan laughed with her. 'Sorry, I'm bad at this.' He glanced towards the door almost involuntarily.

'Do you know if Oliver is coming?' Eavie asked.

He shrugged, trying to act casual. 'I dunno. Haven't spoken to him since the show.'

'Me neither, and I feel awful about how we left things,' Eavie said.

Zoë rolled her eyes. 'He was being a prick and you stuck up for yourself. You shouldn't feel bad.'

Eavie fiddled with her hands. 'Yes, well. I think the stress was getting to all of us.'

'I know,' Imogen said earnestly, 'I started running out of outfits.'

'Yeah, the outfits,' Declan said, looking at Imogen instead of the door. 'That's what I was worried about.'

They rejoined the group in the living room. Maeve was lounging on a brightly patterned floor pillow and Declan plopped himself next to her, letting the girls take the last spots on the sectional.

He waited until the room was buzzing with conversation before turning to Maeve, and murmuring: 'So, where's Oliver?'

Maeve frowned. 'I'm not sure he's coming,' she said. 'I tried his phone again just now, but couldn't get a hold of him. He was pretty busy this week; he wasn't sure he'd be able to get away.'

'Oh,' Declan said woodenly, even as his heart sank. 'Already rehearsing, then?' He tried to sound aloof, even though he'd gone so far as to look through the upcoming schedule for Oliver's dance company and knew their rehearsals wouldn't start for another week. The thought of buying tickets to the next performance had crossed Declan's mind more than once.

'Well, actually...' Maeve said, guilt etching her features, 'he got the New York job, so he's moving at the end of the month.'

'Oh.'

Not only was Oliver not coming to the party, but he was moving across an entire ocean. Declan couldn't find it in himself to be angry. It was fitting for Oliver to run off to New York and fulfil his lifelong dream. Declan couldn't keep him from that – he was just a boy Oliver had kissed twice on a rather strange holiday.

'I'm so sorry,' Maeve said, putting a hand on his knee.

Declan nodded absently, his mind creating increasingly unrealistic scenarios of Oliver's perfect life in New York as he tried to fight the sour taste building in his mouth.

He didn't pay much attention to the party after that, choosing to focus on drinking and making sufficiently engaged facial expressions to keep the attention off him.

He didn't know what he'd been thinking – that he'd come out and Oliver would come crawling back to him? He had come out for himself, and he had quit boxing for himself too. But Declan had thought that maybe without those obstacles between them, and after he'd apologised, there would be nothing stopping him and Oliver from picking up where they'd left off.

Ever since Paige had told him what she'd done, he'd held on to one last shred of hope – never once had he let himself consider that this would be the end for them.

Noticing his drink was empty again, Declan forced himself off the floor and walked to the kitchen, Imogen following behind him.

'What is it?' Imogen whispered when they were out of earshot of the others. 'You're back to zombie Declan, and I don't like it.'

Declan didn't look at her as he reached across the island and refilled her wine glass. 'I don't know what you mean.'

'We're down one ballet dancer at tonight's festivities,' she continued. 'That wouldn't have anything to do with your peppy mood, hmm?'

'He's not coming,' Declan said, staring into the empty cocktail shaker in front of him.

Imogen sighed. 'You can't give up,' she said, putting a hand on his arm. Declan pulled away and poured bourbon into his glass distractedly.

'He obviously doesn't want to see me,' he said, taking a sip and enjoying the burn down his throat. 'And I don't blame him.'

Imogen looked like she wanted to say more, but he left before she could get another word in. He chose a spot between Jack and Owen, determined to do a better job of hiding his heartbreak.

'So, how's the new place?' he asked Jack, trying for a smile.

'It's a shoebox,' Jack said. 'Even winning £50,000, I'm still on a teacher's salary.'

'He's being modest,' Maeve cut in. 'He's been promoted to head of the English department at his school.'

Jack grinned. 'Yes, well,' he said, 'it doesn't come with much of a raise, but it does come with an office that's bigger than my new flat, so...'

Declan laughed as the doorbell rang over the blare of the music. Maeve popped up from her spot on the floor and yelled out, 'Coming!'

'You'll have to have me ov—'

'Well, look who finally decided to show,' Jack interrupted, and Declan turned to see a damp Oliver walking into the room. The group met him with shouts of welcome.

'Hey,' Oliver said, waving as Maeve grabbed his jacket, shuffling him more firmly into the room. 'Sorry, got caught in the rain.'

'You just didn't want to face my wrath after trying to steal my girl. Not cool, bro,' Jack said, pulling him into a hug.

'You caught me,' Oliver deadpanned, finally glancing at Declan. He wished he could tell what Oliver was thinking, but besides an awkward smile, he gave Declan nothing to go on.

'This one's just been to visit Niall,' Jack said, grabbing Owen and tugging him over to Oliver. Declan lost the end of his sentence as the others restarted conversations around him.

He watched Oliver laugh at something Owen said, then looked away quickly, feeling self-conscious. As he scanned the rest of the group, hoping no one had seen him staring, he made eye contact with Imogen, whose eyebrows were so raised they practically blended into her hairline. She nodded pointedly towards Oliver.

Declan stood before he could think better of it, walking over to where Oliver was talking with Jack and Owen.

'His sister, she's absolutely obsessed...' Owen was saying, but trailed off as Declan came to stand between him and Jack.

'Sorry,' Declan said uncomfortably.

'We were talking about Niall and Stella,' Oliver said to Declan.

'How are they?' Declan asked.

'Grand,' Owen said. 'They've moved in together already, you know.'

'Wow,' Declan said, still looking at Oliver.

'Shocking, isn't it?' Jack said, grinning. 'How many of us managed to find love in the madhouse?' He was looking at Owen as he said it, no doubt making a light-hearted jab, but Declan was worried that his expression gave away everything.

There was an excruciating moment of silence as Declan stared at Oliver's hands, noticing they were empty and seizing on the excuse. 'Want a drink?'

'Yeah, thanks,' Oliver said, following Declan to the kitchen.

He leaned against the counter as Declan got to work, slicing an orange and dropping sugar and bitters into the shaker. They were closer together than they'd been in weeks, and Declan was having trouble breathing. He caught the scent he'd come to associate with Oliver, earthy and sweet, and he closed his eyes for a moment. He fiddled with the muddler, doing a shoddy job of mimicking Holly's technique, his limbs moving unnaturally.

'How are you?' Declan's voice came out rough.

'I'm good,' Oliver said, finally cracking a smile. God, Declan had missed that smile. 'Great, actually.'

'I heard from Maeve that you got the New York job. Well done,' Declan said. 'I know you worked hard for it.'

Oliver cocked his head. 'Honestly, just getting accepted was a huge accomplishment.'

'So… when do you move?' Declan asked, fighting the urge to clench his teeth. At least he got to have one last conversation with Oliver. He could apologise and they could part as friends.

Oliver looked at him, eyes dancing. 'I'm crashing with a friend in Brixton.'

'I meant, when do you leave for New York?'

Oliver laughed. 'You dolt,' he said fondly. 'I'm not going to New York.'

'You're not?' Declan said, faltering.

Oliver shook his head. 'I'm not.'

'Why not?' Declan asked. He felt like he was missing something vitally important.

Oliver shrugged. 'Things changed.'

Declan's brain short-circuited. 'Oh.' He shook the drink mechanically, catching Oliver watching the lines of his arms, and then put the shaker down so hard it made a loud clanging noise.

'Easy on the counters, King,' Jack called.

'Sorry,' Declan said, too quietly for Jack to hear him. Oliver wasn't going to New York; Oliver was staying in London. Oliver was here, looking at him, not going anywhere.

Declan poured the drink into a glass, sloshing some of it onto the counter.

'Shit,' he muttered, grabbing a hand towel and wiping the spill. Oliver put a hand over his, and Declan finally looked up. They stared at each other. Declan tried his hardest to form a coherent thought, but kept getting stuck on the exact green of Oliver's eyes.

He swallowed. 'What changed?'

'I think you know.'

Declan supposed he did. He pulled his hand out from under Oliver's. 'Right, well,' he said gruffly, finally breaking their eye contact.

That wasn't what he had wanted to say. It wasn't the down-on-his-knees apology he'd envisioned for when he saw Oliver again. He shook his head and continued, 'I fucked up. When you left – Paige told me what you did for me – I never wanted to put you through that.'

'You didn't,' Oliver said, and Declan scoffed.

'I helped,' he said, squeezing his eyes shut. 'What I mean to say is… I'm sorry.'

Oliver picked up his drink and took a sip, letting out a contented sigh. 'This is really good.'

'Thanks,' he murmured, 'I'm studying to be a bartender.'

'Oh?' Oliver asked, amused.

Declan shrugged. 'I dunno. I'm still figuring out what I want to do.'

'Well, well,' Oliver said, downing the rest of the drink, 'never thought I'd see the day.'

'Me neither,' Declan said.

'Want to get out of here?' Oliver asked, and he nodded eagerly. 'Hey, guys, sorry to cut out early,' Oliver called to the rest of the group, his eyes still on Declan. 'My flatmate texted that he's locked out.'

'Oh, come on,' Jack whined. 'You literally just got here!'

'No, he should go,' Maeve said, looking between them. 'Decs, you heading out too?'

'Yeah,' Declan said, finding his voice. 'He's on the way, figured I could give him a ride.'

Chapter 28

Declan

'Right, um,' Declan said, fiddling with his keys. 'This is me.' He glanced back at Oliver, as he had several times on the drive from Maeve's apartment, to make sure he was still there. Oliver stared back at him, eyes soft, and Declan swung the door open.

His flat had always felt too big for the time he spent there, with the windows lining the far wall offering a view of the street below. The surprisingly tall ceilings for this part of town had only ever left Declan feeling exposed.

He switched on a lamp, casting the flat in low light, and watched as Oliver wandered around, inspecting his sparse decor. Declan categorised Oliver's reactions as he studied the Jimmy King poster above his couch, ran his fingers along the spines of books nestled on two large bookcases in the corner, and finally came to stand in front of the open French doors that led to Declan's bedroom.

Oliver turned to look at him, and Declan realised he hadn't moved from his spot by the door. This was the first time they'd ever been truly alone together, with nowhere else to go and no one to look out for. Something like panic ran through his body.

'I didn't know you read,' Oliver said.

Declan shrugged, walking over to the bookcase absentmindedly. 'I do sometimes.'

'You'll have to give me recommendations, now that I've got more time. It's kind of amazing, having a life again.' Oliver moved over to Declan's bar, examining the bottles curiously.

'What have you done so far?' Declan asked.

'You'll never believe it,' Oliver said. 'I actually spent a few days visiting my family.'

'Oh?' Declan asked, surprised. 'I thought you didn't get on.'

'We don't,' Oliver said, picking up a bottle of whisky and pouring himself a drink. 'But it'd been too long since I'd been home.'

'How did it go?' Declan said, eyeing the line of Oliver's throat as he drank.

'I told them about you,' Oliver said. 'Well, I told them about me, I suppose.'

Declan had got the sense that Oliver's parents were traditional. 'What did they say?'

Oliver's eyebrows drew together. 'To be honest, it was the best conversation we've had in years. I basically told them they have to give up on trying to get me to move home, get married and have five kids.'

'And?'

'They said, "Okay".' Oliver laughed, looking younger somehow. 'And that they wanted to see me at Christmas. I think they've actually missed me.'

'Yes, well, you're easy to miss.' Heat crept into his cheeks at the look Oliver gave him. 'I mean, I missed you' – he swallowed – 'about as soon as I lost you.'

Oliver gazed at him from across the room, the glass of whisky hanging limply in his hand. Declan stared back, hoping Oliver could see everything he was thinking.

Oliver didn't shrug so much as slump against the corner of the bar, resting there as if he could no longer hold himself upright.

'That's... good.'

Declan wanted to respond, but his brain settled on Oliver's fingers wrapped around the glass.

'I didn't stay for you,' Oliver said, after a moment.

'And I didn't come out for you,' Declan said.

They stared at each other, the flat so silent that the aircon clicking on was a roar.

Oliver broke eye contact first. 'I didn't want to go to New York,' he said. 'The only reason to go would've been to prove something I didn't feel like I needed to prove any more. My life is in London, and leaving didn't make sense.'

'I felt the same way,' Declan said, absently thumbing his wrist. He was having a hard time reckoning with how coming out could feel so monumental and yet inconsequential in all the ways that mattered. 'Living like that wasn't going to be enough for me any more.'

Oliver put his drink down. 'But you didn't have to quit boxing.' Declan felt too hot under his gaze.

'No,' Declan said, 'but I wanted to. And I don't have a lot of practice knowing what I want, so I figured I should seize the opportunity.' He could no longer stand still, moving slowly forwards.

Oliver took two steps, meeting him in the middle of the room. He was close enough to touch, and Declan was over-whelmed with relief at not having to hold himself back any more.

He reached out and grabbed Oliver's sides, digging his fingers into the flesh of his hip bones. Oliver inhaled sharply, his hands skimming Declan's arms, one stopping to drape over his shoulder as the other snuck up the back of his neck.

Declan closed his eyes as fingers grasped at the ends of his hair. He let out a long slow breath, feeling himself lean more fully against Oliver.

'And what else do you want?' Oliver murmured into the skin of Declan's throat, teeth grazing along his Adam's apple.

Declan shivered, feeling his hands tighten involuntarily, rucking up the hem of Oliver's shirt and feeling a hot flash of skin.

'I thought it was obvious,' Declan said, running his hand over Oliver's bare spine.

'Humour me,' Oliver said, and Declan could feel his smile against his cheek.

He pulled back to look at him more closely, taking in Oliver's green eyes, lit dimly from the streetlights outside.

'You.'

Chapter 29

Oliver

Six Months Post-Finale

Oliver sat idling outside King's Gym, rubbing his hands together while making mental calculations of their arrival time. He glanced down at his phone, thumbing at the last message he'd sent in the earnest hope that refreshing would result in a new message.

A knock at the window made him jump, and Oliver turned to see Declan's grinning face.

'Hi, you,' Declan said, as Oliver opened the door and stepped out to greet him. The kiss he dropped to Oliver's cheek made him instantly forget his worries about their tardiness. 'Sorry for the wait.'

'It's fine,' Oliver said, leaning into the warmth of Declan's neck for just a moment and breathing in the familiar scent of him. 'Better now.'

'Old softie,' Declan teased, deftly stealing the keys from Oliver's hand. 'Let me drive. You had a long day.'

Oliver walked over to the passenger side. 'Just two more weeks and then the season will end.'

Declan flicked on his turn signal to merge onto the motorway. 'Which reminds me, Dad asked about your next show. Shall I bring him?'

Oliver blushed at the idea of Declan's dad seeing him in tights. In the last few months, Jim and Oliver had bonded over their love of *Bake Off* and he'd even designed Oliver a few training programmes to help him with his lifts.

'Of course, I'd love for him to come.' Oliver reached out to clasp Declan's hand resting on the gearstick. The cold March rain pattered on the windshield, drowning out the low static of the radio. 'And your day?'

Declan shrugged. 'Good. I taught swimming to the under-eights.'

Oliver laughed, delighted by the image of Declan surrounded by children in arm bands. 'And how did that go?'

'Well, no one drowned,' Declan said, glancing at him with a grin.

'I'm adding swimming teacher to the list,' Oliver said, pulling out his phone. His and Georgia's shared note where they kept all of Declan's potential careers grew daily. In the weeks following his retirement, Declan had fielded multiple brand campaign offers and sponsorship deals, but ultimately decided to take a step back from public life altogether. He'd since disabled his social media channels, and was threatening to turn his iPhone in for an old flip phone.

'Oh, would you stop it?' Declan grumbled. 'I don't like how chummy you two are getting.'

'You're just jealous that she likes me more,' Oliver teased. Georgia absolutely adored the Royal London, and had been attending nearly weekly with Declan always by her side. Soon after he'd caught her eyeing his outfit with distaste, PR packages of designer clothes had begun showing up at the flat mysteriously. Georgia claimed to know nothing about how brands had got their address, but Will was taking full advantage.

'Well, Will loves me,' Declan said, wagging his eyebrows. Will had made that particular proclamation at their last pub quiz night with Oliver's mates. Declan had successfully listed the last ten boxing all-stars from the UK, a question that no one else had even a chance of getting correct. They'd won that night, and if Oliver had enthusiastically snogged Declan as a reward, well, Declan's competitiveness must be rubbing off on him.

Declan's phone pinged and he tossed it to Oliver. 'Probably Jack.'

Oliver nodded, reading the message. 'Yeah, he and Maeve just arrived. The hotel is "swanky". His words.'

'Obviously.' Declan laughed.

They were heading up to Bristol for Niall and Stella's engagement party. Declan had snorted when they'd got the invitation, but Oliver knew he was secretly excited at the prospect of seeing their castmates again. It would be the first time they'd all be together since the summer.

'Oh God,' Oliver cackled, reading Jack's next message. 'He's found a karaoke bar nearby.'

'Absolutely not,' Declan deadpanned.

'I dunno, Holls says she's in,' Oliver said.

'Don't you remember Jack in the shower?' Declan groaned. 'The man is completely tone-deaf.'

'Exactly, this is going to be hysterical.'

'I am not singing,' Declan declared.

Oliver squinted at him. 'I think I could convince you.'

The quick glance Declan shot his way was full of bravado. 'Oh, yeah?'

Oliver nodded, eyes wide and innocent. He leaned over the console, pressing his lips to the shell of Declan's ear. 'Absolutely.'

–

In the end, it didn't take much to get Declan up on stage. They'd barely had time to check in and drop off their bags before Jack had found them and dragged them out to the bar. Maeve, Holly and Owen had joined them during their third round of beers, then someone suggested tequila and Declan and Jack were on stage belting out the chorus to 'Mr Brightside' not long after.

Oliver had bowed out after the first round of shots, but watched, enraptured, as Declan threw back his head, dramatically playing air guitar while Jack gyrated against the mic stand.

He liked when Declan got like this; it wasn't often that he allowed himself to let loose. Even with stepping back from the spotlight, he never seemed fully relaxed when they were out in public. There was always a part of him on guard, but Oliver had had the satisfaction of seeing that part of him slowly unclench since they'd got together.

'I need a refill,' Maeve said, the slurp of her straw barely audible over the music. 'And I can't possibly watch any more of this.'

'Oh, you love it,' Oliver said, slinging an arm over her shoulder as they made their way back to the bar.

'Two G&Ts please.' Maeve could hold her drink, but Oliver knew from the bright pink of her cheeks that she was shit-faced. She narrowed her eyes at him as if she could read his thoughts. 'Don't look at me like that.'

Oliver raised his hands appeasingly. 'Like what?'

She pointed a finger at him. 'We should hang out more.'

'We should,' Oliver agreed, grinning at her. 'But you're too busy for me. With all your soliciting internationally and such.'

'Pfft.' Maeve waved her hand like his comment was an annoying gnat, then returned to her pointing. This time her finger poked at Oliver's sternum. '*You're* too busy for *me*.'

'Hey, don't I know you?' came a voice, and Oliver turned to see a man hanging off the bar, staring at them. 'Shit, you're Maeve and Oliver! From *Summer of Love*?'

Oliver glanced at Maeve, who shrugged. Being recognised by random people didn't happen that often any more, but it still wasn't something that Oliver had got used to.

'Oh, this is so cool,' the guy said, pulling out his phone. 'Do you mind if I get a pic? You were my girlfriend's favourite couple. She was gutted when you left the show, Ollie.'

'Aww, that's sweet,' Maeve said, throwing an amused look at Oliver. 'What's her name?'

'Sara, and I'm Tim,' Tim said, bringing his phone up for the picture. Oliver felt himself smile robotically, hoping the photo wouldn't make it online, but also knowing that it probably would.

'Sorry,' Tim said, glancing between them. 'But are you, like... together now?'

'I'm still with Jack,' Maeve said, laughing and pointing.

Tim seemed to finally register the people making fools of themselves on stage and his jaw dropped. 'That's... that's Declan King.'

The awe in his voice wasn't unusual; Declan still seemed to have that effect on the straight male population.

'Indeed,' Oliver said wryly, catching Declan's gaze from across the bar and raising his glass. Declan's grin was wide and open. Oliver felt very warm all of a sudden, and he couldn't solely blame the alcohol. Jack belted out the final words of the song, and the two stumbled off the stage.

'Oh God, he's coming over here,' Tim said.

'He'd probably take a picture if you'd like,' Maeve said. Oliver shot her a warning look.

'Made a new friend, have we?' Jack asked, sidling up to her and taking a sip of her drink.

'He's a fan of the show,' Maeve said, eyes crinkled with amusement. 'He thinks Oliver and I were the best couple.'

'Er,' Tim flushed and stammered out, 'I mean... you two seem great too.'

'Good enough to win,' Declan said, throwing a mock punch at Jack.

Tim seemed at a loss for words, staring at Declan unblinkingly. But Declan was too far gone to notice, wrapping a hand around Oliver's waist and tucking into his side.

'You have a fan,' Oliver murmured in his ear. Declan turned to the man with his real smile still in place, reaching out his hand.

'Hi, I'm Declan.'

Tim blinked at Declan's hand for a moment before shaking it. 'I love you.'

From the look of terror on his face, Oliver guessed that wasn't what he'd meant to say.

'I mean you, and your brother. And your father, really. Great family. Really great.' Tim squeezed his eyes shut as if willing himself to stop talking. Oliver traded amused looks with Jack. 'The best,' he finished lamely.

'Thank you,' Declan said, graciously ignoring the awkwardness. 'Aaron is having an amazing year. Couldn't be prouder of him.'

'I bet.' Tim swallowed nervously; there was a beat where no one said anything. 'Well, um, good to meet you. I don't want to take up any more of your time.' To Maeve, he said, 'Thanks for the photo.'

She raised her glass to him as he walked away.

'God,' Jack said, 'that was next level. Do you get that all the time?'

'Only sometimes,' Declan said, nuzzling his face into Oliver's neck, his breath smelling faintly of tequila. Instead of being disgusted, Oliver found it oddly endearing.

'I'd like it to be known that I was actually recognised first,' Maeve said, pouting. 'I'm much more famous than Declan.'

'Of course you are, sweetheart,' Jack said, kissing the side of her head before looking around. 'Hey, where did Holls and Owen go?'

Oliver grimaced. 'I think they went to the bathroom... together... rather a bit ago.' Holly and Owen had been all over each other at their table, so he was grateful they'd chosen to take their canoodling to a slightly more private area.

Declan's hand came to rest on Oliver's hip. 'Being much more civilised, I think we'll go back to the hotel now.'

Maeve resumed her pointing, this time at both Declan and Oliver. 'Make sure to set your alarm before you get too distracted. The engagement party starts in...' She checked her watch and shuddered. 'Seven hours, for some ungodly reason.'

Jack rolled his eyes. 'It's the exact time of day Niall and Stella laid eyes on one another during the hit TV show *Summer of Love.* The producers assured them they'd be the perfect match...'

'And, somehow, they were right for once,' Oliver finished, grabbing Declan's hand and squeezing it. He saluted Maeve and Jack with his unoccupied hand. 'We'll see you at 10:13 on the dot.'

'Wouldn't miss it for the world,' Declan said, putting a hand on his heart. 'Unless Oliver doesn't wake me and force me to go, in which case I'll probably miss it. But, y'know, I'll see you around.'

Oliver pulled him outside the karaoke bar and into the brisk night with a wave to the others.

To his surprise, a few flakes of snow were falling. Some of them landed in Declan's dark hair, and Oliver ruffled it.

'I don't feel cold,' Declan said, staring with wonder at the snow falling in the little space left between them. His eyes refocused on Oliver. 'I love you.'

Oliver couldn't stop himself from smiling every time Declan said those words, even though he'd heard them thousands of times already. 'I love you too.'

—

'We're gonna be late.'

Oliver stepped out of the hotel bathroom, a tie in one hand and a comb in the other. 'I'm nearly ready,' he said, trying to smooth his hair into a presentable state and failing.

Declan grabbed the tie from his hand. 'You're hopeless, you know that?' he asked wryly, looping the tie around Oliver's neck and making quick work of the knot. Oliver watched his fingers move at the collar, blinking at him in amazement. 'I do know things,' Declan grumbled, and Oliver kissed him.

His phone vibrated as they pulled apart. 'Probably Maeve wondering where the hell we are,' he said, grabbing the phone off the side table. He laughed as he skimmed the messages. 'Will and Georgia are absolutely eviscerating you in the group chat right now.'

Declan sighed. 'I don't know why you insist on sending blackmail material of me to our mates.' Oliver had managed to snag an incriminating video of Declan on stage the night before, saving the moment for posterity.

He pulled Declan in for another kiss, feeling the drag of his stubble as he pressed closer, tasting the toothpaste he'd used that morning. He looped his arms around Declan's neck, grinning stupidly when Declan's hands circled his waist.

'We're going to be late,' Oliver said as Declan leaned in, mouthing at his neck and the sensitive corner of his jaw.

'Let's skip it,' Declan said, bringing his lips across Oliver's cheeks. 'Niall and Stella won't miss us.'

Oliver paused, considering. 'Actually, they might be too wrapped up in each other to notice.'

Declan pressed a kiss to his lips. 'Exactly what I'm saying.'

'Unfortunately,' Oliver said, 'Jack will have no qualms with ratting us out, once he realises we're skiving. The traitor.'

Declan groaned as his jacket pocket vibrated. 'That's Holly,' he said, declining the call. 'Let's go.'

The party was taking place in the garden of their bed and breakfast, so it took little time for them to twist through the corridors and make it outside.

'Bloody Stella,' Declan muttered, stuffing his hands under the arms of his wool coat. Only Stella would think to have a party on the spring solstice, when it was still freezing outside.

'Here,' Oliver said, retrieving a pair of gloves from his pocket for Declan.

Declan looked at him in wonder. 'You're a miracle.'

'*I* check the weather forecast,' Oliver said, spotting a large tent by the edge of the woods.

As they entered the tent, Oliver looked around for Niall and Stella, but couldn't spot them in the crowd.

'Oi!' someone shouted from their left. Oliver turned and saw Jack, Maeve, Holly and Owen shivering in their coats. He and Declan joined them, exchanging hugs. 'We're planning on getting plastered,' Holly said.

'Oh?' Declan asked, cocking his head.

'It's the best kind of winter coat,' Jack explained.

'And you know, hair of the dog, and such,' Maeve said, with a wince.

'I'd best catch us up, then,' Declan said, squeezing Oliver's hand before letting it go. 'G&T for you?'

'Please,' he said. As Declan left them, Oliver turned to Holly. 'I never got to ask you last night – how are things in Manchester?'

'Great,' she replied animatedly. Oliver thought she might be a few drinks in already. 'Though this one keeps trying to get me to move to London.' She rolled her eyes in Owen's direction.

'We'll wear you down eventually,' Oliver said cheerfully, slapping Owen on the shoulder.

'Hey,' a familiar voice greeted from behind them. Oliver turned to see Eavie, stunning as ever, with a familiar-looking man at her side. Oliver peered at him for a moment, trying to place him, before bending down to give Eavie a hug.

'Nice to see you.'

'You, too.' Eavie turned to her companion. 'This is my boyfriend, Samir.'

'Oh!' Oliver said, blinking. 'I should have recognised you – it's been years. I'm Oliver, a former happy customer.'

'I know who you are,' Samir said gravely. 'The boy who insulted my scones on national television. One doesn't forget that sort of thing.'

Eavie smiled. 'But you did bring us together, so there's that. You were right, he *is* a softie.'

Samir had a firm and deliberate handshake, but his tone was warm as he introduced himself to the group. 'It's so nice to finally meet Eavie's friends from reality television.' He said the words as though he wasn't quite sure what they meant.

As the group resumed their smaller conversations, Eavie turned to Oliver. 'How's the Royal London treating you?'

He grinned. 'I'm enjoying a leisurely rehearsal schedule these days, spending more time teaching.'

'Are the kids still taking years off your life?'

'Ha,' he said. 'They're better behaved than the last batch, and I've coerced Will into helping me run things. He can be very stern when he needs to be.'

They were interrupted by an enthusiastic greeting from Jack. 'Faye! I didn't know you'd be here!'

Oliver turned and saw Faye approaching them.

Just then, an arm wrapped around Oliver's waist, a drink deposited into his hand. Declan had entered the circle, to his left.

'Hiya, Faye,' Declan said, grinning.

'This is Declan,' Oliver explained to Samir, and then looked at Faye, 'my boyfriend.'

Faye made a comical expression as she glanced between the two of them, eyes finally resting on where Declan's arm encircled Oliver. 'Wow,' she said finally. 'That does explain a lot, doesn't it? How long?'

'Six months now,' Declan said. 'At that party Maeve threw for Jack in September. I think you were there.'

'I'm starting to think that party was less for me and more for these two,' Jack chimed in, with a glance to Maeve.

'I did nothing wrong!' she protested, her cheeks reddening. 'I threw you an excellent party, and yes, maybe I had a *tiny* ulterior motive or two.'

'Two?' Holly asked, raising her eyebrows.

'A girl has to have some secrets,' Maeve said, taking a sip of her mulled wine.

Samir, who had been staring at Declan since he'd arrived, finally spoke up: 'I know where I've seen you before. You're that boxer.'

'The amateur bartender,' Holly quipped.

'The even more amateur photographer,' Jack said.

'The mushroom-foraging expert,' Imogen put in, joining the circle with Zoë at her side. 'Are we naming Declan's weird hobbies?'

'No,' Declan said firmly. 'We are accepting that I am going through a phase of enlightenment and self-discovery, since retiring from my incredibly stressful, and successful, athletic career. I appreciate the wholehearted support, so thank you.'

'Once you *find yourself*, oh wise one,' Jack said, 'what will you grace the world with, among your many talents?'

Declan gave a pensive look around the group. 'There are too many ways I can be useful to society. It's an impossible choice.'

'Professional reality TV contestant?' Zoë teased.

Declan wrinkled his nose. 'I've got absolutely *everything* I could possibly get out of reality television already.' He looked sideways at Oliver.

There was an uproar of applause from the crowd around them, and Oliver saw Niall and Stella entering the tent from a flap next to an ivy-covered lattice frame. There was a small stage in front of it with a microphone set up.

Stella showed no signs of being affected by the cold, beaming at Niall as he helped her onto the stage.

'Thanks so much for coming, everyone,' she said. 'Niall and I wanted to have a small gathering to celebrate the changing of seasons and our love.'

Niall stepped forwards, bending over the mic. 'While we have you gathered here anyway, we thought it might make sense to just get married now.' He looked at Stella. 'I don't want to spend another second not married to her, to be honest.'

The group exchanged shocked looks.

'Did you know?' Eavie asked Oliver. He shook his head, mystified.

Stella scanned the crowd. 'Is Jack Obiaka in attendance tonight?'

Jack gave a whoop. 'You know I am!'

She waved at him. 'Jack, you once said you were going to become an ordained minister. I hope you've kept your promise.'

'Oh, Stella.' Jack put a hand on his heart dramatically. 'I do.'

'Hey, that's my line!' Niall cut in.

'Come on up,' she said, gesturing him onto the stage.

Jack gave Maeve a parting kiss on the cheek, thrilled to be put on the spot. When he made it onto the stage, he addressed the audience: 'Can I hear a round of applause for the beautiful couple?'

There was a deafening roar from around the tent. 'Okay, that's enough,' Stella called, laughing.

'Please ask me properly,' Jack said, turning to Stella. 'I won't do it unless you get down on one knee and everything.'

She nodded gamely, kneeling. 'Will you, Jack Obiaka, marry me, Stella Reyes... to him' – she pointed to Niall – 'Niall O'Connell?'

'I will,' Jack said solemnly, and Stella stood up, smoothing out her dress. 'Well, we've gathered here today under false pretences, which seems to be in opposition to holy matrimony.' He broke out in a wide grin. 'But we'll ignore it for the sake of two people in love. Are your vows prepared?'

They nodded.

'Ladies first,' Jack said, looking at Stella.

The couple stood there, facing one another and holding hands, for a long moment before Stella spoke.

'Niall,' she said, her voice wavering with emotion, 'since the moment I met you in the most manufactured setting possible, you have been the most real thing I've ever known. They say the key to a successful marriage is to be surprised by your spouse every day. I disagree with that. Niall' – she gazed at him, tears steadily streaming from her eyes – 'I am never surprised by you. Your steadiness and your compassion never surprise me, because they are fundamental to you. My love for you never surprises me. It is steady and true, like you.'

Niall's voice was shaky: 'Stell—' He broke off, wiping his eyes. 'Fuck, well, I'm clearly a mess over you,' he said, gesturing to his blotchy face, 'but I wouldn't have it any other way. You make everything, every hard moment I've been through in my life, worth it, because it brought me to you. I may be steady and true, but you are the person that keeps me steady and true. The person I am with you, I couldn't be for anyone else. I love you, Stella.'

Oliver thought he saw Stella mouth *I love you too*, impossible to hear over the cheers from the crowd. As he looked around, he found he wasn't the only one in the group who was affected. Zoë and Holly were crying, and even Declan surreptitiously wiped a tear from one eye, giving Oliver a silencing look.

'Everyone gathered here today, may you be blessed with a love like this one!' Jack shouted, and Oliver thought his eyes were on Maeve. 'By the power vested in me by Getordaine-donline.uk, I present to you, the married couple.'

Stella grabbed the microphone. 'I do,' she said, with a pointed look to Jack.

'I do,' Niall concurred, grinning widely through his tears.

More cheers arose as Niall pulled Stella into his arms, kissing her and carrying her off the stage. A band appeared from nowhere, setting up as the merriment continued.

'Come on,' Declan said, grabbing Oliver's hand. 'Let's get another drink.'

Oliver glanced at his gin and tonic, realising he hadn't drunk any of it yet. 'Okay,' he agreed, looking into Declan's bottomless eyes.

'You'd go anywhere if I asked you nicely enough,' Declan teased.

'True,' Oliver agreed. 'Try not to abuse that power.'

'It will be difficult,' Declan said, looking him up and down. Oliver felt incredibly warm all of a sudden.

When they got to the bar area, Declan walked straight past it, out of the tent and into the garden.

'I thought you wanted another drink,' Oliver said, confused.

'No,' Declan said. 'I just wanted a moment without anyone else around. I like having you to myself.' They stood there, looking at each other, for a long time.

Acknowledgements

When we started writing this book, it was on a whim. The pandemic had emptied our calendars and life had become monotonous and we thought, *what if we just wrote that book we've been talking about writing?*

Since then, life has been anything but monotonous! The first draft that we never showed anyone turned into the second and third and fourth, ones that we politely and apologetically forced our friends to read. Their feedback is the only reason this book could be published.

Thanks to our first set of readers, who loved Declan and Oliver enough to keep the project alive: Emily D., Emily O., Kallie, Miranda and Natalie. And thank you to our friends who read every subsequent draft until we felt like it was something we were proud to share: Aditi, Ally, Andie, Arjun, Jordyn, Leah, Lidia, Mika and Sam.

Thanks to our friends who didn't read the book but emotionally supported us through this process. We still love you, though maybe slightly less: Andrew, Austin, Ella, Emily G., Emily M., Jack H., Jack W., Jacob, Katie, Kelsey, Meredith and Phillip.

Thanks to our families: our siblings, Becky and Ellis, Madeline's partner, Kelly, and our parents, without whom we would not be the people we are today.

Thanks to Elizabeth Held and Laura Hankin for being our bridge to the romance-reading community in Washington D.C.

Thanks to Miriam Plotinksy. It was in her creative writing class that we first had an inkling that we could write a book.

Thanks to Kate Rizzo and the team at Greene & Heaton for believing in this story from the start and guiding two debut authors through this process. Your support over the past two years dealing with the chaos of publishing has meant so much to us.

And, finally, thanks to Emily Bedford and the team at Canelo for wanting to show this book to the world.